ABOUT THE AUTHOR

Tony Park was born in 1964 and grew up in the western suburbs of Sydney. He has worked as a newspaper reporter, a press secretary, a PR consultant and a freelance writer. He also served thirty-four years in the Australian Army Reserve, including six months as a public affairs officer in Afghanistan in 2002. He and his wife, Nicola, divide their time between Australia and southern Africa. He is the author of twenty-two other novels about Africa and several biographies.

ALSO BY TONY PARK

Far Horizon

Zambezi

African Sky

Safari

Silent Predator

Ivory

The Delta

African Dawn

Dark Heart

The Prey

The Hunter

An Empty Coast

Red Earth

The Cull

Captive

Scent of Fear

Ghosts of the Past

Last Survivor

Blood Trail

The Pride

Vendetta

The Protector

Part of the Pride, *with Kevin Richardson*

War Dogs, *with Shane Bryant*

The Grey Man, with John Curtis

Courage Under Fire, with Daniel Keighran VC

No One Left Behind, with Keith Payne VC

Rhino War, with Maj Gen (Ret) Johan Jooste

Bwana, There's a Body in the Bath, with Peter Whitehead

DIE BY THE SWORD

TONY PARK

Ingwe
PUBLISHING

For Nicola

PROLOGUE

THE BATTLE OF ISANDLWANA, ZULULAND, 22 JANUARY 1879

It was his time to die.

For a moment, less than a second, the pounding of blood in Gregory's ears, the crack of the rifles, the thump of passing bullets, the screams of the wounded and the Zulus' battle cries were gone.

The acrid scent of burned powder and smoke were like smelling salts as the realisation hit him. The terror was there, making him clench, but it was as if the fear of the unknown had paralysed him, rooting him to this place at the foot of Isandlwana, the Sphinx-like hill behind them. The rock would be here for millennia; his blood would feed the soil like Johnson's, lying next to him, and the warrior at his feet, his heart run through with Gregory's own bayonet.

The Zulus were behind them; their fate was sealed. Sub-Inspector Peter Gregory reached into the leather pouch at his belt, drew a round with burned fingers and thumbed it into the breech of the Martini–Henry carbine. He brought the rifle up into his shoulder, and barely needed to take aim. The phalanx of Zulus was almost upon them. He squeezed the trigger and felt the kick in his already bruised shoulder. The smoke obscured the shattered face of the warrior in front of him and the man fell backwards.

Frightened cattle and forlorn humans bellowed behind him. 'Run! We're done for.'

To Gregory's left and right were men he knew. The flotsam and jetsam of the colony, their commander had fondly dubbed them. Old soldiers, miners, rogues and failed farmers – men for whom life was the rolling hills of Natal, a campfire under a sky ablaze with stars, fresh meat sizzling on hot coals, the call of the lion at night. Some in the colony hated the Natal Mounted Police. Gregory had come to love the unit.

'Look left!' Jenkins, standing beside him, aimed across Gregory's body and his rifle boomed, felling a Zulu Peter hadn't noticed in the melee. 'That's a beer you owe me, Peter –'

A warrior's assegai silenced Jenkins, striking him just under his rib cage. Blood poured from his mouth. Gregory turned, reversed his rifle and drove the butt into the side of the Zulu's head, knocking him sideways. The man had begun to remove the stabbing spear from Jenkins' torso, and Gregory reached down and beat the fighter to the shaft, drawing it from his friend's body and slashing the blade across the staggering enemy's face. He saw, now, that the man who had killed his friend was young, perhaps in his teens. Gregory drove the spear into his belly. His hands were wet with the blood of friend and foe.

Gregory and the remaining men of the NMP, distinctive in their dark-brown tunics among a sea of British redcoat soldiers, had rallied around Durnford, the only senior officer on this blood-soaked slope who had any idea what he was doing – and now he, too, was doomed to die.

'Ammunition, here!' a high-pitched voice called.

Gregory tossed the assegai aside and reached into his pouch for one of his few remaining rounds. He looked up and saw that the call had come from a drummer boy, even younger than the last soul Gregory had taken, half dragging, half carrying a stout box of cartridges. The boy had a bayonet in his hand, and as he set the crate down he tried to get the point of the blade under the lid to lever it open. Gregory was half deaf from the boom of gunfire. He watched on helplessly as another shot caught the drummer boy in the shoulder and knocked him backwards. A policeman stepped in, picked up the bayonet and went to work on the crate.

Steel blades clanged on rifles, men yelled. A British officer with a pistol fired into the oncoming mass of muscled flesh and glinting assegais until the hammer of his weapon clicked on an empty chamber. He was overrun.

Gregory worked the lever under his rifle, sending the empty cartridge flying, then took another from his pouch, loaded, closed the lever, aimed and fired again. His bullet passed through the neck of one warrior and into the chest of another slightly below. It was nothing, though. The wave of men came on, up the slope onto which his comrades had retreated. The policemen, who made up the majority of this, one of several stands against the human tide, were shoulder to shoulder. Gregory looked around and saw the drummer boy lying on the ground, crying.

Two Zulus snatched up the body of one of their own and, taking an arm each and shielding themselves behind him, propelled the corpse onto the bayonets of two redcoats, who fell backwards. One warrior leapt over the tangle of living and dead while the other dispatched the soldiers with downward thrusts of his assegai.

The man who had broken through made for the drummer boy. Gregory scrounged in his pouch, but he had just fired his last round. He turned and strode to the fallen lad, rifle out, and charged at the Zulu who was now raising a spear, aiming at the young bandsman. Gregory ran at him, but the African turned at the last second, perhaps sensing Gregory behind him, and Gregory's bayonet only just sliced across the front of the man's torso.

An assegai flashed, cutting through the weave of Gregory's tunic and into the skin on his chest. Gregory felt the sting as he lurched backwards. He tried to bring his empty rifle up, but the man had closed on him. Gregory felt his weapon crushed against his body as the Zulu tried to bring his spear around his back and into his kidneys. Gregory dropped the rifle and, instead, swung his fist into the side of the Zulu's head.

Around them the clamour of battle continued its ceaseless din – gunfire, war cries, pleas for mercy, and ruthless swearing as blades sank into flesh. Gregory heard the roar of blood in his ears again, and looked into the eyes of the latest man who was trying to kill him. Dark pupils, bloodshot whites; the other's sweat stung the inside of Gregory's nose as their breath mixed. They danced on the battlefield, locked in a terrible embrace. Gregory felt the other man's strength, the muscles as hard as steel cables, the righteous rage of a man defending his homeland. *My home.*

In another time he and the man he was fighting could have been neighbours, brothers. And yet Gregory clawed at him and raised his knee into the man's groin. The man stabbed him – not a good strike, because Gregory held him too close – but Gregory felt the skin behind his left shoulder open nonetheless.

But the man was pushing him, and his rage was greater. Gregory took a step back and then another. He was aware of more shooting, of redcoats and police firing faster; perhaps they had managed to open the box of cartridges the drummer boy had brought up. Maybe there was hope for them, but the heel of Gregory's right boot hit a rock, made slippery with blood and entrails. He fell.

The fall, compounded by the weight of the Zulu, drove the air from his lungs. He tried to take a breath but felt only pain. He swung his fists again and tried to get a hand in the man's short hair.

It was his time to die.

The man above him raised his right arm and the blade of the assegai glinted as the sun caught the steel. Gregory put a palm to the man's bare chest, slippery with sweat. The warrior grinned down at him, safe in the knowledge that in this, the ultimate contest, he had won. The arm came down, as if in slow motion. Gregory closed his eyes.

He was smothered. When he opened his eyes the cheek of the warrior was against his. The man's body quivered and his chest rattled as the life burst from him. Gregory craned his head to the left and saw the drummer boy, his face streaked with red lines and tears, staring down at him, a bloody bayonet in his right hand.

Gregory rolled the now-dead Zulu off himself and saw that the lad had pierced the man through the back of the heart. The drummer boy's eyes were wide with the horror of all that he had seen, all that he had done, and his face was white from the loss of blood from his left shoulder. Drained of strength by the effort it had taken to save Gregory, the injured drummer boy dropped to one knee. Gregory got to his feet.

'No!' He would not let this boy die.

A horse came towards him, a blue-coated transport officer in the saddle, and Gregory held up his hand to the man.

'Out of the way, damn you,' the officer said.

As the officer galloped past, Gregory reached up, grabbed hold of the man's pistol belt and hauled him from the saddle. The force of the pull nearly wrenched Gregory's arm from its socket. The startled horse reared up as the falling man landed hard in an eruption of dust.

Spitting dirt, the officer tried to stand. 'Damn your eyes, man.'

Gregory snatched up his Martini–Henry and, even though it was empty, aimed it one-handed at the fallen man's head. 'Help me put the boy on the horse or you die, now.'

The man wiped the back of his hand across a face smeared with dirt from his fall. Gregory put down his weapon and started to lift the boy.

'Do it yourself, man. And get away while you can, but be warned, I'll have you charged for insubordination if you survive this bloody mess. The Zulus are behind the hill now. We're outnumbered, surrounded, done for. It's every man for himself.'

The officer was right about the Zulus. The British were being out-manoeuvered by their enemy's simple, yet masterful strategy, based on the anatomy of a bull. The most seasoned warriors in the centre of the formation, the 'chest' of the bull, were hammering at the redcoat line, while the 'horns', regiments on the left and right of the advance made up of fleet-footed younger men, had pushed out and around in order to encircle their foe.

The drummer boy was barely conscious. The transport officer swung back up into his saddle.

'Wait.' Gregory coughed from the dust and smoke. The transport officer looked down at him. 'If you leave without this boy I'll shoot you in the back.'

The battle raged around him, pressing in closer. Gregory feared he would have to drop the wounded drummer – he was a teenage lad, no mere child; he was too heavy. The officer looked like he might risk taking a bullet from Gregory.

'Let me help,' a deep voice said.

Gregory looked around, saw a Zulu and for a moment thought he was dead. Then he saw the man's tunic; he was a member of the Natal Native Horse and he had just dismounted. The other man took one of the drummer's arms and together they were able to lift him up and over the rump of the transport officer's horse. Gregory slapped the horse and it, and its rider and young passenger, galloped away.

Every man for himself. Gregory spat his disgust at the words into the dust and rock. He looked to the diminishing knot of police and redcoats protecting Colonel Durnford, and the Zulus massing for the final attack.

'Come with me, *Nkosi*,' the African horseman who had helped him said. Gregory recognised the man now – he'd seen him fighting and killing in the donga alongside Durnford, and the colonel had ordered this man and his comrades to retreat, yet here he was. He stood eye to eye with Gregory, dressed in a khaki tunic and boots, an assegai in his hand and two more throwing spears up-ended in a pannier strapped to his saddle.

Gregory shook his head. 'Go.' He knelt by the body of a redcoat, shot through the forehead, and scrounged the last three cartridges from one of the man's pouches and two fallen rounds from the dirt. He glanced up at the African soldier, now back in his saddle, but hesitating. For the briefest of moments, Gregory was tempted to flee, but the revulsion he'd felt at the transport officer's words brought him back to the unassailable truth. His place, his fate, was with those men around Durnford, firing and loading, clubbing and stabbing with their rifles. He had nothing in life except his honour and the uniform he wore.

He glanced over and saw the back of the fleeing transport officer and his horse's rear end disappear over a rise, downhill towards the river. At least the drummer boy was safe.

Then there was a yell behind them and a young Zulu, in the vanguard of the encircling right horn of the army, leapt over a boulder and sprinted towards them, spear outstretched.

The horseman wheeled his mount around so he was almost between the oncoming warrior and Gregory, who worked the lever of his Martini–Henry, slid a cartridge into the breech and locked the rifle closed. He raised the weapon to his shoulder, aimed around the brave man defending him and squeezed the trigger.

Click.

'Hell.' Gregory worked the lever to clear the misfire and saw the grit and dirt ejected along with the filthy cartridge that had jammed. If the native horseman galloped away now – as he should, he could save himself – then Gregory would have to take on this latest fellow with his bayonet. His throat was parched, his limbs heavy.

The horseman reached behind him, dropped his assegai and picked up a longer throwing spear. As the warrior ran past him, the horseman drew back his arm and hurled the spear downwards, into the back of the oncoming Zulu. The man fell at Gregory's feet.

'Come with me, *Nkosi*,' the horseman repeated, more forcefully this time.

Gregory shook his head. 'No, thank you. I'll stay and fight –'

His world went black.

It was his time to die.

1

BHANGA NEK, KWAZULU-NATAL, THE PRESENT

The full moon broke free of the layer of cloud hugging the horizon and cast a pillar of silver on the Indian Ocean as it climbed.

It was beautiful, and should have been perfect, but Adam Kruger frowned.

He strode across the empty white sands of the beach at Bhanga Nek, eyes scanning left and right, just as he had done during his time in the army, on patrol in Angola. Tonight, he looked not for danger but for life. In rugby shorts, a Rip Curl T-shirt and bare feet he was neither hot nor cold. He was at one with his environment, as much a part of it as the turtles he searched for.

Adam was at peace, yet still he felt his right arm bend at the elbow as he walked while his left arm remained straight. It was the same as when he and Sannie had hiked in the Drakensberg three weeks earlier – the muscle memory kicked in whenever he walked in the bush or somewhere quiet and remote, like the beach. As his eyes scanned the terrain for threats, so, too, did his hands imagine they were holding a gun.

He shook his head and his arms as he walked to try and clear the stupid notion. The canvas satchel slung across his body bounced on his back with every step; Adam heard a distant rumble and looked to the horizon again. The cloud was a front, and he knew from the forecast it was heading towards the coast, and his turtles.

Adam plucked at his T-shirt as he walked on, thinking, cursing, sweating. Even at nine o'clock at night the humidity was still high. He'd done one up-and-back survey already, covering eight kilometres. The beach curved in a gentle crescent as Adam approached the northern end for the second time that evening. Here the strip of sand was at its narrowest and rose steeply to a high dune. Behind that was a belt of thick vegetation, a tangled jungle of lala palms, strelitzias and umdoni trees.

The impending storm worried him and added to feelings of unease that were not related to turtle hatchings. He and Sannie had argued, again, on the phone. He should call her.

But phone signal was patchy here. It was only when he was in the Ezemvelo KZN research buildings, in the KwaZulu-Natal national park authority's encampment at the southern end of Bhanga Nek, and had wi-fi access, that he could be reasonably sure of being able to contact her.

'Yes, Adam, I hear that you want to stay to help these new students, but you said yourself *last week* that your work there was finished for the season,' Sannie had said to him the last time they had spoken.

He should have been in his *bakkie*, on his way back to Pennington – to Sannie and the house they had shared for over a year.

Adam had wanted to call her again today, but the wi-fi had been down. He wanted to tell her about the unusually high tides and the nest of eggs that had been washed away during the last storm. All the indications were that the front that was heading their way – he glanced to the right again as he caught a far-off flash of lightning – would be even worse.

Adam saw tracks. 'Shit.'

He quickened his pace and came to the place where the female leatherback had just laid her clutch of eggs. It must have happened while he had been trudging down the other end of the beach. Adam kicked himself. If he'd looked back over his shoulder, he might have seen the turtle emerging from the distinct riptide off to his right, but he'd been preoccupied thinking about Sannie.

Adam stood there, hands on hips, fuming. The indentations of her flippers were stark, accusatory in the now-bright moonlight, but the thunder was louder to the east. He looked over and saw the cloud rising up towards the moon. A stiff breeze chilled the sweat on the back of his T-shirt.

The turtle had laid her eggs in the same place she had probably chosen for the last twenty years, but it could not have been a worse location. This was the narrowest point of the beach and Adam could see that this area had been inundated and carved away by the last run of bad weather. It was no secret that the storms were becoming more frequent and violent along the coast – the Easter before Adam had returned to South Africa from Australia a few years earlier, more than three hundred people had been killed in devastating storms that had hit Durban and the KZN coastline.

Adam looked around him. From the direction of the research camp to the south, he saw two people approaching, walking on the hard-packed wet sand near the water's edge. He checked his watch. The tide was coming in. He recognised them and waved to them; it was Jenny and Thabo. Perhaps sensing his urgency, they started to jog.

Adam dropped to his knees, shrugged the satchel off his shoulder and started digging in the sand at the place where the sea turtle had stopped and made her nest. He was scooping sand into a pile when the two research students arrived.

'What's happening, Prof?' Thabo Radebe, in board shorts and a long-sleeved bush shirt, was panting, hands on his knees. He was a heavyset young man.

Adam gestured over his shoulder with a flick of his head. 'Storm's coming, and when she hits, the waves will wash this nest away.'

'You're going to relocate the eggs.' Jenny Ellis was bent at the waist, looking down into the hole he was excavating. Her long, straight red hair fell like a curtain around her face. She brushed a strand aside. She wore cut-off jean shorts and a white tank top.

Adam looked up at her. 'Yes. But we haven't got much time. The tide won't quite reach here, but this storm's going to bring some hectic waves.' A crash of thunder and a bolt of lightning that hit the ocean punctuated Adam's words.

'We need a box, and a blanket maybe,' Jenny said.

Adam nodded. 'Exactly. Can one of you please go back to the camp and get what we need?'

Thabo cast a look down the long beach.

'Thabo, you stay here and help the prof,' Jenny said. She reached into a pocket and pulled out an elastic, then drew her hair back into a ponytail. 'I'll run back to camp and fetch the Polaris. 'OK, Prof?'

'Yes,' Adam said. 'Quick as you can, please, J.'

She nodded and jogged off. At fifty-five, Adam was probably the fittest of the three of them, although he had seen Jenny running on the beach.

Thabo lowered himself down next to Adam.

'Careful as you dig, Thabo. We should be getting near the eggs. They'll be about –'

'– fifty to sixty centimetres below the surface.' Thabo scooped at the sand, but Adam could see he was taking care with his big hands.

'Well done, Thabo.'

Thabo nodded. 'What are our chances of saving them, Prof?'

Adam was still getting used to being called 'Professor'. He liked it. How could he explain to Sannie that he was happy to spend a few extra days helping these students, even if they weren't technically his responsibility, just because he appreciated their interest in science, turtles, and the environment? And how could he explain why he would sometimes rather be here on the beach alone in his thoughts in the middle of the night than home in bed with her? It was easier to think about turtles than relationships.

'I've done it before, Thabo, and we saved most of them. Some people say we shouldn't try and artificially incubate the eggs, but there are sometimes good reasons – like now, if we know the nest is going to be wiped out in a storm.'

'And there's an argument that with rising temperatures, we need to move some eggs to a cooler environment to ensure a viable population of males remains in the wild.'

'Yes.' Thabo was right – the temperature of the sand in which turtle eggs were laid determined whether the hatchlings were male or female, and with coastal temperatures rising worldwide, more females than males were being born. 'Man's created this problem, so we're within our ethical rights to step in and try to fix it.'

Adam opened his satchel and took out a black Sharpie permanent marker.

'I'm getting to the eggs, Prof.' Thabo had slowed his digging and was now brushing grains of sand from the tops of the first visible white eggs. Each was the size of a ping pong ball, and there would be about a hundred in the nest. Extracting and relocating them would be a time-consuming job.

'These are leatherback eggs,' Adam said, 'which makes it even more important that we save them.' Both loggerhead and leatherback turtles used Bhanga Nek for nesting, but the leatherbacks were rarer and more threatened. While adult loggerheads stayed in the waters offshore from where they were born, leatherbacks roamed the world's oceans and, as such, were at far greater risk of being caught and killed as unwanted 'by-catch' by commercial fishermen.

They both turned at the sound of an engine, revving hard from the south. 'It's Jenny,' Adam said. 'She must have sprinted.'

Jenny roared along the shore on the Polaris, their four-wheel drive all-terrain vehicle, and pulled up just short of where they were digging. She hopped off, bringing three boxes with her. 'I hooked up the trailer as well,' she said.

'Good thinking,' Adam said. He took the lid off the Sharpie and Thabo moved over to make room for him. Adam knelt down and started carefully marking black dots on the top of each egg. 'Do you know why we do this?'

Jenny answered. 'Unlike a chicken, a turtle can't turn its eggs over, so the hatchlings develop by attaching themselves to the inside of the eggshell, so they can draw nutrients from it, and a pool of liquid forms above them, inside the egg, at the top. If you were to take an egg out of the nest now and tip it over, the turtle would drown in the fluid, inside the egg.'

'Correct.' As he marked each egg, Adam carefully removed it and handed it to either Thabo or Jenny who in turn placed it on a beach towel that lined each of the boxes, with the black dot from Adam's marker uppermost. Adam took a temperature sensor from his satchel – it was the size and shape of a ping pong ball, just like one of the eggs. He paused to move a few of the eggs and place the sensor in amongst them. He went back to handing the embryonic turtles to the research students and when they had extracted all the eggs and filled the three boxes, he removed the egg-shaped thermometer. He noted the temperature – they would keep the eggs at that same level.

They loaded the boxes in the trailer and Adam told Thabo to get in the front seat of the Polaris next to Jenny. 'I'll walk.'

'You sure, Professor?' Thabo said.

Adam grinned. 'I'm not that old – yet. Besides, I want to walk alongside you to keep an eye on these eggs. Drive on slowly, Jenny. No rush.'

Jenny nodded, got in, and started the engine. They moved off at a brisk walking pace – Adam's default setting – sticking to the firm sand just above the rising tide.

As he walked, Adam felt spots of rain on his face. The sky darkened as the clouds consumed the moon. The wind picked up and Adam shivered a little. The thunder sounded like a creeping mortar barrage and another lightning strike made him catch his breath. Fortunately, the students were talking to each other and not looking back at him.

Jenny was still attuned to her surroundings, though. 'Professor?'

Adam looked up from the trailer full of turtle eggs. Jenny was pointing down the beach.

'Is that a . . . turtle?' Thabo said. He had to raise his voice over the roar of the surf. The waves were growing with each set and Adam was now being pelted by fat raindrops. Thabo and Jenny had some shelter from the roof over the ATV's small cab.

Adam looked to where they were pointing and Jenny slowed the Polaris to a crawl.

'What the hell *is* that?' Jenny took one hand off the Polaris's steering wheel and put it over her mouth. 'Oh, no! Is that a body?'

'Keep driving, Jenny,' Adam said. She was right. 'Thabo, get out, walk alongside the trailer and keep an eye on the eggs.'

Jenny stopped the vehicle and Thabo alighted. 'We'll come with you. We can help you.'

Adam moved to her side of the ATV and blocked her from getting out. 'Jenny, you're young – both of you. I hope that in your life you don't have to witness a violent death, but you have to believe me, when you do, you can't un-see it, ever.'

She looked into his eyes. 'You were in the army, in the war, in the old days, right?' She pointed to the parachute emblem tattoo on his arm.

'Yes, I was a Parabat. In Angola.'

Thabo looked past him, to the dark inanimate object that had washed up on the shore. The waves were making it roll. Thabo swallowed hard. 'Let's get the eggs back to camp, Jenny.'

Adam clapped Thabo on the arm. 'Good call, *bru*. Let's salvage some life. This weather is turning to *kak*. Get those eggs indoors.'

Thabo nodded. Jenny pressed the starter.

'I'll be back, just now,' Adam said. 'Call the police when you get to the camp, Jenny.'

'Will do, Professor.'

The rain was stinging him as he went to the water's edge. The surf receded, though each new set of waves was bigger than the last, the whitecaps whipped to a frenzy by the onshore wind. The details were revealed to him.

It was a man, dark-skinned but not African. He wore jeans, but the right leg was gone below the knee. The head was a mess, half missing, which would make identification difficult. The shirt had been ripped from the body, and the torso had been opened by a shark. Adam stood over the remains. *No heart.*

Adam walked into the water until it was over his ankles, grabbed an arm and the good leg, and dragged the body up onto drier sand. He searched the trouser pockets – nothing. The man wore a diving watch, mid-range. The foot that remained was bare. The jeans puzzled him. This was no hapless fisherman, nor a local who'd gone for a swim after too much to drink.

Adam straightened again and looked down the beach. Jenny and Thabo were almost at the camp. Adam would walk down and bring the Polaris back, along with a plastic tarpaulin in which to wrap the body. The police would need to inspect it, but as the dead man had come from the sea – there were no tracks on the beach to suggest otherwise – there was no crime scene to contain. He'd call Sannie, as well, to ask her if there was anything else he should be doing until the local police arrived – and that could take hours.

Adam glanced down at the man again and closed his eyes. He breathed in the smell of the sea, listened to the waves crashing and concentrated on the rain pelting his skin, but he could not stay in the moment, as his shrink would have suggested. He was in Angola again, the *crump* of mortars replacing the thunder, the stench of death and cordite dispelling the freshness of the ocean and of peace.

He turned away, walked a few paces, sucking in the night air and the rain that cascaded off his nose and onto his lips and plastered his shirt and shorts to his lean, hard body. Adam put his hands in his close-cropped silver-blond hair and tried to cram the memories back into his head.

Turning towards the sea, he noticed something bobbing, half submerged and tumbling in the waves. He waded into the water again and reached for the object. It was squarish, and bulky from being swaddled in several layers of plastic bubble wrap, which had kept it afloat.

Adam picked up the package and returned to the dry sand, giving the body a wide berth as he tried not to look at it. The rain eased, then stopped. The clouds parted, like a chink in a nosey neighbour's curtains, and the effect was to send a beam of moonlight onto the troubled ocean and illuminate the object in his hands.

It was heavy – maybe three or four kilograms. He unwrapped it with wet fingers made soft by the rain, and fumbled with the sticky tape. Someone had really wanted this thing to stay dry.

The plastic wrapping snapped in the wind as he rolled the object over in his hands. He had uncovered a casing of some kind and it looked old. It was made of a metal – maybe brass or copper – which gleamed in the moonlight. When he had finally freed it he thought it looked like a prop from some kind of ancient history or fantasy film. It was like a mini treasure chest, inlaid with what looked like decorative metalwork and what were probably fake or semi-precious stones.

Adam paused to bundle the discarded bubblewrap and stood on it so that it didn't blow into the ocean. Looking back at the object he found a latch, which he opened, revealing a book inside the small chest. It looked like a medieval Bible, and when he opened the stiff, worn leather cover he saw words inside on yellowed parchment. They were like a monk's calligraphy, but they were not in English or Latin. They were in Arabic.

He glanced again at the body. Did the plastic-wrapped book, perhaps an antique copy of the Koran, belong to him?

2

AFTER THE ANGLO-ZULU WAR, NATAL, 1880

There was a knock at the door. 'Compliments of Hellfire Jack, Mister Gregory, sir,' the voice called from outside. 'You've an appointment with a dead body and a journalist.'

Peter Gregory opened one eye in the dim, two-room thatched farmhouse that smelled of woodsmoke, mould and woman. Preeti, Harpreet Naidoo, who now wished to be known as Grace, stirred beside him, warm under the sheet and blanket.

'Go away, Phillips,' Gregory croaked. 'It's Sunday, a day of prayer and rest.'

Sergeant Gavin Phillips brayed. 'Very good, sir. But the major was most adamant. Your presence is requested *now*, sir. And might I come in? It really is raining quite heavily outside.'

Phillips was twenty, seventeen years younger than Gregory. In the British Army he would have been a second lieutenant, a wet-behind-the-ears whelp in his first command, but he'd been brought up in the colony, the son of a wealthy cane farmer, so had joined the local force. Phillips had enlisted in the Mounted Police with the hope of seeing action, but had been too late – the war had finished before he could fire a shot in anger. However, so many police had been killed at Isandlwana that Phillips had been propelled up the ranks from constable to sergeant in quick time.

'No.' Gregory ran a hand through his unwashed, thick, dark mane, which hung down to his collar.

Black eyes framed by a matching curtain of silky fringe peeked over the top of the blanket and blinked at him. Gregory winked back.

Phillips thumped on the door. 'Sir, the major told me I must not return to camp without you, or he'll have my guts.'

Gregory reached for his pocket watch on the sawn-off stump that served as a bedside table. The back of his hand brushed the empty square-faced gin bottle, which toppled and landed on the slate-hard floor of polished and hardened cow dung with a crash. Grace started and pulled the covers back over her head.

He swung his legs over the side of the timber-and-rope bed and pulled on his cavalry breeches and boots. As he stood, he hitched the braces over the shoulders of his collarless, grimy undershirt. Thunder rumbled, like Chelmsford's four-pounders firing in the distance, and a crack of lightning sounded like a bursting shell.

Gregory lifted the wooden latch from its stay and opened the door a fraction. Phillips paused, fist up, ready for another knock. Rain streamed from his off-white pith helmet onto the thick corduroy of his dark brown Natal Mounted Police uniform tunic. Gregory caught a whiff of horse and sweat.

'I'll be out in fifteen minutes, Phillips. Wait in the barn. Ask Samuel to –'

'I've already told the bloody –'

Gregory held up a finger. 'Please ask *Constable* Khumalo to saddle my horse.'

'I've already done so, sir. And if you don't mind me saying so, that . . . *man*, Khumalo, has something of a superior attitude, unbecoming in a native.'

Gregory reached for his own police tunic, hanging on a hook. 'That's because he's a prince, Phillips, a member of a Zulu royal family. Best not to forget it. If you were back home in London, he'd have you cashiered and horsewhipped for insubordination. I'll be out directly.'

Gregory waited long enough to see Phillips trudging through the mud to the barn before closing and latching the door again. He tossed the uniform jacket on the bed, then went to the hearth and prodded the fire's near-dead embers with the tip of a rusted Martini–Henry bayonet.

It was May and the Natal Midlands was colder in the approaching winter than any of Gregory's estranged family back in England could have imagined. The unseasonal late rain, some of which was finding its way through the thatch roof, just made it more miserable. Gregory laid a taper on the glowing coals until a flame appeared and used it to light a thin cigar from a tin box on the simple brick mantelpiece. He coughed.

Grace emerged again and wiggled up the mattress until her back was against the bedhead. Though she held the sheet up, Gregory saw the shadow of one dark, wayward nipple peeking around a fold. He felt a tightening in his lower belly.

She frowned. 'I'm not inclined to agree with the current body of medical evidence that smoking is conducive to good health and an improved respiration.'

'Preeti . . .'

She frowned. 'Grace.'

'I liked your Indian name better. Now that you're a God-fearing, baptised Christian lady, you should be repenting for what we did an hour ago, not lecturing me about smoking.'

She drew the sheet up to cover her face completely. 'You are a perfectly horrible man, Captain Peter Gregory. I shall pray for your soul.' Grace liked to refer to him by his former army rank, captain, which he'd held before joining the police, as she thought it sounded more important than his police position as a sub-inspector. Still in her twenties, Grace was big on social standing. She blinked at him again, the bedclothes now revealing only her eyes. 'Do you have to go?' she purred.

He put his cigar in an ashtray made from a giraffe's vertebra he'd scavenged from the remains of a lion kill on the banks of the Umfolozi River, shrugged on his tunic and buttoned it up. 'When Hellfire Jack Dartnell calls, one doesn't say no.' Gregory took his pistol belt from the back of the chair and buckled it on. 'Besides, no one else would employ me.'

Gregory drew his revolver, thumbed back the hammer and spun the chamber. Satisfied that it was clean, he slid it into its holster.

'You had the night terrors again, Peter,' Grace said.

He looked in her direction, but let his eyes rest on the white-washed wall above her head. His mind projected a magic lantern image of a field of naked bodies, each sliced from sternum to groin, the viscera spilling out. Fires flickered at the corners of the scene; a single gunshot silenced a horse's dying whinnies. He screwed his eyes closed. Gregory remembered, now, waking in the small hours of the morning, screaming.

'Peter . . .'

He opened his eyes and manufactured a smile. 'Probably the tinned fish we had for supper.'

Grace shook her head. 'There is no need to make light of it. Your soul is injured, but your pain may come from one of your past lives.'

Gregory gave a snort. 'I doubt your new friend the Baptist pastor believes in your Hindu notion of reincarnation, Preeti.'

'Grace . . .'

He put his spike-topped pith helmet on and adjusted the chin-strap. 'I don't believe in past lives.'

'You were troubled before . . . when I first met you, Peter. Karma teaches us that we can change our situation, our present life, no matter what grievances we suffered in the last.'

Gregory picked up his cigar and took another drag of it, the tobacco enlivening him even as he coughed again. He stubbed it out. Gregory looked at Grace, in bed, and revelled in some impure thoughts for a few moments. He sighed. 'I must away.'

She lowered the sheet a little and gave him a smile to accompany the improved view. 'You won't reconsider?'

Unless he drowned himself in gin, she was the only thing that *could* currently make him forget the horrors of the last twelve months. It felt like a curse that even in her arms, in their warm bed, the terror bubbled up inside him like a cancerous growth, eating him from within.

It was a wrench, but he also knew that doing something, even riding in the rain, helped. 'Phillips will be back looking for me soon. Best he finds you in your maid's clothes, dusting.'

She lowered her eyes with the exaggerated slowness of a music hall actress. 'Yes . . . sir.'

He almost ripped his jacket off again, but instead he opened the door and walked out into the rain. Grace was on the right path in her life, at last. She didn't need him and his melancholy dragging her down or ruining her reputation when she was making a very good effort at salvaging it.

Grace had been grateful of his offer of refuge on his farm, but she had also, in a polite and businesslike manner, made it clear to him that despite whatever attraction they felt for each other, she did not intend to remain there.

'I escaped from life as an indentured worker on a farm, and I have no intention of spending the rest of my days mucking out stables or milking cows,' she had told him, only half in jest. 'For goodness' sake, Peter, you can't even afford labourers.'

Her words had stung, but they were true. He was living off his police wage, and, lately, supporting her as well. Part of his problem, he knew, was that as hard as he tried, he could not wash the blood from his memory, nor the stain of guilt from his soul. Unless he was out riding, in search of some criminal, he found it hard to even get out of bed, let alone work the farm.

Grace had also made no secret of her designs on the Baptist pastor. 'He's handsome, and I think he likes me,' she had said. It was frank, casual comments like this that let him know she would soon be on her way. It was probably for the best.

'Captain.' Samuel led their horses from the stable as Gregory approached. The rain had eased to drizzle. Phillips came out, his hands wrapped around a tin mug of steaming tea.

'*Sawubona*, Your Highness,' Gregory said.

Samuel smiled. 'Sergeant Phillips says we have work to do.'

'That we do.' Gregory put a foot in Bullet's stirrup and hoisted himself up into the saddle on the black stallion's back. He slid his Martini–Henry into the rifle bucket. 'Come along, Phillips.'

Samuel was in the saddle and closing on Gregory before the young sergeant was even mounted.

It was two hours' ride on muddy tracks that cleaved Natal's emerald-green hills like freshly puckered scars until they reached the mix of ramshackle thatch-roofed huts, timber houses and brick edifices of the colonial capital, Pietermaritzburg.

The air hung heavy with damp, and when the sun did make the effort to cut through the clouds it made the thick wool of their uniforms and the horses' coats steam in the creeping warmth. It was still preferable to the coast, where Grace hailed from, where the Indian labourers sweated in the oppressive heat and humidity while they hacked at the sugar cane that lined the farmers' pockets and fuelled the engine of empire.

The war against the Zulus had brought more building, more people, more roads, more colonists, more soldiers and more sin, and while the people of heaven, as the Zulus called themselves, were defeated, more than one man and woman on the roadside cast a sideways glance at Samuel. Those who did could not hold his fierce glare for long; he might have worn white man's clothes, but with his straight-backed bearing, spears and rifle he was the very essence of a warrior.

Samuel stayed outside to mind the horses when they arrived at the imposing, two-storey brick headquarters of the Natal Mounted Police. A uniformed sergeant led Gregory and Phillips inside and an elderly Zulu woman trailed them along the polished wood-floored hallway, mopping the water and mud they left in their wake.

'Major Dartnell will see you now, Sub-Inspector Gregory,' the sergeant said when they reached the commanding officer's door.

'Right, well.' Phillips shifted his weight from one foot to the other, waiting to see if he would be invited in as well. There were no further instructions. 'I'll see you anon, then.'

Gregory nodded and knocked.

'Come.'

He opened the door, saluted, and took off his hat. Dartnell sat behind a large mahogany desk; the cloud-dimmed light from outside was supplemented by an oil lamp that burned hot and hazy on the major's desk. He looked up from his writings and ran the thumb and forefinger of his right hand down the length of his short, pointed beard.

'Gregory.'

'Sir.' Gregory took a seat.

Dartnell was thinning on top, but he was perhaps only a year or two older than Gregory. His eyes fixed on Gregory like he was prey. Hellfire Jack had earned the respect of his men not only through his straightforward manner and loyalty to them, but because of his history of service. During the Indian Rebellion he'd been recommended for a Victoria Cross after being first up the ladder to storm an enemy fort, and he'd later served in Bhutan, and in the Zulu War. Dartnell put his elbows on his blotter and leaned forward.

'Are you clear-headed, Gregory?'

Gregory was taken aback, but casually covered his mouth while pretending to stroke his moustache. 'I've not been drinking this morning, if that's what you mean, sir.'

'No. That is not what I mean, Gregory. Some men are afflicted by their experiences on the battlefield. A malaise settles upon them and they are unable to shake it off. They withdraw from polite society . . . take refuge in one improper substance or activity or another.'

'I am in good health, sir.'

The major looked him up and down and snorted. 'If your mind still works, I have a task for you. I recall how you brought that chap Blundell to justice.'

Gregory nodded. 'Said his wife had shot herself in the head using her right hand, when some simple enquiries revealed she was left-handed. He was a gambler with outstanding debts and a mistress.'

'Hmmm. Not the most difficult of cases, but you saw it through to the end, and the fellow admitted his crime.'

'Yes, sir,' Gregory said, wondering what the back-handed compliment was meant to achieve.

'There's been another murder,' Dartnell said. 'A former army officer, killed and slit open, in the manner of the Zulus.' The major picked up a pen, dipped it in ink and began scratching on a piece of paper. 'This is the name of the deceased, and his farm, on the road to Dundee.'

'Yes, sir.'

Dartnell stopped writing and looked up at him. 'Some local farmers are up in arms, as it would *appear* to be the work of Zulu renegades.'

'I wasn't aware that we'd had any problems with the Zulu since their defeat last year, sir,' Gregory said, 'and certainly not here on the Natal side of the border with Zululand.'

The major slid the piece of paper across the desk and Gregory took it. 'We haven't, which is why I'm sending you to investigate the killing.'

Gregory glanced at the note. He knew the rough location of the farm. He looked up at Dartnell. 'Phillips said something about a journalist, sir?'

'Suspected journalist.' Dartnell shuffled through a sheaf of papers on his desk until he found the one he was looking for. He consulted it. 'But, yes. A woman *and* an American to boot.' He grimaced and looked up from the sheet, raising his eyebrows. 'A titled woman, Lady Beecham, one Teresa O'Kane. She is quite the independent traveller, now being estranged from her former husband, Lord Beecham, and claims to be a close acquaintance of the Empress Eugénie.'

It took Gregory a moment to recall something he'd read in the *Natal Witness*. 'The mother of the late Prince Imperial of France, sir? Is she not on her way to the colony, sir?'

'Here already.' Dartnell's chest swelled as he drew a deep breath, frowned and nodded. 'Her Majesty has come to commemorate the first anniversary of Prince Louis's death, on the first of June, just around the corner. The empress has embarked on a pilgrimage to retrace her son's footsteps and to be present for the unveiling of a new memorial at the site of his death.'

Gregory nodded. Just over a year ago all their lives had changed. Had it been a year already? If one event had eclipsed the undying shame of thirteen hundred British, colonial and native troops being overrun and slain at that damned rock, Isandlwana, it had been the death in a small skirmish of a single Frenchman – the great-nephew of Napoleon Bonaparte himself in an unnamed donga, a dry tributary of the Tshotshosi River in Zululand.

'Miss O'Kane,' Dartnell continued, '*Lady* Beecham, seems to have it in mind that she will be reunited with the empress and attend the memorial service. We have yet to ascertain the validity of her claims – enquiries are ongoing – but the lady will require an escort as she seems intent on visiting the key battlefields of the late campaign, as well.'

'Sir . . .'

Dartnell held up a hand. 'Still your inevitable protest, Gregory. Yes, I need to assign some poor fellow to chaperone the good lady, but there's another reason why I'd like it to be you who retraces the steps of Lord Chelmsford's campaign.'

Gregory pinched the bridge of his nose with thumb and forefinger. He felt dizzy and silver spots began appearing at the extremities of his vision, even as he closed his eyes.

'Gregory!'

He opened his eyes. 'Sir.'

'Pay attention.'

'Yes, sir.'

Dartnell exhaled, and his shoulders sagged a little. 'You are one of my best officers, Peter, and undoubtedly the cleverest, if not when it comes to affairs of the heart.'

Gregory drew a breath and was ready to reply, but Dartnell shut him down with a raised hand.

'Enough. What goes on between you and your Indian *housekeeper* is none of my business. No, Gregory, there is something else I need you to do for me.'

Gregory held his tongue. Dartnell sifted through more papers, until once again he found the one he was looking for. 'I have here a missive from Lord Chelmsford. What I am about to tell you, Gregory, is in the strictest confidence. No one else must know of the contents of this correspondence. Do you understand?'

Gregory nodded. 'Yes, sir.' Chelmsford had been the overall commander of the invasion of Zululand at the start of the war, in January, 1879. It was he who had made the terrible error of splitting his forces and leaving his supply wagons exposed and under-defended at Isandlwana. They had been massacred, almost to a man. The heroic defence and British victory at Rorke's Drift, which followed the disaster at Isandlwana, had not been enough to save Chelmsford's job, but even though he was relieved of his command he led a final incursion back into Zululand. Chelmsford defeated the Zulu king, Cetshwayo kaMpande, at his imperial capital, Ulundi, before Chelmsford's successor, Garnet Wolseley, could arrive to take the glory.

Dartnell's eyes scanned the page, then he looked up. 'When Lord Chelmsford returned to England after Ulundi, he sought and was granted an audience with the Empress Eugénie. His purpose, as well as conveying his condolences over the death of the Prince Imperial, was to return the young prince's sword to his mother.'

Gregory pulled his head back a little in surprise. 'They found Napoleon's sword, sir?' The way he'd heard it, the Zulus who had ambushed the small scouting patrol that the prince had been on had killed the heir to the Bonaparte dynasty, as well as two British soldiers and a Zulu scout working for the British. They then stripped the bodies, mutilated them, and took their weapons and uniforms.

Dartnell arched his eyebrows. 'You say, "Napoleon's sword", Gregory. What do you mean by that? The prince's weapon, or that of a more famous forebear?'

Gregory shrugged. 'The latter. I remember some stories, sir. A friend of mine in the Royal Artillery, whose younger brother had trained with the prince in England, said that Prince Louis carried the sword of his great-uncle, Napoleon Bonaparte. He said the blade was that carried by the French Emperor at the Battle of Austerlitz.'

'Indeed.' Dartnell consulted the letter again. 'But Chelmsford wrote the following to me: "*On presenting the sword to Her Majesty she affected a look of surprise, followed by profound dismay, whereupon she told me that this was not her son's sword, nor that of her husband's uncle, Napoleon Bonaparte*". It seems Chelmsford had the wrong sword.'

'How did Lord Chelmsford come across the sword?' Gregory asked. He found himself leaning forward, elbows on his knees. There was something about a puzzle, a mystery, an odd question that excited him. It also had the welcome effect of pushing any other problems or maladies in his life into the background.

'You remember the situation between the Zulus and our forces in the lead-up to Ulundi?' Dartnell said, answering with a question.

'Sir.' Gregory nodded. 'We wanted revenge after Isandlwana, but even when the second invasion happened, the Zulus did not rush to the fight again.'

'Yes,' Dartnell said. 'King Cetshwayo may have basked briefly in his early victories, but he knew what the reaction would be. Accordingly, he sent out several envoys to try and negotiate with Chelmsford. However, His Lordship was intent on crushing the Zulus. One party of Zulus, under a senior officer named Mfunzi, approached a British patrol below the Mthonjaneni Heights, en route to the White Umfolozi River, under a white flag, and handed over the Prince Imperial's sword. They claimed it was the weapon taken during the encounter and that they had since learned that their men had killed a great warrior, a nobleman from Europe. They offered the sword as a sign of good faith. Chelmsford took the sword, but refused to negotiate, and the rest is history. Except...'

'Except it wasn't the prince's sword?' Gregory asked.

Dartnell shook his head. 'Oh, it was a French sword all right, but a common cavalry officer's weapon. According to the empress it was certainly not the rather ornate blade carried by Bonaparte at Austerlitz – that one was apparently covered in rather ornate engravings.'

Gregory thought a moment. 'How the hell would a French cavalry sword end up in Zululand?'

Dartnell leaned back in his chair, which creaked with the movement. Outside, cicadas screeched in the sun now that the rain was gone. He folded his hands over his stomach, fingers interlaced. 'Exactly. And where is Napoleon Bonaparte's famous sword now?'

Gregory looked his commander in the eye. 'Sir?'

Dartnell leaned forward again on his elbows, closing the distance between him and Gregory. 'I want you to make some enquiries, Gregory, discreetly, but posthaste. With the empress here now it is Lord Chelmsford's wish that we do our utmost to find the *real* Napoleon's sword and present it to her.'

'But surely the army, sir –'

Dartnell held up a hand. 'As you very well know, Lord Chelmsford was officially relieved of his post just before the Battle of Ulundi and was supposed to hand over command to General Wolseley. As it happened, Chelmsford snatched victory from the jaws of his own reputational defeat and Wolseley arrived too late for the last big battle of the war. There is bad blood between the men, and if Wolseley found out that Chelmsford had embarrassed himself by handing over the wrong sword then Wolseley would sully Chelmsford's reputation further. It is a matter of honour for Lord Chelmsford.'

Gregory took in the information. In his experience, the foolish pride and honour of generals more often than not ended with the death of soldiers.

'The empress is known in London as a woman of great generosity, who rewards the favour of those who serve her well,' Dartnell added.

Sweetening the pot? The good Lord – and his newly minted servant Grace – knew that Gregory was proving to be a failure at farming. Perhaps Dartnell had also learned of Gregory's parlous financial state. The funds from England had dried up with the death of his mother, and though nothing had yet been communicated formally, Gregory couldn't help but wonder if word of his shame had reached the rest of his estranged family.

'What is occupying your thoughts, Captain?'

Gregory realised he'd been lost in his own troubles. 'Er, nothing, sir. Do you have any avenues of approach in mind as to where I can start looking for this missing sword?'

Dartnell ignored the question. 'I know what troubles you, Gregory. I've read the full report of what happened at Isandlwana, and the accounts of the very few survivors of the battle.'

Rout, more like it. 'Sir.'

Dartnell stroked his neat beard. 'I wish that more people in the colony could have read that document – it would still some of the . . . innuendo. You and I know what happened.'

'With respect, sir, I was unconscious for much of it.'

He nodded. 'Yes, yes, yes, I know that. But we both know that those with idle hands and simple minds will gossip, and I am not unaware of how that has affected your social standing in the colony, Gregory. This mission, quest, whatever you will name it, to assist the empress, will be an opportunity to demonstrate the thoroughness and sense of duty and honour that I know you possess.'

Gregory wasn't sure what to say. There it was – the ink blot of his life, not only indelible, but still spreading. Peter Gregory – cad, drunkard and coward. He needed to change the subject lest he find himself pressing the barrel of his revolver to his temple, as he'd done once before after imbibing to excess. 'And the murder, sir?'

Dartnell sat back again, then searched among his papers. 'Yes, here are the details. And when you asked about avenues of investigation, this is the first. A passing traveller found the man dead on his smallholding on the Dundee road yesterday. It appears he had been stabbed to death and then treated in the Zulu manner – that is, his stomach was slit open. You know the drill.'

'Yes, sir. Do we know who he is?'

Dartnell consulted his piece of paper and handed it to Gregory. 'Indeed we do, Gregory, indeed we do. He is, or was, Major Harry Morrison, late, in every sense of the word, of the 17th Lancers. He was one of a number of officers who elected to stay on once the hostilities were over and farm a piece of land.'

Gregory sat up straighter in his chair. 'I know of the man, sir. In the course of my investigation into the Blundell case I learned of some unsavoury allegations about a man of the same name. I was planning on paying him a visit.'

Dartnell nodded. 'Find out everything you can about this Morrison chap, Gregory.'

'Yes, sir. And the missing sword, sir?' Gregory prompted.

'As it happens, Morrison was the adjutant of the 17th. According to Lord Chelmsford's letter, Morrison was also,' Dartnell leaned back in his chair again, and permitted himself a small smile, as if enjoying the drawing out of this briefing, 'the officer who was presented with the Prince Imperial's sword by the Zulu emissary Mfunzi.'

3

KWAZULU-NATAL, THE PRESENT

Lieutenant Colonel Sannie van Rensburg took the M7 on-ramp from the N2 and turned away from the Indian Ocean and the sprawling industrial outskirts of Durban.

She was leaving the laid-back south coast lifestyle she had come to appreciate, but also the stifling humidity of office politics. And she was leaving Adam Kruger's home, albeit temporarily.

'Bar-One?' Warrant Officer Marilyn Msani extended the chocolate bar to her with a sly smile from the front passenger seat of Sannie's Toyota Fortuner.

'No, thanks.' The reply was instinctive. She'd been watching her diet, exercising more and drinking less. She'd wanted to lose six kilograms and look her best for a holiday she and Adam had been planning. Now there was no holiday – it was postponed indefinitely due to Adam's work. She reconsidered. 'What the hell. *Ja.* Sure.'

Marilyn broke the chocolate and caramel treat in half and Sannie closed her eyes very briefly in a moment of rapture as she bit down on it.

'I don't know why you worry about your weight, Colonel,' Marilyn said.

'Who says I worry about it?'

Marilyn shook her head. '*Ai, ai, ai*, you're always "no to the chips", "no to the chocolates", what-what.'

Sannie frowned. But she enjoyed the chocolate. She indicated to pass a truck – there were so many of them on this stretch of road – and accelerated uphill through a sweeping curve. 'I'll show you chips – we'll stop at the Windmill and you can try one of their homemade pies. They're the best in KwaZulu-Natal.'

Marilyn tutted. 'We shall see. All that talk of stolen beef is making me hungry. I'm looking forward to getting out in the country and away from the heat. And give me cattle rustlers over cash-in-transit heists and murders any day.'

Sannie watched the thermometer on the Toyota's dashboard. The temperature had already dropped from thirty to twenty-six degrees, and looked to be falling further by the minute. She was less keen than her new partner on their temporary duty assignment, but there was no escaping it, and it may have come at a good time.

'You used to work in Stock Theft and Endangered Species, Sannie – you'll be perfect for the job,' their commanding officer at the Directorate for Priority Crime Investigation, Gita Kapahi, had said to Sannie when she had briefed her in her office at the Hawks' headquarters in Port Shepstone.

'Colonel, when I headed up the STES unit at Skukuza we were more interested in rhino poaching in the Kruger Park than stolen cattle,' Sannie had protested. 'I don't know one end of a cow from the other.'

Gita had frowned. 'I thought you told me you grew up on a farm, Sannie?'

'A banana farm, Colonel.'

Sannie's immediate task was to take over the STES unit until its regular commander, Lieutenant Colonel Sibuya was fit to return to duty. Sibuya had been in a car accident the week before and was in intensive care, in hospital, in Durban. Gita had told her that Captain Derick le Roux, the second-in-command, would have filled in, but he had just announced that he was leaving the police service and moving to New Zealand and was due to finish this week. All that was why Sannie had been plucked from the Hawks at Port Shepstone and, along with Marilyn, sent out here to the KZN hinterland. Sannie was still wondering, *why me*, when Gita dropped her bombshell.

'I'M SENDING YOU, SANNIE,' Gita had explained, 'because no fewer than sixteen dead rhinos were found at a place called Virginia Farm. It appears that the elderly owner of the farm and a game reserve, David Gregory, killed them himself. On top of that there's been a spike in stock theft cases recently, with a very organised gang behind large numbers of cattle being stolen.'

Now on the N3, the countryside changed the further Sannie drove. It was one of the amazing things about KZN – and South Africa as a whole – how quickly the landscape, culture and people morphed from one thing to another, within relatively short distances. They had left behind the cloying heat of the subtropics and were soon passing through green fields of cows and horses that would have looked at home on a postcard from England.

Sannie remembered how she'd been so cold when she visited London that the first place she went to was a street market, to buy an overcoat. That brought back memories of her second husband, Tom, the father of her third child, Tommy. She bit her lower lip.

'You OK?' Marilyn screwed up the chocolate bar wrapper.

Sannie nodded. 'Fine.'

'Speaking of *fine*, how is that man of yours – the surfer dude with all the muscles?'

Sannie puffed her cheeks and exhaled. *Like my second husband*, she wanted to say, but held her tongue. Tom had been a policeman in England, a protection officer and bodyguard, and she'd met him when he'd been on a job in South Africa that had gone horribly wrong. They'd fallen in love, married, and Tom had come to live with Sannie and her children in the Lowveld, near the Kruger Park, but Tom had found it hard to get used to not working – he couldn't at first, on his spousal visa – and had drifted into work as a contract bodyguard working for the United Nations in Iraq. He was far from the only ex–law enforcement or military person chasing the big bucks in the Middle East, but the job had cost him his life. He had been killed in a terrorist rocket attack. To her dismay, Sannie felt like she was going through something similar with her new boyfriend, Adam.

'He's busy supervising a research project up at Bhanga Nek.'

'Where's that?' Marilyn asked.

'Between St Lucia and Kosi Bay, in the iSimangaliso Wetlands Park. Up near the border between KZN and Mozambique.'

'Never been there.'

Sannie sighed. 'It's beautiful there. Adam's researching sea turtles. He's a professor now, at Durban University.'

She'd been so proud of Adam, how he'd turned his life around from having to work as a car guard at a shopping mall to make ends meet, to finishing his PhD as a mature-aged student, and then getting tenure as a professor. His age and his background were against him – there was pressure in the university to appoint people from formerly disadvantaged backgrounds to permanent positions – but he'd excelled and proved to be a brilliant teacher.

But, like Tom, it seemed as though he still felt he needed to prove something to her. And she couldn't help feeling that Adam sometimes preferred to be alone. At least he wasn't working in a war zone, and Bhanga Nek was probably the safest place in South Africa to work – even if Adam was fond of freediving with sharks.

'I don't like the ocean,' Marilyn said.

Sannie looked at her. 'But you live at Ramsgate and you're dressed by Roxy half the time at work?'

Marilyn smiled. 'I like the beach vibe; I just don't like getting wet. And there are sharks.'

Adam had been researching sharks when Sannie first met him. She gripped the steering wheel a little harder. 'I know.'

John Parker's phone pinged in the breast pocket of his khaki safari shirt, which was emblazoned with the uBhejane Game Reserve logo of a black rhino. He stopped his Land Rover game viewer, took out his Samsung and read the message.

Urgent. Intruders on Virginia Farm. The message came from Adella Mdluli, David Gregory's domestic worker.

The male cheetah lifted its head as John turned the key. The starter motor whined for a few seconds until the tired old engine finally caught. The cat stared at him with its haunting red-gold eyes. John had enjoyed the rare moment of peace; his was the only vehicle at the sighting. There were no guests, virtually no staff, and not enough diesel in the reserve's tanks to fill another Land Rover even if someone did want to go for a game drive.

John slipped the phone back in his pocket, put the Land Rover into gear and accelerated as fast as he could along the rutted, ungraded game-viewing road. He passed a small herd of zebra and a lone male giraffe, a big old bull, and was back at the lodge within ten minutes. Jan-Maree Ball came out, lithe and sexy and still in the Esjay activewear she'd worn on her early-morning run. She must have seen from his high-speed approach that something was wrong.

'What's happening?' Jan-Maree asked. Her accent was still notably Australian, even though it had softened from her time in South Africa. Here, the first part of her name, Jan, was a boy's name, and she was forever telling people that it pronounced 'Jan as in January, or Janet'. John loved everything about her, even her accent.

'Old David. Intruder at Virginia.' He saw the concern in her face, and for the hundredth time in the last two weeks he wondered how a woman like her had fallen for him and into his bed. She brushed some stray strands of ash-blonde hair away from her blue eyes.

'Oh, bloody hell. You're going?' Jan-Maree asked.

John was already out of the Land Rover, striding past her into the lodge manager's house where he lived. Jan-Maree still had her little flat, on the smallholding outside of Dundee, but she had moved some things in since breaking up with Deon, and they'd talked about her moving in fulltime. 'Of course I'm going.'

'Don't. Please.' Jan-Maree followed him into the small two-bedroom dwelling.

By the time she got to the bedroom, John had the semi-automatic LM5 assault rifle out of the gun safe and was fitting a curved thirty-round magazine into it. He grabbed the cocking handle and pulled it back, chambering a round.

Jan-Maree laid a hand on his arm. 'Armed response and the police will be there just now. You don't need to go.'

He shook his head. 'I do. David would come if it was me.'

Jan-Maree screwed her eyes closed. 'These bloody farm attacks. I hope David doesn't try to fight back. Shall I come with you?'

'No,' John said. 'Hopefully I won't be long.'

John took the spare magazine, already filled with rounds, from the safe, and strode out the door. He got into the Land Rover, took out his phone and tapped on the WhatsApp Farm Watch group: *Parker, responding.*

Others were on their way. The local armed response security company left a voice note on the group. John tapped on the message to listen to the recording as he sped down the dirt access road from the lodge towards the main gate.

'*Ja, it's Deon here from Viking Security. Responding, but I'm just coming from the other side of Dundee now. I had another call-out which turned out to be a false alarm. I'll be at David's in . . . ten minutes.*'

John frowned. He had no wish to see Deon, but there would be no avoiding it. He glanced at his watch, then geared down and floored the accelerator. When he reached the gate he had to get out, undo the padlock and slide the heavy barrier open, and then close it after him. Once out and on the tar road he pushed the old Land Rover up to its ninety-kilometre-per-hour maximum.

David's farm was five kilometres down the road. The two properties were joined – David owned uBhejane Game Reserve as well as Virginia Farm – but it would have taken longer to drive the neglected internal roads. John came to the rusted entry gate and saw that it had been broken open.

John followed the weaving road towards David's home, but stopped three hundred metres short, near an earth-walled dam. John took his LM5 from the passenger seat and got out. Dairy cows stared at him from beyond a fence as John moved forward, the butt of the rifle in his shoulder.

John squeezed the rifle's pistol grip tighter. His senses were on full alert; he hadn't felt this focused since he'd faced down a lion that he encountered while taking some guests on a guided walk at uBhejane. Unlike David, who had served in the Border War, John, at the age of twenty-eight, was born after military conscription ended in South Africa. As a safari guide, however, he was a proficient marksman.

A man burst from the front door of David's house, out onto the covered *stoep*.

John raised the barrel of the rifle and looked down the sights. 'Hands up!'

The man was young, trackpants hanging low, white T-shirt, and carrying a rifle. He swung around and stared at John.

'Gun down, now!'

The young man raised the rifle. It looked like a heavy-calibre weapon – maybe one of David's. John fired two shots, a double tap. The young man fell. John moved forward. One bullet had caught the man in the heart; the other had winged him in the shoulder. John was breathing hard, adrenaline coursing through his body.

John broke into a run, and as he reached the house, the window next to David's front door erupted as three gunshots echoed around the yard. John dived to the ground and rolled, seeking cover behind David's red Toyota HiLux *bakkie* parked in the driveway.

A shadow moved behind the shattered window. John, lying flat on his stomach, took aim and fired twice. A hand appeared, holding a pistol. John lowered his face to the grass and four shots thudded into the vehicle above him. A fifth ploughed into the grass next to his head. John rolled away, and then crawled to the rear of the *bakkie*.

A bullet pinged off the Toyota's bodywork and a second shattered a window above John. He winced and checked his watch – Deon from the security company should be there soon. As much as they disliked each other, John couldn't wait for the big Afrikaner to get to the farm.

'Shit.' John stood up, took a deep breath and sprinted for the house. At any second he expected to see the gunman at the window, or to feel the thud of a bullet knocking him off his feet. His blood pumped in his ears and he was blowing hard as he threw himself against the plastered exterior wall of the house.

There was the sound of glass shattering, perhaps from the far side of the farmhouse. John edged along the wall, towards the rear. He ducked as he passed under a bedroom window, then paused as he reached the back corner of the building.

John raised the barrel of his rifle again, ready to shoot on sight, then swung himself around the corner.

A man stood there, broken glass on the ground next to him from where he had smashed out a window and jumped. He spun and saw John, and brought his pistol up at the same time.

John fired twice and the man fell back. John went to him, and as he stood over him the man raised his gun hand again. John fired a third shot.

He went to the back door, found it locked, and kicked it. The wooden frame splintered on the third attempt. John realised David must have dead-locked the door from the inside, which was why the man had broken the rear window to jump out.

John moved down the hallway, his rifle still at the ready, then went into David's living room.

'No!'

Sannie called the Stock Theft and Endangered Species Unit at Glencoe from the hands-free device in her car. She was only ten kilometres from town. A Sergeant Nyathi answered. Sannie introduced herself. 'Can I speak to Captain Le Roux, please?'

'I'm sorry, Colonel, but everyone's out, including the captain. There's been an incident at Virginia Farm.'

Sannie recognised the name. 'The place where those sixteen rhinos were killed?'

'Exactly, Colonel. The captain said that you would want to visit there, and that I should tell you when you arrived that you should go straight to the farm and meet him there.'

'*Ja*, OK,' Sannie said. 'Can you send me a pin?'

'Will do, Colonel.' Nyathi hung up.

Sannie passed her phone to Marilyn. When it dinged, Marilyn checked it. 'You can turn right up ahead, Sannie. We're not far.'

Sannie made the turn and accelerated. Marilyn guided her past green fields and farms, and through a rural area with modest houses made of brick and tin. Goats and cows grazed in small fields and on the side of the road. Twice, she had to slow to let cows cross.

Marilyn pointed through the windscreen. 'This is the place, coming up on the left.'

Sannie saw a sign that said *David and Zelda Gregory, Virginia Farm.* Below the name of the farm and its owners was the logo of the agricultural chemical company that had sponsored the sign. Sannie turned in through the wide-open gate and the Fortuner bounced along a rough gravel road.

A kilometre on, they approached a farmhouse. Parked outside was a green Land Rover Defender game-viewing vehicle; a police *bakkie*; a Ford Ranger painted black and bristling with radio antennae, with the words *Viking Security* on the side; and an older model red HiLux.

Sannie pulled up just short of the vehicles and she and Marilyn got out. As they moved forward, a pair of uniformed police officers, a man and a woman, rounded a corner of the farmhouse. Sannie introduced herself and held up her ID.

The female officer, the more senior of the two, greeted Sannie in English and Marilyn in Zulu.

Sannie looked past the officers and saw the body of a young man in the grass. 'What happened here?'

The female officer looked to the man and then gestured with a flick of her head to the rear of the house, where they had just come from. 'There's another one out the back. You should speak with Captain Le Roux. He and the others are inside.'

Sannie thought there were probably enough boots trampling this crime scene, so she and Marilyn waited outside the farmhouse. A procession of men emerged a minute later.

A man in his late fifties or early sixties – Sannie couldn't remember how old he was – walked out first. He was balding, with a ring of grey hair, and wore a blue polo shirt, tan cargo pants and hiking boots. He had a Glock in a holster on his hip and his SAPS ID around his neck. He gave her a broad smile. 'Colonel van Rensburg, it's good to see you again.'

They shook hands. Sannie had met 'Oom Derick' Le Roux a few times over the years at STES conferences. He was friendly, jovial, and well respected in the SAPS.

'And you, Oom. Please call me Sannie. And this is my partner, Warrant Officer Marilyn Msani. How are you?'

'*Sawubona*, Marilyn,' he said, and shook her hand. 'Yes, I'm sorry, but this place is a mess. There's another dead *oke* inside, and old David . . . he's gone as well.'

'David Gregory, the owner of the farm?' Sannie said.

Le Roux nodded.

'And his wife . . . Zelda?'

'Died two years ago, cancer,' Le Roux said.

Two more men emerged from the house. The first was a two-metre-tall muscle-bound young man with a crew cut and fade with body armour and a pistol in a holster on his chest. Sannie didn't need to see the uniform tactical patch to know he was from Viking Security. The second man was also in his late twenties, but of a slighter build, shorter, blond and handsome, in a khaki safari shirt and shorts and *vellies*. Le Roux introduced him first.

'This is John Parker, manager of uBhejane Game Reserve. It is – was – also owned by David. It's about three thousand hectares, adjoining Virginia Farm. John was first on the scene.'

Parker lifted the brim of his uBhejane baseball cap in greeting to Sannie, looked at her, but seemed to fix on a point beyond, or through her. His face was pale. She'd seen those signs before.

'John, ah, *accounted* for the two outside, but he was too late for old David.'

Parker blinked at Sannie. 'I was . . .' he swallowed hard, as if to compose himself, 'I was worried about David . . . I thought that maybe I could save him.'

Le Roux put a hand on Parker's shoulder. 'It's all right, John. You don't have to go through it again. I've got your statement. It looks like the thieves were after David's guns – one of the dead men had his .375 hunting rifle and another had his pistol. They were busy taking his TV and other stuff. Typical farm invasion.'

'I'd like to take a look inside,' Sannie said.

'Of course, Sannie,' Le Roux said. 'It'll be your case anyway.'

'Thanks,' Sannie said to Le Roux. 'I'll want to talk to Mr Parker as well, and the security guy.'

Parker was walking slowly towards his game viewer, but turned at the sound of his name. He looked like he was still in shock.

'I did take his statement already, Sannie,' Le Roux said, 'but I know how thorough you are.'

Sannie smiled and nodded. It was a shame Oom Derick was leaving the service and the country. He would have been the perfect choice to head up the local stock theft unit – he'd lived in the area for decades – but in the way of the SAPS he was unlikely to be promoted to a command position. She would read the statement the older policeman had taken, and get to Parker herself eventually.

Le Roux nodded to the tall, fit security guard, now leaning against his *bakkie* and talking on his phone. "That's Meyer. I'll tell him to wait for you. Meanwhile, I'll also hang around here for you if you want to take a look inside yourself, Sannie.' Le Roux took a packet of cigarettes from his pocket. 'A fresh pair of eyes is always a good thing.'

Sannie walked inside David Gregory's home and her senses ratcheted up a notch. The house smelled musty, but was clean and well kept. The walls of the hallway were crammed with pictures – prints – showing soldiers and battlefield scenes from long ago. Marilyn paused to inspect a trio of portraits of Zulu warriors, which seemed to date from the nineteenth century. There were bedrooms on either side, with guest beds made up, but no signs of life. The living room was at the rear.

They stepped around a flat-screen television leaning against the hallway wall.

'This place is like a museum,' Marilyn said as they emerged into the living room.

Its keeper was dead. David Gregory, Sannie assumed, was sitting, his hands tied behind him and to the frame of a chair, in the middle of his lounge room.

Sannie swallowed hard. It was one of the goriest murder scenes she had ever seen. David Gregory, if that was who it was, had been slit from sternum to groin, and his entrails were falling out of his body. Blood had splattered the wall and the richly patterned rug beneath an antique coffee table, and had soaked into the carpet around him. Sannie went to the body, breathing through her mouth. Marilyn had her hand clamped over hers.

Sannie looked on the floor and saw a bloodied assegai, a Zulu stabbing spear, lying next to Gregory.

Marilyn walked around the body, slowly, watching where she put her feet, then bent at the waist to take a closer look. 'There's an exit wound in his back. It looks like he was shot.'

Sannie just nodded, then began inspecting the white-painted plaster wall behind him. As in the hallway there were more antique prints, all with a military setting. Half-a-dozen Zulu shields, elongated oval shapes made of cowhide, hung next to them, as well as crossed assegais and knobkerrie clubs. Two rifles were mounted on either side of a large open fireplace, each set at an angle of forty-five degrees, pointing inwards above the mantelpiece. Below each of the rifles were two more matching collections of assegais, each set of six fanned around a central point.

Above the mantelpiece, two stout timber doors hung open, either side of a recessed cavity in the wall. There were two racks, which Sannie imagined had held the television. An open padlock lay on the floor in front of the fireplace.

'The thieves must have dropped the TV when they heard John Parker arrive,' Marilyn said.

Sannie nodded. 'But they were here long enough to force David to give them the keys to the gun safe and television cabinet.'

The furniture was mostly dark leather, chesterfield lounge suites and two wing-back chairs. There were three glass-fronted display cabinets containing sets of campaign medals and old-style sun helmets which Sannie thought were probably British Army, and various antique cups, bottles, utensils and old bullets and bullet casings. On a wall behind her was a framed red uniform tunic.

She turned her attention to the dead man. Almost incongruously he was wearing a Senqu T-shirt and shorts and sandals. He sat on a wooden dining room chair and his hands had been bound using long plastic cable ties.

Sannie heard a knock at the door.

'Crime scene team's here, Colonel,' Le Roux called from the end of the hallway.

They retraced their steps and Sannie led Marilyn to the left, into what seemed to be the master bedroom. There was a king-sized brass bed, fully made, with throw cushions on it.

Sannie went to a wardrobe and opened it. 'Nothing here, just empty hangers.'

'It might be his wife's,' Marilyn said.

Sannie nodded and went to the corresponding door. David Gregory's clothes were hanging in there, and a gun safe stood open. Having seen enough for now, Sannie and Marilyn walked out into the sunshine. While the KZN south coast was hot and steamy, here one seemed closer – too close – to the sun. She felt the burn on her face.

'*Meneer* Meyer?' she called to the knot of men by the vehicles.

The two-metre-tall man in the uniform walked over to her.

'Hello, I'm Lieutenant Colonel van Rensburg.'

'*Goeie middag, Tannie*,' he said.

She frowned. 'I'm not your aunty, I'm an investigating police officer,' she said in Afrikaans. 'Name?'

'Deon Meyer, ma'am.'

Sannie raised her eyebrows. '*Rerig*?'

He smiled. 'No, not really.' He continued in Afrikaans: 'My real name is Matteo Meyer, but I've liked the crime writer Deon Meyer's books since I was in school, and the other kids started calling me "Deon". It stuck. I even wanted to join the Hawks, and be like that hero of his, Benny Griessel, but the police didn't want me.'

'I like his books as well.' Sannie gave him a smile and wrote Meyer's real name in her notebook. Up close she saw just how big he was – barrel chest and shirtsleeves straining over big biceps. 'Tell me what happened here . . . Deon.'

He put his hands on his hips. 'I already gave my statement to Oom Derick.'

'Yes, well, *Captain* Le Roux is leaving the service, as you may know. I'll be taking over this case.' She needed to let these people know that she was here now, and that she was taking over the STES unit and everything it was investigating. 'I'll talk to you again soon about what happened here today, but tell me, what security was on this farm when the rhinos were killed here?'

He recoiled from her. 'Not me!'

She held up a hand to allay his fears. 'Don't worry, I'm not looking for scapegoats – not yet, anyway. Did Mr Gregory employ security here?'

Deon shifted from one foot to another. 'Yes and no.'

'What do you mean?

'I mean, he used our company, Viking, for a while, and we did a *lekker* job. We know the people around here, and we have a good source of intelligence in the local communities. We know who the local *tsotsis* are, and one time, when one of those criminals was planning on coming through the fence, we heard about it first and were able to set up an ambush and catch the guy. No shooting, either – we arrested him. He got out on bail, but the locals, they *moered* him. Mr Gregory used to employ a lot of people, gave money to the local creche and school. The people liked him.'

Sannie gestured to the house with a flick of her head. 'Not these people.'

Deon shook his head. 'I don't recognise any of them. I checked the bodies. They're not any of the local *skelms* that we know.'

'Why did David stop using Viking Security?'

Deon sighed. 'Shame, he couldn't keep up with his bills. He had to let nearly all of his staff go. You know, everyone is suffering. Oom David, Mr Gregory, he used to work as a guide on the Zulu battlefields – Rorke's Drift, Isandlwana, the place where the French *oke* was killed and what-what-what. It was a good sideline for him, and his clients used to stay at his lodge at uBhejane, but his business never really recovered after COVID. I love rhinos – I even did some moonlighting for him on the weekends, but my boss gave me *kak* for that so I had to stop.'

'So, he had no security?'

Deon rocked his big head from side to side. 'Yes and no. He used these,' Deon made air quotes, '"volunteers", from some overseas veterans' organisation. They were all from the British and American armies, and had served in Afghanistan and Iraq and places like that. Oom David also used them to help him care for the younger rhinos. I visited once – these big tough men and women were crying, shame, feeding the little ones. David said it helped their PSTD or whatever.'

'PTSD,' Sannie said.

Deon rubbed a hand over his crew cut and yawned. '*Ja*, that.'

Sannie focused on one of the bodies, now being photographed by a crime scene tech. She didn't imagine Big Deon would be losing any sleep over seeing David and the two suspects killed. 'The action here was all over before you got here?'

Deon shrugged. '*Ja*, I had a false alarm, across the valley over at the MacGregor farm. Mac's wife, Kate, called to say she'd seen an armed intruder outside their farmhouse enclosure, but when I got there we couldn't find any signs of trouble. Shame, if that hadn't happened, I might have been able to sort these chaps out.'

Sannie looked around. 'Looks like John Parker did that, although he was too late to help David.'

Deon sneered. 'I didn't think that *soutie* had it in him.'

'What do you mean by that?' Sannie was not referring to the derogatory Afrikaans term for an English-speaking South African. A *soutie*, or *soutpiel*, was someone with one foot in Africa, the other in the UK, and his *piel*, his prick, in the ocean.

'Parker's a bunny-hugger.' Deon clenched his fists by his sides. 'He hates hunters, and thinks it's *lekker* to sleep with another *oke*'s girl-friend and steal her away.'

Sannie looked up from her notes. 'Your girlfriend?'

Deon gave a short, sharp nod. 'My Jan-Maree. That snake stole her from me.'

Sannie made a note. 'Jan-Maree . . .?'

'Ball,' Deon said. 'She works as a waitress in The Shed, the pub in Dundee, but she's also a real brain. She's studying for her doctorate or whatever at university, in history.'

Sannie looked towards Parker, who apparently had stolen Jan-Maree away from Deon. He was deep in conversation with Captain Le Roux. Deon was looking Parker's way as well, and Sannie could see a vein pulsing on the side of the tall man's head. She needed to keep him calm, and talking. 'So, what happened with the farm secu-rity here?'

'*Ja*,' Deon refocused on Sannie, 'so the veterans came and did their thing, and there were plenty of pictures taken and even a TV crew came from England or somewhere, and it was all peace, love and Kumbaya, and then David decided that he could do without Viking Security. He didn't have the money to pay us in any case. But it didn't work out.'

'Why?' Sannie did not have all day, but Deon seemed to like taking his time telling a story.

'The way I heard it from Jan-Maree was that David and the guy in charge of the veterans were arguing in The Shed a couple of weeks ago.'

'Who's the boss of the veterans?'

'A *rooinek*, a proper ex–British Army officer, only he's Welsh or something like that. Guy by the name of Tustin.'

'A real-life "redneck"?' Sannie said, using the old Anglo-Boer War term for a British soldier.

'*Ja*. This one moved here from the UK. He's another *fundi* on the

Anglo-Zulu War, or so he says. He's written a couple of books. David and him used to argue all the time.'

'Argue over what? Security? Protecting the rhinos?'

Deon shook his head. 'No, they'd get the *moer* in, arguing like "Private Smethurst was over here", "Corporal Jones was over there", all that sort of *kak* on the battlefields. I went out with them a couple of times, when I was still interested in all that. I got *gatvol* of all the bickering.'

'Oh, so it wasn't a serious argument in the pub, then?' Sannie asked.

Deon licked his lips, then cast a wary eye back at the house, as if not wanting to invoke some evil spirit. 'Jan-Maree – this was before she lost her mind and left me – said that this boss of the veterans organisation, Major Richard Tustin, was ready to kill old David, in the restaurant.'

'*Kill* him? Why?' Sannie brushed a fly away from her face. She imagined them buzzing already around the dead bodies. The fly made her think of something important, though she couldn't quite remember what it was. It might have been something that she had missed in her quick look through David Gregory's farmhouse. But Deon was just getting to the good part of his story. He leaned closer to her and grinned.

'Tustin told David he'd kill him, because Jan-Maree said that David had just threatened to kill Tustin.'

'What was all this over?' Sannie asked.

Marilyn barged up to them. 'Colonel, we've got to go.'

'What is it?' Sannie asked.

'Captain Le Roux just got a call. Shots fired on a farm near here. Stock theft in progress.'

4

NATAL, 1880

The rain cleared and the resurgent sun lit the veld bright green as Peter Gregory, Samuel Khumalo and Sergeant Gavin Phillips made their way cross-country towards the retired Major Morrison's farm on the outskirts of Dundee.

Reedbuck, skittish creatures at the best of times, squeaked and took flight at their approach. Gregory took a deep breath and tilted his face to the azure sky. *This* was what it was like before last year, before Isandlwana.

As his horse, Bullet, cantered along, it felt like the breeze in Peter's face could almost blow away the memory of the stench. These hills had been beautiful once, a paradise, but one awaiting fools. How had he, and so many others, believed that it would be theirs and that they could take it without consequence?

This was the land of the Zulu, the people of heaven, and they would no sooner surrender it to some foreigner than Peter's father would have relinquished his corner of Buckinghamshire to an invading nation. God forbid the pretenders would have been of a different colour.

Cetshwayo had been no saint, but nor was he a benevolent tyrant. The only reason Samuel was at Peter's side, and had been serving the colony for the past two years, first as a trooper and later as a police constable, was because his own king had wanted him dead.

They crested a hill and a valley revealed itself, so picturesque it made Gregory want to believe again. Grace would have dropped to her knees and given thanks. He smiled at the thought of her. He had not returned to the farmhouse to tell her he would be gone, but that wouldn't worry her. Grace had been born into poverty and her life had become worse ever since. Being shipped to South Africa to either provide female company for a cane worker or perform menial labour as little more than a slave might have crushed a weaker person. Grace, however, was a survivor. She had escaped her indentured fate by setting herself up in business as a sly girl: a dishevelled skivvy in a curry house by day, but an alluring courtesan by night and, more recently, a decent Christian woman with a fondness for the shepherd of her new-found flock.

As he rode, Gregory remembered the first time he'd met her and the first time he'd heard Morrison's name.

HE DUCKED his head to pass through the low-beamed doorway into the darkened interior of the Red Lantern tavern in Pietermaritzburg. There was a fug of smoke, pipe tobacco and something else, opium perhaps. The lanterns inside did more to caress rather than illuminate the hands, limbs, ankles and painted faces waiting in the shadows. A piano playing a music hall favourite stopped.

'It's the bloody snuffs,' a voice said.

'And I'm sure there's nothing untoward to see here.' Gregory's parade-ground voice had cut through the hubbub. A man swore in the darkness; a woman laughed; the revelry resumed. He was investigating a man, Alfred Blundell, whose wife had apparently committed suicide. Gregory had his suspicions about the man and had learned that he was a frequent visitor to this establishment. The Red Lantern was not just a pub but also a well-known bawdy house and illegal gambling den.

'I am Scheherazade.'

Gregory turned at the lilt of the woman's voice – a woman he would later come to know as Grace – and the touch of her hand on his arm. He paused, snagged in her eyes. 'Are you going to tell me a story?'

She smiled at him, and it trapped him like a fly in honey. She passed him a tankard of beer. 'From the master of the house. He says we are to make you most welcome.'

Gregory took the mug. 'I'll get to him in due course. Do you know a man by the name of Alfred Blundell, a regular here?'

She batted her eyelashes. 'Most prefer not to use names here, sir, at least not their real ones. Perhaps we could go somewhere . . . private, to talk?'

He'd straightened. 'I'm not here for that.' And more was the pity. He found himself wanting to spend more time interrogating her. 'Don't you want to know why I'm looking for this man?'

Scheherazade had given a little shrug and he'd been mesmerised by her bare shoulders above a bodice that barely covered her nipples. From the waist down she wore a hooped skirt of red velvet. She waved a fan in front of her face and let it settle over her mouth, as if she was sworn to secrecy.

'He killed his wife.'

Her captivating eyes widened in surprise. 'No.'

'A physician examined the good lady's body. There was evidence of bruising . . . of other unmentionable degradations.'

'Blundell.'

He stared at her. There was no question, no inflection in the way she had said the name. As she lowered the fan Gregory could see she was biting her lower lip. She turned and walked deeper into the fug. Gregory followed her, eyes fighting to stay fixed forward.

Scheherazade waved to an African woman, clicked her fingers and sat at a table. She motioned for Gregory to sit. The serving woman returned and placed a glass in front of Scheherazade.

'Gin?' he asked.

'Rose water. One needs to keep one's senses in a place like this.' Scheherazade wrapped her hands around her glass and stared into it, not drinking. 'There are nice men, sometimes, but there are very many bad men.'

Gregory sipped his beer. The music, the singing, the laughter couldn't hide the smell of this place. Sweat, perfume, spilled beer . . . sin.

'There are men . . .' she paused, unable to look up at him, 'who like to hurt the girls here. To beat them, soundly, in order to do what it is they have come to do here.' She shuddered.

'I am sorry . . .'

She looked up at him and fixed him with eyes that were now as cold and hard as stone, and in control. 'And there are some men who like to be hurt.'

He put a finger in his collar to try and loosen it from his skin. It felt hot in here. 'Which kind is Blundell?'

'The former. And as bad as he is, there are some who are worse.'

'Worse than striking a defenceless woman?'

She gave him a little smile. 'We're not all defenceless, Mr . . .'

'Gregory, Sub-Inspector Peter Gregory. At your service, madam . . .?'

'Miss. And it's usually the other way around in here. But at least you seem like a gentleman, unlike most. And even the gentlemen aren't very gentle in the Red Lantern. At least not the likes of Blundell and Co.'

'Worse, you said?'

She nodded and took a sip of her drink. 'There are some,' she gave a shiver of revulsion this time, 'who ask for younger. Girls and boys. In my culture a girl can be married at twelve, but there are some men who take pleasure in children even younger than that. The master here says he does not cater to men like that, but it doesn't stop them asking, nor others from finding poor children who are then . . .'

Gregory's beer tasted sour. He set it down. Such abhorrences against nature were not limited to the colony, or to Africa – there was enough such evil back in Britain. But it was against the laws of man and nature, and it sickened him as much as it revolted this woman. 'Blundell? Is he one of those men?'

'He gambles, Inspector Gregory. Gamblers lose, and when they are short of their winnings, they will do anything, find anything, sell anything to get enough money to get back to the card table, or get their hands on the dice again.'

Blundell had made a poor show of grief when Phillips and Gregory had interviewed him, following the report of his wife's apparent suicide.

When Gregory had confronted Blundell, and said he'd never heard of a woman killing herself by putting a gun to her own head, Blundell had fobbed him off, claiming his wife had been a melancholic, especially given her inability to provide Blundell with a child. When Gregory and Phillips had gone back to him and reported the discovery of bruises on the woman's body, Blundell had said his wife had recently fallen from a horse, and was accident-prone.

'I think this man Blundell murdered his wife, and made a clumsy attempt to stage the scene so that it appeared the poor woman had shot herself. I know for a fact that the deceased was left-handed, yet her husband's revolver was found in her right hand.'

Scheherazade had peered around him at that point. 'Here he is.'

Gregory turned his head. 'Who?'

'Your Mr Blundell,' Scheherazade said. She raised a hand, smiled and waggled her fingers. 'He's seen me. He likes me,' she lowered her voice, 'the irksome toad.'

'You'll . . . entertain him?'

'Not by choice,' Scheherazade said.

Gregory made a fist and touched it to the tabletop. 'If only I could get him to confess, to make some admission about his wife.'

Scheherazade put her drink down. 'He's a talker. When he . . . when he is in the company of a lady, he likes to brag. In fact, he won't shut up. The girls say it's better if he's talking, because then he is not hitting.'

Gregory looked at Scheherazade. She was plotting. 'No. And even if you were able to entice him to say something, we would need another witness. Someone –' He stopped himself, but it was too late.

She cast her eyes downward. 'Someone respectable.' Then looked up: 'Or someone white.'

'Miss Scheherazade, I meant no –'

'Stow it, Sub-Inspector. Do you want this bastard or do you not?'

He took a breath. 'I do. But how?'

Scheherazade beckoned to the African serving girl, who came to her and curtsied. 'Miss Scheherazade?'

'Tombi, take the sub-inspector to the special room.' Scheherazade winked. 'You know the one.'

The young woman put a hand over her face, perhaps in false modesty, but nodded and walked away.

'Follow Tombi. She will position you somewhere . . . most advantageous.'

'I –'

She made a shooing motion with her hands, then stood, straightened the front of her bodice and waltzed through the press of men and women towards Blundell.

Tombi threaded her way between patrons and into a corridor with rooms on either side. A lantern with red glass burned at the far end, giving off a glow that was part enticing, part evil.

'This way, sir,' Tombi said.

Gregory heard the rhythmic thumping of a bedhead against a wall, a high-pitched scream, animalistic grunting as he passed each door.

Tombi opened a door at the very end of the hallway and ushered Gregory inside.

'What the . . .?'

If he'd been expecting a chamber with a big bed, a washbasin and perhaps a strategically placed looking glass, he was wrong. This was a cell akin to those at the Durban prison. 'I say . . .'

Tombi squeezed past him, into the bolthole. It was no more than two yards long, and barely wide enough for him to stretch his arms out to either side. A paraffin lantern hung from a hook, burning, making the interior of the enclosure hot and fetid. A bench ran down one side and on the wall opposite, Tombi slid back a small wooden panel set in two tracks.

'Look, sir.' She pointed at the aperture.

Gregory moved inside and put his eye against a small hole that had just been revealed. On the other side of the wall was a bedroom, more like what he had expected. The door to that room opened and, to his surprise, Scheherazade walked in, leading Alfred Blundell by the hand. Blundell was carrying a brandy bottle; he swigged from its neck.

Tombi curtsied again and reversed out of the cubicle, unhooking and taking the lantern with her. She shut the door behind her, leaving him in darkness. Gregory felt most peculiar, closed in here on his own. Scheherazade had come very close to the wall and was fussing with her hair. Gregory realised there must be a mirror some-where on the wall, perhaps partly obscuring the peephole. She gave him a wink and he felt himself blush.

Blundell, a big man with luxuriant mutton-chop sideburns and a fleshy, ruddy face, began unhooking his suspenders from his shoulders.

'How can I be of service, sir?' Scheherazade asked him. Gregory heard her voice through a series of smaller holes that had been drilled in the wall next to the peephole. He guessed that the plaster or other surface of the bedroom wall on the other side must have been of such decrepitude that the spyholes blended in.

Blundell unbuckled his leather belt. 'Bend over the end of the bed, wench. Prepare to take your punishment.'

Scheherazade put the back of her hand to her forehead. 'Oh, kind sir, mercy, please, I pray of you.'

Gregory allowed himself a small smile at Scheherazade's very amateur theatrics. He had a feeling it was not the first time she had put on such a show. Scheherazade moved to the end of the bed and did as she was told.

Blundell sidestepped to the door of the bedroom, turned the key in the lock and pocketed it.

Scheherazade looked sideways. 'Sir, please leave the key –'

He put a finger to his lips. 'Shush, my pretty. All part of the fun, yes? You've nothing to fear from me, really. Nothing you don't deserve.' Blundell folded the belt in his hands, raised his arm and brought it down with a lightning-fast lash.

'Sir!'

He laughed. 'That bustle and your petticoats protected you, wench. You'd not be able to take a lash on that pretty backside of yours.'

'Oh, sir,' Scheherazade cooed, 'I doubt you could truly hurt this very bad serving girl. I'm not as innocent as I look, and I have read the works of the Marquis de Sade. I'm sure you're too much of a pussycat to really indulge in such pleasures.'

Blundell stepped back, grasped the folded belt in his two hands and pulled the two lengths taut with a *snap*. 'You don't know *what* I'm capable of, lass.'

Scheherazade turned her head around from the mattress to make eye contact with Blundell. 'Try me,' she said in a flat voice.

Blundell strode back across the bedroom floor, bent and lifted Scheherazade's skirts and petticoats and flicked them up over her back. Gregory was shocked to see she was not wearing undergarments. He pressed his two hands against the wall in the dark and only then noticed that all of the plaster and most of the timber battens had been removed from his side. He felt the rendering on the other side start to give a little. The wall between them was the flimsiest of structures. He felt his cheeks burn and his heart thump at the sight of the woman's nakedness.

If Blundell was moved by the vision of flawless skin, then it triggered him to violence. He brought the belt down again with a blow that pushed Scheherazade forward and made her scream into the soiled duvet.

'Doubt I could truly hurt you now?'

Scheherazade sniffed, then raised her head again. 'I've known children's nannies who could deliver a stripe better than that, you popinjay.'

'Ha!' Blundell seemed to rise to the challenge and delivered three more lashes to the backs of her legs in quick succession. Gregory was ready to stop this sadistic farce when Scheherazade turned to Blundell again.

'Does my suffering please you, sir?'

'Very much, you cheeky little miscreant.'

She wiggled her rear end in defiance of him. 'Imagine, good sir, what it would be like to live like this all the time, with a willing slave girl at your disposal, day and night, to attend to your every need, and do so willingly.'

Blundell paused in his ministrations to grab the brandy bottle from where he'd left it on a side table and take another long swig. He set the bottle back down, and Gregory noticed he was becoming unsteady on his feet. Blundell wiped his mouth and moustache with the back of his hand and burped. 'That . . . would please me. To have a woman who was more . . . pliable.'

'I could even . . .' Scheherazade paused, her mouth curling into a small smile, 'I could even find another *servant* for you. Perhaps someone younger – much younger.'

Blundell cleared his throat. 'No, I'm not interested in children.'

'But one of the other girls said you were asking, sir.'

'That was for someone else. A retired army major, Harry Morrison, farming up towards Dundee. If you were to find a child for him, there'd be money in it for you, girl.'

Scheherazade nodded, as if filing away the titbit of information and so, too, did Gregory. Gregory would be paying the former major a visit soon. Scheherazade slipped back into character like a music hall actress. 'Are you not married, sir?'

Gregory noticed how Blundell stiffened. He was supposed to be the grieving widower, yet here he was, his wife's body barely cold, indulging his every vice in a whorehouse. 'Was.'

Scheherazade kept looking back and Gregory fancied she was making eye contact with him, as well, behind the wall. 'And were you not able to make your own wife bend to your will, sir? Surely it would have been her duty to . . . to respect your particular desires, to please you in whatever way you saw fit?'

Blundell took up the bottle again and his Adam's apple bobbed as he took a fierce amount of the strong liquor into his gullet.

'Or were you incapable, sir,' Scheherazade continued, 'of even bringing your own wife to heel?'

Gregory drew a breath. He reached down to his belt and unbuttoned the flap on the holster of his pistol.

Blundell drained the bottle, then set it down, its glass base rocking for a moment on the tabletop. He stood there, his back to Gregory, and clenched his fists. Gregory willed Scheherazade to stay silent.

But she started to stand up, and half turned to face Blundell. 'And here I was thinking you knew how to treat a woman. You couldn't tame a dog.'

Blundell let out an animalistic roar and went for Scheherazade. She raised her hands to try to fend him off, but he barrelled into her, using his considerable weight and bulk to push her backwards onto the bed, where he pinned her with a meaty hand around her throat.

Gregory drew his revolver. Enough was enough.

'Wait!' Scheherazade gasped. Gregory saw she was trying to look around Blundell and her eyes met the hole in the wall. Gregory thumbed back the hammer on his weapon.

Through a voice constricted by Blundell's hand, she said: 'If you didn't have a wife, if you could put me in her place, you could do whatever you want to me. I want it. I want the pain, sir.'

'I'll do whatever I want with you,' Blundell said. 'And if you try and say no –'

'If I try and say no, what, sir?' She gagged from the force of his hand, and Blundell was now forcing her legs apart.

'I'll . . .'

'You'll what? You're all talk, all bluster and wind like a lying politician, as limp as a wet rag.'

Blundell screamed again as he fumbled for the buttons on the front of his trousers. 'You be quiet and take what you deserve, or I'll kill you like I killed her. I'll put a gun to your head and no one will ever know it was me who did for you.'

That was it. The woman had given Gregory what he needed. Gregory drew back his gun hand and threw his weight behind a punch that shattered the plaster on the other side of the wall and made a fist-sized opening. 'Get off her, man. Natal Mounted Police!' he called through the hole.

Blundell released his grip on Scheherazade, who rolled away from him. He tumbled off the bed, and, pulling up his trousers, turned to see the gun pointed at him. Blundell snatched up the duvet in a meaty hand and tossed it at the wall. The quilt snagged on Gregory's hand for a moment and Blundell used the distraction to move to the side table. He snatched up the empty brandy bottle by its neck then smashed it against the bedroom wall.

Scheherazade had darted to the bedroom door and tried the handle, forgetting it was locked. As she turned, she saw Blundell starting to swing the broken bottle at her. Sheherazade grabbed his wrist. She was strong, and while she stopped him from slashing her, Blundell punched her in the face with his free hand.

Gregory drew himself back then raised his right leg and kicked at the timber battens and plaster. His leg went through. Frustrated, he pulled his leg back inside the hidden chamber, turned side-on and threw his whole weight into the wall. He crashed into the bedroom in a cloud of white plaster dust and dropped to one knee. He held up his revolver.

'Drop it,' Blundell said. He had pulled Scheherazade to her feet, and, not having enough time to unlock the door and escape, he held her hostage. He had one arm around Scheherazade's neck and the jagged end of the broken bottle pressed against her slender throat. Blood streamed from her nose. 'Put your gun on the floor and kick it to me.'

'Don't do it,' Scheherazade sniffed, her eyes full of unbidden tears. 'Don't let this bastard get away.'

Recognition dawned on Blundell's face as he looked at Peter through his mantle of dust. 'You – the bloody snuff who was poking into my affairs.' Blundell squeezed Scheherazade harder and a trickle of blood ran down her neck from where a shard of broken glass had nicked her. 'I'll kill her. Drop the gun, peeler.'

Gregory held his revolver pointed at the murderer, but Blundell had positioned himself so that Scheherazade covered virtually all of his body. Gregory was a good shot, but he didn't trust himself or the accuracy of his pistol to be able to hit Blundell in the eye.

'I'll kill her,' Blundell said again, pushing the bottle even deeper into the woman's neck.

She flinched and seemed to change her mind. 'Do as he asks, please, Sub-Inspector.'

Gregory looked into her eyes. He saw not terror but steel forged in fires the likes of which he could probably not imagine. Beautiful, clever, confident and shrewd – what misfortunes had brought her to this place, he wondered, yet left her so in control of her emotions and surrounds? Blundell had one of her arms pinned against her side, but her free hand, unnoticed by her captor, was in her hair, ostensibly as if she was clutching at her head. Gregory could see the fingers of her right hand fidgeting. Blundell was focusing on him.

Gregory held up his left hand, palm first. 'All right, Mr Blundell, I'll comply with your request, just let the young lady go.'

Blundell gave a half-smile. 'Slowly, now.'

Gregory bent at the waist and lowered the revolver to the floor.

Blundell's eyes followed Gregory's hand, and as the man inclined his head, momentarily distracted, Scheherazade pulled a long bone-handled hairpin from her hair. Blundell's right eye was right beside her left cheek, and, quick as a flash, she drove the pin into his eyeball.

Scheherazade sidestepped as Blundell screamed, but her captor turned and followed her to the door, scrabbling at his eye with one hand and slashing the broken bottle wildly with the other. The broken glass caught Scheherazade on the back of the neck. Gregory scooped up his revolver, aimed, and fired.

Gregory had dragged Blundell out of the Red Lantern, the other man squealing like a two-year-old from the flesh wound in his shoulder and his stabbed eyeball. Scheherazade had said she could walk, but once they were outside, followed by the mob of revellers from within, Samuel had taken charge of Blundell and Scheherazade had fainted.

The master of the house, who had dealt with his fair share of shootings, stabbings and beatings, had bandaged Blundell's eye and the gunshot wound, and sat with him and Samuel until two more snuffs could be fetched. Blundell had been conveyed to the cells after a visit with the town's inebriated surgeon, who'd been located in another tavern.

Gregory had carried Scheherazade away from that place in his arms, holding her like a child – she was not much heavier than one. She had come to and looked up into his eyes; neither of them had said anything. He'd cared nothing for the few lewd remarks, nor the cheers from the working girls who were well rid of Blundell and his brutal ways. Scheherazade had clung to his back on his saddle, her heart pressed against his. Gregory had taken her to his farm, where he had bathed her wounds, made her tea and soup, and discovered she preferred to be called Grace, over her real Indian name.

In the days that followed she had been nervous, at first, like a wild animal brought indoors to have an injury tended to, not fully trusting. But Gregory had put her in his bed and slept in the outbuildings with Samuel.

'You are mad, Captain,' Samuel had said to him on the first night they had shared his room. 'There is a beautiful woman in your bed. You should be there with her. If you don't, I'll offer her half a crown to come out here and sleep with me, and you can go back to your soft mattress.'

'You'll do no such thing, Samuel.' But Gregory had laid on his back on the straw palliasse as Samuel had blown out the lantern, thinking of what it would be like to be next to the woman.

Her wounds had run deeper than those inflicted by the cut glass and she had been quiet for several days. Unbidden, she cleaned the farmhouse – it needed it – and began cooking for the two men. She filled the home with the scent of aromatic curries and fresh-cooked rotis and made tea in the morning and washed their clothes.

'You must have your bed back,' she said to Gregory after a week.

'But where will you sleep?' he had asked.

'I actually also find the bed quite comfortable.'

COMING OUT OF HIS REVERIE, Gregory pulled on Bullet's reins as he, Samuel and Phillips approached the Morrison farmhouse.

According to his information the body was still inside. The prospect of seeing a dead man didn't overly perturb Gregory – he had seen hundreds of them during the war, and several in the course of his duty as a police officer.

But this one would be different. This was, most likely, no innocent victim of murder, nor a soldier or snuff cut down before his time.

The body inside this house was that of a recently retired British Army major: a man who had allegedly offered money to others to fulfil his evil lusts, and who may have known what happened to the missing sword of an emperor.

5

KWAZULU-NATAL, THE PRESENT

Adam Kruger poured coffee for Jenny and Thabo in the open-sided, thatch-roofed kitchen of the research camp, situated in the thick vegetation behind the dunes at Bhanga Nek. A vervet monkey leapt onto the counter, grabbed a rusk and scampered off.

'Little bugger,' Jenny said.

Adam smiled. 'His kind was here first, before all of us.'

It was still early, not yet seven, but they all rose with the sun that streamed into their accommodation, canvas tents on timber decks under thatch. The storm had passed. The morning sky was clear and the temperature was pushing into the mid-twenties already, with not a whisper of wind. Adam was barefoot in board shorts and his Rip Curl T-shirt, and his students were in a similar uniform. A trumpeter hornbill cried like a baby in an umdoni tree somewhere nearby.

'You got in late, Prof,' Thabo said, taking a rusk from the plate for himself and his cup from Adam. Thabo looked over his shoulder at where Adam's personal *bakkie*, a Ford Ranger, was parked, further away than usual. They all knew there was a body in the back, wrapped in a plastic tarpaulin.

Adam nodded and checked his watch. 'The police should be here in about an hour.'

'How was it; the body?' Jenny asked.

'It was what it was. The sharks had been at him. It wasn't pretty.'

Jenny nodded. 'Had he been swimming?'

Adam sipped his coffee. He didn't want to involve his students in what he'd done. That would make them complicit and mean that they would be subjected to an interview by the police. He'd been through that shit before, and he wouldn't wish it on anyone, although he reminded himself that it *was* how he'd met Sannie. 'No. I think he must have fallen off a boat.'

Thabo looked out to where they could hear the surf breaking on the beach. 'Out there, in the middle of the night? Fishing off the marine reserve?'

Adam shrugged. 'Maybe. I don't know.' *No.* The clothes were all wrong. And the hand was soft, not just from being in the water, but it wasn't scarred or calloused like a fisherman's and the clothes were good. What the hell had he been up to out there?

'Local guy?' Jenny took a rusk.

Adam was about to say that he didn't think so when his phone pinged. He checked the screen; it was a WhatsApp message, which he read.

'The cops have just come across a serious car accident – one person killed, one seriously injured,' he told the students. 'They're going to be delayed a couple of hours. Somone will also come to collect the body as well – some time. They'll message me when they're mobile again.'

'Eish,' Thabo said.

Adam felt restless, and a little unsettled after his night's labour. He was also curious about how the body had washed up. 'I'm taking the RHIB out for a while,' Adam said. The rigid-hull inflatable boat was their research vessel.

'Cool,' Jenny said.

Thabo slurped his coffee. 'Let me get my gear.'

'Me too,' Jenny said.

Adam set down his cup and held up his hands. 'Hold on, take it easy, you two. I want to go out by myself.'

'Why?' He saw the challenge in Jenny's eyes.

Should he lie to her? If he told them he wanted to go look for male turtles cruising offshore then they would want, justifiably, to come with him, because that was related to both of their studies. He could say he just wanted time alone – that was partly true.

'Someone needs to wait for the cops.'

'They just confirmed they'll be, like, two hours.' Jenny narrowed her eyes. She had a child's dusting of freckles on her cheeks. 'You're going to look for evidence, aren't you, Prof?'

He was no good at lying to women. Never had been, so he tried not to. It helped him as often as it hindered him. Sannie was a cop – there was no fooling her. She knew he wasn't up here again just because of the university schedule. 'I'm not sure what I'm looking for.'

'The guy on the beach, do you think he was, like, shipwrecked, Prof?' Thabo asked.

Adam couldn't discount the possibility. 'I don't know. I guess that if there was one man washed up, there could be others.'

'They might be in trouble,' Jenny said. 'We should totally go. You'll need more eyes out on the ocean.'

Thabo drained his cup. 'I'll be back in five.' He turned to Jenny. 'Do *not* go without me.'

She nodded. 'Affirmative, *bhuti*. I've got your back.'

'Be quick,' Adam said. 'I want to be back well before the police arrive.'

When Thabo had gone, Jenny reached out and put a hand on Adam's forearm. The gesture surprised him and he almost recoiled.

'Prof?'

He looked down at her hand.

She removed it. 'Are you OK?'

'What do you mean, Jenny?'

'Sorry. But, I guess, well, it probably wasn't easy for you last night. I just thought that maybe you might need a mental health check.'

He started to laugh, then stopped when he saw the hurt in her eyes. 'Sorry, my bad. It's sweet of you to ask, Jenny.'

She screwed her mouth into a frown. 'I'm not being *sweet*, Prof. My dad was in the war, in Angola, and he had some tough times. He went to a shrink for a while. There are more guys talking about PTSD and the effects of the war these days.'

He smiled at her concern. 'Thank you, but I'm good. How are the turtle eggs?' He wanted to change the subject.

'Fine. Thabo and I checked the temperature this morning and it's exactly where it should be.'

'Good.' He'd done the same, but he wanted to see if his students were self-starters, capable of doing their job without being told.

Thabo returned, a little breathless. 'Ready.'

Adam finished his coffee, and while the two students walked to the beach, he got in the camp's HiLux and reversed the boat, on its trailer, out into the sand. With Jenny guiding him he backed the RHIB down into the shallows and the two students then unhitched the boat. Adam drove the *bakkie* back into the shade of the trees before joining the others. The three of them heaved on the inflated sides of the vessel and Adam jumped in. Jenny and Thabo stood waist-deep in the water, steadying the boat with her nose into the oncoming waves.

'Climb aboard!'

The pair of them hauled themselves up over the side as Adam gunned the big outboards. He'd timed his run well, and the students sat on the sides of the boat and held on to the ropes as the bow reared up over a wave and coasted down the other side. Adam opened the throttle again and soon they were clear of the shore break and out on the glassy morning water.

'What are we looking for?' Thabo called over the roar of the outboard.

'Anything floating,' Adam said. 'Lifejackets, rubbish, a fuel tank maybe.' He didn't add 'bodies'. *What was that guy up to, and what was with the antique book?*

Adam headed north, the wide arc of Bhanga Nek beach on his left and the sun coming up on his right. The students scanned the water on either side of the RHIB. Further ahead of them, about thirty kilometres away, was the coast of Mozambique. It was no secret that the border between South Africa and her neighbour was a transit corridor for nearly every illegal product consumed by man, from stolen cars and drugs through to guns, illegally mined gold, diamonds, black-market cigarettes, and human beings.

Had the guy been a smuggler?

'Look!'

Adam and Jenny turned to follow where Thabo was pointing. Adam felt a stab of adrenaline, remembering the body.

'Dolphins,' Jenny said.

Adam swung the boat to move closer to the sleek grey forms porpoising through the water. They may as well have some fun while they were out here.

'I'm sorry, Prof.' Thabo looked sheepish.

'Don't be. It's good that we can enjoy a sighting like this, just the three of us, but we *do* have work to do. Keep an eye out for turtles as well.'

They tailed the pod of twenty dolphins for a while, and just as Adam began cutting back towards the beach Jenny saw a leatherback coming up for air and pointed it out.

'Well spotted.' Adam swung the wheel. 'Thabo, suit up.'

Thabo was already pulling on his fins. Jenny shrugged off her T-shirt and buckled on her weight belt. Adam kept his eye on the spot where he had seen the turtle's head submerge and set the throttle to idle as he coasted up.

'Over the edge, quick as you can,' he said.

Thabo pulled on his mask and snorkel, tightened the strap, then placed a hand over the lenses and rolled backwards into the water with a splash. Adam leaned over the edge of the RHIB, watching Thabo and searching for the turtle. Jenny exited over the other side of the boat.

. . .

JENNY EXHALED AS SHE DIVED, purging the air from her lungs as she finned her way towards the bottom. The morning sun streamed in above her and the water was warm.

Bliss.

She felt so proud, spotting the turtle. Jenny scanned left and right as she descended. If she could find it, and it was a male, it would make her day and the professor would be proud of her, which would be the icing on the cake.

Jenny was jolted out of her reverie by a flash of movement in her peripheral vision. She looked to the left and saw a fully grown leatherback turtle cruise past her. She turned, finned hard and followed it as it headed for the sea floor. The turtle's shell was more than two metres long; it had to be a male. Jenny needed air, so she slowed and swam for the surface.

'Prof!' She waved to Adam, who turned around and saw her. She heard the thrum of engines, but not from their boat. 'I found him. Leatherback, huge. Male.'

'Good work. Go get him.'

She trod water. 'Really?'

'Yes, go for him, J. There's another boat coming. I'm going to put out a float and keep them away from us. We don't want to lose your leatherback.'

My leatherback. She grinned. 'OK, wish me luck.'

He waved her on her way. She took a deep breath and finned down through the clear green water, passing Thabo on the way and giving him a thumbs up. He'd soon work out what was going on and, hopefully, come and help her.

Finning with purpose she made for the bottom, eyes scanning for danger and looking ahead for the turtle. She saw its big oval shape, its barnacle-encrusted shell dark against the paler sand below. It was bobbing about next to something that looked like a rock or mini-reef. As she headed down, and closer, however, she could see straight lines and sharp angles start to appear. That was not natural.

The turtle was suspended in the water, head extended, and seemed to be eating, nibbling on something. As the gloom of the ocean depth came into focus Jenny slowed her finning. It was a boat. On the seabed.

She made for the turtle, her prime reason for being down there. The big male was preoccupied, so she was able to come up behind him without him noticing her. It was only when the turtle was almost within arm's reach that she saw what he was nibbling on.

ADAM HELD his hand up to his eyes and watched the boat come towards him. It was a Zodiac black rubber inflatable, similar to the research vessel, but without the fibreglass hull and with just a single outboard on the back, a seventy-horsepower by the sound of it. Four men were on board. Adam tried waving the skipper off, but the other boat bore down on him.

Adam pointed to the day-glo orange buoy and flag bobbing in the water ten metres from where he idled, indicating there were divers below. The skipper of the other boat must have at least seen that, because the nose of the oncoming craft settled in the water and they slowed.

'Divers below!'

The man at the helm gave him a thumbs up. 'Morning.'

'Howzit,' Adam called back in reply.

'Good thanks. You diving on something interesting?'

The other skipper's accent was English. His passengers, all male, looked to be in their thirties or maybe early forties. Like many scuba divers they looked fit. Two, including the skipper, were in board shorts and the others had camouflage wetsuits on, rolled to the waist to reveal washboard abdominals. They all had short hair, and their skin was uniformly red and tattooed. Tourists, Adam thought.

'We're doing research, department of marine biology, University of KZN,' Adam said as the other boat coasted slowly in, giving the buoy a wide berth.

'Are you the turtle people?' the Englishman asked. He had black hair and a beard and was built like an upside-down triangle – broad shoulders and narrow waist, with big biceps sticking out.

'You could say that.'

'Diving for turtles today?'

Adam smiled. 'Always.' It wasn't unusual for other divers or tourists to ask him and his students about their work and Adam was usually happy to spare a few minutes explaining what they were up to. But today was different. 'I'm sorry, but I've got a couple of students in the water right now. Need to keep an eye on them.'

'No problem,' the Englishman said. 'We might just take a look as well.'

It was an open ocean and there was nothing Adam could do to stop them from diving wherever they wanted to, but he didn't need sightseers getting in the way. 'We're just trying to catch and tag a male turtle now. Maybe you can let us do that first – you're welcome to snorkel on the surface and watch, or wait for us to land it.'

'What's wrong with us diving and watching?' The man was smiling. Two of his three comrades had already begun zipping up their wetsuits and shrugging on their BCD vests and cylinders.

'Nothing, except you might ruin our day's work. Diving for turtles with cylinders on is like going birding with a vacuum cleaner on your back. The noise and the bubbles can spook them. That's why we free dive.'

The skipper seemed to take that on board. He turned to the others. 'Jones, Willis, stand down.'

'Thanks,' Adam said as the men took their buoyancy vests off again. 'Won't be long.'

The other boat's skipper removed his shirt and picked up a weight belt. 'I'll take a free dive as well then. As long as you don't mind . . .'

Adam waved a hand with a flourish. 'Be our guest.'

'Thanks.' The man put on a mask, snorkel and fins.

Jenny surfaced. She pushed the mask off her face. 'Prof!' She trod water and spun in a circle, trying to orientate herself, and Adam could see that she had just noticed the other boat.

'We've got company,' he said.

Jenny nodded. It seemed to Adam as though she had been bursting to tell him something, but for some reason had decided not to. Perhaps she felt self-conscious, showing how excited she was around strangers. Adam looked at her and saw her look down and to one side, as if gesturing to something underwater.

'Do you need some help down there?' Adam asked.

'Um, yes, please.'

Thabo surfaced. 'I saw the turtle, Prof. Going down again.'

'No, wait, Thabo. I need you up here in the boat. Get everything ready for the tagging. I'll go with Jenny.'

'Oh, OK.' Thabo looked a little disappointed, but he took off his mask and hauled himself back up over the side of the RHIB unassisted.

Adam clapped Thabo on the arm. 'Good man. This will be good experience for you – they're harder to land than they are to catch.'

Adam slipped on his mask and flippers and slid off the boat backwards. In the water, he finned down after Jenny. She was a natural free diver and made the descent look effortless. Adam saw the turtle, floating contentedly off to one side, but Jenny was ignoring the creature, and him. He followed her down.

By the time Adam reached the ocean floor he could see what Jenny had found. It was a sunken boat. It looked like a small fishing or pleasure craft, a twenty-four-foot ski boat, he reckoned, with a half-cabin that Jenny was now looking inside.

Adam finned over, and as he approached her Jenny moved to one side. He saw now what she had wanted to tell him about – inside was the body of a man. Adam could see that the face had been attacked by marine life, possibly the turtle, and that the body appeared half trapped in the cabin and partially tangled in a rope net. Jenny looked at him and Adam motioned to the surface with his thumb. Jenny nodded.

As they ascended they saw the man from the other boat coming down towards them. Adam pointed wildly at the turtle, hovering nearby, and then at the surface. The man looked down, but as he had already slowed his descent he would not have had enough air to get to the bottom. The three of them surfaced within a couple of seconds of each other.

Adam pulled his snorkel from his mouth. 'Saw another turtle down there, on the floor, but we won't worry about it.'

'Anything else?' the man asked.

Adam wondered what he meant. If he'd had concerns about a missing boat or crewmen, he would have said something. 'Like what?'

The man shrugged in the water. 'Like sharks, or rays or whatever.'

Adam shook his head. 'Just the usual suspects, plus the turtle. Want to help us capture and tag the male?'

The man looked to Jenny and gave her a wink. 'Sure.'

Adam reached out a fist. 'I'm Adam.'

'Andy.' They fist-bumped in the water.

Adam couldn't put his finger on exactly why he didn't trust the man. He could have asked him to help them dive on the wreck and free the body, but there was something about the look of the quartet of fit divers that seemed incongruous. Most divers Adam knew would have been excited at the prospect of seeing a fully grown sea turtle, let alone the prospect of helping to capture and tag one, but this guy was just acting like it was any other routine dive trip. And if he was the divemaster, as the skipper of the boat, why wasn't he calling to the others on his boat, to share the discovery?

'Let's do it before he gets away,' Adam said.

The three of them dived and finned down towards the turtle, which hadn't moved. Adam guessed it might be sleeping. He swam around the creature and when he got to almost within arm's length, the turtle opened its eyes. Adam grinned. He loved being this close to these prehistoric creatures.

Jenny had moved behind the turtle, along with Andy, and as the turtle woke it did what Adam hoped it would do – it turned itself on its side to present its carapace to him. This exposed the big male's belly to Jenny. Adam and Jenny grabbed hold of the placid reptile between them and then finned for the surface. Adam saw Andy cast a look down into the depths, but the wrecked boat was too deep to be visible from this close to the surface. Andy also headed for fresh air.

Adam took hold of the turtle's front two flippers and guided them up towards where Thabo was waiting for them, leaning over the side of the boat. When Thabo took hold of the flippers, Adam boosted himself up and into the boat and together, he and Thabo started hauling, while Jenny and Andy pushed from below.

'This thing is bloody heavy,' Andy said.

'Maybe six hundred and fifty kilograms,' Adam said. He grunted and half fell backwards as he and Thabo manhandled the turtle over the side and landed it. Thabo held it down while Jenny climbed into the boat.

Andy swam around to his boat, which the others had rafted up to the research vessel. The other men were watching on.

'What do you do with it now?' Andy asked as he climbed back aboard his craft.

Adam already had a battery-powered drill in his hand. He placed the bit against the side of the centre ridge of the turtle's carapace. 'On leatherbacks like this one we drill through and tie a satellite tracker to the shell.'

The drill whirred and Jenny fetched the tracker, which she threaded through the newly drilled hole. 'Now we cover this with some epoxy and smooth it down. This allows us to track the turtle for as long as the battery lasts – maybe six months. And we'll take some blood and tissue samples as well before we let it go.'

'How long will you be here?' Andy asked.

'About an hour,' Adam said. 'You sticking around?'

Andy looked to his fellow passengers, then out at the water around them. 'No, I think we'll move on. Maybe find another spot to dive.'

What was wrong with this one? 'Plenty of ocean out here.'

'That there is,' Andy said. 'Rough weather lately.'

Adam was bent over the turtle. Thabo was scraping barnacles off the carapace near where they would fix the tracker. They had work to do. 'That's for sure.'

'You guys check the beach, don't you, for turtle eggs?' Andy said.

Adam kept his eyes down. 'We do.'

'You must see all kinds of stuff washed up.'

Thabo handed Adam a can of epoxy and Adam busied himself

with it so he didn't have to look up. 'Sometimes.' Now was Andy's chance to ask if he'd seen the wreckage of a boat, or the body of a missing friend.

'Yeah, well, maybe we should leave you in peace,' Andy said.

Now Adam glanced up at the Englishman. He might have been paranoid, but it looked to him like Andy was staring at him, trying to read him. 'As long as *you* aren't looking for anything I can help you with? Sharks? Turtles?' Adam said lightly.

'Oh, we're just diving for the fun of it.' Andy smiled with his teeth but not his eyes.

'Enjoy.' Adam kept working.

One of Andy's offsiders – Jones, a big bear of a man – cast off the line. To Adam it looked like he knew what he was doing. Adam noticed one of the tattoos on Jones's arm – a globe flanked by laurel wreaths on each side and a crown on top.

'Good luck with your research,' Andy said as he put the throttle in reverse and backed away.

'Thanks.'

Adam kept busy with the turtle. They needed to minimise the time it was out of the water. Jenny watched the other divers go, then turned back to help Adam spread the epoxy around the transmitter, moulding it into the contours of the carapace so that they left a smooth surface.

The other boat turned and moved off. Adam saw how all the men on board seemed to take up stations, sitting astride the inflatable sides of the boat and looking out over the ocean. Their heads moved as though they were scanning for something.

Maybe they were looking for sharks or dolphin fins. Or maybe they were searching for something else, like the wreckage of a sunken boat. Or maybe, Adam thought, missing cargo. For now, Adam had another body to retrieve.

6

KWAZULU-NATAL, THE PRESENT

Sannie and Marilyn raced through the KZN countryside past commercial farmers' fields dotted with fat cattle and kraals where goats wandered from between modest tin and brick houses out onto the road.

'It is very difficult to kill a goat,' Marilyn said as Sannie braked yet again.

'That's reassuring,' Sannie said.

Marilyn nodded. 'Cows, quite easy; donkeys – well, donkeys have a death wish, my father always said. Cows are stupid and will wander into the path of a car by mistake, while donkeys will just stand in the middle of the road waiting to be hit. But a goat . . . no, a goat is fast and clever.'

Although Sannie had grown up on a farm she'd had very little to do with livestock as a child. She was learning a good deal in her short time in rural KwaZulu-Natal.

Marilyn checked her phone. Captain Derick le Roux had sent them a pin on WhatsApp. 'Turn right, here.'

Sannie swung the Fortuner and for the second time that day they found themselves heading up a long dirt driveway towards a farmhouse. This time, they were drawing their pistols.

Le Roux's *bakkie* was parked outside the house. The building was single-storey, plastered and painted a pale grey-blue on the outside and surrounded by a wide colonnaded *stoep*. The garden was a beautiful riot of colour.

Derick le Roux emerged from inside, followed by a grey-haired woman in jeans and a khaki shirt, a shotgun cradled in her right arm.

'Colonel van Rensburg,' Derick said as Sannie approached, 'this is Lettie Pienaar.'

Sannie greeted the woman in Afrikaans. 'And this is my partner, Warrant Officer Msani.'

The older woman shook hands with both of them and greeted Marilyn in Zulu.

'English?' Lettie said to Marilyn.

'If it's OK with you, ma'am. My Afrikaans is not so *lekker*.'

Lettie gave a tight smile. 'Fine. My dogs started barking,' she said as if continuing a story she had begun before the women arrived. A Jack Russell and a Rhodesian ridgeback trotted out from the house as if on cue. 'They know not to make a fuss unless it's something serious. There was a man out in one of the cattle yards. He was herding my stock away through the far gate.' She pointed with the tip of the barrel of her gun. 'Second time this month.'

'You've lost some stock?' Sannie asked.

Lettie nodded. 'No doubt. I haven't checked yet, but I'm sure they're gone.'

'Lettie's farm was hit three weeks ago,' Le Roux said.

Sannie took her notebook out of the back pocket of her jeans. She started a new page with the date, time and location. 'How many, ah …'

'Head,' Lettie said. 'Of cattle. Brahmans. Twenty-four last time, and we'll see soon enough this time. I expect they're on their way to Lesotho by now.'

'Lesotho?' Marilyn asked.

'The Mountain Kingdom's a prime destination for South African stock,' Captain Le Roux said. 'They're either consumed there, used for breeding by local farmers, or exported back out through South Africa to Mozambique. It's big business.'

'How are they transported from here?' Sannie asked.

'The locals round them up from here, sometimes with horses,' Lettie said, 'then they're loaded somewhere quiet onto trucks. When they get close to the border of Lesotho they're herded across again. *Ag*, this country, the authorities are hopeless.' She glanced at Le Roux. 'Sorry, Derick, I know you do your best, but we need another thousand like you.'

Le Roux shrugged and looked at Sannie. 'What can I say? I don't need to tell you about budget and manpower shortages in the SAPS. And I'm tired; that's one of the reasons I'm moving to New Zealand.'

Lettie put a hand on his arm. 'We don't blame you, Derick. We all know you do your best. I'd follow you overseas as well, but everything I own is tied up in this farm. It's all I've got, since . . . Well, who would like a cup of coffee?'

Sannie had more questions, but Le Roux smiled at Lettie: 'Yes, please.' Sannie and Marilyn politely declined. When Lettie walked back inside, her dogs in tow, Le Roux added in a quiet voice: 'Her husband, Johannes, was killed last year. Farm murder. Here. Shame, poor woman.'

'My goodness,' Sannie said. She wondered at the staying power of the old widow, living out here by herself, except for her staff.

'She's a tough one,' Le Roux said, echoing her thoughts.

'The murder?' Sannie asked.

Again, he shrugged. 'Open case. Some stock were taken as well, along with firearms – a hunting rifle and a pistol.'

'No leads at all?'

Le Roux shook his head. 'Some of the stock theft is done by local *skelms* and we round them up soon enough, but ever since Johannes was killed we've had trouble solving as many cases as we used to. I think there's a professional gang that moves through KZN and the Free State and then back again. They're organised – we're sure they use large vehicles to transport the stock – and they've got brains and money.'

'These criminals you mention,' Marilyn asked, 'where are they from? Lesotho?'

He shook his head. 'I don't think so. If they were, we'd be able to pick up their vehicles, with Lesotho plates, pretty easily, but they seem to move like ghosts. This is a big-scale operation. They're dealing in hundreds, maybe thousands of head of cattle per year, not dozens. Based on the losses we can't account for, we're talking maybe three million rands' worth this year so far alone.'

'I see.' Sannie's phone vibrated in her pocket. She took it out and saw that it was Adam calling. She hit the cancel button.

'You need to get that, Sannie?' Le Roux asked.

'Later. How widely do you think this stock theft gang operates? You said the Free State?'

He nodded. 'From here over to Clarens at least. You know that area – the "green highway".'

'Yes.' Sannie had heard the term. 'The main smuggling route for marijuana grown in Lesotho comes over the border and through the town of Clarens into South Africa.'

'*Ja*, and diamonds, if you believe the stories,' Le Roux said. 'The word is they're coming from the DRC.'

Sannie had heard those rumours as well, that conflict or 'blood' diamonds illegally mined in the Democratic Republic of Congo were being 'dry-cleaned' and released onto the world market via other diamond-producing countries. Murder, drugs, diamonds, cattle rustling – it seemed that she'd landed up in an organised crime hotbed rather than the sleepy *dorpie* she'd expected.

Lettie came back outside with a cup of coffee for Le Roux. 'Sure you don't want one, ladies?' she said to Sannie and Marilyn. They declined again.

'How soon will you know how many cattle are missing?' Sannie asked the older woman.

'My manager, Desmond Sibisi is out doing a count now. He should be back here in half an hour, I think. He's also looking for tracks and breaks in the fences.'

'Did you use your firearm?' Sannie asked.

Lettie was about thirty centimetres shorter than Sannie and twenty years or more older, but she squared up to her. 'I did. And I'll do so again next time someone enters my property uninvited.'

Sannie didn't condone vigilantism, but she now knew what had happened on this farm. She nodded. 'I'm assuming that shotgun is licensed.'

'It is. As is my pistol. I'm competent with both.'

Sannie didn't doubt it. 'Was the man who entered your yard armed?'

There was just a moment's hesitation before she replied. 'Yes. Of course.'

Sannie wrote in her notebook. 'Can you describe the weapon?'

'Pistol. Nine-mil, I would say.'

'Where were you standing, and how far was the intruder from you?'

'I was on my *stoep*. He was . . .' She looked out to the fields and pointed. 'Over there by the perimeter fence.'

'Inside the fence or outside?' Sannie noted that the fence was maybe seventy metres from the *stoep*. It was a long shot for a shotgun, or a pistol.

'I wasn't taking any chances,' Lettie said. 'He fired at me, and I let him have both barrels.'

'Did you see the bullet strike?' Sannie asked, knowing the answer.

She shook her head. 'No. He missed me.'

'Where on the *stoep* were you standing?'

'By the front door.'

Sannie looked at the wide frontage of the farmhouse. 'And his bullet didn't hit the house at all?'

Lettie looked to Le Roux, who gave a little tilt of his head.

'It's not my fault if he was a bad shot,' Lettie said.

Sannie made a note. 'Did you hit him?'

'No. I fired over his head. A warning shot.'

The lies were tumbling from her. 'Even though he had fired at you, you aimed high?' Sannie said. It gave her no pleasure to catch the older woman out.

'Yes, well, I could tell I'd scared him off by then.'

'I see.' Sannie remembered the time in Hazyview when she and Tom still lived on the banana farm. A man had come to kill them, and her children. That man had not left the farm alive. 'Can you describe him?'

Lettie drew a breath, thought a moment. 'Medium build. Dark clothing – like black jeans, long-sleeved dark-grey top, beanie. Gloves and a ski mask.'

'A bit overdressed for the weather,' Marilyn chimed in.

Almost comical, Sannie thought, like a parody of a cat burglar. Or was this another lie?

'You didn't recognise the person – nothing about their build or height?' Sannie asked.

Lettie shook her head. 'No. No. Not at all.'

Something was going on here. Sannie closed her notebook. 'Thank you, Mrs Pienaar. We'll be in touch.'

'That's it?'

'Yes,' Sannie said. 'Unless you have anything else to add? Marilyn will give you her phone number.'

Warrant Officer Msani wrote her number in a page of her notebook, tore it out and gave it to Lettie.

'*Baie dankie,*' Lettie said. Marilyn nodded. 'I'll WhatsApp you when I find out from Desmond just how many beasts were stolen. I'll need it for the insurance claim in any case.'

Sannie had started to walk to her car, but stopped. 'Insurance? For cows?'

Le Roux gave a small laugh. 'There's insurance for everything in this country, Colonel, because, as you know, everything gets stolen. If we're done here, Sannie, it's probably time I settled you into the office.'

They walked out into the yard to their respective vehicles.

'Probably.' Sannie opened the passenger-side door of her Fortuner and said to Marilyn: 'You drive. I need to make a call.'

•　•　•

ADAM PUSHED the boat's throttle full forward and rode down the face of a breaking wave. The combination of the outboards' thrust and the ocean's swell sent the RHIB skidding up the beach until, completely free of the water, it listed to one side.

Thabo hauled himself over the side first, doubled over and dry-retched. He'd thrown up twice already since they'd pulled the dead man aboard. Jenny was staring down at the body, her face white.

Adam's phone vibrated in the waterproof pouch around his neck. He took it out. The freakish patch of phone reception he had picked up out on the open water, when he tried to call Sannie, was holding up.

'Howzit,' he said to Sannie.

'Fine and you?'

He slid over the inflated edge of the boat and walked a short distance away from the others. He ran his free hand through his damp hair. '*Lekker*. Well, not so *lekker*, actually.'

'Same here, as it happens. Busy morning.'

There was a forced formality to her voice. He had himself to blame for that. 'Are you alone?'

'I'm in the car, with Marilyn.'

'*Sawubona*, Marilyn.'

The young officer replied in Zulu, asking if he was well, and he told her he was tired and wet.

'Come home to your woman, she misses you,' Marilyn said in isiZulu. Adam allowed himself a sad smile. He knew, as did Marilyn, that Sannie spoke next to no isiZulu.

'When I need your help as a relationship counsellor I'll ask for it, sister,' Adam replied in isiZulu, 'but thank you.'

'What are you two talking about?' Sannie interjected.

'The weather.' Marilyn laughed.

'*Ja*, well, maybe one of you can share the weather joke with me later. Is everything all right, Adam?'

He exhaled, long and loud, and looked to the boat. Jenny was out and rubbing Thabo's back. He'd hoped to spare them this. 'Not so good. The ocean's served up two dead bodies here in the last twenty-four hours.'

'Oh, my word,' Sannie said. 'Drownings?'

'Looks like it. One washed up on the beach last night and the other we just found trapped in a sunken ski boat.'

'Local police on the scene yet?'

'Still waiting.' Bhanga Nek was a long way from anywhere. 'They were supposed to be here, earlier, but they called me to say they'd been delayed by a traffic accident. Adam looked down the beach to their research headquarters at the southern tip. 'I can see a white van now. That might be the medical examiner, or coroner or whatever. The police said someone else would come for the body as well. Any advice on what I should do?'

'Adam, you can't really conduct your own investigation. Can you secure the scenes where you found the bodies, until the police get to you?'

He started walking back to the boat and his students. 'The first one was a guy who washed up on the beach last night. I couldn't leave him there overnight. The second crime scene is at the bottom of the Indian Ocean, about five hundred metres offshore. We had a big storm last night, so it might have foundered there, but the second guy we found was trapped in the wreckage, in a net. The guys look like foreigners, maybe Middle Eastern, and from what they were wearing and what was on board it was clear they weren't fishermen. I'm thinking smugglers. I might be able to find out what they were smuggling if we go back for another look. I found an antique book.'

'The local police will have to make the call. You said "we" found the man?'

'Jenny found the second body. We were catching a male turtle.'

There was a pause. 'Well, I guess you won't be coming home anytime soon, then.'

'No.' He felt a defensive wall come up. 'We spent the evening rescuing about a hundred eggs from a tidal surge last night, as well as picking up a dead body.'

Before, when he'd called her, he had been looking forward to hearing her voice. But now he felt under attack.

'Adam, I'm just tired. I didn't mean –'

'I should get going,' he said.

There was another pause. 'Remember to check the dead guys' pockets, make a note of any valuables or jewellery, and their IDs if they have them. Stuff like that can go missing, but might be important to the detectives later.'

'OK.'

'Adam?'

'Yes?'

'How stable is the wreck of the boat?'

He rubbed his stubbled jaw. 'We've got more bad weather coming and the ocean's been rough. The boat's no battleship. It's a small ski boat – like for fishing or pleasure.'

'Maybe you can take another look. Goodness knows how long it will take our people to get police divers to your location. That would be a big help.'

'Sure.' He tried to think of something else to say to her, to keep her on the line, but she sounded tense, busy.

'Adam . . .'

'Yes?' He tried to hide the note of hope in his voice. It was his fault they were apart, even though he didn't see himself as having done anything wrong by staying on at Bhanga Nek for a while longer. Sannie had made it plain she wasn't happy about it, but here she was, riding about KwaZulu-Natal like some modern-day Wild West sheriff.

'I . . . well, take care. Stay safe. You can look for evidence but don't go doing anything foolish.'

He had thought she was about to say that she missed him, but his pride wouldn't let him say that he felt that way right now. 'You too. Take care. Don't get run over by a cow.'

'A what?'

He smiled. 'Google it. More people get killed by cows than by sharks every year.'

'I've got to go. Bye.'

Sannie ended the call. Adam walked along the beach, back to their boat. Thabo was standing upright, which was an improvement. 'How are you doing, *bru*?'

Thabo swallowed hard, nodded and smiled, maybe at the term of endearment. 'Um, good, Prof. Sorry.'

'No need to be. Shows you're human.'

Jenny put her hands on her hips. 'And what am I, Prof, a robot?'

He smiled at her. 'No, you're a fish. We might need to go out and dive on that wreck again, take a look around her.'

Thabo coughed. 'OK.'

'No, Thabo, I want you to check on the turtle eggs. They're our actual priority right now. I need temperature checks, everything.' Adam knew that going back to the boat might trigger more pain for Thabo. Adam had seen every possible reaction to death in his time in the army, from revulsion and physical sickness to casual cruelty. It was hardest on the thinkers, the sensitive ones, like Thabo. It had been hard on Adam himself.

'Yes, Prof,' Thabo said.

'I'll go get the Polaris,' Jenny said.

Adam was about to tell her to go and help Thabo, but she had looked death in the face, had held the body in her arms as the pair of them had hoisted it into the boat. Just as there was nothing in Thabo's genes or upbringing – he was the son of a wealthy doctor and a banker from upmarket Sandton, in Johannesburg – that would make it easier for him to cope with trauma, nor was there any indication that Jenny, the daughter of a Johannesburg goldminer, would be any less likely to be affected by trauma.

'All right,' he said to her.

The two students set off down the beach and Adam climbed into the boat again.

Like the man who had washed ashore, this body was neither black nor white. Adam had guessed them to be Middle Eastern, maybe, but he couldn't be sure. The antique book was a clue. This man might have come from the same part of the world as the other, but he was different.

His shirt was mostly unbuttoned and Adam saw an old scar low on the torso, round and puckered. He knew what that was, a bullet hole, but from long ago. There were tattoos on the man's arms, as well, faded and blurred because this man had been older than the other, maybe in his fifties. Adam lifted an arm and examined the underside. There was a tattoo of a rifle, an AK-47, and a crest or badge of some kind. He took out his phone and snapped a picture of it.

He also took pictures of a gold wedding ring on the man's left hand, and a chunky gold necklace. On the man's wrist was a heavy watch, white gold. Adam let out a low whistle when he zoomed in. It was a Rolex. Adam didn't know enough about watches to know if it was real or fake, but the man's chinos and polo shirt were branded, and he wore brown yachting shoes.

Adam checked the man's pockets. There was a wallet with no credit cards, but a sodden fold of US dollars. Adam snapped another shot of a soaking fan of five green hundred-dollar bills, two fifties, and three twenties.

'What were you doing out there, *bru*?' Adam asked out loud.

He was about to get out of the boat when he noticed a bulge at the bottom of the man's trousers, just above his shoe. Adam bent down and pulled up the hem of the chinos. There, strapped just above his ankle, was a holster with a pistol in it. He looked about the boat and picked up his T-shirt, then used that to extract the weapon, using his covered fingertips. It was a Russian-made Makarov. Adam wrapped the pistol in his T-shirt. He felt that it was better if he secured it somewhere and handed it to the police when they arrived, rather than leaving it on the body.

Adam looked up the beach, northwards, towards Mozambique. The border was close here and it was a very quick run down the coast by boat. Adam was becoming more and more certain that these two men had been up to no good. He seriously doubted they were tourists or fishermen. Neither was dressed for that part.

Smugglers.

Adam thought about the antique book – the Koran or whatever it was – that was currently in his tent. He wondered if that was being moved into or out of South Africa. He guessed it was the former. But who wanted it, and why? Money, he guessed. The land border with Mozambique was mostly bush and very porous. It was well known that illegal goods moved both ways, but why had these guys come by boat? Adam was sure that plenty of contraband was moved by sea, but why a historic book? The ornately decorated text must be valuable, but it was not very big – surely it would have been just as easy to smuggle it through a land border post? Adam knew that tourists and locals staying further north of Bhanga Nek, up around Kosi Bay, sometimes illegally walked up the beach to go to the bars in Ponta do Ouro to feast on Mozambican peri-peri prawns and drink Dois M lager, with the border authorities rarely batting an eyelid. Why risk rough seas and a night crossing to deliver something that small via the ocean?

Maybe there was more on the boat.

Adam and Jenny had been preoccupied with freeing the body from the cargo net and getting it to the surface, so they'd done little more than a quick visual scan of the sunken boat. It was time for them to get back out there.

He heard the growl of the Polaris and looked up to see Jenny racing along the hard wet sand along the waterline. She pulled up close to him.

'How's Thabo?' Adam asked.

'More at home playing mother hen to turtle eggs than picking up dead bodies.'

Adam nodded. 'I don't blame him. You sure you're OK?'

'Strangely, yes. I always liked biology at school, which is part of the reason I chose a science degree. I never minded dissections. I didn't know how I'd feel if I ever saw a dead human body, but now I do.'

'And how do you feel?' he asked.

'Sad for him, I guess, but also intrigued. I mean, rather than feeling sick, like Thabo, I want to know what happened to the guy. It's like I want to help him. Is that weird?'

Adam shook his head. 'No.' He remembered the first time he'd seen a dead person – it had been a fellow soldier, a friend. He closed his eyes.

'Are *you* OK, Prof?'

He took a breath. 'I'm fine, Jenny, but thanks for asking. This stuff is never easy.' He gestured to the boat. 'I searched him. He was carrying a gun.'

'Serious?' She looked almost excited.

Adam heard the far-off drone of an outboard motor. Looking out to sea, he spotted the low silhouette of the Zodiac, with Andy, the man they'd encountered earlier, and his three burly comrades on board, racing for the shore.

7

NATAL, 1880

He could smell death even before he reached the building.

Peter Gregory dismounted outside the farmhouse. It was a modest affair of mudbrick plastered with white-washed dung and a thatched roof. Some hungry cows lowed from a nearby kraal. Perhaps they were in need of milking; cattle were not Peter's forte.

Samuel and Phillips followed him on foot. Gregory heard the buzzing of flies before he opened the door. He drew a deep breath before he went inside.

The dead man lay on his back in the centre of the room, which was not unlike Gregory's home, if his hut could be called as such. Unlike his abode – which was much improved since Grace had been there – this house was filthy. Phillips turned at the doorway, went out into the yard and emptied his breakfast in one go. Gregory didn't know if it was the odour or the sight of a man slit from groin to sternum that upset the lad more.

Samuel looked over his shoulder. 'A Zulu did not do this.'

'How do you know?' Gregory asked.

'He still has his jacket on. We would have taken it.'

Gregory nodded slowly, breathing through his mouth. He remem-

88

bered the field of bodies, opened like this one, but bare from the waist up.

Samuel walked around him and bent, placing his hands on his knees. 'Also, his rifle is still here. One of our warriors would have taken that.'

It was interesting that Samuel used the word 'our'. He'd been cast out of his royal home, but still thought of the Zulu as his people. Had the French Prince Imperial still thought of the citizens of France as his subjects? Probably. This was why wars were fought, why men had their innards spilled.

Gregory looked around. There was a wooden dining table with one chair and a dirty plate and bowl. Ants were climbing over the crockery, scavenging the remains. Gregory reached down and picked up one of the man's outstretched hands. The fingers were stiff. 'He's been dead a while, a couple of days.'

'Do we know his name?' Samuel asked.

'Morrison. Used to be a major in the 17th Lancers,' Gregory said. 'Retired.'

'He does not look very old to me,' Samuel said.

Gregory moved to a bookcase made of rough-hewn timber. 'According to Grace, and something I overheard in the Red Lantern, Major Morrison had some perverse weaknesses of the flesh. Hardly what would be considered the behaviours of an officer and a gentle-man. And looking at the state of this place,' Gregory pointed to two empty gin bottles on the floor, 'he seems to have well and truly fallen from grace.'

Gregory picked up a book from the shelf. It was a volume of Dickens and there were pieces of card and paper in it. He opened the book. 'What have we here?'

Gregory took out half-a-dozen postcards with an assortment of lithographs and drawings of naked women and girls in lewd poses, and one of two young men in Arab dress – or, rather, partial undress. He snapped the book closed. Further back in the book he found a sheet of paper which he unfolded and read.

· · ·

Harold,

It was with great sadness that your mother and I learned of your 'resignation' of your commission. It was our fervent hope that a spell in the army would cure you of your perverse and loathsome tendencies. One can turn a blind eye to certain peccadillos, but not to the sort of behaviour that you have evidenced. I wrote to your commanding officer, whom I knew from my time in the military, and reading between the lines it would seem that your time in the warmer climes of the colonies has rather inflamed your unhealthy passions. While I understand that you now find yourself without means, I must inform you that your mother and I have decided to decline your request for remittances. It is time that you learned to conduct yourself as an honest, moral, decent Christian gentleman and we do not believe that this will be encouraged by sending you charity. You have brought shame and dishonour on our family. Word has already reached Whitechapel of your 'resignation' and there are rumours of both cowardice and moral lassitude attached to it. You are not welcome in London.

Your father.

CLEARLY MORRISON'S resignation had been forced. Gregory checked the date on the letter; it was six months earlier. Judging by the state of the house Morrison was living in – and the remaining clothes on the body, which seemed threadbare and unclean – the former major had been living a life of borderline subsistence as a rural pauper.

And he'd been murdered.

Phillips appeared at the door, wiping his mouth and looking up at the smoke-stained rafters and blackened internal grass of the roof. 'Renegade Zulus, I expect?'

'No,' Gregory said. 'Samuel?'

'Yes, Peter?'

Gregory noted how Phillips frowned at Samuel's familiarity, but it bothered him not. 'I want you and Sergeant Phillips to search this place. Turn it upside down.'

'What are we looking for, sir?' Phillips asked.

Gregory looked around the room. 'I don't know.' Gregory replaced the volume of Dickens on the bookshelf then selected the next tome, a leather-bound notebook. When he opened it, he saw it was a diary. Good. He held it close to him.

'Sir?' Phillips looked baffled.

Samuel smiled at Phillips. 'He does this. The captain wants us to look not just with our eyes.'

'Then with what, man?' Phillips turned his exasperation on the Zulu.

'Our *minds*,' Samuel said. 'To find what is here – and perhaps, what is not here.'

Gregory gave a sharp nod. 'Exactly.' When Phillips persisted with his perplexed look, Gregory offered him some clues. 'Murder weapon, evidence of theft, evidence of other crimes. Indications as to the state of mind, social standing and means of the dead man. Like Samuel said, use your brain.'

'Sir.'

Gregory walked outside into the fresh air. He breathed deep and took a moment to steady himself. The cloying scent of decay was carrying him back in time, to more than a year ago. He had a purpose, he reminded himself: to find who had killed the less-than-innocent Major Morrison, and to find out something that the dead man might have known – the whereabouts of the missing sword.

Gregory opened the diary and began leafing through it as he walked towards the cattle kraal. The entries began in late 1878, when Morrison seemed to have embarked in England on his voyage to Africa. Peter flicked past reports of the sea voyage, leave in Cape Town (though he noted with some unease in his stomach a reference to a 'comely' young girl), and slowed when he came to an account of Morrison visiting the battlefield at Isandlwana after the slaughter.

Although he wanted to move ahead, Gregory stopped and leaned on a rough-hewn fence post. He ignored the cow that came up to him and tried to nuzzle him through the railings as he read:

· · ·

WE CAME across a vision of hell such as none on earth has ever seen. All around me, as far as I could see, were the decomposing bodies of British and colonial soldiers. The natives had defiled each and every one of them, slitting them open. It is said that this is a mark of respect, but to me it was pure evil. I must confess to a certain fascination as I pondered the strength of character needed to perpetrate such horrors. Is there not a purity, something to be admired, about a warrior who can dispatch a fallen foe in such a merciless manner?

GREGORY SHOOK HIS HEAD. Morrison had misunderstood the Zulu ritual, which was about freeing the spirit of the fallen foe so that it could not stay on earth to haunt the warrior who had done the killing and drive him insane. Yes, the Zulu were allowing their victims to ascend to their version of heaven, but they were also indulging in a form of self-preservation. Gregory had no idea if there was any basis in such superstitions, but at this point in his life he was willing to try anything to free himself of the spirits that haunted him. Strong liquor put him to sleep when nothing else worked, but the nightmares still came, eventually.

As much as Gregory respected the martial prowess of the Zulu and their allegiance to their clans, Morrison's diary gave a rather twisted view of the Zulus' ability to dispatch a foe without mercy. *Purity* was not a word Gregory would have chosen.

Gregory flipped through more pages. There were some sketches that made his stomach turn. This was, truly, a window into the innermost thoughts of a man who had lost his moral direction in life – if he had ever had one. Gregory found an upturned milk pail and sat on it. A word leapt off the page at him: *Sword.*

WHILST ON PATROL we were approached by a pair of natives. Judging by their age and bearing they were men of some seniority, confirmed by the fact that they introduced themselves as emissaries of King Cetshwayo himself. The senior of the two was named Mfunzi. He said the Zulu were keen to parley, which was not surprising since we have invaded their lands in force and it is common knowledge that we come with a firm desire to exact justice for the abominations of Isandlwana and the rebel ruler's temerity to defy England.

Mfunzi said that Cetshwayo wished to enter into negotiations with Lord Chelmsford and offered a gift to be conveyed to our commander as a sign of good faith. Thereupon he produced a sword, minus its scabbard, and told our party that the blade had belonged to an important nobleman, who had died most bravely in battle. The sword was curved in the manner of some Saracen weapon of old and there were some words engraved in French in the steel.

GREGORY LICKED HIS LIPS. The cow beside him lowed and stuck her head through the railings again, reaching for him. The interior of its kraal was ground to mud. The animal could wait – he felt a tightening in his chest at the mention of the French writing. He wet his finger with his tongue and turned the page.

WE TOOK possession of the sword, and while we were sure – and hoped – it would not assist in any negotiated settlement of the impending hostilities, there was much excitement in the headquarters that evening. It seemed that we had, in fact, become the custodians of the young French Prince Imperial's sword and that this same weapon had been carried by the late prince's famed great-uncle, Napoleon Bonaparte himself!

Naturally I was flushed with honour when the commanding officer decreed that I should take custody of the emperor's prized possession and keep it safe until it could be delivered to Lord Chelmsford. This possession, whose value must be incalculable to some Bonapartist, had been handed down to his heir, lost, and then found once more. I must confess that I considered this important trust placed in me to be a feather in my cap.

NO DOUBT. Gregory shook his head. 'Pompous arse.'

Gregory read on, then skimmed the next few pages, but there was no more mention of the sword.

'Sir?' Phillips called from the farm hovel, and stepped outside.

There was more to read, but Gregory shut the diary, stood and slid it into the pocket of his tunic. 'What is it?'

'I –'

Samuel came through the door, stood next to Phillips and stared pointedly at the young sergeant.

'That is, Samuel discovered something interesting, sir.'

'What is it?'

'That man, Morrison, was shot,' Samuel said.

'Was he now?' Gregory walked to them.

Samuel led the way back inside, then dropped to one knee. He took hold of Morrison's left arm, disturbing a cloud of flies, and rolled the body over. 'See here,' Samuel said, pointing to three holes in the rear of Morrison's coat. 'The killer has stabbed him in the back, in the rear of the heart, with an assegai. I think he did this to cover the true nature of his death.'

Gregory squatted beside the body, doing his best to ignore the stink. He looked where Samuel was pointing. 'The tunic is burned there, which would have been in the centre of the chest. And I can see the edge of a bullet hole.'

Samuel nodded and lifted up the coat and Morrison's bloodied shirt. 'Same here, on the body. The killer has used the spear to try and cover his dirty work, but this hole in the skin is too big. This is where the bullet exited.'

'It would be interesting to see the bullet,' Gregory said.

Samuel smiled and reached into a pocket of his uniform jacket. He opened his palm and Gregory took the flattened lead slug from it.

Gregory stood and held it up to the weak sunlight coming in through the window. 'Looks like a .44 calibre, perhaps from an Adams revolver. Smaller than a bullet from a Martini–Henry rifle.'

'British Army issue,' Phillips said.

Gregory nodded. 'Where did you find it, Samuel?'

Samuel also stood and walked to the rear wall, the one facing the door. He pointed to a vertical wooden beam, partly exposed. 'I dug it out of here.'

Gregory looked at where Morrison had fallen. 'So, the not-very-good major opens the door and someone shoots him through the heart, and proceeds to make it look like a Zulu warrior has killed him.'

'So it would seem,' Phillips said, as if he'd somehow been part of this discovery. 'Anything of interest in that book you took outside, sir?'

Gregory shook his head. 'Nothing pertaining to this incident.' That was true – Hellfire Jack had told him to be discreet in his enquiries into the missing sword, so Samuel and Phillips didn't need to know about that for now. But was it a bizarre coincidence that one of the men Gregory would have interviewed about the missing heirloom had turned up dead even before his investigation had begun? 'I'm presuming our man lived alone?'

Samuel nodded and cast a glance around the squalid interior. 'No sign of a woman in here, no wife, not even a domestic.'

'Some sort of a recluse, sir? A hermit?' Phillips ventured.

Gregory sniffed the fetid air. 'Worse. No self-respecting person would want to live here. Search the barn and the yard. And do something about that cow. It seems . . . distressed.'

Samuel laughed. 'Ah, you'll never make a farmer.'

Gregory scowled. 'Go about your duty or I'll let Phillips here whip you.'

Samuel took a menacing step towards Phillips, who backed off. Samuel laughed.

The other two went outside and Gregory poked about. Off the main room was a bedchamber which, had it not been for the stench coming off the body, would have smelled even worse than the filthy living room. Yellow sheets had been disturbed and the mattress tossed.

On the wall above the bedhead was a collection of six swords, mounted on wooden racks. Gregory leaned over the filthy bed and inspected the weapons. He recognised a standard cavalry sword; a Royal Navy cutlass, with its curved blade; and another that he thought might have been from India. There was no empty rack where a French emperor's weapon might have been, but if Morrison had been in possession of Napoleon's sword then Gregory doubted the ex-major would have been stupid enough to have it on show. There was no sword hiding in the wooden wardrobe, just some of Morrison's clothes, and his cavalry dress uniform, which was covered in a dusting of white mould.

Clearly, Morrison was a collector. Had he happened to have a standard French cavalry sword, which he switched for Bonaparte's weapon last year? Was it this substitute that Chelmsford had presented to the empress?

Even in the pallor of death it was clear that Morrison had a drinker's face, and the cluster of empty bottles by the bed confirmed this. Gregory recalled the letter from Morrison's father, advising that his son would not be welcome in London.

London. It seemed a lifetime ago, and indeed it could have been. Gregory had known soldiers who had lived fewer years than he'd been away from his birthplace in the green fields of Buckinghamshire. Sometimes, if he narrowed his eyes and the sun was not too fierce nor the sky marbled with lightning, and the rivers of Zululand were not running red with blood and mud, he could see those patchwork meadows in the rolling hills of Natal.

But Gregory had been back to England only once in the past twenty years, since joining the army as a seventeen-year-old ensign. His father had been titled, but his elder brother inherited that so, as was the custom, Peter, the second son, went into the army. He'd arrived too late for action in India, in the aftermath of the mutiny in 1859, but had been 'blooded', as his commanding officer in the British West India Regiment put it, eight years later in the British possession of Honduras, in Central America.

There his action had been limited to skirmishes with indigenous Indian tribes who kidnapped white planters as part of a nascent uprising against the colonial power. In an action to free a settler, he had run a man through with his sword and shot another with his pistol. In the mess his brother officers had toasted him and joked about each taking of a life, but Peter had sought the refuge of his tent and letters to his mother to try, as best he could, to examine and explain his feelings. On the one hand he'd felt proud to have done his duty, but on the other, the men he had killed returned to him in his dreams, most especially when the malaria took hold of him during a later posting to the Gold Coast where he commanded a lonely fort outside of Accra.

His first-hand observance of people fighting for their own freedom, land and beliefs gave him a respect for the Zulu traditions of war and combat. He had prayed at the drumhead religious services on Sundays, but that did not stop the night terrors. What were the Zulu practices, such as setting free a dead foe's spirits by eviscerating him, other than a bloody prayer? Samuel did not seem unduly burdened by the memories of the men he had killed in inter-tribal battles; for him it had been part of the life of a warrior.

Gregory looked out through the grubby window pane, at Samuel taking charge and Phillips pretending to.

Gregory tapped on walls, looking for a hidden cavity, and moved an opened steamer trunk to see if it concealed anything underneath it. The floor was solid, the same as that in Gregory's home – cow dung mixed with water and soil and then dried to a solid finish. It had not been disturbed.

As well as the bookshelf there was a battered writing desk in a corner of the room. Samuel and Phillips had been through the drawers and some papers were scattered on the desktop. Gregory picked up two and inspected them.

'Gambling chits,' Samuel said from the open doorway. 'I was going to mention them to you, but the bullet hole in the body seemed more important.'

Gregory nodded. 'It was. But it's all important. Anything outside?'

Samuel shook his head. 'He was not much of a farmer. About as good as you.' Gregory smiled. 'The barn is as disgusting as the house. More so. Chains, belts, even some leg irons.'

'Really?'

'*Yebo*. I don't like this place. There is plenty of rubbish in there. More empty liquor bottles. Evil.'

Gregory felt a chill on the back of his neck. The Lord – or Satan – alone only knew what had gone on in this place. He had an urge to put the farm to the torch, but he had an unpleasant feeling he would need to return here.

He riffled through the paperwork and sorted the gambling chits into a single pile. Together they totalled fifty pounds, a significant sum indeed. Some were made out to the Red Lantern. Other chits were owed to individuals and Gregory recognised a couple of the names – a lawyer and a man who ran an import–export business with warehouses down at the Bluff.

'No weapons, other than the pistol by his side, the swords in the bedroom, and the shotgun in the corner?' Gregory nodded to the long-arm propped against the wall next to the fireplace.

'No, sir,' Phillips said.

Samuel shook his head. 'There are some tracks outside – not ours. Sergeant Phillips discovered them.'

Gregory looked to him and raised his eyebrows. 'Yes?'

'Two men, on horses. One big, heavy, one shorter, lighter.'

Gregory rubbed his chin. 'Not a man and a woman, perhaps?'

'No,' Phillips said.

'And what do you know about tracking, Sergeant?' Gregory asked.

'Er, not very much at all, sir. But there are no women in the army, of course, and those tracks that I found are both from British military-issue boots.'

Gregory looked to both of them and gave the smallest of nods. It was good work. They were no closer to finding a killer – and part of Gregory didn't care whether or not the murderer of Major Morrison was ever found – but he had another mystery to solve.

'Samuel, a word, if you please?'

Gregory led Samuel away from Phillips, who looked at the distressed cow and made a sympathetic clucking noise. When they were out of earshot, Gregory briefed Samuel on his mission to find the missing Napoleonic sword. Samuel was older than Phillips, and he knew that if he told his friend to keep the information to himself, then he would. The young sergeant, however, might be tempted to run off at the mouth the next time he was in a tavern. Gregory saw promise in Phillips, but he needed to get the full measure of him. He shared the information he had found in Morrison's diary with Samuel, and also explained about his other task, to provide an escort for the American woman, Lady Beecham – Phillips would learn of that soon enoguh.

'I know Mfunzi, the former king's emissary. The one you say presented this prince's sword to the British,' Samuel said. 'He was a friend of my father.'

'Can you find him?' Gregory asked.

'If he is still alive, yes. So many men were killed in the war – they say every household lost someone.'

'Will it be safe for you to travel to his home?'

Samuel shrugged. 'The king is in exile, but there are those who would still support him. All I have to protect me is my uniform. But I don't fear Mfunzi. He was an honourable man. If he lives, I can find him.'

'See what you can find out about the sword, and if anyone can remember what it looked like.'

'You think that perhaps the Zulus did not give back the prince's actual sword, the one carried by this French king?' Samuel asked.

'It's a possibility, so we need to rule it out.'

'I understand,' Samuel said. 'I will meet you at Kwa Jim's on the day before the full moon.'

Kwa Jim's was the common Zulu name for the old mission station-turned-fort at Rorke's Drift, which had once been trader Jim Rorke's home. Gregory shook hands with his friend.

'*Hamba gahle*, Samuel.'

Go well, Gregory repeated to himself as Samuel mounted and rode off. *And be safe*. As Samuel had said, there was evil in the air.

8

KWAZULU-NATAL, THE PRESENT

The South African Police Service station at Glencoe was a single-storey brick building with a tin roof. Marilyn parked out the back and she and Sannie went inside. The interior was like every other station Sannie had ever entered or worked in. There was a faint smell of bleach and sweat, and other worse odours, and a rattling inefficient air conditioner that would never truly be free of the smell of stale nicotine.

A female sergeant behind the charge counter greeted them.

'Colonel van Rensburg, Warrant Officer Msani. Welcome, we've been expecting you. It's good to have you here,' the sergeant said.

'Thank you, and nice to meet you . . .'

'Sergeant Nyathi, Eva.'

'Ah yes, we spoke on the phone,' Sannie said.

Marilyn exchanged greetings with her in Zulu. Derick le Roux, who had arrived before them, emerged from a corridor and waved at them to follow him.

'Welcome,' he said.

Le Roux pointed out people in offices on either side of the hallway as they walked, giving them no time for more than a wave. At the end of the corridor was a conference room. On the door was a poster of an image of a rhino crossed with a man, who was dressed like a soldier and armed with an AK-47, which he pointed towards the viewer.

Marilyn pointed to the poster. 'Clever.'

Le Roux smiled as he led them into the room. 'My wife, she's a whiz with Photoshop. Please take a seat. This is the stock theft briefing room.'

A woman in a domestic's simple uniform of a dark blue polyester dress came in. 'Coffee or tea?'

Sannie and Marilyn both greeted the woman and ordered coffee. Le Roux already had a cup in his hand with *BOSS* emblazoned on the side. 'I'm going to miss you, Precious,' Le Roux said to the woman.

She smiled at him, then sniffed and lifted a hand to her eyes. Le Roux crossed the room and wrapped his arms around her. 'No, no, please don't cry, Precious.'

The woman wiped her eyes. 'I am sorry, Captain. But you know we will all miss you.'

He nodded, and Sannie saw how Derick's Adam's apple bobbed. Precious left and Derick coughed into his hand, clearing his throat.

'Forgive an old man,' he said to Sannie and Marilyn. 'I don't want to get emotional, but it's hard to be leaving after so long. Come, let us get this briefing done.' He forced a smile. 'I've got a farewell *braai* this afternoon.'

'We'll try not to keep you,' Sannie said.

'Where to start?' he asked.

'As you know, we were sent here to take over temporary command of the unit and assist with the investigation of the killing of the rhinos on David Gregory's property, but that seems to have taken an unexpected turn, with him being murdered,' Sannie said. 'Connection?'

Le Roux set down his cup. 'Yes, the allegation was that David shot all sixteen of his rhinos in their bomas on Virginia Farm, adjacent to his uBhejane Game Reserve. For the record, it was an ongoing investigation and I'd said nothing to the press, but someone in the provincial government leaked the details. As you know, they've taken a hammering over the number of rhinos they've lost in the Hluh-luwe-iMfolozi Park this year and they wanted to be seen to be taking a tough stand on rhino poaching.'

Sannie nodded. From her own experience of rhino poaching she knew that even though the Kruger National Park, where she had worked for several years, and the surrounding game reserves had improved their security and ramped up their anti-poaching efforts, the problem had simply moved to other, less-prepared parts of the country. As Oom Derick had alluded to, it was also a highly political issue.

'David claimed he was the victim of poachers who had got into his rhino bomas at night and killed and dehorned all his rhinos in silence. It seemed fanciful – he thought that maybe the poachers had used silenced rifles, but we all know it's impossible to make a weapon as quiet as it appears in the movies and on TV. He would have woken to that much noise, and the rhinos would have been squealing once the killing started.'

'Deon Meyer said David let his security go?' Sannie said.

Le Roux nodded. His face was grave. 'Poor old David. I felt sorry for him, in a way. He had no money and couldn't afford to pay for anti-poaching. He had a falling out with those foreign Rambos he used to have on the property and even young Deon, who you met, couldn't stay on as a volunteer. It was our theory that David staged the attack, but really killed the rhinos himself.'

Sannie nodded. 'As you know it's not the first time a private rhino owner's been accused of killing his own rhinos and trying to make it look like poachers did it.'

'*Ja*,' Derick said, 'the cost of protecting rhinos has become astro-nomical. It drives owners to break the law – smuggling horns out of the country – or crazier things.'

'I get it,' Marilyn said. 'Some rhino owners dehorn their animals to make them less attractive to poachers, but they have to keep the horn secure and register it with the authorities. If they do the deed themselves and claim poachers took the horns, then they can sell the stuff on the black market. But where's the evidence?'

Le Roux shrugged. 'Not a lot. It's why I asked for reinforcements – that and because I'm retiring.' He spread his hands wide. 'To be honest, I needed someone else, a fresh set of eyes, to take a look at the case, interview David and those who knew him. I couldn't get a confession out of him.'

'But you did find some rhino horn?' Sannie knew some of the details of the case from Gita, even though not everything had been released to the press.

'That's right. We found six horns, placed inside a plastic rubbish bin which was buried in a field about two hundred metres from David's house. We got an anonymous email tip-off from someone who said they used to work at the farm, and that David hid his cash and other valuables in a hole in the ground. There was some night-vision video, like from a camera trap, of David going to the spot with a spade, digging it up and depositing something in the cache. The video was grainy and it was hard to make out what it was he was hiding there. It was longer than his arm and cylindrical, curved, and wrapped in a blanket. One of his rhinos was a big old cow with a *moer* of a horn on her.'

'And were the horns in the buried bin?' Sannie asked.

'Yes and no.' Le Roux stood and went to the pinboard fixed to one wall of the conference room. Sannie had noticed it on the way in and assumed Le Roux would get to it in due course. 'David,' he pointed to a colour portrait photo of a distinguished, grey-haired man in a button-down shirt pinned to the top centre, 'had been keeping some stuff in his hidden safe deposit bin.' Le Roux tapped a picture showing an overhead view of an excavated hole with a plastic container embedded in it. 'He kept his late wife's jewellery in there, as well as R200,000 in cash – enough to make us mildly suspicious – as well as the deeds to his farm and two small ingots of gold. His excuse was the number of farm robberies and killings. He said he kept some cheap jewellery, watches and cash in the house in case he was ever broken into. As I mentioned, there were also six horns of varying sizes.'

Sannie got up and went to the board for a closer look at the next image Le Roux was pointing at. It was a crime scene–style photo of plastic zip-lock bags on a bench, opened, with the contents, rhino horns, next to them, and a ruler in the shot for scale. 'But no big horn?'

'No,' Le Roux said. 'Our theory was that he sold that one, and nine others, and the six in the bin were the remainder from his sixteen dead rhinos.'

'So he was at least guilty of illegally dealing in rhino horn,' Marilyn said.

Derick shrugged. 'Although it's against the law, many private rhino owners fervently believe they should have the right to humanely dehorn their rhinos and sell the horn. It's the age-old debate of pro-trade versus anti-trade. The environment department might have been on to him, though. They seized some horn at OR Tambo airport a while ago and wanted to do DNA testing on various populations to see if the horn had come from a live rhino in private hands. David was in the picture – they were planning to come and check his herd.'

Precious returned, carrying a tray with two cups of coffee and a jug of milk. She set them down in front of the women, who thanked her.

Elsewhere on the board were pictures of dead rhinos. Sannie hated viewing such images – she had seen more than her share of slaughtered animals when she worked in the Kruger Park. She did notice that the animals in the pictures had yellow tags in their left ears.

'He tagged all his rhinos?' Sannie asked.

Le Roux nodded. 'Yes, there were small GPS trackers in the tags. A gift from an NGO a few years ago.'

'What did farmer David have to say about your theory about the horns in the cache?' Marilyn asked.

Le Roux looked to her. 'He'd found himself a lawyer by that stage,

Marilyn, and was refusing to answer questions – or so the lawyer said. David slipped up in the interview when we asked him about the rhino horns. He said that he had dehorned some of his rhinos when the poaching problem first started to get worse, around 2012, he thought, and that he'd stored six of the removed horns in his underground hidey-hole.'

'What was he going to do with those horns?' Sannie asked.

'At that point his lawyer told him to shut up, and he did. He just sat there with his arms crossed, glaring at us. He was angry.'

'So, he might have been doing some illegal dealing,' Sannie sat down again, 'but did he kill his rhinos?'

'He was adamant in every interview that he did not, but there was some more evidence against him. Each of the rhinos was killed with a bullet from David's .375-calibre hunting rifle. The bullets taken from the animals were an exact ballistic match and the rifle was in David's house.'

Marilyn shook her head. 'He was that stupid?'

Sannie took out her notebook and began making some entries. Writing down the facts she knew already, or had just learned, helped her to order them, and to spot any anomalies or patterns. 'You mentioned he was under financial pressure?'

'Yes.' Le Roux sat. 'He'd borrowed heavily to build a new camp, just before COVID, on the game reserve part of his farm. He fell behind on his repayments and the bank was about to foreclose on him.'

'Why didn't he just sell his rhinos, if he was short of money and couldn't afford to protect them?' Marilyn asked.

Sannie guessed the answer, but Le Roux beat her to it. 'No one wants rhinos. They cost too much to keep safe and they cost a fortune to dart and transfer. David said he was negotiating with the African Parks people – the NGO that helps run a number of national parks across the continent, and sometimes gets involved in animal translocations – but admitted he wasn't having much luck.'

'What sort of person was he?' Sannie asked.

'A good man.' Le Roux threw his hands up in the air, as if unable to explain why some people turned to crime. 'His family have lived on that farm forever. He had a great-great-great whatever – grandfather or uncle or something – who fought in the Zulu Wars with the Natal Mounted Police, and he used to run tours of the main battle sites. He was well liked by the local community and shared the wealth from his farm and game reserve in various community projects. Until the money ran out, that is. Things started to go wrong, then.'

'Wrong?' Marilyn asked.

'When David had to pull his funding from a local primary school, a bigwig from the ANC started agitating in the community, saying David's ancestors had stolen their land and that he should give the farm and the game reserve to the village as compensation. The ANC guy, George Tshabalala, lodged a new land claim on David's property.'

'That name sounds familiar,' Sannie said.

'*Ja*,' Le Roux said, 'he was in the newspapers a year ago. He was arrested for the murder of an ANC mayor in the province. The allegation was that he wanted his job. He beat the murder charge, but he failed to take over the municipality. Although he's ANC, George is a Zulu and he says his ancestors were robbed. He wanted the farm and the game reserve for himself, not the community. He even broke through the game reserve fence and herded some of his cattle into the reserve. We had to help David chase them out.'

'Anyone else have a problem with David?' Sannie asked.

'When the story came out about us investigating David over the killing of his rhinos it sparked a furore on social media,' Le Roux said. 'There were people from Australia to Zimbabwe, and plenty here, calling for him to be strung up or castrated or locked up for life. Also, his security people left on bad terms.'

'Yes,' Sannie paged back through her notes, 'Meyer also said there was a falling out with an NGO run by a Richard Tustin.'

Le Roux gave a dismissive flick of his head. '*Major* Tustin, if you please. David used that bunch of crazies – they call themselves Wild-Force – for about six months, but it all ended in tears.'

Sannie made a note then looked up. 'How so?'

'Tustin's men were manning an observation post with their fancy night-vision goggles and guns one night and they watched a seventeen-year-old kid from the local village enter David's land. He came in under a fence where a warthog had been burrowing and was walking through the bush when the ex-soldiers called out to him to stop. He panicked and ran and one of them shot him.'

Sannie was wide-eyed. 'What? Was the suspect armed?'

Le Roux shook his head. 'No. Luckily, they didn't kill him – shot him through the leg. The volunteers gave him first aid – did a pretty good job according to old Dr Nel in Glencoe – but the *kak* hit the fan.'

'I can imagine. Volunteers like that shouldn't have been carrying firearms,' Sannie said.

'Of course,' Le Roux said. 'The guy who fired the shot, a former US Marine, got around the fact that foreigners can't be licensed to own a gun in South Africa by bringing his own from the United States. He'd told Customs at the airport when he arrived that he was here on a hunting trip and that was David's story when we went to investigate. I could tell that David was furious, but he didn't want to get in trouble and he *had* covered himself by providing us emails and so forth saying he was offering hunts on this property. Major Tustin and David gave statements saying that the WildForce men were on a night-time leopard hunt and that the intruder had been carrying a stick – if you can believe that – which looked like a rifle, and he pointed it at them when they challenged him.'

Sannie thought the cover-up sounded ludicrous and any half-decent lawyer in South Africa would have shot it down in court. 'What happened to the shooter?'

'He was on the first flight out of South Africa to New York the next day. I got an affidavit from him – more bullshit – but we couldn't proceed with any charges. The kid who'd broken into the property said he'd been going to check a snare that he'd set for bushmeat, and that he wasn't carrying a stick or any other kind of weapon. In the end, though, the victim didn't want to give a full statement and David didn't want to press charges for trespassing.'

'Strange. Why?'

'I think Tustin paid the kid's family off. He's a wealthy *oke*. Made his money running a private military contracting business in Iraq and Afghanistan after he got out of the army. David didn't want the bad publicity that would come with his volunteer security guards shooting an unarmed boy and George Tshabalala was doing his best to whip the local community into a frenzy over the incident. It all died down.'

'Hmmm.' Sannie checked her notes again. 'Meyer said his former girlfriend, Jan-Maree Ball, who works at The Shed in Dundee, told him that she overheard David and Tustin threatening to kill each other.'

'I don't know anything about that, but I do know they didn't part on good terms. One minute Tustin's crew were playing their anti-poaching war games and the next minute they were gone.'

Le Roux glanced at his watch once more. Sannie could tell that he wanted to wrap this briefing up, so he could go to his farewell *braai*. She was sympathetic, but she had a job to do. 'What prompted the call to David's farm this morning?'

'David's domestic worker, Adella Mdluli, showed up to clean the house and saw an unknown man appear at the open front door. She panicked and ran off and sent a message on the local Farm Watch WhatsApp group.'

Sannie mentally ticked herself off for not asking her question when she first arrived at the farm. 'Did you interview her?'

'*Ja*, of course,' Le Roux said. 'She came back to the farm before you and Marilyn arrived. She was in a terrible state so I let her go home. I don't think she could add much more, but I can give you her details if you also want to interview her. I'm afraid the robbery at David's property was part of a pattern. Tshabalala's supporters knew that David was on the ropes. Someone broke into his farm shed last week and stole a trimmer and some tools. There were reports of poachers with dogs hunting buck on uBhejane two weeks ago, and more cattle being driven into the reserve. It was almost like he was under siege. All but his most loyal staff were gone – he couldn't afford them and had reduced the wages of those he could keep.'

'So you don't think the killers were part of this organised stock theft gang that you mentioned?' Marilyn asked.

Le Roux shook his head. 'Since we got the call from Lettie later, I'd say no. Pretty unlikely that they'd be hitting two farms at more or less the same time. David had been selling off his cattle in any case, to try to make ends meet. Lettie, however, is more of a target for stock thieves. She's also living on her own, and her herd is some of the best in the district. She's been hit before.'

Sannie tried to get her head around all this information. It seemed there was more going on here than she had ever expected.

'Where can I find this Major Richard Tustin now?' she asked.

'I'm not sure,' Le Roux said. 'Last time I checked on the WildForce Facebook page they were talking about moving into another game reserve somewhere close to the coast, near the iSimangaliso Wetland Park. Around that Phinda and Mkuze area. There were some pictures of his gunslingers on a fishing trip and doing some scuba diving. Also some talk about protecting turtles and conducting 'maritime operations' to protect the coastline, if you can believe that sort of rubbish.'

'I'll have a look on their Facebook page.' Marilyn took out her phone and started searching.

Le Roux stood and went to the other pinboard. At the top, in the centre, was a glossy colour print of a cheetah. The big cat stared down at them through red eyes that almost glowed.

'This is everything, well, visually at least – you'll find more in the various case dockets – that we know about the stock theft gang.' Le Roux tapped the picture on top. 'We call them the Cheetahs, because they're fast – much quicker than us – and they are cheat-*ers*. Get it?'

Sannie gave a polite smile at Oom Derick's dad joke. 'Yes.'

Le Roux gestured to a map of KwaZulu-Natal and tapped six different dots as he spoke. 'They hit farm after farm, sometimes less than two days after the previous raid, and then we don't hear from them for maybe a month. We figure that they move the cattle or sheep, or goats even, to a holding area, then move them en masse to their destination in one or two big shipments.' He looked at the two women. 'The six recent attacks represent only what's happened in the last two months. This has been going on for a year.'

Sannie studied the board. There were random pictures of cows and sheep, probably just to keep the problem top of mind for any officer who happened to look at them, and a shot from a security camera of a large truck transporting livestock. She pointed at it. 'The vehicle?'

Le Roux glanced back at the image. '*Ja*. This part of the country is not Joburg or Cape Town. We don't have cameras everywhere, but in some of the towns there's an active community watch and sometimes, if the people have enough money, they put up some cameras. After a farm was hit three months ago we put out a call for camera vision and we did get some video of some cattle trucks – five, in fact. We could see the licence plates of four of them, and they checked out to be reputable livestock carriers, but this one,' he pointed to the image, 'had a front plate that was obscured with mud, or paint. We asked all the trucking companies we could find and none of them recognised this truck. We think the criminals were using it.'

There was a knock at the door. It was Precious again, but she had changed out of her domestic's uniform and into a yellow sundress with flower prints. 'Sorry, sir, but everyone's gathered for the *braai*.'

'Thank you, Precious. I'll be there just now.' Precious nodded and left, and Le Roux held his hands wide. 'I'm sorry, Sannie, truly I am. I wish I had more time to talk you through it, but, like I say, I truly think it's a blessing in disguise to have someone like you take another look at all this – the rhino horns and the Cheetahs.'

Sannie had plenty more questions, but knew it would be unfair to try to keep Le Roux here on his last day at work. 'Of course, Oom Derick,' she said.

'Of course, you're both most welcome to join us for the *braai*,' he said.

They all stood and Le Roux smiled, then excused himself and left them. Marilyn looked up from her phone. 'Isn't your boyfriend based at a place called Bhanga Nek?'

'He is.' It still felt weird having Adam described that way, especially as they'd seen so little of each other lately.

'This Major Richard Tustin's veteran anti-poaching strike force or whatever they call themselves are there now.'

'Really?'

Marilyn handed Sannie her phone and she looked at the screen. She saw a video taken from within a black rubber inflatable boat. Men in camouflaged wetsuits coloured in different shades of grey sat or lay facedown on the sides of the craft, posing like Navy SEALs about to raid a foreign country. The caption superimposed on the screen said: *Ready for action, patrolling the Indian Ocean coast looking for bad guys.*

Just who the 'bad guys' were or what they were after wasn't spelled out, but the video, set to music that Sannie vaguely remembered was from the first *Top Gun* movie, had been posted that morning and already had more than a thousand likes. The next clip showed dozens of tiny sea turtle hatchlings scrambling across the sand, headed from their nest to the water.

'What rubbish,' Sannie said.

Marilyn took her phone back. 'Kind of sexy, I would have said. Especially the big guy at the front of the boat.'

Sannie closed her notebook. 'The waters off Bhanga Nek are a marine sanctuary and that stretch of coastline has been patrolled and monitored by South African park rangers and researchers since before you were born, Marilyn. The community's on board and the main threat those little turtles face is from crabs and other predators, or if they grow up and cross the ocean and get caught in some fishing trawler's net. These clowns are just pretending they're doing something useful.'

'Why?' Marilyn also gathered up her stuff. 'Money?'

They headed for the door. 'Maybe,' Sannie said. 'I know some people from NGOs who worked in the Lowveld around the Kruger Park and they talked about "rhino fatigue". There's been so much coverage here and abroad about rhinos being killed for their horns that donors get tired of giving to the same cause all the time. We know that Tustin and his veterans lost their contract at David Gregory's farm, so maybe they're trying to reinvent themselves as seaborne warriors or marines.'

'Are we seriously going to go to a *braai* right now, at a station where we don't know anyone?' Marilyn asked.

Sannie took her car keys out of her handbag. 'Not when there's a murder to solve and a cattle-rustling gang to catch.'

9

KWAZULU-NATAL, THE PRESENT

'Help me cover the body,' Adam said to Jenny.

She took one end of the vinyl boat cover, which had been stowed in the rear of the RHIB, and helped Adam unfurl it and then place and tuck it over the corpse.

'Not a word,' he said. She nodded.

Andy guided the Zodiac in to shore and up onto the sand with the same skill Adam had shown. The lighter rubber craft *shushed* even further up the beach than the research vessel had.

Andy and his men climbed out and Andy came to Adam as, without a word, the others picked up their Zodiac and started carrying it off the beach, in the direction of the municipal camping ground, through the dune vegetation. Andy waved and smiled. 'Hello again.'

'Good diving?' Adam asked.

Andy held out a hand palm down and wiggled it from side to side. 'Not bad. Visibility's not great because of the storm. How did you fare with your turtle?'

'Fine, thanks.' Adam started walking away from the RHIB, with Jenny by his side. 'Fitted a tracker to it.'

Andy raised his right hand in a salute. 'Hello again, ma'am.'

'Hi,' Jenny said.

'Andy.' He held out his hand and she took it.

'Jenny.'

He smiled. 'Lovely to meet you. Come across anything else on your trip?'

Jenny looked to Adam, then back to Andy. She tucked a strand of hair behind her ear. 'Like what?'

He grinned wider. 'I dunno. Buried treasure? Shipwrecks?'

Jenny forced a laugh. 'What? No.' She looked over her shoulder at the vast ocean. 'Not out there.'

Andy looked to Adam again. 'Sea's a hungry beast. You never know when and what she's going to eat, eh, Adam?'

Andy's tone of voice and smile made it look they were old friends, but the other man's stare was like a laser locking on to a target. Adam had to fight to hold it. 'True, that.'

Andy pointed to a tattoo on Adam's arm. '1 Parachute Battalion. They call you guys the Bats, yeah, short for Parabat?'

Adam nodded.

'Respect, bruv. I served with a couple of your veterans, ex-Bats, in Iraq. Tough guys. Were you on the border?'

'Yes,' Adam said. Like all white South African men his age he'd been eligible for conscription and had done his time in South Africa's Border War. The new South African National Defence Force had not been involved in America's war in Iraq, so Adam guessed the men Andy was talking about were private military contractors. He remembered the tattoo on one of the other men in Andy's boat. 'I was in Angola in 1987. You're all ex-military?'

'Royal Marines, and SBS. I did two tours in Afghanistan and worked as a contractor in Iraq, and maritime security on cargo ships. Good money, if you're interested. Plenty of pirates out there on that big ocean.'

'No thanks,' Adam said. Credentials had been established, but Adam still wondered what Andy and his band of seaborne warriors were up to. 'Here on holiday? R and R?'

'Partly, though none of us is currently working. We're here with a charity, WildForce. One word, two capital letters. You might have heard of us?'

Adam shook his head. 'Afraid not.'

'We recruit military veterans to work on anti-poaching projects in Africa. Mostly it's capacity-building, training local rangers in basic military skills and first aid. Also some strategic advice. A few of us,' he used his thumb to indicate his comrades, now disappearing over a dune into the trees, 'have amphibious warfare skills so we're scouting for new projects that we might be able to help out with on the coast.'

'We don't have any armed poaching threats here, if that's what you're interested in,' Adam said. 'The main threat to sea turtles is becoming by-catch in commercial fishing nets. You might have more luck in Mozambique where their navy and maritime law enforcement agencies are even harder up for cash than ours.'

Andy nodded. 'Thanks for the tip. We are planning on visiting Mozambique at some stage on this recce.' He glanced over at the research boat. 'You do a little fishing of your own while you were out there?'

'No.' Adam was conscious of the large irregular shape of the body under the boat cover.

Andy held his gaze for a couple more seconds, as if trying to bore into his mind to see if he was lying. In the end, he smiled again and stuck out his hand. 'We're here for a few more days. Swing by the community campsite and let me know if you think of anyone who could use our help. Or just come for a beer.'

Adam shook Andy's hand. 'Will do.'

Andy turned to Jenny again. '*Lovely* to meet you, Jenny. The offer stands to you and your friend . . .'

'Thabo,' Jenny said.

Something about Andy knowing all their names unsettled Adam, especially as he noticed the other man giving a small nod, as if committing them all to memory.

Andy took another long look at the RHIB before turning and walking up the beach in the direction the others had taken their boat.

'There's something not right about that guy,' Jenny said quietly. 'Is that why you didn't tell him about the dead guys?'

Adam watched Andy's back disappear. 'Yes. Also because he didn't ask, and he didn't say he was looking for any missing friends or anything like that.'

'Speaking of dead guys . . .' Jenny began.

Adam rubbed his chin. 'Change of plan. Please take the Polaris back to the camp, and can you come back with the HiLux and the trailer?'

'I get to drive the truck as well?' She opened her mouth in mock amazement. 'And don't even ask if I can reverse a trailer, Prof. My father was a keen fisherman when he wasn't underground and I've been launching and pulling out boats since I was fifteen.'

'OK, quick as you can, please, J.'

JENNY GUNNED the throttle of the Polaris and sped back to the research base.

Thabo came out of the lab building. 'What's happening?'

'Can't stop.' Jenny jumped off the all-terrain vehicle and then into the Toyota *bakkie* Jenny found the keys in the ashtray, where they were usually kept. She slid the driver's seat forward and adjusted the rear-view mirror.

Jenny was about to drive off when the passenger-side door opened. 'I'm coming with you.'

She glanced at Thabo and realised there was no reason why he shouldn't come along. 'OK, hurry.'

'Where's the fire?'

Jenny told him about Andy and his prying questions. 'He even mentioned sunken shipwrecks, or something like that.'

'I thought there was something slightly off about that guy.'

As they drove down the track leading to the road that ran behind the beach, a car suddenly came into view heading towards them and Jenny had to brake hard. Neither of them had bothered putting on a seatbelt and their heads snapped forward.

'Careful,' Thabo said.

'Police.' Jenny didn't feel like reversing back to the lab so she put on the handbrake and got out. An officer in a golf shirt and chinos met her. 'Sorry,' Jenny called to him.

'I'm Warrant Officer Mkhizi, how are you?' He looked to be in his early thirties, fit, with a neatly trimmed pencil moustache and bulging biceps.

'Jenny Ellis. Fine, thank you.'

'I understand there is a body?'

'Two, in fact.'

The officer rubbed a hand over his shaved head. '*Two?*'

'My colleague, Thabo, can take you to the first, um, deceased person,' Jenny said. 'I'm going to get the other.'

'We cannot disturb a crime scene. I will come with you.'

'Warrant Officer,' she said, 'the crime scene was under twenty metres of water. The other guy's in a boat and we were just going to fetch him.'

Mkhizi sighed. 'Very well.'

Thabo had been listening and got out of the *bakkie*. 'I'll show you the way, sir.' Thabo opened the door of the police vehicle and got in. Mkhizi drove on.

Free of the cops, Jenny resumed driving. This time she buckled her seatbelt. This wasn't Johannesburg, but the road was a single lane for much of the way in and out of Bhanga Nek and sometimes there were tourists or locals speeding along the rough surface.

The narrow sandy road meandered through a jungle of thick bush behind the dunes fronting the beach. Although she was studying marine biology, Jenny had a fascination for most things in nature, including trees. Gnarled umdonis, waterberry trees, bent and reached across the road, forming a cool, green tunnel, their branches enmeshed with luxuriant lala palms. This coastal green belt provided a habitat for monkeys that scampered through the branches, and troops of banded mongooses who patrolled the sand looking for bugs, lizards and the inevitable human rubbish.

Jenny sighed as she drove past the public picnic areas. Beer bottles and cans overflowed from boxes or lay scattered on the ground near the *braai* places where cooking fires had been made. Where picnickers had been 'thoughtful' enough to leave their rubbish in plastic bags, the local wildlife had ripped into them in search of edible morsels and the disposable diapers, plates and cutlery had spilled out. She and Thabo would be returning on one of their volunteer trash patrols later in the day.

She passed the community campground. Amid the trees, almost like a military encampment, was a circle of green tents and a pair of new-model Toyota HiLux *bakkies* with camouflage vinyl wraps and signage reading *WildForce* on the sides. As she slowed, she saw the men who had been out on the water, and their black rubber Zodiac boat. They turned to look at her. One was still in his camouflage wetsuit, while the others were in various stages of dress, from just board shorts to T-shirts and shorts. They were buffed, heavily muscled and tattooed. Two waved at her and she waved back.

Andy, their leader, emerged from the narrow laneway through the bush leading to the beach and he also waved to her. She smiled and returned the greeting, then carried on a little further to the beach access road.

The newcomers were uniformly handsome, if you liked that over-muscled he-man look – and part of her did – but she felt a shiver despite the oppressive heat outside the open window. Maybe it was Adam's reading of them that had rubbed off on her, or perhaps it was the way each of the tents seemed to be precisely spaced apart, and that their gear was stacked up in green plastic carry cases. She wondered what was in those trunks.

Jenny bounced up the access road, reached down and engaged low-range four-wheel-drive as Adam always did, and drove onto the beach.

She swung the HiLux in a wide arc then started reversing down to where Adam was waiting.

'Did you see our friend Andy?' Adam asked her when she pulled up and got out to help him attach the boat to the winch on the trailer.

'Just now. You should see the camp they've set up. Looks like a military base. The cops are here – finally. Thabo's taking them to the other body.'

'Good.'

'Poor Thabo.' Adam looked at her. 'I mean, he's sensitive, Prof. You saw how he acted when we pulled the other guy in.'

He nodded. 'What makes you so tough?'

Unusually, she didn't want to make eye contact with him right then. Instead she turned to the ocean, the only place she truly felt at ease. 'I've seen a dead body before. I didn't want to say anything last night. I never want to talk about it, really ...'

'It's OK, J. I'm sorry I asked. I didn't mean to be insensitive.'

When she turned her head she was met with his kind eyes, holding their own memories of sadness, she was sure. 'No. It's all right. I mean, it *does* help if I talk with someone . . . with someone who understands.'

He said nothing, but nor did he shut her down. She felt sure he understood.

'My father killed himself,' she said. There it was. And as the images went spooling through her mind, she made herself continue. 'He was a gambler. He drank too much. He lost just about everything we had – Mom, me and him. He shot himself in the bathroom at home. I wasn't meant to find him, but I wasn't feeling well and the teacher let me go home early from school. I was the first person on the scene ...'

'I'm so sorry. From the way you spoke about him, I got the impression your father was still alive.'

'Sometimes I think he is.' She held up a hand. 'It's fine. I've had some help, talked to a shrink about all this. I know I wasn't to blame, but I felt, like, *How could you do this to me?* I know it was selfish, but he didn't say anything to me, or ask for help. He and Mom were fighting all the time by that stage, but I was supposed to *mean* something to him. He always told me I was the most important person in his life and he ...' She sniffed and the tears came.

Adam came to her and put his arms around her.

.   .   .

FOR A MOMENT ADAM had thought he was having a heart attack. There was a real pain in his chest after he'd eased himself away from Jenny. He felt so much for her that it was like his own heart was breaking.

He'd lost friends in the war, worn their blood on his uniform, and Jenny's tears had threatened to bring on his own, but he had stayed strong for her. They were all broken – him, Jenny and Sannie, each carrying their own grief.

After they'd loaded the boat onto the trailer and driven back to the research base, Jenny introduced him to the police detective.

'Jenny, how about you take a break, maybe find Thabo and the two of you organise some sandwiches for us all?' Adam said.

'Of course, Prof.' She gave him a smile, her earlier grief shelved.

Thabo was nowhere to be seen, obviously having left the immediate area before the first body was unwrapped from its plastic shroud. It was exposed to the sun now, already bloating as the police detective, Warrant Officer Mkhizi, wearing rubber gloves, conducted his examination.

Adam unzipped his daypack and withdrew the pistol wrapped in his T-shirt. He held out the package to Warrant Office Mkhizi and let the material fall away.

'A gun? Where did you find this?'

'On the other body,' Adam said.

'Ah, yes, I understand we have a second body, in the boat.'

Adam nodded.

Mkhizi started walking to the boat. 'You found the first body when?'

'Last night. After midnight. I was monitoring turtle hatchlings and nests.'

'And you found this other man in the wreckage of a boat on the ocean floor?'

'Yes,' Adam said. 'This morning. As well as the body there are some waterproof boxes – like lockers – still in the boat.'

Mkhizi ran his eyes over the second dead man and exposed the deceased's empty ankle holster with his gloved fingers. He looked up at Adam again. 'Do you have any idea how long it will take me to organise a police dive team to come up here, Professor Kruger?'

Adam shrugged. 'Not today, I'm guessing.'

The detective laughed. 'Not this *week*. Do you think you could make a dive on the boat, to retrieve whatever is down there? It's important we find out what these men were up to – fishermen don't wear chinos and carry concealed firearms.'

'Yes, of course,' Adam said. 'We have all the gear.'

Mkhizi went back to checking the body. 'No ID on this one?'

Adam shook his head.

'Why?'

It was clearly a rhetorical question, but Adam was wondering the same thing. 'Do you think they might be smugglers?'

'We'll know more when we discover what was on their boat,' Mkhizi said.

Adam thought about the antique book. He knew he should tell the detective about it, but he justified withholding the information because the object had washed up on the beach. Theoretically, it could have come from anywhere. Also, technically, it was now Adam's property. He was no thief, but he loved books and his study in his house back in Pennington was lined with textbooks, novels and a collection of scientific and natural history books his grandfather had cherished.

'You live here, yes?' the detective asked, breaking into his thoughts.

'Temporarily, yes,' Adam said. 'Whenever the university has research students in residence, like now. I've been here a month.' It was funny; the thoughts of his books made him miss home. The vision that had accompanied them was one of Sannie, on a Sunday morning, sitting in the armchair by the window, a cup of coffee on the low table beside her as she read. He missed her.

'Have you seen any suspicious characters around here lately?'

Adam could have answered glibly, that there were 'suspicious characters' on every street and in every town, village and city in the country, but the question brought him back to this morning. 'Did you see the campground on the way in?'

'*Eish*, that looked more like an army camp, with camouflage *bakkies*, army-green tents and so forth. Who are those people, the A-Team?' He laughed.

'They *are* ex-military, part of a veterans' not-for-profit. They call themselves WildForce. They're looking for anti-poaching work. I told them we won't need them here.'

Mkhizi rubbed his chin. 'The sunken boat you mentioned – was there anything you noticed that might make you think these foreign veterans had an interest in it? Those waterproof boxes you mentioned?'

Adam thought. 'I'd need to take another look, but the trunks I saw on the boat could have been military. They were a dark colour, but it was hard to see. We were free diving so I couldn't stay down there long. I'll have a look when we go back with our scuba gear.'

'Please do,' Mkhizi said. 'Oh, and Professor?'

'Yes?' Adam said.

'This is going to be a difficult investigation for me to carry out. I'll have to travel two hours each way to get here and back to the station. I have few staff and virtually no resources.'

'I understand.'

'Do you?' He nodded in the direction of the community campground. 'I'm going to pay those men in the army tents a visit, and ask them if they know anything about what you found on the beach and in the water.'

Adam took a deep breath. 'I didn't share with them anything about what I've found – the two bodies. I'm not sure about them.'

'You're worried about them? Do you think they are dangerous?'

Adam straightened his shoulders. 'I can take care of myself.'

Mkhizi nodded slowly. 'I can guess that, by your tattoo. What I'm saying, Professor, is that you and your students are a long way from help. If there are armed smugglers operating along this coast, then I can't be here to protect you if you happen to get in the way. It is the job of the police to investigate crimes, not well-meaning amateurs.'

'I would never put my students at risk.'

'Good. Please check the wreck for me, and call me if you find anything.' He took a business card from his pocket and handed it to Adam and waved to the men from the coroner's van. They had apparently been waiting for this signal, sitting in their vehicle with the doors open, to stay cool, and now got out and began removing a stretcher. 'Just because I'm asking you to dive on a sunken boat for me does not mean that you are a – what would the Americans call it – a "deputy sheriff".'

'I understand,' Adam said again.

'Stay safe, Professor, and call me, please, if you learn anything. On sea or land.'

Jenny came out of the research building just as Adam left the policeman and turned to head inside.

'Food's ready. How did it go?' she asked him.

Adam shrugged. 'Not much they can tell at this stage.'

Soon enough Andy and his band of merry men would find out that Adam had found a sunken boat and two dead bodies. Hopefully the anti-poaching volunteers knew nothing about the wreck and had nothing to do with any smugglers or valuable Middle Eastern artefacts.

Somehow, Adam doubted it.

10

NATAL, 1880

Gregory and Sergeant Phillips wrapped Morrison's body in an oilskin tarpaulin they had found in the barn, strapped it across the back of one of two horses that were stabled there, then headed back to Pietermaritzburg.

'Where did Constable Khumalo go?' Phillips asked.

'Family business,' Gregory replied.

As they approached the capital, Gregory said, 'We'll let old Dr Hughes have a look at the body – see if he can tell us anything else about the man. I have a lady to meet. Get yourself and your horse fed and watered, Gavin. Meet me in two hours at the Imperial Hotel, ready to ride out again.'

'Oh.' Phillips' mouth turned down at the edges. Gregory figured that a murder investigation had been the highlight of the young sergeant's year to date. 'Very good, sir.'

Gregory made his way, alone, through the town. A stray dog yapped at his horse, then ducked out of his way; two young boys pointed at the suspicious bundle wrapped and tied across the horse that Gregory led. A woman strolling with her maid on the wooden boardwalk lining the edge of the muddy street cast him a glance and he touched the brim of his pith helmet. A dung-smelling herd of

124

cattle was being driven through town ahead of him, the crack of the owner's whip echoing like random gunshots. There was the clang of a blacksmith's hammer, and the smell of curry cooking in a street vendor's pot made his stomach rumble.

He made his way down a side street to the doctor's surgery, but found that Hughes was out. Possibly in a bar, Gregory thought. He had two of the doctor's servants take charge of the spare horse and body and told them to give his compliments to the doctor and that he would be back later.

He rode on and hitched his horse to the post outside what he still thought of as the Oaks Hotel, a sprawling brick affair with white columns lining the front. It had been built as the mayor's house before being converted to lodgings. Above the double doors was the establishment's new name, the Imperial Hotel. It had been changed in honour of the late Prince Imperial, Louis Napoleon, who had stayed there prior to departing on his ill-fated excursion into Zululand. A Zulu in footman's livery opened the door for him and Gregory removed his helmet as he walked in. His boots clacked on the tiled floor as he walked to the polished wooden reception counter, behind which stood a smiling man with oiled hair in topcoat and pince-nez glasses. They exchanged greetings.

'Sub-Inspector Peter Gregory. I'm expected by one of your guests, Lady Beecham.'

The man's smile was undermined by his eyes. 'Ah yes, our *American* guest.' He tapped a brass bell on his desk and the doorman strode over. 'Jacob, please be so kind as to tell Her Ladyship that Sub-Inspector Gregory is here to see her.'

'Sir.'

'Lady Beecham is checking out this morning.' The man sounded relieved. 'Perhaps you'd care to wait for her in the courtyard.'

'I know the way.' Gregory walked to another set of doors and let himself through into the enclosed, open-air area within the hotel. A worker was busy putting a fresh coat of whitewash on the walls and a woman mopped the floor. 'This old place is looking smart, now, yes?' he said to the painter.

The man looked down at him. 'Yes, sir. I had to repaint the inside for the French queen.'

Gregory nodded. By 'queen', he was sure the man meant the Empress Eugénie, widow of the late Napoleon III and mother of the Prince Imperial, killed in action last year.

'Captain Gregory?'

Gregory turned. It was her eyes he noticed first, which were the most vivid green he had ever seen, set off by auburn curls that a bow was unable to completely restrain. She wore a jacket whose cut was almost military, the colour complementing those eyes, and though severe, there was no hiding the woman beneath. Her skirt, which matched the jacket, ended just high enough to show brown leather riding boots.

'Indeed.' She was quite striking – so much so that he forgot to correct her use of his former rank. 'Lady Beecham, I presume?'

She came to him and presented her hand, which he took before bowing at the waist. He composed himself; attractive she might be, but he had no great desire to play nursemaid to a foreigner. 'At your service, it would appear, ma'am.'

'"It would appear"?' She did her best to copy his colonial accent. 'My my, do I detect the faintest hint of resentment already?' she drawled in an accent Gregory had heard from mining prospectors in the colony who had travelled from America. 'I know I can be a handful,' she lowered her voice, 'just ask that popinjay on the front desk, but surely you're not regretting this assignment already just because I'm a woman?'

Gregory was momentarily taken aback, although an outspoken woman was nothing new to him – she and Grace had that in common. He chided himself; she'd read his feelings through the slightest inflection of his voice. 'On the contrary, and my apologies, madam, if it seemed that way.'

She tilted her head. 'I won't say you're forgiven – you'll have to earn that – but I can tell I'm not going far by myself, so I'm saddled with you.'

Saddled? 'Perhaps a cup of tea?' he ventured.

'Coffee.' A hotel staff member walked across the courtyard and Gregory signalled to him and ordered. They took seats at a courtyard table.

'I understand, Your Ladyship, that you are an acquaintance of the Empress Eugénie?'

She fidgeted with her hair and looked in the direction of the painter. 'Why, yes. I am.'

'It's also my understanding,' Gregory went on, 'that the empress has passed through Maritzburg already. Did you miss her?'

This time she busied herself picking non-existent pieces of lint off her skirt. 'So it would appear. I could have sworn she said that she was staying here, at this hotel, but in fact she breezed through the town on her way to tour some of the spots where her son, Louis, served.' Now she aimed her green eyes at him. 'I'm counting on you, Captain, to find us some kind of a short cut through the wilds of Africa so that I can cross paths with my dear friend the empress and, especially, be with her when she reaches the spot where the Prince Imperial was killed.'

In his time as a policeman Gregory had learned to spot a liar at a hundred paces. He'd yet to meet one as attractive as Lady Beecham, but she was as much a dissembler as any confidence trickster or pickpocket he'd met.

'Your Ladyship . . .'

She smiled at him, and her eyes glowed like liquid emerald. 'Please, call me Teresa, and you are . . .?'

He cleared his throat. 'Sub-Inspector Gregory, ma'am.'

'I was told you were *Captain* Gregory.' She wound an errant curl of hair around a finger.

'My former rank, in the army, madam. Some people still refer to me as such. I think it would be best if we referred to each other –'

'I think,' she interrupted, 'that we're not in London, nor in New York. We're here in *Africa*, and I think this wild, untamed land deserves a certain rewriting or dismantling of the old rules. I shall call you Peter, and you shall call me Teresa.'

'How did you –?'

'How did I know your name? Why, that curmudgeonly old Major Dartnell told me he would assign one of his best officers to escort me through Zululand, and that I would be advised of his name in due course. Naturally, I asked around the police building and found out that you had been summoned to see Major Dartnell. You fit the description my source gave me.'

'Your *source*? How did you get a member of the constabulary to reveal all of this information to you, a civilian, ma'am?'

She gave him a sweet smile. 'I have my ways, Peter.'

'Sub-Inspector Gregory, ma'am,' he said stiffly.

Her smile broadened. 'We'll see.'

'You say you're an acquaintance of the empress, ma'am?'

'I am.'

'Perhaps we can get word to her party. I have a sergeant, a reasonably reliable young man, who can ride ahead of us, catch up with her escorts, and advise her you are en route.'

Their coffee arrived and Teresa waited for the servant to depart. 'Let's not spoil the surprise.'

Gregory sipped from his cup. 'The *surprise*, ma'am?'

She fluttered a hand in front of her face. 'Oh, that Eugénie. She and I are such a couple of kidders. We like playing little tricks and surprising each other by showing up unannounced. Also,' she leaned conspiratorially towards him, 'I don't know that I want to see *every* inch of ground that poor Prince Louis trod, Peter. I'd rather just be with the empress when she gets to the place where . . . well, where it happened.'

'Where the Prince Imperial was killed?'

'Er, yes.'

'And it is there that you wish to *surprise* your friend the empress, at the scene of her son's death, because you are a, what was the word? *Kidder*?'

She cleared her throat, took another sip of coffee, then narrowed her eyes and stared at him. 'Are you a good officer, Captain Gregory?'

He returned her look, no smiles now. 'That depends on how one defines "good".'

'Do you follow orders?'

'Lawful orders, yes.'

'And what are your orders with regards to me, as they stand at the moment?'

'I am to meet with you –'

'You are, and I quote, "to provide an escort for Lady Beecham through Zululand so that she might rendezvous with the Empress Eugénie and her party, subject to further clarification."'

She had read, or been told of, the same communication that Hellfire Jack had read to him.

'Well, *Captain* Gregory?'

He smoothed his moustaches. 'You appear remarkably well informed, ma'am.'

All trace of her smile disappeared. 'Then let's saddle up, cowboy.'

'Excuse me?' Gregory said, taken aback.

Teresa looked over her shoulder. 'Good. At least someone in this damned country understands time.'

Standing in the entry to the courtyard were two porters and, behind them, Gregory could see a small mountain of luggage – steamer trunks, carpet bags, hatboxes and wooden crates. Lady Beecham, it appeared, did not travel light.

'Close your jaw, Captain, I've paid for a horse and cart.' She pushed her half-drunk cup of coffee across the table and stood. 'Let's get a move on.'

He also got to his feet, out of habit, but Gregory was damned if he was going to dance to this woman's tune like some trained monkey. 'I have duties to perform before I leave Maritzburg, ma'am.'

'They can wait until you get back.' She turned to leave.

'Madam.'

Teresa stopped and looked back at him.

'No, my duties cannot wait,' Gregory said. 'They concern a most sensitive matter.'

A look of realisation turned to wide-eyed joy. 'Oh. The murder! Well, that's all right then. I can get two stories for the price of –'

He raised an eyebrow. 'Stories, ma'am? I did hear that you were a correspondent for one or more newspapers in America. But surely your meeting with your *friend* the empress is not something as spurious or trivial as a "story"?'

Her cheeks flushed. 'No, no. Of course not. I meant that I'm here to write about the colony of Natal and its varied wildlife and its . . . its noble and fascinating people.'

'I'm sure the hotel staff can help you load your wagon. My sergeant and I will be back in an hour and we can set off then.'

'But . . .'

He put on his hat and gave her a short bow. 'I have police business to attend to, Your Ladyship. I'll return directly.'

Gregory walked through reception and out into the street where there was, indeed, a horse and cart, presumably waiting to be loaded, and a fine chestnut mare with an expensive saddle tethered to the rear of the wagon. He unhitched his own horse, Bullet, mounted, and set off.

He rode through town, dodging people and stray animals crossing the main street and past the tavern where he and Grace had captured Blundell. Gregory diverted to the NMP headquarters.

The duty officer, another young sergeant, told him that Dartnell was out, so Gregory couldn't report on the infuriating American woman's spying and conniving, and nor could he seek an update on whether or not the French empress wanted to meet with Lady Beecham. Frustrated, but with his other mission to occupy him, he made his way through the building to the cells.

'Prisoner Blundell,' he said to Sergeant Lloyd, who was acting as sergeant of the guard, in charge of the town's prison. Lloyd was a jolly, rotund fellow, who led Gregory down a stone-flagged corridor to a steel door, which he unlocked.

'No trouble in front of the officer, now,' Lloyd said to the prisoner, who didn't get up from his bed, a shelf attached to the wall.

Gregory took off his helmet. 'Your friend Morrison's dead. Murdered.'

Blundell spat on the cell floor. 'Weren't no friend of mine.'

The cramped room smelled of mould and piss. 'I found a sheaf of gambling debts in his farmhouse. They were not insubstantial. How was he going to pay you?'

'Pay me for what?'

'Don't play dumb with me, man,' Gregory said. 'How was he going to pay you for the child that he wanted you to procure for him?'

Blundell looked at Gregory, as if sizing him up. 'And why should I tell you a bloody thing?'

'You're probably going to swing for killing your wife.' Gregory had no desire to show any mercy to this odious specimen who had murdered a woman and had been prepared to sell a child into misery. 'But Morrison could have been involved in yet another crime. If I can solve it, and you were shown to have helped the police, then, well, perhaps a judge might take that into account.'

'And what? Shoot me instead of hang me?'

Gregory shrugged. 'Who knows, perhaps your sentence might be commuted to life imprisonment.'

Blundell spat again. 'Fat chance.' He seemed to think a moment. 'I can tell you something, but I want a payment in return.'

'What sort of payment?'

He looked Gregory in the eye and leered. 'A woman. Before I meet me maker, I want one more cunny.'

Gregory shuddered. The man was disgusting. A thought crossed his mind. 'Very well.'

Blundell narrowed his eyes. 'You agreed to that very quickly. Do I have your word? As a gentleman?'

A *gentleman*? 'Yes, as an officer and a gentleman. I promise you I will have a woman who has sold herself brought to you for a period of two hours. Is that long enough?'

He laughed and slapped his thigh. 'Oh, yes, yes. My word it is.' He became serious. 'Don't worry, I won't kill her.'

Gregory nodded. 'Now tell me about Morrison.'

Blundell leaned back on his bed, his body relaxed, legs spread. He scratched his privates. 'The good major,' he gave a chuckle at the expression, 'had his debts, but he was about to come into a great deal of money, so he was.'

'How so?'

'He didn't say what, exactly, but he did tell me that he owned something of great value, that many people, including foreigners, would pay big money for.' Blundell winked. 'He said he'd found a buyer for this . . . thing, whatever it was, and he was expecting to receive enough money to start a new life.'

'And indulge his disgusting vices,' Gregory said.

Blundell spread his hands wide. 'Who am I to judge – or you, cavorting with that very tasty little Indian.'

Gregory took two steps towards the repulsive figure and raised his right hand, forming a fist. He had the satisfaction of seeing Blundell cringe away from him in fear. He stopped short of hitting the man. 'Did you ever go to his farm?'

Blundell shook his head. 'No.'

'Did you ever see Major Morrison in the company of other people, any other men or women?'

'No. He was a loner. Bitter. It seemed the army had turned its back on him after he'd been cashiered; his family disowned him as well.'

Gregory stared hard at the man, trying to work out what else, if anything, he might be holding back. He wished him dead. He'd seen too many good people killed in the war and it seemed criminal that a specimen such as this had been allowed to live and prosper for so long. The same could have been said of Morrison, and while his death might have been fitting, it was, in itself, a crime.

'Why was he drummed out?'

'Why do you think?' Blundell smirked. 'The army was good at killing Zulus, in the end, but they couldn't stomach certain things. Men being men, if you like, and Morrison's, well, predilections, were too much for even the most lenient of officers to overlook.'

Justice of some kind. Perhaps Morrison really had been killed by a Zulu, someone he had wronged. Gregory wanted to keep an open mind, but such a theory didn't really fit. Morrison had been shot, then butchered to make it look like a Zulu had killed him. There was more to this. And if there was an object of high enough value to kill a chronic gambler's debts then Gregory and his party had found little evidence of it in their search of the farm. Whatever it was could have been stolen, perhaps by the person who was purportedly going to buy it.

'Your story sounds fanciful,' Gregory said. 'There's not a shred of proof to substantiate anything you say. You were right, earlier – I agreed to your demand too soon.' He made to turn around. 'Goodbye.'

'Wait.' Blundell held out a hand.

Gregory paused at the door to the cell. 'I'm listening.'

'There was a man . . . once. He came to the bawdy house with Morrison. The two of them drank, in a corner, keeping to themselves, like they was plotting.'

Gregory waited, but Blundell volunteered no more. 'Name?'

Blundell affected a pompous, upper-class drawl: 'Second Lieutenant *The Honourable* Llewellyn Walters. He made sure everyone knew that.'

Gregory nodded. 'And you say he and Morrison were friends.'

Blundell nodded. 'Same regiment, 17th Lancers. If that old villain Morrison had ever sired a son – and let's just say I can agree that would not be a good thing – then Walters would have been him to a tee when it came to sins of the flesh. Walters was often in the Red Lantern, though he wasn't there looking for children. Young and handsome; the girls loved him, at first.'

'At first?'

'There were a few tears later in the evening. One of the girls said Walters was too rough with her, but, hell, if they can't take a bit of that then they shouldn't be in the game, right, Captain?'

Gregory sneered down at him. His skin was crawling in this creature's presence. He would need to find and question this Lieutenant Walters. He opened the cell door again.

'You won't forget our little deal, Captain?'

Gregory looked over his shoulder. 'No, I won't forget it.' *And neither will you.*

Gregory returned to NMP headquarters. Hellfire Jack was out, but Gregory found a desk, wrote a letter, sealed it in an envelope, and commandeered a young constable who was lounging about with nothing much to do.

'You know my farmhouse?' Gregory said to the constable.

'Yes, sir.'

'Ride out and take this to the lady there who is . . . in my employ.' He handed the constable the letter. 'You'll then escort her to the town lockup.'

'Very good, sir.'

GRACE CAME to the police lockup later that day, carrying the leather fishing rod case one of her grateful clients had given her as a gift. She liked fishing. Her rods were not in the case today, though.

When the constable had arrived at the farm, she was already packing to leave, but the man had brought with him a note from Peter, with an invitation to report to the cells.

She smiled as she walked down the dank stone corridor behind Sergeant Lloyd. The prison keeper had grinned at her when she arrived and said she was here to visit an inmate, Alfred Blundell. Grace fancied Peter had let Lloyd know about her visit.

Lloyd took his ring of keys from his belt and inserted one into a door.

''Bout bloody time,' Blundell called from inside as the heavy steel door creaked on its hinges. 'You can bring me my meal and you can come and take these bloody leg irons and wrist cuffs off me. You ain't taking me nowhere.'

Lloyd swung open the door. 'Hush now, prisoner. I've brought a visitor for you.'

'What . . .?' Blundell's scowl turned into a broad smile as Grace entered the cell. 'Aye. Good old Captain Gregory, true to his word, and sharing his favourite sweet tart with me. You can take the cuffs and irons off, Sarge, I told the captain I'd be a gentleman.'

Lloyd ignored him and looked at Grace. 'Twenty minutes, ma'am?'

Grace nodded demurely. 'I believe that should be ample time, Sergeant.'

'I was told two hours,' Blundell interrupted.

Grace cooed: 'Oh, Mr Blundell, I doubt you'd last that long with me. Leave us, please, Sergeant.'

Lloyd nodded. 'Very good, ma'am. As per the sub-inspector's orders I'll leave the prisoner in chains.'

'Thank you, Sergeant.'

Lloyd let himself out and locked the door behind him.

'What? No . . .' Blundell began. The protest died on his lips and his face turned white as Grace unbuckled her rod case and drew out a long, hippo-hide sjambok whip.

11

____

KWAZULU-NATAL, THE PRESENT

Sannie and Marilyn drove ten kilometres from Glencoe to the town of Dundee and found The Shed, a pub and restaurant along a quiet street off the main road.

Sannie pulled into the car park in front of the eatery. As its name suggested, the place was unpretentious from the outside, a single-storey building with a tin roof.

'We can get a late lunch while we're here.' Sannie had called before leaving the police station to make sure Jan-Maree was at work.

Sannie and Marilyn walked inside. The place was open and airy with a tiled floor, bar at one end, and a few tables and cane chairs inside. Most of the diners were sitting outside on a wooden deck that overlooked a lake in a park setting. A waitress in a red shirt and black jeans welcomed them. Sannie asked if Jan-Maree Ball was available.

'Sure, just let me check,' she said.

The waitress returned with a woman perhaps in her early to mid twenties, with long, straight blonde hair. She stood close to two metres tall. Sannie's first impression of her was that she could have been a model.

The woman took off her apron. 'Hi, I'm Jan-Maree. My manager said I can take a break now.'

They introduced themselves and exchanged pleasantries and the waitress who had greeted them escorted them to a table inside.

'Thanks,' Jan-Maree said. 'I could use a rest.'

Sannie slid into a padded booth chair next to Marilyn. 'We shouldn't keep you too long.'

Jan-Maree placed her palms down on the wooden table and exhaled. 'Take your time. I won't complain.'

The waitress took their orders – Cokes for Sannie and Marilyn and tap water for Jan-Maree.

Sannie smiled and took out her notebook. 'Thanks for seeing us. May I ask, your accent?'

She folded her arms. 'Australian. But don't ask me about rugby. I don't follow it. My Dad's from Pretoria, but his family moved to Australia when he was young. He met my my mum, who's Aussie, and I was born there. I studied in Australia, but we came over here a few times on holiday and I decided I wanted to stay here, to further my studies. My mum's mother's name was Jan – like in Janet – so that's why she gave me a South African boy's name.'

Sannie nodded. From the delivery it sounded like *Jan*-Maree was sick of telling the story. 'A man by the name of Deon – Matteo – Meyer said you might be able to help us.'

Jan-Maree folded her arms and leaned back in her seat. 'Deon's my ex-boyfriend.'

'So I heard.' Sannie decided to get straight to the point. 'Deon told us about a recent conversation you overheard between Mr David Gregory and a Major Richard Tustin. Are you aware of what he might have told us?'

Jan-Maree looked up at the roof. 'Jeez. Can't he keep his bloody mouth shut? I told him to keep that quiet, and the first thing he does is go and tell the cops.'

Sannie made a note. Marilyn asked: 'Why would you ask Deon to keep quiet about two men threatening to kill each other? Are you aware of what's happened to Mr Gregory?'

Jan-Maree nodded. 'My . . . friend, John Parker, told me.'

'Of course,' Sannie said. *The new boyfriend.* 'Tell me about David Gregory and Richard Tustin.'

'David was broke. He only came here to eat because Richard offered to buy him lunch sometimes. Shame, the poor old guy just couldn't catch a break. First COVID, then the riots, then all the land claim protests started by the Tshabalala guy. Deon's company had to stop pulling security for David's game reserve, and then when David had the bust-up with Richard, well, it looks like he thought the only way to save himself and his family's farm and reserve was to kill all his own rhino, make it look like poachers did it, and sell the horn on the black market. It was a shame Richard left. He...'

Sannie said nothing. Marilyn also waited.

Jan-Maree looked from woman to woman. Their waitress came back and took their food orders. Sannie settled for a cheeseburger, Marilyn the ribs and wing combo, and Jan-Maree a salad. Sannie had felt that Jan-Maree was about to add something, but the waitress arriving had given her a reprieve.

'You were saying, about Richard?' Sannie prompted.

She shrugged. 'Too bad he had the fallout with David. He's ex-military. He's passionate about wildlife and history.'

Sannie waited again while Jan-Maree fiddled with a silver ring on her left index finger. 'That's nice,' Sannie said, nodding towards it.

Jan-Maree glanced up. 'It's Celtic.'

'English?' Sannie asked.

She shook her head. 'Irish.'

'Where does one find such a beautiful piece of jewellery in Dundee?' Sannie asked with a smile.

'I . . .' She waved her hands, palms uppermost, as if to say she didn't know, which was not possible.

Sannie could see that Jan-Maree's cheeks had coloured. The girl looked around, as if searching for her salad. Sannie could see she was trying to hide something.

'Look, am I in trouble?'

'No, Jan-Maree, you're not in trouble,' Marilyn said across the table.

'Did Richard give you the ring?' Sannie asked. 'He's from the UK, yes?'

Jan-Maree looked down again. 'Yes,' she said, her answer barely audible. She placed her right hand over her left, hiding the ring from them.

'Do you only work here in The Shed?' Sannie asked, changing tack for a moment.

Jan-Maree looked up again. 'I'm studying for my master's in history and I tutor high school kids and work as a part-time tour guide as well.'

'Busy. You said Richard was passionate about,' Sannie made a show of checking her notebook, 'wildlife and history. And you?'

'Both.'

Their food and drinks came, giving Jan-Maree another respite from answering questions. They still hadn't talked about the fight between Richard Tustin and David Gregory, but Sannie felt it was better to take this slowly. She took a bite of her cheeseburger. 'I liked history at school. What era are you studying?'

Jan-Maree was picking at her salad. 'The Anglo-Zulu War.'

'You're a battlefields guide?'

She nodded.

'Tell me about the fight between Richard and David, please, Jan-Maree.' She ate some chips while she waited. They were superb.

The young blonde woman set down her fork. 'Whatever Deon told you, Richard did not want to kill David.'

'So, the word "kill" was not used?' Sannie asked.

Jan-Maree puffed out her cheeks and exhaled. 'Look, Colonel, you know men. They say stuff they don't mean when they're angry. And Richard *was* angry. He and David had a fight about the guy that was shot on David's game reserve. You heard about that, right?'

Sannie nodded while chewing.

'Yeah, well like the Saffers say, that was not so *lekker* and Richard made sure the American who shot the poacher was on the first plane out of South Africa – not to protect him, but because Richard wanted him gone-gone. He told me later he regretted letting him come to the country in the first place. He said the American had broken their rules of engagement and that he should not have even been carrying a firearm that night. He was pissed off at the guy. Richard apologised to David about what happened. Richard also paid compensation to the family of the wounded poacher, and covered the guy's medical bills.'

'But David didn't accept Richard's apology?' Sannie asked.

'David was a stubborn old goat. He told Richard that he wanted him gone from the reserve and that was what they were arguing about. When Richard said to David something like: "OK, so who will protect your rhinos now?", David said, "I'd rather kill them all and sell the bloody horns than have one of your Rambos kill a human being".'

Sannie wrote the alleged comments down in longhand in her notebook. And while she was doing so, Marilyn picked up the questioning. Sannie trusted Marilyn; she was young, but she learned fast and her instincts were good.

'But surely David must have known the risks involved in owning rhinos and protecting them against armed poachers?' It was the same question Sannie would have asked.

Jan-Maree shrugged. 'I guess, but old David was the sort of person who would insist something was black if you told him it was white. He was in favour of legalising the trade in rhino horn to protect the species, while Richard was very much opposed to legitimising the sale of horn. He said it was the "commodification" of wildlife that he and his men were fighting against, and I sided with Richard.'

'Did you have much to do with David?' Marilyn asked as Sannie continued to write.

'Yes,' Jan-Maree said. 'He was probably the local area's foremost expert on the Zulu War battlefields. He actually oversaw my guide's qualification exam. He has – well, had – the most amazing collection of memorabilia as well. His great-great-uncle was at Isandlwana and was one of the few white people who survived the battle there. David even showed me one of his relative's diaries and I used it to help write a paper about the Natal Mounted Police and their role in the war.'

Sannie stopped writing. 'So, you were friends with David?'

Jan-Maree grimaced. 'As much as anyone could be a friend of his. He was the original grumpy old man. But I respected him, hugely. He knew so much about the battlefields and the times. I kept telling him that he should write a book, but he wasn't interested. I think he was also not happy when I . . .'

It was as if the younger woman had just realised she had said too much. 'When you what?' Sannie asked. 'Became friends with Richard?'

'How did . . .?' Jan-Maree parked her question. 'Richard is also an expert on the Anglo-Zulu War. We had a good deal in common, so, yes, we had much to talk about.'

She was skirting around the nature of her relationship with the English military veteran. Sannie felt it went deeper than she was letting on, and for some reason Jan-Maree didn't want to talk about that. Why? Because of Deon? Because of her new boyfriend, John Parker?

Sannie nodded and made a note, then picked up her cheeseburger. 'Had Richard been to war?'

Jan-Maree widened her eyes in surprise. 'What? Why would you ask that?'

'It's just a question,' Marilyn said.

'Um, yes. He was in Afghanistan with the British Royal Marines.'

'Did Richard ever get angry, or anxious, Jan-Maree? I know veterans. Sometimes they can be quick to anger.' She thought about Adam. Although he was never, ever violent towards her, he had a short fuse occasionally.

'Both of them had tempers,' Jan-Maree said. 'It was why they were arguing here, in public, but they also had disagreements on battlefield visits – especially out in the field. Mostly it was good-natured.'

'And his service?' Sannie pressed.

Jan-Maree sighed. 'He did two tours in Afghanistan. His first was with 40 Commando as a young lieutenant in 2002, then he went back in 2013 as a major. He told me that things were quiet in '02, and when he deployed ten years later there was much more fighting, but by then he was a company commander, so he didn't actually fire his rifle in anger. So, if you're asking if he has ever killed anyone, then the answer is definitely no.'

Sannie nodded. 'You said that Richard's arguments with David were "mostly" good-natured?'

Jan-Maree set down her fork again with a *clink*. 'Look, I'm telling you, Richard did *not* kill David. I told Deon they'd had words here, and threatened to kill each other, but I added something like, "as usual", which Deon must have neglected to say to you. That's all. Although they fell out, I think they still respected each other as experts in the history of this area, and as military men. David served with the Umvoti Mounted Rifles in the Border War and was proud of his time in the army.'

Interesting, Sannie thought. David would have known how to defend himself in case of an armed invasion at his farm, yet he seemed to have been overpowered without warning.

'Do you know where we can find Richard Tustin now, today?' Sannie asked. Jan-Maree looked up, over Sannie's shoulder, and her mouth opened with surprise.

'Behind you,' a male voice said.

Sannie turned around to see a man standing behind her, maybe just over six foot tall, early-to-mid forties, well built, with neatly trimmed, thick dark hair with a few strands of grey and a matching moustache. He wore tan cargo pants and a blue polo shirt and was smiling. She started to stand.

'Don't get up.' He reached out a hand as he slid into the booth seat next to Jan-Maree, opposite Sannie and Marilyn. 'Richard Tustin.'

Sannie was taken aback, but took his hand and shook it. 'Lieutenant Colonel Susan van Rensburg, South African Police Service. Major . . .?'

He smiled. 'Retired.' Tustin offered his hand to Marilyn. '*Sawubona.*'

Marilyn nodded and shook. 'Warrant Officer Msani.'

'The pleasure is all mine,' he said. 'Can I help you ladies with anything?'

Sannie consulted her notebook. 'We were just talking to Jan-Maree here about the events of this morning. You've heard?'

He nodded. 'Poor old David. You know, he and I fought like a couple of old bull elephants, but I was shocked to hear what happened. For all his faults he did not deserve to go like that.'

'Like how?' Sannie asked.

'In a farm invasion, of all things. He was good to the local people,' his eyes flitted to Marilyn, 'even if that local nutter of a politician Tshabalala was trying to stir up a vexatious land claim against David's property.'

Sannie posed an open question: 'What did you fight about?'

He sat back in the booth. 'I suppose it might be better to ask what *didn't* we fight about? British and Zulu troop dispositions at Isandlwana; the materials used to construct the defences at Rorke's Drift; global politics; rugby, the weather – you name it, Colonel. He was a cantankerous old so-and-so, but then, some people would say the same about me.' He looked to Jan-Maree.

Sannie detected a colouring in Jan-Maree's cheeks.

'Did you ever threaten to kill him?' Sannie asked.

Tustin snorted. 'Probably. Why? You don't –'

Sannie made a note then looked up. 'Mr Tustin –'

'Richard is fine.'

She continued: 'We understand that you were asked to withdraw your volunteers from providing security for Mr Gregory's game reserve after an incident in which an intruder was shot.'

'That's about right,' Tustin said. The waitress reappeared and asked him if he wanted anything. 'Coffee, please. Americano. No milk.'

Sannie decided to change tack. She had more than one investigation running in parallel and wondered if she could find any links between them. 'Who do you think killed David Gregory's rhinos?'

Tustin puffed out his cheeks, then placed his hands back on the dining table, palms down. 'I hate to speak ill of the dead . . .'

'You think David killed them himself.'

'It was a threat he'd made to me, in the past.'

'So I've just heard. When you argued,' Sannie pressed.

He nodded. 'Yes. Here, in the restaurant. That was a particularly heated debate, I seem to remember. David had given us our marching orders, after the shooting incident, and at the very same time he was complaining that with no security on his reserve his rhinos would probably all be killed within a matter of weeks. He said he had a mind to kill them himself and sell the horns on the black market.'

Sannie read back over her notes. Jan-Maree had said the same thing. She looked Tustin in the eye. 'And what did you say to that, Richard?'

'I said, "Over my dead body, David", and he said that he would be happy to oblige me.'

'And what did you say next?' Sannie asked.

The waitress returned with Tustin's coffee and Sannie used the break in questioning to finish her cheeseburger. She pushed her plate to the side. Tustin sipped his coffee and as he leaned back he reached out his left arm and placed it on the back of the seat behind Jan-Maree, as if he was about to put it around her. He looked at the younger woman. 'What did I say next?'

Jan-Maree's cheeks went bright red now. 'Um . . . you weren't happy, Richard. That much I remember. But your exact words . . .'

'Hmm.' He tapped his lips with the index finger of his right hand. 'Ah yes, I remember, I said, "If you kill those defenceless animals I'll put a bullet in your head myself, you stupid old goat".' He craned his head forward a little as if trying to read Sannie's notes. 'Did you get that verbatim, Colonel?'

She finished writing. 'Pretty much, yes.'

'I was joking, of course.'

'It doesn't seem to me like it was lighthearted banter between friends.' She looked to Jan-Maree. 'Was it?'

Jan-Maree shook her head. 'No, but Richard didn't mean it. Of course he didn't.'

Tustin took some more coffee. 'The day after that altercation I went out to David's farm. I found that he and his staff had corralled all the rhinos into the bomas near his farmhouse. I asked him why he'd done this, and what he planned to do with them.'

Sannie raised her eyebrows. 'And?'

Tustin grimaced. 'All he said to me was, "None of your business". And then he told me to get off his property or he would shoot me. I tried to reason with him, to offer our services, along with a guarantee that there would be no more accidental shootings. I actually think he was beginning to show some early signs of dementia. My mother went that way – it's a terrible thing to witness. I asked him if I could make him a cup of tea and he went inside and got a shotgun and came out and pointed it at me. That was when I left.'

Sannie made some more notes, trying to picture the scene as she wrote. 'Forgive me,' she looked back over the last page, 'it was clear that you'd had your differences, but are you telling me that David Gregory was prepared to kill all his rhinos and see his game reserve left unguarded from poachers over a disagreement with you, even after you had settled the matter with the local community?'

Tustin shrugged. 'Like I said, in my opinion he wasn't thinking straight. You're right – no matter how he felt about my volunteer shooting the young person, the matter had been resolved. I was offering free security in exchange for billeting my volunteers, yet he'd dug himself in to his position.'

'He was like that,' Jan-Maree added. 'Once he took a stand on something, whether it was to do with running the farm or a historical point, he'd defend it all the way, and never concede.'

'When did you next see David?' Sannie asked Tustin.

'I didn't. It was after that last argument, a day or so later I think, that I heard that his rhinos had been found dead. He'd called the local stock theft unit, saying there were criminals on his farm in the night, and he'd heard gunshots, and when he went to check the next morning he found his rhinos had been killed.' Tustin held his hands out, palms up, as if he couldn't believe the account. 'I heard that David told the cops he had fired a few shots out of his bedroom window into the night, in the direction of the boma where the rhinos were, and that he thought that would scare the poachers off.'

Sannie noted that this version of events was different to the statement David Gregory had given to the police. Derick le Roux had said that David claimed the poachers came and went in silence, presumably using suppressed weapons. David had lied to someone, which further implicated him in being involved in a crime. And in Sannie's experience hardened rhino poachers would not have been deterred by a couple of wild shots – not with sixteen horns up for grabs. More likely, they would have opened fire on the homestead and killed David. There were too many unanswered questions in this case.

'More likely,' Tustin continued, 'David went through with his threat to kill his own rhinos and had only got halfway through the job when someone called the police and told them what was going on.'

'Someone?' Marilyn asked.

'A staff member, maybe?' Tustin said. 'He employed good people. It's likely that at least one of them was as outraged with what David had done as the rest of us were.'

'Can you give us the names of any of his staff who we could talk to?' Sannie asked.

'John,' Jan-Maree said. 'John Parker is David's head guide on the game reserve. He was devastated by the loss of the rhinos.' Jan-Maree gave them Parker's phone number.

Sannie made a note, then looked up at Jan-Maree again. 'I understand that you and John are in a relationship.'

Jan-Maree's cheeks coloured. 'Yes.'

Sannie noticed that Tustin had turned away. 'Your men, Mr Tustin. Your volunteers – where are they now?'

He faced Sannie again. 'They're no longer "my men", as you put it, Colonel. I've had many volunteers pass through Dundee over the years, but there was no more work for this current crop. They left – they went to the coast,' he said. 'Taking a bit of R and R, from what I've seen, and scouting out some new opportunities of where Wild-Force might help in the fight against poaching. They're near Kosi Bay.'

'Really?' she said. 'Do you know where exactly?'

'A place called Bhanga Nek,' he said. 'Do you know it?'

Sannie closed her notebook and nodded. 'I do, as a matter of fact.'

12

KWAZULU-NATAL, THE PRESENT

Adam stood on the wooden deck outside his permanent tent. He took a deep breath, inhaling the scent of the sea. He and Sannie lived on the beach in Pennington, on the KwaZulu-Natal south coast, but it was a long drive from here. He wanted to be with her, always, but he'd also only just found his true purpose in life.

He wished she could be here with him now, and even though she was financially independent, he didn't feel like he could ask her to drop everything and leave her job so that she could come and live *his* best life with him.

His phone rang and when Adam checked the screen he saw, spookily, that it was Sannie. 'Howzit,' he said.

'Fine and you?'

'Same. Where are you?'

'Going to a game reserve to interview its manager.'

'Half your luck,' Adam said.

'I came here to bust cattle rustlers and find out who killed some rhinos, but today I've been investigating a murder,' she said.

'Oh.' Her job was not easy, but he knew from their time together so far that she was good at it and that she was proud to be doing something to help her country in the fight against crime.

Adam wasn't sure what to say next. He didn't want to rekindle an argument with her.

Sannie broke the short silence. 'I don't suppose you've noticed a bunch of overseas military veterans hanging around Bhanga Nek, have you?'

He was taken aback. 'In fact, I have. Big guys. Fit. Military tattoos. They're here on a diving holiday.'

'Do they look like they know what they're doing, in the water, I mean?'

'Yes. Camouflage wetsuits, black Zodiac boat; they look more like they're preparing to invade a foreign country than going spearfishing. I spoke to their leader, a guy called Andy. He's English. They're from some charity . . .'

'WildForce,' Sannie said.

'Yes, that's it. How did you know? They're looking for work here, they said.'

'I just interviewed one of the charity's people here in SA, a retired major named Richard Tustin. He's ex–Royal Marines. They were working on a game reserve up here near Dundee, but had a falling out with the owner, who's turned up dead. It seems one of the veterans shot a poacher and then left the country, but it cost them their contract here.'

'Middle East veteran?' Adam asked.

'Yes, Tustin served in Afghanistan.'

'Sannie, the guys whose bodies we found here – they were Middle Eastern, maybe. One was armed. They could be smugglers.' He told her about the antique holy book he'd found on the beach.

'Was there anything else that might indicate they were smugglers?' she asked.

'I'm sure they weren't on a sightseeing or diving cruise. The local cops want me to check out their sunken boat. When we retrieved the second body I could see plastic storage crates on board but we didn't have scuba gear so couldn't investigate. Jenny and I are going to take another look.'

'Jenny? Is she the one who's been sharing posts on your Facebook?'

'Yes, one of my students. I'm sure I mentioned her to you. She's a natural in the water.'

'Hmm, yes, well, don't go dragging your students into anything you're doing to help the police, Adam. You should be more responsible – you have a duty of care to those students.'

'Yes, Colonel.'

'Adam!' He heard her draw a breath. 'Tell me about the book – the Koran or whatever it is,' Sannie said.

'I took some pics of it and sent them to a colleague, a history professor at the university – he's Muslim. His specialty is religious history, so I'm hoping he'll know what it is, and its significance.'

'And you say it was wrapped up?' Sannie asked.

'Yes, it looked like it was packaged up to be waterproof, like maybe it was going to be transported to shore.'

'Too bad the dead can't talk,' Sannie said. 'Is it a coincidence that this band of ex–special forces soldiers are diving around the same beach where this all happened?'

'I'm going to try and find out,' Adam said.

'Just in the water, Adam. Dive on the wreck and see what you can find, and message me the name and number of the detective in charge of the investigation. Don't go snooping around these soldiers' camp. OK?'

'OK,' he said. And after a pause: 'I love you.'

'*Ja*. Love you, too,' she said, then hung up.

ADAM EASED the throttle back and handed over control of the RHIB to Jenny as they approached the site of the wreck, which Adam had recorded on the boat's GPS. Adam accepted what Sannie had said about his responsibility for his students' safety, but it would also have been irresponsible and impractical for him to go diving alone.

'Stay on this heading,' he said to Jenny. She nodded.

Adam went to the rear of the boat and, sitting on the floor, shrugged on his BCD and cylinder. He strapped his diving knife to his right calf and slid a steel pry-bar between the strapping and his leg. Lastly he put on his fins and mask.

'Coming up to the wreck now,' Jenny said.

They could just see the shore from this far out. Adam stayed low as he moved next to Jenny, on the side of the boat furthest from the beach.

'Cut to dead slow.'

She nodded and eased back the throttle. Adam shifted his bottom up onto the inflated side of the RHIB and put his hand over his mask. 'You know the drill?'

She nodded again. 'I'll move up and down the coastline, like I'm looking for turtles. In fact I *will* be looking for turtles as I want to get in the water again today.'

'Good,' he said.

'Adam?'

He lowered his hand. 'Yes?'

'Be careful.'

Jenny looked to the GPS screen and gave him a thumbs up. Adam held on to his mask again and rolled backwards into the water.

The calm settled around him as he finned downwards. It was always like this. In the water, he felt complete, assured of himself, and at peace. On dry land, around others – even people he loved, such as Sannie – he was often worried that he was saying the wrong thing or, increasingly, that he'd lost the ability to read people. Especially Sannie. Perhaps it wasn't just him – maybe it was her, as well. And sometimes, like the past couple of days, things reminded him of Angola and the war. Dead bodies, guns, to name just a couple.

But here in the warm green embrace of the Indian Ocean he felt at home, in his element. He adjusted his course slightly when he caught sight of the wreck, lying on the ocean floor. Visibility was better today, though still not perfect, as the water had not completely cleared from the turbulence kicked up by the storm that had probably swamped the smugglers' boat. If that's what they were.

Out of habit he swivelled his head, looking for sharks or other signs of danger. Some fish, red romans, swam past him.

Adam let more air out of his buoyancy vest, allowing him to descend further, until he reached the wreck. A stingray, startled by his arrival, shot out of the half-cabin, and Adam had to lean back to avoid being hit by it.

On the deck he saw the waterproof cases that he and Jenny had first spotted when they retrieved the body of the second man. He finned to the biggest, a long, narrow case. It was green, military-looking, and judging by its dimensions he thought it might contain a rifle. Adam grabbed hold of a carry handle at one end and tried to lift the box. It was heavy – as evidenced by the fact that it hadn't floated when the boat sank. He ran his fingers along the side of the hinged upper lid and came to a catch that secured it. There was a padlock. When he continued feeling along the lid edge he found a second catch and lock, and then a third.

Adam raised his right knee towards his chest and slid the pry-bar from behind his dive knife. He thought for a moment. Was whatever it was that was locked inside the box valuable? Probably. Would it be damaged or destroyed by sea water if he opened the box? Maybe. He thought of the antique Koran. It had been wrapped securely, so perhaps the same precautions had been taken with everything onboard. He could not carry this box to the surface himself – he'd need a winch or an inflatable buoy of some kind, and rope, to send it upwards. His curiosity got the better of him.

Adam worked the narrow end of the pry-bar between the plastic of the case's lid and the metal catch securing it, and started to worry the heavy steel shaft up and down.

Finding purchase, he gave a strong heave and the first of the three catches snapped away from the box. He started work on the second, mindful that if it took him this long to open one of the fastenings, he would not have much time to search the rest of the boat after opening all three. Glancing around as he worked he saw the two other, smaller cases, but decided to carry on trying to open the largest box.

Adam's thoughts wandered to Sannie again. He wanted to be with her, but he wanted her to understand that sometimes, for whatever reason, he needed to be by himself, even if it meant being physically away from her occasionally.

He saw a flash of movement in his peripheral vision.

Adam stopped his work and looked to his right, heart pounding. It was a small reef shark. He breathed easier into his regulator. The predator was too small to be a bother to him and must have been curious about what he was up to. Adam resumed his work, jiggling the pry-bar under the second lock. He worked faster now that he was able to sense where the weakest spot was on the lock. The second catch gave way.

He wondered what Jenny was doing, topside, and whether she had, in fact, found a turtle for them to dive on and catch later.

The third lock was proving more stubborn for some reason, or maybe, Adam thought, he was losing patience the more he thought about Sannie. He cursed to himself as the pry-bar slipped free of the catch.

The reef shark cruised by again and Adam tried to focus on being in the moment, and not letting his frustration redline. He slowed his breathing, then checked his dive watch. He was fine for time. He needed to slow down, concentrate on what he was doing, and then make his way to the surface again. Jenny would be coming back for him in twenty minutes. Strictly speaking, it wasn't good safety protocol for him to be on the ocean floor without a boat above him, in case something went wrong, but he'd been to war, faced the prospect of death several times, and nearly been killed by being shot and run over a couple of years earlier.

Adam eased the pointed end of the bar in behind the catch again and pulled back on it. He felt the lock start to give.

Then he couldn't breathe.

Adam drew a breath, but instead of inhaling a life-sustaining mix of oxygen and nitrogen he took in a mouthful of sea water. He spluttered and turned as he noticed a high-speed stream of bubbles rising up from his air hose, which had just been severed. Adam tried to see what or who had cut his supply, but an arm clad in black neoprene was now around his neck.

Adam flailed as he realised another diver had come up behind him and was choking him. He registered white skin on the man's hand as he reached behind him to try and get a hold on his attacker. Adam saw a glint of light, as if a silver fish had just come into view, then realised it was the blade of a knife, catching the sun from far above. Adam twisted in the man's grip as the sharp edge ran across his chest, opening his wetsuit. Blood coiled up from the wound.

The man tried to stab him, but the tip of the blade snagged in Adam's BCD. Adam realised he couldn't reach his own dive knife, strapped low down on his right leg, so instead, he contorted his torso backwards, into the man and, at the same time, unsnapped the clasps holding his BCD closed. As Adam reversed his move, now leaning forward, the vest and heavy dive cylinder fell back on his assailant, forcing him to release his grip on Adam.

With his knife momentarily stuck in the vest, which was now weighing him down, the other diver struggled to regain a level position. Unencumbered, Adam hung there in the water a moment, held down by the weight belt he still wore. He'd wondered how the man had got to him, with no sound of a boat's engines, but then he saw, on the ocean floor, a black DPV, a diver propulsion vehicle. The hand-held device used a silent, battery-powered propellor to drag the diver through the water. The man could have launched from the beach.

Adam needed to get to the surface, but what then? If he stayed up there, waiting for Jenny to return, the man could take his time, circling him under water like a shark until he found the right moment to – what? Kill him?

Adam could only assume the man had come for whatever was in the boat. If he left him there, on the bottom, would the diver in the black wetsuit be content to take whatever he was looking for and leave Adam alone? *No way.*

It was a moot point. He needed air, so he finned for the surface. At any moment Adam expected to feel the tug of the man's hand on his ankle or fin, the cut of the knife again.

His head burst clear into the sunshine, and Adam coughed out sea water. He looked around. Jenny was following his orders and had not returned early. He could swim for shore, but that was probably what the man expected him to do. Adam was an accomplished swimmer, but with his DPV the other man would easily catch him. Adam checked his watch – twelve minutes until Jenny was due back. He did the last thing the man would expect.

Adam drew a deep lungful of air, then duck-dived and finned back down into the depths. As he suspected, the man probably thought Adam was trying to escape now, and that he would deal with him later. Like Adam before him, he was focusing his attention on the storage box. However, instead of trying to open it, he was fastening a length of rope to a carry handle at one end of the box.

Adam reached down and drew his diving knife from its sheath.

He kicked hard, sliding through the water with the purposefulness and intent of a great white shark. When he hit the other diver he did what the man had done to him, and sliced through the air hose connecting the man's cylinder to his regulator. Bubbles streamed out as the man stopped what he was doing and flailed about. Adam swam on, staying clear of the man in order to watch and wait for his next move. Adam contemplated going for the man's DPV, but it was too far away.

The man did what Adam had done: unclipped his BCD and let it fall to the sandy bottom of the ocean. Instead of heading straight for the surface, however, he looked around him.

Adam floated, knife hand out. *What are you doing?*

From the other side of the sunken boat another diver appeared, dressed in camouflage and being towed by another DPV. This man had a spare dive cylinder trailing from a cable attached to the underwater scooter.

Seeing what had just happened, the man with the DPV made

straight for his comrade, who floated there, with no oxygen, waiting. The man was a cool customer – he'd ignored the urge to strike for the surface, perhaps knowing that Adam would follow him and possibly finish him off.

The diver with the DPV stopped his vehicle next to the first man, took his regulator from his mouth and put it in the other man's mouth. The first diver sucked in some oxygen, then returned the regulator and took over the DPV and spare tank.

Outnumbered and running short of air, Adam finned for the surface again. Whatever advantage he'd won he had now lost.

Adam broke the surface again and swivelled his head. Still no sign of Jenny. *Shit*. He sucked in air again, and dived once more.

On his way down he saw the second diver coming towards him. Beyond him, Adam could see that the first man was putting on the spare BCD and cylinder. It was now two against one.

Adam saw, almost too late, that the man coming towards him was armed. He carried a spear gun in his right hand. Adam reached for the clasp at his waist and flipped it, freeing the weight belt he was wearing. He ripped it from his body and held it out as he continued to descend.

They were on a collision course and Adam saw the other man extend his right hand and take aim at him. They were closing on each other, no more than ten metres apart when the man pulled the trigger.

Adam, directly above the other man, let go of his weight belt at that same moment and the heavy lead and fabric webbing twisted and turned through the water. The spear glanced off a weight and its trailing line became entangled in the belt. The pointed shaft missed Adam, who gave two more strong kicks and propelled himself into the other man.

Adam slashed down, fighting hard against the water. The man let go of his spear gun, which was still tethered to him by a wristband, and tried to parry the blow. Adam's knife cut into his wetsuit, drawing blood from the man's forearm. Adam pushed his hand into the man's face, grabbed hold of his dive mask and tried to wrench it free.

But the other man was strong, heavily muscled. Adam looked into his eyes as they grappled with each other. It was not Andy or one of his other men from the boat he and Jenny had encountered, but that didn't mean there weren't more veterans at the campsite.

The man was able to keep Adam's knife hand away as he, too, tried to get to Adam's mask. He wrapped his arms around Adam and in that moment, Adam realised what he was trying to do. The man, who was breathing oxygen and nitrogen through a regulator, was going to hang on to Adam until he drowned.

Adam struck again with his knife, but being crushed to the other diver's chest meant that all he could do was slash and stab against his captor's vest and dive cylinder. Adam looked into his eyes. The bastard was grinning at him. Adam tried to stab lower, but the other man anticipated his move and twisted his body. Adam's blow lacked speed and power because of the water pressure and while he felt the point of the knife pierce the man's wetsuit somewhere low on his side, it was not enough to make the man stop smiling. He seemed to be mocking him.

Blood curled in the water around them, from the wounds Adam had inflicted and the cut the first man had made to Adam's chest. Then something slapped against him from behind, sending him lurching through the cool green water. Its touch was rough, rasping on his wetsuit like sandpaper. Adam saw the look in the other man's eyes turn from smug triumph to wide-eyed terror. The man relaxed his grip, allowing Adam to twist and turn. The bronze-grey flank of a two-metre bull shark, which had just whipped Adam with its tail, glided by. The man was right to be scared.

His breath nearly exhausted from the dive and the fight, Adam needed to get to the surface. He finned towards the dappled sunlight above, the shark cruising just beneath his feet. Adam had completed a PhD in sharks, so it was good to think this one might have saved his life – as long as it didn't eat him.

As he tasted fresh air again, he heard the welcome hum of outboard motors. He waved his hand.

Adam spun in the water and saw Jenny in the RHIB. She changed course, slightly, indicating she'd seen him, and opened the throttle wide. *Thank heavens.* Adam started swimming towards the oncoming boat.

Lifting his head as he swam, he saw the nose of the RHIB start to settle. Jenny was slowing down, about to coast up to him. He stopped to wave again, beckoning her towards him as he bobbed in the swell. 'Keep moving!'

'What?' Jenny called back.

'Faster, don't slow! Come get me.'

Jenny got the message. He heard the note change as she nudged the throttle forward again. She aimed just off to one side of him and moved to the side of the boat, then leaned over the edge with her arm out.

Adam knew he had one chance to get this right or they would both be in danger. As the boat churned towards him he reached down underwater and removed his fins, letting them float away. He held up his right arm, and although the RHIB was not moving fast he grunted as he felt her hook him and heave him up. Adam flipped his right leg up and over the inflated side of the boat and rolled inside. Without Jenny at the helm, the boat was starting to turn of its own accord.

'Quick,' he gasped. 'Full speed ahead.'

'Which way?'

'Any way. Away from here!' he said.

'Why . . .?'

Jenny couldn't finish asking what was happening. As Adam hauled himself to his knees he saw what she had just seen. The man who was after him had surfaced and was treading water, holding his spear gun, which he had reloaded.

Jenny pointed. 'Who's that?'

Adam was on his feet. He needed to get Jenny out from behind the wheel, to protect her. He needed to get them to a safe distance away from these men, and to patrol the coastline, waiting to see where they emerged. 'Out of the way, Jenny. Get down!'

Jenny was transfixed as the man took aim at them. Adam tried to knock her out of the way, but the man fired. The spear shot towards them.

Jenny fell backwards, the blood bright on her white T-shirt.

13

NATAL, 1880

They travelled under a dome of perfect blue with not a single cloud in sight. Gregory, Phillips and Lady Beecham – Teresa – were on horseback, and an elderly Zulu, Mathias Mpofu, drove the wagon loaded with the American woman's considerable baggage, as well as their tentage and other stores. They had flour, a crate each of red wine and champagne, bottles of gin and beer, dried fruit and boxes of vegetables and biltong – dried game meat. Phillips, who fancied himself a marksman, would shoot fresh meat and game birds for the pot and Mathias would double as chef.

The mornings were crisp, the days sunny and warm, and the nights freezing. Ahead of them was a series of endless hills whose emerald sheen was slowly fading as the winter dry season took hold. The grassy slopes were punctuated with grey granite outcrops, rocky crags where an elusive leopard might be hiding or sunning itself while scanning the wilderness for prey.

A couple of reedbuck – a male with recurved horns and a shaggy khaki coat and his slighter, bare-headed female – gave a warning squeak at their horses' approach, and bounded away down a wide valley in front of them.

Lady Beecham rode like a man, legs astride her mount, with

a confidence and upright posture that reminded Gregory of Grace. He wondered how she was faring with her pastor, and he hoped she had enjoyed exacting a measure of revenge on the prisoner, Blundell. For now, he expected this titled lady with the American accent would be enough of a handful for him to manage.

'You ride well,' Gregory said to Teresa as he cantered alongside her.

'Thank you, as do you.'

He blushed. 'I simply meant . . .'

'Relax, Captain,' she said. 'My daddy wanted sons but all he got before my poor mom passed during childbirth was me. I grew up in New York, but he sent me to the best educational institutions, even to finishing school in Geneva. I spent my vacations learning to ride and rounding up steers on a ranch in Montana.'

'I see.'

She looked at him askance. 'You're wondering why I'm travelling alone, and where my title comes from, given that I'm American. Most folks usually do ponder those things – some are even rude enough to ask.'

He said nothing, but she continued.

'I was sent to London to stay with an aunt and to make my debut. Daddy's money came from oil – though the ranch was his first love – but he wanted me to have the manners of someone well bred, someone British. I think he secretly wanted to marry me off to some titled gentleman and, well, he got his wish.'

'Lord Beecham?'

She gave a sound, most unladylike, which was half-snort, half-laugh. 'Freddy? Yes. The *dis*honourable Lord Beecham. I fell for him. He took what he thought was his right to take and pretty soon we were husband and wife, with me swelling up like a heifer with calf and on a ship to New York.'

'You have a child?' Gregory knew he should have been more circumspect, but she was being decidedly candid and his words tumbled out.

Teresa looked away from him, out over the distant, winding dragon's tail of mountains. 'Didn't make it all the way.'

'I'm sorry,' he said.

She looked back to him. 'Thank you. Most men, I find, don't like talking about such things. Freddy had already been staying out late, coming home smelling of expensive liquor and cheap perfume, and he was gambling away his money faster than his mommy and daddy could send it to him. Once I lost the baby, Freddy tried to convince himself, and others, that our marriage wasn't real, because we'd got hitched in a municipal office in Portsmouth before we boarded the ship and not in a church. Later, I found he'd bribed the clerk there to lose the paperwork.'

'My word,' said Gregory.

'Exactly. Bounder *and* a cad, right?'

Gregory scanned the hills out of habit. Coming back through this countryside reminded him of the events of a year ago. Peace, of sorts, had come to Zululand, but there was still the possibility, however remote, that thieves or angry warriors might decide to rob a lightly protected party. Samuel was somewhere ahead of them, across the Tugela River and deep into Zululand by now, looking for the king's emissary, Mfunzi. 'So it would seem, Your Ladyship.'

'We live separate lives now. He went back to England and I haven't seen him for a couple of years. To hell with him.' She gave Gregory a beatific smile.

Gregory frowned. He was well used to men using bad language, but not women. There was something quite different about this woman.

Phillips, riding ahead of them, glanced back at Gregory. 'Riders.'

Gregory lifted his chin and saw the dark specks coming down the slope of a hill, off to their right. As they came closer, he glimpsed blue uniforms, with white facings.

'Cavalry,' Gregory said. Red and white pennants fluttered from the lances carried by half-a-dozen troopers. An officer rode at their head.

Phillips kept them on course, following the valley along the edge of a stream that tumbled and gurgled invitingly on their left. The waters slowed at a shallow ford.

'We'll stop and water the horses here, and top up our canteens,' Gregory said.

'Yes, sir,' Phillips said.

Phillips reined in his horse, next to where Gregory and Teresa stopped. 'What are you gawping at, Phillips?' Gregory asked.

'Er, nothing, sir. Nothing at all.'

Clearly, he was captivated by Teresa, and it was not hard to see why. She dismounted with the ease of a leopard alighting from a tree branch, and if Gregory had been standing closer he would have clipped Phillips on the back of his head for the way his eyes stayed fixated on Lady Beecham's bustle.

Gregory brought Bullet to the stream and he drank while Gregory knelt and refilled his water bottle. He took a long drink of cool, clean water then refilled his bottle and stoppered it. He heard the jangle of horse brass and the clump of hooves and turned to see the mounted troopers rein in nearby.

Their young officer dismounted and gave his horse's reins to another trooper to take care of. 'Who's in command here?'

Gregory eased himself to his feet and hung his canteen from the pommel of his saddle. He walked around the horse to the officer, who stood waiting, hands on hips.

'Good day,' Gregory said.

'Are you in command?'

Gregory narrowed his eyes. The man – boy, really – had been in Africa a while. His cheeks were burned red, his lips cracked from the unforgiving heat and the bitter cold, yet he'd learned nothing of the pace of life here, especially the importance the local people placed on manners. The officer's cap badge was a skull and crossbones with a banner reading *Or Glory* under the head – the 17th Lancers, the same unit Major Harold Morrison had belonged to.

'Sub-Inspector Peter Gregory, Natal Mounted Police. How do you do,' he looked at the man's single rank pip on his shoulder, 'Lieutenant?'

'I'm fine.'

Gregory was sure he caught sight of a sneer at the corner of the man's mouth. Cavalry officers, he remembered from his own time in the army, often thought themselves a cut above mere mortals and the 'Death or Glory' boys were no different. 'As am I. And yes, Lieutenant …?'

'Walters.'

Gregory kept his expression unchanged, but the name made him start. This was the same man Blundell had mentioned, who had visited the Red Lantern with Morrison.

'Yes, I'm in command of this party, Lieutenant Walters. Might I enquire as to your business out here,' he gestured with a hand, 'in the middle of nowhere?'

'I was going to ask you the same thing, especially as I see you have a lady accompanying you.' Walters touched the brim of his pith helmet in a gesture of greeting to Teresa, who was keeping her distance and, surprisingly, from what little Gregory knew of her already, her silence. 'Ma'am.'

Teresa nodded. Gregory returned his attention to the officer. 'I'm escorting the lady on a journey into Zululand, in order for her to rendezvous with an acquaintance.'

'That's intriguing,' Walters said. His men had dismounted and, like Gregory's party, were leading their horses to the stream. 'I'm tasked with providing outlying security for the Empress Eugénie's party. You've no doubt heard of her pilgrimage to the colony.'

Gregory nodded. 'I have.' He gave a flick of his head. 'The lady accompanying me –' He smelled Teresa's perfume; she had covered the distance between them in just a few long, quick strides.

'– is here to photograph birds, Lieutenant,' Teresa interjected.

Gregory was surprised for the second time in a few minutes. He had no desire to ingratiate himself with Walters, now that he knew who he was – assuming this was the same young second lieutenant Blundell had spoken of – but nor did he want to alienate him. Indeed, Gregory wanted to question Lieutenant Walters at some point.

Teresa caught his eye. 'Isn't that right, Captain Gregory.'

'Yes, quite.'

'*Captain*?' Walters asked.

'My previous rank, in the army,' Gregory said, making it clear he had outranked Walters.

'So, you have a camera?' Walters said to Teresa. 'I'd be intrigued to see it.'

'That would be my pleasure. Come, take a look.' Teresa turned on her heel and walked to the cart piled with her luggage. She unbuckled a heavy strap, moved one box and then lifted off a second, which Gregory assumed had contained a hat. When she undid another fastening and lifted off the lid she did, however, extract a camera. 'Perhaps you'd allow me to take a picture of you and your men.'

'We've no time for such frivolity. I need –'

'Go on, sir.' A cavalry sergeant, a barrel-chested man with an impressive moustache, perhaps ten years older than the young whelp who commanded him, had come up behind Walters. 'I'd accept the lady's offer, if I were you, sir. There's a good officer. I'm sure the lads would like to be immortalised.'

Walters looked back at the sergeant. He was annoyed yet seemed to be somewhat under the sergeant's control. 'Oh, I suppose so, then. Very well. Have the men form up, Sergeant.'

'Splendid, you won't regret it, Lieutenant, and I'll make sure you get a copy,' Teresa drawled.

She went back to the wagon and with some help from Phillips and Mathias, extracted another trunk with a tripod inside, which she set up. When she had fixed the camera to the tripod she went to Walters, who stood to the left of his troop of cavalrymen. Gregory smiled and smoothed his moustache as he watched her.

'Oh, Lieutenant,' she cooed, 'you've got a speck of lint on your tunic. May I?'

Walters cleared his throat. 'Of course.'

Teresa stroked his uniform, then moistened her fingers with her tongue in order to peck at another imaginary speck of dust. 'We have to have you looking your best, don't we?'

'Um, quite.' Walters coughed into his hand. 'I'm tasked, madam –'

'You can call me Mary,' she said.

'Yes, well, Mary, I am tasked with ascertaining the whereabouts of a female *journalist*.' His mouth puckered in disgust after the last word.

'Annoying creatures, reporters,' Teresa said. 'You've got a stray lock of that lovely dark hair. Do you mind if I fix it for you, Lieutenant . . .?'

'Er, Llewellyn, madam . . . Mary.' One of the troopers in the rank behind him sniggered.

For a man with a reputation as something of a cruel beast in a whorehouse, Walters seemed to be disarmed, like an inexperienced teenager, in the close presence of Teresa, who for some reason was hiding her true identity. Walters seemed an arrogant young prig and Gregory enjoyed seeing him flustered.

Teresa tucked some hair behind his ear, beneath the rim of his pith helmet. Gregory fancied he could see Walters' chest swell, and suspected he might be taking a deep inhalation of Teresa's floral perfume, which Gregory had also been distracted by on first meeting her in the hotel.

'You say you're here to photograph birds,' Walters said as Teresa took a pace back to check her handiwork.

'Oh yes. I find that the birds here in Africa are the most beautiful I've seen. Have you ever come across anything as lovely as a lilac-breasted roller, Lieutenant?'

'I, I can't say that I have . . .'

'Or the simply stunning purple-crested loerie?'

Walters tugged at his collar and shot a glance over his shoulder at another trooper, who muttered something that elicited a laugh. 'I . . . regrettably, I'm too busy soldiering and protecting the frontier to waste my time on ornithology, Miss *Mary*, you say?'

'Yes, Mary. Mary O'Brien, ornithologist and photographer.'

'You're not, by chance, taking pictures for a newspaper or periodical, I trust?'

'Perish the thought.' Teresa shook her head as she turned and walked to her camera. 'Perfectly still, now, gentlemen.' She bent behind the apparatus and pulled a small cape over her head. She clicked a button on the end of a cable and then re-emerged.

Walters started towards Teresa, but Gregory intercepted him. 'A word, if you please, Lieutenant.'

'Certainly, er . . .'

'I think you'll find "sir" is the word you're looking for, since I outrank you, Lieutenant, and did so when I was still a commissioned officer in Her Majesty's army.'

'Very well . . . sir.'

Gregory ushered him away from the woman. 'It's a matter of some discretion, best discussed away from the lady, and your men.'

Walters looked back, but allowed himself to be led further along the stream bank.

'You knew a Major Morrison?'

Walters jutted his chin out. 'What of him?'

'You heard what happened to him?'

Walters nodded. 'Murdered. By Zulus. There was to be an investigation, I heard.'

'Quite,' Gregory said. 'I'm the investigating officer. We've heard nothing and seen no signs of Zulu unrest in the hills this side of Pietermaritzburg, where Morrison had settled.'

'The bastards are everywhere,' Walters said. 'They're resentful of us, still, nearly a year after being quashed.'

'Wouldn't you be,' Gregory said, 'if a foreign army deposed Queen Victoria and invaded England?'

'You talk of them as if they're equal to us.'

Gregory shook his head. 'Oh, no, Mr Walters, they're not equal. They believe they're superior to us. I admire them for it. I don't think Morrison was killed by some random Zulu raiding party out for revenge on a soldier-turned-farmer.' He pointed to Walters' belt and the holster that hung from it. 'He was shot dead with a British service-issue pistol, just like that one you're wearing.'

Walters nodded. 'And like yours.'

'Exactly, but rarely a Zulu weapon of choice.'

'They say Morrison was opened up with an assegai, the way the

Zulus do after they've killed a foe, no matter how the man was executed.'

'Who's "they"?' Gregory asked.

Walters shrugged. 'Talk around town, in Maritzburg.'

'Where?'

'The pub, I suppose.' Walters looked back to his men. 'I must be on my way, Captain.'

'Could it have been talk in the Red Lantern? The pub and whorehouse you frequent, Lieutenant Walters?'

Walters' face reddened even more. 'You must be mistaken. I've never been to such a place.'

Gregory took a pace closer to the young officer, so that his nose was just a couple of inches from the other man's. 'Oh, I don't think I'm mistaken at all. And leaving aside what I'd like to do to a man who gets his pleasure from hurting women, I've a very good reason to believe you visited said establishment in the company of that other pig, Morrison. Why, Walters, would you be seen with that odious specimen? Do you like the idea of fornicating with children as well?'

'I . . . no. Never.' He looked away again. 'Not that.'

'But you knew Morrison. What dealings did you have with him?'

Walters took off his helmet and wiped sweat from his brow as he ran his hand through his thick, dark hair. 'Yes, all right. I knew Morrison. He was my company commander when I first arrived in Natal, and ended up the adjutant before, well . . . before retiring.'

'When did you come over?' Gregory asked.

'Last year, with the reinforcement drafts that came over after Isandlwana.' Walters raised an eyebrow. 'I understand you had experience of the engagement.'

Gregory gritted his teeth and searched the other man's eyes.

Walters sneered. 'Or do you not recall much of the battle, since I understand you departed rather early on in the piece?'

Gregory felt the vein in his temple start to pulse. It was clear Walters had known who he was all along. How much did he know of Gregory's mission? Gregory reached out with his left hand and grabbed Walters by the front of his tunic and drew back his right fist. Walters, damn him, just smiled back at him.

'Go on.' Walters' words were barely audible.

'Sir!' called a voice.

Gregory heard the footsteps and jangling kit of cavalry troopers heading his way.

'Peter,' Teresa cried.

Gregory felt like he might draw blood, so hard were his fingernails digging into his right palm.

Walters mouthed a single word. *Coward.*

Gregory thrust Walters away and felt ready to retch from the smell of hair oil and cologne, horse and leather, and the memory of slipping on the brains of a dead redcoat. He stood there, exhaling through his nostrils like a blown cavalry mount, and when he closed his eyes for a moment he heard the bellowing of terrified cattle, the useless rattle of Martini–Henry rifles and the drawn-out, menacing Zulu war cry. *U-su-thu. U-su-thu.*

'Everything all right, sir?' the big cavalry sergeant asked Walters as Gregory opened his eyes and managed to focus on the people around him.

Walters brushed down the front of his uniform jacket and put his helmet back on. 'All is well, Sergeant. Isn't that right, *Captain*?'

To his shame, Gregory felt a string of drool escaping the right side of his mouth and Walters grinned at him as he wiped it away with the back of his hand. 'I'll see you again,' he said to Walters.

Walters nodded and touched the brim of his helmet with the fingertips of his right hand in a mocking approximation of a salute. 'Oh, I don't doubt it. In fact, I almost look forward to it.'

'Peter, come.' Teresa took his left elbow in her hand, but he shrugged it off.

'And you, Miss Mary, Mary, quite contrary, I wish you well with your bird spotting and photography.'

Teresa glared at him, hands on hips.

'And a word of advice for you, Your *Ladyship*,' Walters said.

'You do me the honour of a title I don't have. What is your *advice*?' Teresa asked.

'I'm told the Empress Eugénie, for all her many charms, likes birds about as much as she likes nosey foreign journalists.'

'I'm sure I have no idea what you're talking about.'

Walters ordered his men to mount, then did so himself. As he wheeled his horse around, he paused and looked back at Gregory. 'The empress has ordered that no visitors or spectators are to infringe on her privacy. Especially a certain American journalist. Keep her away. I'm sure a man with your experience is good at keeping his distance, consorting with the camp followers.' Walters spurred his horse in the flanks and galloped off.

Gregory stood there, staring after him, hands clenched.

'I say,' Phillips came to his side – Gregory had caught sight of him earlier chatting to the cavalry troopers – 'that chap got out of bed on the wrong side this morning. What was the kerfuffle between you and him, sir?'

'Nothing.' Gregory saw that Phillips had a map in his hand. 'What were you and the troopers talking about?'

'Oh, they were just moaning. You know what soldiers are like. They're on this mission to escort the deposed Empress of France to visit her son's memorial, the place where Prince Louis was speared last year. Seems like they're taking a very circuitous route through the countryside.'

'Show me.' As Phillips unfolded the map, Gregory looked over to where Teresa was standing by the wagon. She was stowing her camera gear but caught his eye, then looked down. His look told her that he would deal with her later.

Phillips used his finger to trace the route. 'You see, from where we are, here, near Greytown, the most direct route to Nqutu, where the prince's memorial is, would be via Helpmekaar, then northeast through Rorke's Drift and Isandlwana. She'd no doubt want to see where the big battles were fought, but the cavalrymen said their commander's taking them on a merry detour to take in Kambula and

Hlobane. That'll add sixty or seventy miles to their trip over very inhospitable terrain.'

Gregory studied the map and scratched his chin. 'General Evelyn Wood's in charge of the empress's party. Lord Chelmsford gave him command of one of the first three columns to enter Zululand. While the world remembers the defeat at,' he swallowed, involuntarily, 'Isandlwana, Wood's force was thrashed on Hlobane Mountain a couple of months later. The next day, however, he had a major victory at Kambula. He's taking this route as much for himself as he is for the empress. From memory, Prince Louis travelled through that area, but you and those cavalry troopers are right – it's a big detour.'

Phillips glanced over at Teresa and lowered his voice. 'And Her Ladyship? The troopers said they'd been warned about a female journalist who's been chasing the empress.'

Gregory gave a slow nod. 'Our orders are to escort Lady Beecham, though her story that she's a friend of the empress appears to be cock and bull, Phillips.'

Phillips' face looked like he had just bitten into a lemon. 'Really? So, what do we do now, sir?'

Gregory pondered the chain of events. General Wood and the empress obviously knew of Teresa's presence in the country and her true identity and purpose – which Gregory was fairly sure now was some sordid journalist's quest to get an interview with – and a tintype image of – a grieving royal on the anniversary of her son's death. It almost beggared belief that a pushy scribe would hound a person in such a way, or go to such lengths to secure a picture of a royal person. What was the world coming to?

Teresa's eyes flitted towards him every now and then as she took her time packing. She was as cunning as she was attractive, and chameleon-like. She had probably purposefully lagged behind the official party like a hyena tailing a leopard, or a pack of hunting dogs, biding her time until she could pick up the morsels she needed to sustain herself. She, too, knew very well she was not welcome around the empress's campfire.

And what of his mission – or missions? Major Hellfire Jack Dartnell had not survived as long as he had in charge of the NMP without knowing how to play politics. He'd sent Gregory on a quest to find a missing sword and in the same breath he had assigned him this fool's errand, to escort an unwanted journalist across the unforgiving hills and valleys of wildest Zululand. His quest to find an emperor's missing sword was one of delicacy and secrecy, and the answer to its whereabouts – or where and how it had gone missing – would most likely be found in these same kloofs and dongas where the Prince Imperial had roamed and been killed, and where the sword had later been recovered. Escorting a meddling reporter would give Gregory just the cover story he needed to carry out the more important task, for his commander. Gregory allowed himself a smile at the major's cunning.

'Sir?' Phillips prompted.

Gregory drew a breath of clean air and reminded himself that he was not on the blood-soaked slopes of that cursed hill, but under a blue sky with the sun on his back, by a cool, clear mountain stream. 'Help Mathias erect the camp. We'll stay here tonight.'

Phillips looked to the sky, no doubt thinking it was far too early to stop, but Gregory's eyes confirmed that those were his orders. 'Very good, sir.'

Gregory walked to Teresa, who had finished packing her camera gear and was running a rope over the boxes. He came up behind her and put his hand on hers, stilling her movement. It was an overly familiar gesture, but she didn't try to remove her hand. Instead, she turned her face to his.

'I don't need to ask you the real purpose of your journey,' he said.

'I don't know what he was talking about . . .' Her protest died under his stare. She shrugged.

'You're not the empress's friend and she doesn't want you anywhere near her, does she?'

Teresa slipped her hand out from under his and stepped away from the wagon, and from him, and put her hands on her hips. 'So, what now? You going to abandon me here out in the wilds?'

He shook his head. 'No. You're going to help me.'

14

___

KWAZULU-NATAL, THE PRESENT

Sannie and Marilyn headed back to David Gregory's farm and game reserve. Sannie was driving and Marilyn had called the number Jan-Maree Ball had given her for David's head guide, John Parker.

'Turn right up ahead,' Marilyn said, checking the location of the pin John had sent her via WhatsApp.

Sannie followed a road that was tarred, but narrow and potholed. On their right ran a two-metre-high fence made of barbed wire and razor wire, topped with electrified strands. On closer inspection, Sannie could see that in some spots the electric wire was snapped and sagging, and here and there were gaps under the fence in places of rough terrain, such as where it crossed a washed-out donga. Some of the gaps were easily big enough for a poacher to crawl under. A kilometre further on they came to a sign announcing the entry to uBhejane Game Reserve.

'It means black rhino in Zulu,' Marilyn said.

Sannie nodded. The entrance was a substantial affair, two pillars clad in a decorative mosaic of rock, with a stout steel sliding gate in between. Beyond was a thatched portico and office. There was no one in sight.

173

Marilyn sent a message and Sannie honked the Fortuner's horn, in case there was a guard inside.

'John's on his way,' Marilyn said a minute later.

While she waited, Sannie checked her emails. There was one from Hudson Brand, a reply to a message she had sent, which she speed-read. All of the local farms that had lost cattle in the last six months, presumably to the 'Cheetah' gang, had been insured with the same company, and it was one that Hudson had worked with in the past. None of that was unusual or suspicious in itself – it would be logical for neighbouring farmers to share details of their brokers. She was just being thorough, and she was using Hudson as a short cut as she did not have time to deal with insurance agencies while she tried to get a handle on a murder. Hudson said in his email that his contact at the insurer was pulling the files for him and would send them through; he offered to take a look at them.

Sannie looked out the window. She could see now that the reserve was on its knees, just as they had heard. The main access point should have been manned twenty-four hours a day, but it was clear there was no security on duty. The thatch on the gatehouse had been pulled apart, probably by baboons, and there were gaping holes in the roof. Sannie opened her door, got out and stretched. It had been a busy first day in her new posting and she and Marilyn hadn't even checked in to their accommodation.

She checked her watch: half-past three. The sun was heading for a distant range of hills and its rays bathed the countryside in soft gold. There was a growl from a valley beyond the gatehouse and a green Land Rover came into view, black smoke puffing from the exhaust. John Parker, dressed in his uniform of khaki shorts and bush shirt, got out. He came to the gate and fiddled with a padlock, then heaved the sliding gate open.

'Come on in,' he said. 'I'll close up after you. The gate motor was stolen the other day.'

Sannie got in, drove through, then got out again.

As she watched John close the gate, she saw there were bags under his eyes and he sported three days' worth of stubble. His shorts needed a wash and had been darned where they had been ripped. When he turned, Sannie saw that the collar of his uBhejane uniform shirt was frayed. On his right hip he wore a holster with a tan-coloured Glock pistol in it.

'Follow me; I'll take you to camp,' he said.

Sannie got back into her car and followed the plume of smoke down the road.

'This place is falling apart,' Marilyn said.

Sannie nodded and moved her sunglasses from the top of her head onto her eyes, to cut down the glare from the afternoon sun. John led them to a camp called Fish Eagle Lodge, overlooking a river, and pulled up next to a parking area where the shade cloth roof hung down, tattered and faded.

'The camp's a little more than rustic these days,' John said as they got out of the Fortuner. 'I can get us a cup of tea or coffee. Or, if you like, I was just about to go out for a drive. There's not much else to do around here to keep one's sanity. I've got a cooler box with some drinks, and a flask of hot water.'

Sannie looked at Marilyn, who shrugged. 'Why not, boss?' Marilyn said. 'I've never actually been on a game drive.'

John looked surprised. 'Never?'

Marilyn frowned. 'We're not all rich Capetonians or cashed-up foreign tourists, you know. Some of us work for a living and I was too busy studying and busting criminals for most of my life to cruise around the bush looking at lions.'

'Sorry, I meant no offence, I . . .'

Marilyn grinned. 'It's all right. I'm only kidding.'

'A game drive sounds *lekker*,' Sannie said. 'You can give us a bit of a feel for the place while we see the sights.'

'All right. Climb aboard, ladies.'

John held out a hand and Marilyn let him help her up into the row of seats behind him, which surprised Sannie. She was normally fiercely independent and outspoken, as her cruel little joke had just proven.

'Why thank you, Mr Safari Guide,' Marilyn said.

Sannie took the seat next to Parker. Despite her comment, she was not here to sightsee and she had plenty of questions for the head guide. She took out her notebook.

'So, it's business as well as pleasure,' John said.

'Always, I'm afraid,' Sannie said. She took out a pen. 'How long have you worked here, John?'

He put the Land Rover in gear and took a rough road out of camp, climbing steeply from the river that roared through the valley behind them. 'Going on ten years now. It was my first job after I finished my bachelor's degree and got my guide's qualification. Originally, I thought I might do a couple of years here before moving on, but this place grows on you.'

'And David Gregory? How was he as a boss?'

John turned to stare at her – she had the feeling he could drive these roads blindfolded at night by the way he took a turn to the right without looking. 'He did not kill his rhinos.'

'That's not what I asked,' Sannie said.

John shifted his gaze forward again, and then right and left, looking for game without catching her eye. 'I guess he was like any boss. Some days you loved him, some days he drove you crazy, but he was committed to conservation above all else. That's why I stayed here so long.'

'Conservation above all else?' Sannie asked.

John nodded. '*Ja*, I'll give you an example. Near the river,' he pointed back over his shoulder with his thumb, 'David started growing some *Warburgia salutaris* – pepper bark trees. Have you heard of them?'

'Yes,' Sannie said. 'I worked in the Kruger for a while. There's a stand of them up north, near Punda Maria camp. The trees are endangered because there's a black market in them. We had them under armed guard, in case of poachers.'

'Serious?' Marilyn said from the back. 'Trees being guarded by rangers?'

John turned to look at her. 'The traditional healers market the bark as a treatment for cold and flu, and the unscrupulous ones claim it cures HIV-AIDS. Anyway, I found a leopard one day, hunting in among the trees, and this rich guest we had, from America, insisted that I drive off-road so she could get a close-up picture. We can drive off-road in most of the reserve, but not in that area, because of the endangered trees.'

'What happened?' Marilyn was leaning on the handrail in front of her bench seat, hanging off John's every word.

He took his eyes off the road long enough to smile back at her. 'I stood my ground and the tourist went to David after the drive – demanded to see him, and that he give her her money back. He told her to leave the reserve.'

'Really?' Sannie said.

Parker nodded. 'He made her and her husband pack their bags, and called the transfer company to come get her. She and her husband had booked for five nights and this was their first drive. He refunded their money and gave them their marching orders.'

Sannie was getting the same picture of David as she had from Richard Tustin and Jan-Maree Ball – that he'd been a rather irascible old man, with little time for people he didn't like, but there was no indication he would have resorted to killing his own wildlife for money. 'What was his position on the trade in rhino horn?'

'You mean, should it be legalised?' John asked.

'Yes.'

'He was for it, but that didn't mean he'd kill his rhinos because he was short of money. As anyone knows, you can dehorn a rhino without harming it.'

'Yes,' Sannie said, 'but you'd need a veterinarian present, someone qualified to dart and sedate the rhino and make sure it was OK, plus plenty of labour.'

'Agreed,' Parker said, 'but that doesn't mean David took a short cut and killed those animals. No way. David did think that private owners of rhinos should be allowed to sustainably remove their horns and sell them, and reinvest that money into anti-poaching and conservation.'

'And you?'

'I'm anti-trade,' Parker said. 'I don't believe in legitimising a phoney market. And there are so many myths about the uses of rhino horn that no one truly understands the actual level of demand. For example, rhino horn used to be shipped to Yemen, in the Horn of Africa, for use as dagger handles, but that market died out. The market in the sixties and seventies was fed by thousands of animals that were killed every year and their horns sold in China, other parts of Asia and Yemen. Yes, things are bad now, but these days it's a market that's fed by less than a thousand horns a year, most of it going to Vietnam. If anything, I think demand is slowly decreasing. Now is *not* the time to flood the market or send a message to the user countries that the trade is OK.'

Sannie nodded. It was an endless debate in South Africa and other African countries with rhinos – whether flooding the market with legally, sustainably sourced rhino horn would end poaching and the illegal trade in countries such as Vietnam, where horn was still prized as a status symbol and for its alleged medicinal properties.

'Everyone was quick enough to believe that *kak* that he killed his own rhinos,' John said. 'David would rather have starved than slaughter one of his own animals.'

'Where were you, John, when the rhinos were killed?' Marilyn asked.

He glanced back. 'I was on leave. It was the first time I'd been away from the reserve for more than a night for two years. I've been working flat out, even longer hours since David stopped paying for security and those idiots from WildForce left. With fewer and fewer guests coming to the reserve, there's been virtually no need for me to guide. I started working nights, pulling security shifts, and sleeping days.'

'Yet it was the night you were away that sixteen rhinos were killed. Coincidence? Or if someone other than David shot the animals, did they have inside information?' Sannie asked.

'All of the above,' John said. He thumped the steering wheel with his right fist. 'Hell, I don't know. Maybe one of the staff here was on the take, and let some of his buddies know I was away. But I doubt that, hey. Like me, just about everyone here has worked at uBhejane for years, and those of us who stayed did so because we love the place. David can barely pay any of us a living wage, but we have somewhere to sleep and something to eat.'

Before Sannie could ask another question, John held up a hand, cutting her off. 'Elephant.'

He stopped the Land Rover and turned off the engine.

Marilyn put her hand over her mouth. 'Oh. My. Word.'

Sannie smiled at her colleague's reaction. The big bull elephant had appeared as if by magic from a dense thicket of bush and was munching on a leaf-covered branch, which he gripped with his trunk. He was no more than ten metres away.

'Are we too close?' Marilyn whispered.

John grinned back at her. 'He's chilled. Isn't he beautiful?'

Marilyn opened her mouth to speak, but seemed to struggle to find words. 'That,' she said finally, her right hand on her heart, 'is the most amazing thing I've ever seen in my life.'

Sannie took out her phone, reversed the camera and leaned over her seat into the rear of the Land Rover so that she could get Marilyn, herself, and the elephant in a selfie. Marilyn shifted over to the left, the side where the elephant was, rested her elbows on the bodywork of the vehicle and her chin in her hands. Her smile lit up the picture.

'Can we go?' John asked.

'Just a few minutes more, please?' Marilyn said.

'Of course. Is it your first elephant, Marilyn?'

She nodded, and when Sannie looked back again she could see Marilyn was wiping a tear from her eye. She leaned over the centre console box in order to talk to John without disturbing Marilyn's rapture. 'There's a suggestion that robbery was a motive for the break-in at David's farmhouse, and his death.'

John shook his head. 'I doubt it. He didn't have any reserves of cash or jewellery or anything valuable in his safe. You could see it in the way he dressed, the beat-up old HiLux that he drove. He put any spare cash back into wildlife and keeping this place going; the farm was borderline subsistence, to keep him and his wife Zelda afloat, when she was still alive.'

'They had no children?'

'No,' John said. 'I know they tried. He used to say . . .' John cleared his throat and for a moment Sannie thought he might be about to cry. 'He used to say I was like the son he never had.'

'Really?'

'*Ja*.' He gave a little laugh. 'But in true David fashion that was good and bad. He thought he could treat me like a kid, ordering me to do menial shit and telling me off in a way you normally wouldn't if it was your staff. I'm sure that if he thought he could have got away with it, he would have beaten me. But he was capable of love, sometimes.'

Sannie thought for a moment about how to frame her next question. 'When will his will be read?'

John started the Land Rover's engine, not bothering to ask Marilyn if she was ready to leave the elephant sighting this time. Sannie had touched a nerve. He didn't answer until they were moving again, and when he did he looked straight ahead, not at Sannie.

'I don't know, and I don't care. Even if he decided to leave me the whole place, I wouldn't want it. We're too deep in debt, and there are too many mouths to feed. With a land claim hanging over the farm and reserve, no one would want to buy it.'

'I see.'

'Well *I* wouldn't mind being left all of this,' Marilyn said.

John stopped the Land Rover and turned back to her, his arm over the back of the middle seat. 'Marilyn, I'm sorry. I didn't even ask if you wanted to stay at the elephant sighting.'

Marilyn reached out and laid her hand on his forearm. 'It's OK. This must be a very stressful time for you. You're forgiven, John. Just this once.'

He smiled up at her. 'Thank you. I feel so privileged to have shown you your first elephant.'

'It was nice . . . but where are the lions?' Marilyn laughed.

'I'll do my best, for *you*.'

Goodness. Was her detective partner flirting with an interview subject? 'Let's move on,' Sannie said.

John drove off again, taking them in and out of one spectacular valley after another, over grassy hills punctuated with granite *koppies* and into deep, thickly vegetated gullies where Sannie fancied there were leopards peering out through the foliage at them. It felt good to be back in the bush and she realised that part of her missed wild places like this, since she had moved to the coast south of Durban.

The thought led her to Adam. To save her from contemplating her relationship she turned her mind to the case, and a link between her and her partner – the presence of WildForce.

'Tell me about WildForce.'

John seemed to think before answering. 'They started off just fine, and they were a godsend to David, because his revenues were way down. David was living hand-to-mouth before COVID came – he'd invested all his spare cash in upgrading the lodge and had taken out a bank loan as well. Forward bookings were looking good, but then the virus happened and it all fell away. I told him we should spend time during the lockdowns maintaining the camp, but he went into a kind of depression. It was all I could do to get him to wake up every morning. I did my best, with the staff, to keep the lodge in order, but the bush eats camps. There just wasn't the money to do essential maintenance, like painting the decks, fixing the thatch roofs. Slowly, the place began to crumble. When we did reopen, the TripAdvisor reviews all said things like: "tired", "in need of TLC", "friendly staff, but substandard accommodation".'

'Shame,' Marilyn said.

'David had to cancel the security contract, so WildForce arrived at just the right time,' John said. 'At first they went well, but then there was the business with the American guy who shot the intruder. And other stuff.'

Sannie made a couple of notes, but she knew most of this already. 'What sort of "other stuff"?'

John shrugged. 'Some of the volunteers would occasionally come and go in the middle of the night. They were working nights, often, because that's when rhino poachers are potentially more active, especially when there's a full moon, but a few times I heard vehicles moving about. One night I went to the gate and a couple of the Wild-Force guys were leaving in a *bakkie*. I asked them where they were going and Randy, the American who shot the poacher, said they were heading into town to find a bar. I told him that nothing would be open around here so late, but he dismissed me and told me they'd find somewhere, even if they had to go to a brothel.'

'You didn't believe them?' Sannie asked.

'Randy was a redneck. He'd made some frankly racist remarks and I had to tell him, and Major Tustin, that he needed to watch his language. Tustin did reprimand him, but it seemed odd that Randy was going out in the middle of the night looking for local women.'

'Do you think WildForce might have been involved in anything illegal?' Sannie asked.

Again, John took his time answering, keeping his eyes on the road ahead. 'They were an interesting bunch. When Tustin first came to the lodge, David and I met with him to discuss the work they'd be doing, and why it was important for the veterans. He said many of them were suffering from post-traumatic stress disorder, and that coming to Africa to train rangers or assist with anti-poaching would give them back a sense of purpose that they had been missing. Tustin also said they wouldn't be taking part in offensive operations – that is, they wouldn't be out hunting poachers or getting into gunfights. I pointed out to them that it would be illegal for the veterans, as foreigners, to own firearms here or use them as security guards. Of course, that all went out the window. And the PTSD thing was *kak*.'

Sannie nodded. 'Why do you say that, about PTSD?'

He held up a hand. 'Oh no, don't get me wrong. I know it's a real condition, but if Tustin's guys were suffering in any way, they had a funny way of showing it. I watched them training one day, on our shooting range here on the reserve. It was just them, and they didn't know I was watching. I parked up on a hill and checked them through my binoculars. It was like they were re-fighting the invasion of Iraq down there. They were doing vehicle ambush drills from a couple of their four-by-fours, fire and movement, snap shooting. They must have fired off about five or six hundred rounds between five of them.'

'Where did they get the weapons?' Marilyn asked from the rear seat.

'Not from us,' John said. 'We have a few old shotguns and David had a hunting rifle. I got a permit for an LM5. When Tustin told me his men wanted to go and shoot some targets, I thought they'd be taking turns with Randy's hunting rifle, which he'd brought from the States. I told them I would be busy guiding some clients on the other side of the reserve, but the clients were delayed so I had some time to kill. He didn't know that I'd be watching. They had AK-47s and pistols and they were firing like ammunition wasn't a problem. I couldn't believe my eyes – at one point they even threw a hand grenade and it went off. Where in hell they found that, I have no idea. I went to David and reported what I'd seen and he and Tustin had a big fight that night. I could hear the yelling from the farmhouse.'

'What happened then?' Marilyn asked.

'The veterans all packed up and left the next day and we've been without security here on the reserve ever since. I can't patrol the whole place myself – I don't have any money for fuel in any case. There are parts of this reserve that I haven't seen for weeks – months, even.'

'Stop! Look!' Sannie and John both turned to see Marilyn pointing off to the left.

'Zebra,' John said, seeing a small herd grazing on the side of a hill about fifty metres away.

'Yes, but no,' Marilyn said. 'Something just glinted, like sun reflecting off glass, or whatever, in those rocks over there.'

John turned the key, but there was just a click. 'Not now, baby!' he groaned. He tried again, but the engine refused to turn over.

They heard the *crack-thump* of a bullet cleaving the air and the Land Rover vibrated as something punched into the left front fender.

'Gunfire!' Sannie drew her Z88 pistol from the holster on her belt as she flung open the door of the Land Rover. 'Get out!'

Marilyn scrambled over the row of seats and started clambering down over the right-hand side of the game viewer. Another shot clanged into the body of the vehicle. A second weapon started firing – this time on full automatic. A burst of three shots rang out. Marilyn screamed, lost her grip and fell backwards off the Land Rover.

Sannie racked her Z88, pulling back the slide on top and letting it fly forward to chamber a round. She darted around the front bumper bar and scanned the hillside and rocks where Marilyn had been pointing, looking for targets.

John had dragged a green canvas gun bag from its cradle on the dashboard of his vehicle. He knelt in the grass next to the driver's side and undid the zip. From the bag he pulled his LM5, the semi-automatic civilian version of the South African Army's R5 assault rifle, and fitted a banana-shaped magazine into it.

Sannie crawled to Marilyn, who had her hand to her shoulder.

'I'm hit.' Marilyn's voice was calm but she was wide-eyed, as if she couldn't believe what had just happened to her.

John reached up into the vehicle, near where he'd been sitting, and grabbed a khaki fleece jacket, which he tossed to Sannie. 'There's a first aid kit in the back. I'll get it when I can.'

'Thanks.' Sannie caught the fleece, moved Marilyn's hand from the deep furrow the bullet had grazed on her right upper arm, and balled and pressed the jacket against it. 'Put your hand on this and keep pressure on it, Marilyn.'

'OK.'

'Give me your spare ammunition.' Marilyn patted her jeans pocket and Sannie pulled out a magazine.

Sannie popped her head up over the side of the game viewer to try and see the shooter, but she was answered by another burst of gunfire which raked the vehicle. One bullet zinged past her head. This was too hot for comfort.

'Who are they?' Marilyn cried, her voice rising in panic as the enormity of what had just happened began to sink in.

'I don't know,' John said. 'Poachers maybe?'

'Heavily armed,' Sannie said.

The land dropped away on the side of the road furthest from the gunmen. John slid down the bank a couple of metres, staying out of sight of them, then turned and crawled in the direction they'd been travelling, towards a couple of granite boulders. Sannie looked behind them and saw the same sort of feature. She copied what John had done.

She was breathing hard as she crawled, trying to stay calm and think. Two gunmen. Automatic rifles. They needed backup more than heroics. She lay on her back in the lee of the road and took out her phone.

'*Fok.*' There was no signal. She put the phone in her bra and started crawling again, until she reached a pinkish granite rock. She heard gunfire, but this time it was from their side. She looked past the Land Rover, further along the road, and saw that John had risen up on one knee behind the rocks. He pumped three rounds in quick succession towards the shooters.

Sannie could see another good firing position across the road, on the same side as the gunmen. The cluster of boulders was halfway up the hill towards them.

'Cover me! Sannie drew a deep breath and stood as John pulled the trigger five more times. She sprinted across the road and up the hill. Legs and arms pumping, she imagined the hammer blow of a bullet hitting her at any moment. She was breathing hard as she slid into the ground at the base of the boulders.

When she carefully raised her head above the boulders, she could clearly see one of the men who had been firing at them. He was wearing camouflage fatigues and a black ski mask and he was exposed, side-on to her. John's barrage must have taken the men by surprise, because the man she was looking at seemed to have no idea she was there – they must have had their heads down when she ran.

Sannie took Marilyn's spare ammunition from her pocket and put one of the magazines on the rock. She brought her pistol up, laid her arm on the smooth, warm surface of the boulder, took aim and fired.

Once, twice, three times the Z88 bucked in her hand, but she squeezed the trigger slowly each time. It was long range for a handgun, more than fifty metres, but just as the man finally worked out where her fire was coming from and turned towards her, one of her nine-millimetre rounds hit him in the chest and knocked him backwards.

Sannie saw a flash of movement down the hill and realised John was up and advancing. She fired off the rest of her magazine into the rocks where she knew the other shooter was still hiding. She saw an arm, and a glimpse of camouflage as the man shifted, perhaps away from her fire.

John was firing on the run as he made for another cluster of rocks.

Show yourself, she willed the man, then yelled to John: 'Magazine!'

Sannie thumbed the release button on her Z88 and the empty magazine slid out. She rammed Marilyn's extra one into the hand-grip, let the slide fly forward, and started firing again.

John went to ground and the remaining gunman fired another burst of automatic fire towards him. The rifleman obviously couldn't risk taking a shot at her; she had successfully outflanked him, and in order to shoot at her he would have to expose himself, like his comrade who lay bleeding and moaning in the grass.

'Police, put down your gun!'

Her words only prompted more firing from the rocks.

Sannie looked for a way to get further up the hill, and behind him. There was some dead ground, a shallow and dry gully, which probably ran like a mini waterfall during the wet season. It snaked down the hill towards her. She would have to cross about twenty metres of open grass to get to it, but once in the depression she could crawl uphill, out of sight of the shooter.

She called out her plan, in Afrikaans, to John.

'*Verstaan*,' he replied. He understood. John started firing.

Sannie got up. If the man shooting at them also spoke Afrikaans, then this would be his cue to shift position so he could get a shot at her.

Sannie tensed again, then ran for the gully. John was firing, but all she could hear now was her blood pounding in her ears. She thought of her children, Ilana, Christo and Tommy, and how unfair it would be on them if she was shot dead on some hillside in KwaZulu-Natal. She pictured Adam, and wished she'd tried harder.

The lip of the depression was just ahead of her, the eroded soil promising temporary protection.

As she ran, she looked over and found she could now see the remaining gunman. He might have heard her, because he moved his head. She raised her right hand and took a snap shot at him, but her bullet went wide.

The man dropped his rifle.

Hell. Was he about to surrender? She could not shoot an unarmed man, even though he'd wounded Marilyn and been doing his best to kill her and John a second ago. Sannie lowered her aim. 'Face down! On the ground.'

She came to the edge of the donga and leapt over the rim. It was like a shallow trench, and as she was still standing, she could keep an eye on the man. He was reaching into the lower pocket on his military-style tunic.

'Hands where I can see them,' she called.

He was looking at her through the eyeholes of his ski mask. He raised both hands and she shifted her pistol so that she could cover him.

'Cease fire, John.' She glanced down the hill and saw the ranger edging up towards them, his rifle still up and in the ready position.

The man in the uniform drew back his right arm and Sannie could now see, for the first time, that he was not empty-handed. He hurled a green orb towards her, then ducked. Sannie's brain tried to comprehend what she was seeing. It did not seem possible.

'Down!' She squeezed off two shots at the man, who had ducked out of sight among the rocks.

The hand grenade hit the ground in front of her, bringing up a puff of dust, then skipped and rolled through the grass until it toppled over the edge of the dry watercourse and landed about three metres downhill from her.

Sannie scrambled up over the edge of the gully, in the direction she'd just come from, ran a few paces then threw herself to the ground.

Her last thought was, again, of her children.

15

KWAZULU-NATAL, THE PRESENT

Adam dressed for war.

Living in Pennington on the subtropical KwaZulu Natal south coast, his winter wardrobe was almost non-existent, but Sannie had bought him a long-sleeve green T-shirt with the North Face logo in black, so he put that on. He pulled on long black track pants, then strapped on a belt, with his diving knife scabbard threaded onto it.

Marilyn had called him with the news. The thought of Sannie and what had happened to her made him bite his lower lip.

Adam pulled the cork from a near-dead bottle of red wine, drank the dregs, and then used the cigarette lighter he kept by the gas burner on the *stoep* of his tent to set fire to the cork. He let it burn a few seconds then blew out the flame and rubbed the still-warm end in streaks up and down his face. When he was satisfied with his camouflage he rubbed black into the backs of his hands and pulled a black beanie over his grey-blond hair.

Adam stood on the *stoep*, listening to the night sounds and, with the light off, he gave his eyes time to adjust to the darkness. Frogs croaked and he heard the hoot of a spotted eagle owl. A predator, just as he had once been.

189

His phone, on silent, vibrated in his pocket. He took it out and looked at the screen. It was Marilyn.

He answered her call. 'How are you?'

'I wish I could say fine. I'm on painkillers, but I feel like I was run over by a taxi. Before you ask, Sannie's still sedated.'

Adam pinched his eyes with the thumb and forefinger of his free hand. '*Ja*, when I spoke to him the doctor said they'd keep her knocked out until tomorrow.'

'She's *alive*, Adam, and she's tough. The doctor was in the army in the bad old days, in your war. He knows what he's doing. He said that the fact the grenade went off in the donga, and that Sannie had thought to lie flat, saved her life. There's nothing broken on her body, but he did pick some small bits of grenade casing out of her. He's more worried about traumatic brain injury, though he says her vital signs are good.'

Adam swallowed. He needed to keep his emotions in check for what he was about to do, but the thought of her lying in a hospital bed, unconscious, was almost too much for him to bear.

'I know you want to be here, by her side,' Marilyn said, before he could say it himself. 'But we have work to do, you and me.'

'How's your arm?' he asked.

'I'm getting out of here as soon as I can. I want to get these bastards, Adam.'

'Me as well.'

'Sannie wouldn't want you to do anything stupid. You know that.'

'Yes.'

'Ah, but me and the colonel, we don't think alike all the time. We know from Tustin, their boss, that he has men at Bhanga Nek, supposedly on holiday. I think that is *kak*.'

Adam couldn't hold back a smile at her straight shooting. 'I think it was one of them who shot my student with a spear gun.' They had already traded messages on WhatsApp, and Adam had let Marilyn know that he'd rushed Jenny to the Manguzi provincial hospital with a spear sticking through her left arm. He'd bandaged the spear in place and she had been incredibly brave on the bumpy drive from the coast to the nearest big town. It was probably just as well that he had to transport her – it would have taken hours for an ambulance to get to them – because otherwise he would have stormed the veterans' camp like a one-man assault force.

'We need proof it was them who attacked you and Jenny. And you need to get it, Adam.'

The mention of Jenny's name brought up an inner tide of guilt that almost hurt. Sannie had been right about not putting his students at risk. He'd messed up, and all because of his curiosity. He needed to make this right, for Jenny and for Sannie. Adam had ordered Thabo to return to his home in Durban, so he, at least, was safe. 'OK. Did you have any info on the men who attacked you?'

'The man Sannie shot was black, but he was wearing what appear to have been US Army–pattern camouflage fatigues,' Marilyn said. 'These guys were armed with AK-47s and hand grenades. The local cop tried to suggest they were rhino poachers, and he brushed me off when I reminded him that David Gregory had supposedly killed all his rhinos. You don't take an assault rifle and a grenade if you're hunting impalas. The police are going to ask around, and talk to Tustin. *I'm* going to talk to him as soon as I get out of hospital, even though I was warned not to.'

'You were?'

'Yes. One of the local detectives is investigating the shooting, but it's a mess here. Their boss, Captain Le Roux, seemed like a good guy, but he's about to leave for New Zealand so no one's in charge here. I've been told, supposedly because I'm now a witness and a victim of crime, that I need to back off.'

'Are you going to?' Adam asked.

'No way. But for your part, you need to check out those guys who attacked you.'

There was a link between all of this. Sannie had been sure of it. Adam could see the way Marilyn's thinking was headed.

'Tustin and his crew are up to something,' Marilyn said. 'I don't believe they're at Bhanga Nek to go snorkelling and looking for Nemo.'

'Agreed,' Adam said.

'Find them, Adam. Work out what they're up to and we'll get them, for Sannie. We'll –'

He felt and shared her rage, but she didn't need to finish her sentence. 'I understand, Marilyn. If you don't hear from me by morning, tell the local cops I went to the municipal camping ground here at Bhanga Nek.'

'Affirmative,' Marilyn said.

She understood. If he didn't call, he would be dead.

AFTER SHE HUNG up from her call with Adam, Marilyn got out of bed and dressed.

A nurse walked into her room. 'What are you doing, Miss Msani?'

'I'm leaving. I've got work to do.'

'But Doctor said you must stay here under observation, at least for tonight, and . . .'

Marilyn took her pistol from the bedside table, and the act of sliding it into her holster silenced the poor nurse. Marilyn had the keys to Sannie's Fortuner, which a police officer had brought to the hospital. It was after five and she walked out into the golden light of late afternoon she took out her phone, checked her WhatsApp contacts, and called Captain Derick le Roux.

'Marilyn, are you in hospital still?'

'I just checked myself out. I'm fine.'

'Sergeant Nyathi called me to tell me about the attack at the game reserve. I phoned the hospital just now and they gave me an update on Sannie. I'd come and visit, but my wife and I are literally packing up the last of our things now. We're driving to Joburg tomorrow and then we're flying out. But I feel terrible to be leaving things like this,' Le Roux said.

'It's fine, Captain. I need George Tshabalala's number.'

'Of course, I'll WhatsApp it to you. Do you think he might have been involved in the attack on you?'

'Do you?' Marilyn replied.

There was a pause on the other end of the line. 'I thought he was mostly just bluster, but there was the business of the rival councillor who was killed. George has made no secret of the fact that he wants Virginia Farm and uBhejane Game Reserve.'

'Yes, but would he have taken out a hit on us, and if so, why?'

'Maybe he thought you and Sannie were getting too close to something.'

'We would have spoken to him at some point,' Marilyn said, 'based on what you told us in the briefing. I need to talk to him.'

'You need backup, Marilyn. Listen, I can talk to my wife. Maybe I can come meet you. Are you planning on confronting Tshabalala in person?'

'I am, Captain. But I'm a big girl. I can look after myself.'

'I'm sure of that, Marilyn, but I'd feel terrible if –'

'It's OK, Captain. Thanks for the offer. Please just send the number.' Marilyn ended the call and a few seconds later her phone dinged. She got into Sannie's car and made another call.

'Hello?'

'George Tshabalala?'

'This is he.'

Marilyn introduced herself and said: 'I'd like to come and ask you some questions.'

'Of course you would.' He gave a small laugh. 'I've been waiting for your call. I heard you and your colleague were in town. Nothing gets past me. I assume you want to talk to me about the killing of the rhinos on David Gregory's farm, and presumably his murder.'

'What makes you say that?' Marilyn asked.

'Come now, Warrant Officer Msani, you must know the answer to that. Because I'm African, you and your police colleagues will automatically profile me as a rhino poacher and criminal. Your whole organisation is still trapped in the era of apartheid stereotypes.'

'Whatever,' Marilyn said. 'Where can we meet?'

He gave her an address in the industrial area outside of Dundee and, using her phone, it took Marilyn less than ten minutes to find him. She pulled up outside the gates of a large compound and warehouse that had *Tshabalala Transport* on a sign out the front. Marilyn told a security guard on the gate who she was there to see, and he let her through.

The yard was filled with large lorries. Some were hitched to trailers made for transporting coal, while others were for bulk goods. There were also two water tankers. Marilyn knew that some businessmen made money from the poor state of the infrastructure in South Africa. In KwaZulu-Natal much of the railway network had yet to be repaired following damaging floods several years earlier, and trucks were carrying minerals that had previously been transported by trains. Likewise, the poor state of water pipes in some areas meant that companies were being paid by the government to deliver drinking water to some municipalities.

George Tshabalala – she recognised him from the picture on Le Roux's briefing wall – walked out of the warehouse and greeted her.

'*Sawabona, sisi*,' he said as he extended a hand.

'I'm not your sister,' she replied in Zulu, 'I'm Warrant Officer Marilyn Msani.'

He laughed. 'OK, we'll play it by the book. But unless you're going to arrest me, I can give you five minutes. I've just closed up and I'm already late for a meeting with the mayor. We can talk while we walk to my car.'

He led her around the warehouse towards a shiny black Ineos Grenadier.

'Imported from England. Cost me nearly two million,' he said.

The watch on his wrist looked like a Rolex. He wore a Lacoste shirt and matching white trainers. None of it impressed Marilyn, even though the businessman seemed to think it would.

'Is that a good look for a politician, a so-called man of the people?'

He smiled. 'Come now, Warrant Officer. You should be applauding me for wanting to help uplift my fellow South Africans. Is it a crime for an African man to be successful?'

'No. Where were you –'

He held up a hand. 'Let me save you some time, Marilyn. I have rock-solid alibis for the dates and times when David Gregory's rhinos were killed and when he was killed. I was at an ANC conference for one – there is even television footage of me there – and in Pietermaritzburg in the party office, in a meeting, for the other. And no, as far as I know, no one employed by me, related to me or in any other way associated with me was present at either of those crime scenes.'

'It's Warrant Officer Msani,' she said again. 'And how do you know?'

He grinned. 'Because I know everything that happens in this town.'

'Then who killed David Gregory and shot his rhinos?'

He laughed. 'Well, almost everything. That's your job. But it wasn't me or my people. I'm a councillor and a respected businessman, Warrant Officer. Why would I jeopardise that over some rhino horn or a cantankerous old white man? Gregory was bankrupt and it was only a matter of time before his farm and game reserve came up for auction, or my claim on it was upheld. Either way, it is going to be redistributed to the people.'

'By "the people", Mr Tshabalala, do you mean you?'

He put his hands together and looked to the now darkened sky. 'The Lord helps those who help themselves.'

She looked around the yard at the rows of parked trucks. A thought crossed her mind. 'Do you transport cattle?'

'I transport anything and everything that makes money. Wait a minute . . . are you going to pin the local stock theft crime wave on me as well?'

'You'd be happy to provide me with a list of all your vehicles and their registration numbers?'

He shrugged. 'I don't see why not. I have nothing to hide. Call my office in the morning, and my secretary, Phumzile, will help you.' He looked at his watch. 'But now I must go, for cocktails with the mayor. Would you like to come with?'

She shook her head. Marilyn had no grounds to arrest him. Not yet, anyway. She took out her phone and began walking around the compound, taking a picture of every truck she saw and their registration plates. She would call Tshabalala's secretary, but she also wanted to make sure that she and her boss didn't leave any numbers out.

ADAM CREPT through the band of thick jungle behind the sand dunes that lined the beach. He could hear the surf's roar off to his right and the continuous rumble helped mask the sound of his movement, though he watched every footfall.

If it had been two of the veterans from the camp who had ambushed him in the water and shot Jenny, then they would know that he would be coming for them. He'd noted that Andy, their leader, was in camp when Adam flew past in the *bakkie*, Jenny sitting pale-faced beside him. Andy had raised a hand and given a half-smile as Adam accelerated along the sandy road.

On the way back from the hospital he'd noted that they were still there, and in greater numbers, though he couldn't be sure if any of them were the divers he'd fought with. Adam was glad, though, that he'd made the decision not to tell the police his theory that the veterans were responsible for hurting Jenny and cutting him. He'd had his own wound, which looked worse than it was, seen to at the hospital when he had dropped Jenny off. The cops – if they'd had the resources to travel to Bhanga Nek – might have spooked the campers into moving on. Adam wanted time to search for more evidence, and a chance to get even.

He heard the sound of a vehicle and ducked into the deep shadows of the foliage. It was a *bakkie*, and as it slowly cruised past, Adam saw that it had the camouflage vinyl wrap livery of WildForce printed on it. A man drove with one hand and swung a hand-held spotlight with the other, sweeping the trees and bushes. Adam was certain now that they were expecting him.

That was fine with him.

He carried on, moving past the camping ground, which was on his left across the sand road. Adam moved to the very edge of the green belt and knelt down. He watched the camp.

Voices carried through the night and he saw the flicker of a campfire in the centre of the circle of evenly spaced green tents. A man walked past the flames and Adam saw the glint of firelight on glass. He was holding a bottle and topping up drinks. Two more men were seated around the fire. Adam heard the tinkle of ice. Someone laughed. They were getting merry, cocksure of themselves, their faith in the roving patrol in the *bakkie*.

Adam thought about what he would do if he was in their situation. The vehicle, he decided, was mostly cosmetic, a show of force and a presence patrol. He would have had sentries posted on the perimeter, in the dark. From what he could see there were three men talking around the fire, though they were too far away for him to make out what they were saying.

There had been four on the rubber boat when Adam had first encountered them. Adam counted the tents. There were six. So far he'd seen four men, but if there was one man per tent then two more were out there, somewhere in the dark.

Adam searched for the best way to approach the camp. The track swung around to the left, inland. If he followed it around the bend he could cross without being seen by anyone in the camp. From that direction a finger of uncleared bush and undergrowth extended almost all the way to the tents, so he could move through there and get closer to the encampment without being seen.

He dropped to all fours and started crawling.

The leaves and dry deadfall in front of him rustled and shook. Adam stopped. Something, perhaps a rat or even a large lizard or snake had just moved across his front. There was danger here in many forms. He took it slow to avoid making any noise, and reminded himself that he was in his natural element, here on the coast of KZN – his enemy was not.

Adam raised his head a little and sniffed the air. He smelled tobacco smoke. He dropped even lower and leopard-crawled as he closed on the bend in the road. The odour became stronger.

He lifted his torso again and saw a small flare of light illuminate some low branches.

There was a man there, sitting in the jungle on *his* side of the road, smoking a cigarette.

Adam had been right – Andy had been smart enough to post a sentry, some distance down the road from the camp, and covering the blind spot Adam had chosen for his infiltration. But, as per the drinking and merriment around the campfire, this man was also sure of himself and perhaps too relaxed.

Fuck them.

Adam waited a few moments, watching the man, who stubbed out his cigarette and raised both hands over his head, stretching. He was tired, or bored, and probably wanted to get back to the party.

Adam eased himself into a crouch, looked at the sentry and then in the other direction, then crossed the road, bent low at the waist. Once on the other side he made for the line of bushes and dropped into them. He paused, listened, watched and waited. No one had seen him.

He figured now that there must have been a lookout posted at the other end of the camp, somewhere in the bush towards the research camp. Adam had been right to move through the thickest part of the dune-side vegetation, because he must have bypassed the other guard.

The bush here was not as thick, so Adam continued to leopard-crawl forward, ensuring his head stayed just below grass height. Away from the coastal breeze the air was still, heavy and warm. He paused to wipe sweat from his eyes.

All of his senses were alert and on edge and he realised he had not truly felt this alive since his days on missions inside Angola in the 1980s. The sounds of the African bush were chillingly similar, even though here he was a stone's throw from the Indian Ocean, whereas in Angola he'd been surrounded by harsh, baking sandveld.

The oily yet enticing smell of *boerewors* sizzling over hot coals made his stomach rumble and he heard laughing. The talking was louder, and he picked up snippets: a joke about a woman, and a mention of 'fucking Afghan', as the British referred to Afghanistan.

Adam crawled closer, then lay still, not more than three metres from the rear of a tent. He was close enough to feel the warmth of the fire. Andy sat in a green canvas director's chair. Adam saw the distinct silhouette of an AK-47 with its curved magazine resting beside the chair. What kind of camper kept an assault rifle by his side?

He heard a chime and the hiss of a radio call. '*Niner, this is two, over.*'

Andy unclipped a handheld radio from his belt. 'This is niner, go.'

'*Niner, can I come back to the fire? I'm getting bloody murdered by mosquitoes and there's no one out here, over,*' said a voice with an English accent.

The other two around the fire laughed. 'Tell him to fucking harden up, Andy,' one said.

Andy held up a hand. 'Two, this is niner, quit your honking, mucker. I'll get loudmouth here to come relieve you in fifteen.'

The man who had joked scrunched an aluminium beer can and threw it on the fire.

'Stop fucking about.' Andy's voice was low but commanding. 'We know he's out there. We've just got to sit this out for two more nights.'

'What about the cops?' the third man asked Andy.

'Remember that cop we slotted in Yemen?' One of the men laughed.

Their leader shrugged. 'Nothing we can do about them, and it was just as well we all happened to be going for a long bushwalk when that detective came snooping around the camp earlier.' He laughed. 'Besides, we're just a bunch of innocent holidaymakers at the seaside, right?'

The man also chuckeld, but it contained no mirth. 'Yeah, I suppose so.'

Adam thought about what had just been said. It sounded like Andy and the others had hidden in the bush when Detective Mkhizi had come to pay them a visit. Perhaps they had seen the undertaker's van and the police vehicle arrive and decided to make themselves scarce.

'Look,' Andy said, 'the DPVs are well hidden, and your camo wetsuits are at the bottom of the ocean. There's nothing the cops can find to link us to what happened, even if they do come back looking for us. We've got what we wanted.' He leaned forward in his chair and slapped his hand on something, but Adam's view was obscured. 'All we need to do is sit tight and wait for the next shipment, if it comes. None of this shit would've happened if those Saudi idiots hadn't drowned.'

Moving on his elbows, toes and knees, Adam reversed back into the foliage. He decided he would crawl further around to the right of the clearing, to get a better view. Once deeper into the bush he could raise himself up onto all fours and crawl faster. His progress was checked, however, by a man-made mound covered in a brown waterproof tarpaulin, which had then been layered with palm fronds and cut branches.

Methodically, he removed the improvised camouflage and lifted the tarpaulin. Underneath it he found a cache of half-a-dozen waterproof plastic cases. He flipped the locks on the first one. Inside there was a drone, a large four-rotor commercial model. He snapped a picture of it with his phone. There was another identical crate underneath, which he assumed carried a second drone.

He opened a different-sized case and found small cardboard boxes stacked inside. He lifted one out. On it was printed *ammunition 7.62x39*. These, he knew, were rounds for the AK-47s Andy and his men were toting. According to Marilyn, the men who fired at her and Sannie had been using the same kind of rifle. He took another picture, then closed up.

Adam gritted his teeth and tried to keep his anger in check as he opened a third crate, which was smaller than the others. Inside, in protective cylindrical containers, were eight M26 hand grenades, with their igniter assemblies stowed separately. The outside of the case was marked *SANDF*. These grenades had been stolen from, or sold by, someone within the South African National Defence Force. Adam thought of Sannie, lying in hospital.

After taking a third picture, he removed two grenades from their cases and then screwed in the other component, consisting of the lever, pin and fuse. Lazy campers had tossed rubbish into this stretch of bushland and Adam extracted a plastic Shoprite shopping bag from a tangle of weeds. He put the two armed grenades and all the remaining igniters into the bag. Amid the crates he also saw the two dive propulsion vehicles that the men who attacked him underwater had been using. Adam took pictures of these as well.

Adam crawled to a position where he could get a better view of Andy and the men around the fire. He checked his watch. It was fifteen minutes since he'd heard the radio call, and the sentry Adam had bypassed came strolling up the coastal sand road, his AK-47 balanced on his right shoulder, a fresh cigarette in his left hand.

'I hope you weren't fucking smoking while you were on picquet,' Andy said.

The man dragged on his cigarette and exhaled. ''Course not, I'm a professional, aren't I?'

Andy scoffed. 'Fucking TA Bootneck more like it.'

Adam thought a moment. TA was an abbreviation for Territorial Army, the old name for Britain's military reserve force, and a Bootneck, he knew, was slang for a Royal Marine. This group was not what they pretended to be – a group of troubled war veterans, looking for salvation by helping Africa's endangered wildlife.

But why were they here? And what was the 'shipment' that Andy had mentioned?

Adam lay in the undergrowth, watching and listening, but the men in front of him had lapsed into a contemplative or semi-drunken silence as they stared into the campfire. A mosquito buzzed around Adam's ear, and even though he could feel it land and start to drink from his temple, he didn't dare lift a hand to swat it.

A rustling noise next to him sounded as loud as a herd of zebras galloping past him. He slowly turned his head and saw it was a mouse, scratching about in the plastic bag he had used to transport the grenades and ignitors. There must have been some food remnants in the bag.

Andy shot up and looked around, staring into the bush in Adam's direction.

'What was that?' one of the other men asked.

Andy left his chair and walked towards Adam, between two of the canvas tents. He had his rifle half up, his right hand curled around the pistol grip. Andy peered into the gloom, and when one of the others started to say something he held up his hand for silence.

Adam held his breath as Andy took two steps towards him.

The mouse continued its scratching, but when Andy kept walking the light behind him cast a shadow, which fell over Adam and the rodent. The movement startled the little animal, which ran off into deeper cover. Andy paused at the very edge of the clearing, no more than two metres from Adam. If he looked down and to his right, he would surely see him lying there.

Adam's knife was in the scabbard on his belt and he could not reach for it without making a sound. All he could do was stay still.

Andy scanned the dense vegetation, then swung his AK-47 around and slung it over his right shoulder. He unzipped his camouflage fatigue trousers, pulled out his penis and started urinating. Adam closed his eyes; he felt the tiniest droplets of liquid bounce onto him from the leaves that Andy was splashing. Adam turned his face slowly so that his nose was in the sand.

Eventually, Andy zipped up, turned and walked back to the fire.

Adam eased his face up and looked at the campfire again. He let his pent-up breath escape slowly through his lips. That had been too close. He had what he needed; it was time for him to pull back, return to his base and call the police. Marilyn's vengeful words rang in his ears, but these guys were toting an arsenal of weaponry – too much for one man to take on. Besides, he had enough evidence with the pictures of the grenades and the ammunition to get the police involved.

Adam started to ease his way backwards.

'Check the cache,' Andy said to one of his men. 'And prime a couple of grenades. We'll string some tripwires out in case anyone comes snooping. That way we can turn in and get some sleep.'

Shit. Adam froze again, watching as the foot soldier stood, picked up his rifle and started walking towards him. He avoided the area where Andy had pissed – thankfully, as it took him further away from where Adam was lying – but he would reach the hidden store of equipment in a matter of seconds. He was clomping through the bush behind Adam, which also cut off Adam's escape route through the finger of vegetation. The fact that he had tampered with the grenades was about to be discovered sooner than he had hoped, so his plan needed to change - quickly.

Andy also stood and went to a parked HiLux. From the rear tray he took a plastic tackle box and, from that, he extracted a roll of fishing line. This was what they would use to string a booby-trap trip-wire. The problem for Adam now was that he was *inside* their camp and needed to get out, and away. Once they discovered the grenades missing there was no telling what they would do. There were innocent Ezemvelo parks staff at the research base. If these thugs decided to mount an armed attack, there would be bloodshed. Adam had no idea why Sannie had been attacked – it seemed like she was only in the earliest stages of her investigation – but it sounded like whoever had shot at Sannie, Marilyn and the lodge manager had been intending on leaving no witnesses.

Adam looked to the campfire again. Andy and the other man with him were preoccupied, rolling out fishing line around the perimeter of their encampment. The man who had walked past him was continuing on to the ammunition cache.

Adam took the two primed hand grenades from the plastic shopping bag and stuffed one into each of his pants pockets. He grabbed the handful of igniters and tossed them far into the bush. He drew his knife, brought himself up into a crouch and, bent double, ran to the nearest HiLux *bakkie*. In the rear he saw a red plastic container, the fuel tank for an inflatable boat. Adam lifted it out and stabbed it. As he withdrew the blade of his knife he let the petrol gush out into the back of the vehicle, then sloshed fuel into the cab and down the driver's side door. As he backed away from the truck he tipped the remaining fuel in a thick trail along the grass and sand.

Adam heard the noise of an engine. He tossed the empty fuel container and ducked down behind the vehicle he had just doused. The smell of petrol was strong in his nostrils.

Headlights swept the camp, but the vehicle pulled up next to Andy and his offsider, some twenty metres from where Adam was, close to the campfire. Things were about to go bad, and Adam would need to make himself scarce, but there was one more thing he wanted to check.

Adam stayed low, using the *bakkie* to shield him from view, and went to the long, plastic storage case that he had first seen on the sunken boat. It was lying in the sand in front of where Andy had been sitting, in the open. Adam knelt and unclasped the one remaining snap lock that he had been unable to prise off when he was diving. He opened the lid.

Inside, sitting on a mass of unravelled bubble wrap, was a sword. It had been drawn from a scabbard, which lay underneath. Adam sheathed his knife and picked up the sword. The blade was about a metre long, and curved, and its hilt was inlaid with a red precious stone on the pommel. Its sheath was also decorated. He thought of the Koran he had salvaged. Were these precious antiques from the Middle East? Were they really worth killing for?

'Andy?' Adam heard the call from the hidden stash in the bushes. 'Boss, someone's been here! The grenades –'

'What?' Andy called.

Adam picked up the sword, backed away from the floodlit circle and turned towards the nearest tent. Carelessly, one of the veterans had left an AK-47 propped against the canvas. Adam snatched it up. He needed to get to his vehicle and get the hell out of Bhanga Nek, but he also had to distract his pursuers, who now knew he was in their midst.

He headed back to the fire as voices called in the night around him, and picked up a burning piece of wood. He tossed it in the direction of the Toyota. The fuel trail lit up, like a fast-moving fuse, and raced towards the *bakkie*. The pool of petrol in the rear tray ignited with a dull *whump* and a second later the whole vehicle was ablaze.

Andy and the others, and the roving vehicle, were blocking Adam from getting back to the research base, so he decided to run away from the camp, retracing his path to the bend in the road, then he'd cross over into the belt of jungle behind the dunes and make his way to the surf. He could then run down the beach, or even get into the ocean and swim to the point where his tent and vehicle were. As plans went, it wasn't a good one, but it was all he could think of.

He heard the roar of the other vehicle behind him as the driver accelerated. When Adam glanced to his right he saw that Andy was in the back, and had the hand-held spotlight. He swung it in an arc and caught Adam.

'There!' Andy pointed.

Another man, next to Andy, opened up with an AK-47 on full automatic.

Adam stumbled, tripped and landed hard, but the fall probably saved him as a burst of rounds sailed over his head, sending a shower of shredded leaves and twigs down over him. Adam crawled for his life. There was no point trying to make a heroic stand – he was outgunned.

The *bakkie* stopped and Andy swept the bush with the light, looking for him.

Ahead of Adam was the gang's Zodiac inflatable boat, the big outboard on the transom, mounted on a trailer for ease of launching. If they had another shipment to deal with, then Adam assumed that would be on the water. He imagined that their plan was to rendezvous with another smuggler's boat.

'*Fok jou*,' he whispered.

Adam rammed the sword tip into the ground and slung the rifle. He took a grenade from his pocket and pulled the pin. He held on to it as the lever flew off, then he stood, retrieved the sword, and ran, grenade in hand. As he expected, Andy picked him out and the HiLux roared into action again, the engine screaming as the vehicle hit soft sand and slowed.

The man with the AK opened up again, but the vehicle was jolting as the driver probably tried to find low range. His bullets went wide.

As Adam brushed past the black rubber flank of the Zodiac he let go of the grenade and it rolled into the boat. He carried on, arms and legs pumping, and when he had made it another thirty metres he dived headlong into the undergrowth.

'He's down again,' Andy yelled.

The driver had the measure of the soft ground now and Adam heard the vehicle closing on him, faster now, as he lay flat, counting down the seconds. He hoped he'd got his timing right.

The hand grenade detonated with a thump that shook the ground, just as the HiLux passed the boat.

Adam felt a storm of debris – dirt, sand, rocks and bits of fragmented metal – wash over him in a blast wave that knocked the air from his lungs momentarily. He heard screaming and swearing and a second later he was on his feet, running again.

'Stop . . .' Andy coughed, 'stop him!'

Adam forced air back into his lungs and kept going, jumping over tree roots. Branches slapped his face and torso and a couple of times he nearly fell again. He didn't look around to see how much damage he had caused.

He crossed the road, headed along one of the access paths leading to the beach, and when he reached the ocean he turned right and sprinted as fast as he could on the firm, wet sand towards the south end of Bhanga Nek and the research base.

His own vehicle was packed and ready. It was time for him to regroup and rearm.

Battle had been joined, but the war was just beginning. He laughed as he ran.

16

NATAL, 1880

'Captain Gregory? Peter? Are you all right?'

Gregory felt his whole body tense, as though he'd just tripped and was falling, about to hit hard ground. The noise of gunfire, the crackle of burning grass and the frenzied yells of Zulus faded. He felt a soft hand on his cheek, and was startled anew.

He opened his eyes. He was lying half in, half out of his bedroll on the dewy grass.

Teresa looked down at him, frowning. 'I thought you were in pain – that you'd been bitten by a snake or scorpion or something. You were screaming.'

Dawn was showing grey over the Drakensberg. He blinked. 'I . . . I'm fine. Just a dream.'

She smiled. 'Hell of a dream, Captain.'

He rubbed his eyes. 'It's Sub-Inspector, ma'am.'

'Whatever. Your men call you Captain, and if you don't like Peter, then I'll call you Captain.'

It was two days after they'd had their brush with Lieutenant Walters, and Gregory had finally extracted the truth from Teresa, refusing to guide her another step from the encampment by the stream until she had told him the real purpose of her mission.

She'd stonewalled for a while, sticking to her story that she was a friend of the Empress Eugénie, out to 'surprise' her by meeting up at the site of the prince's death. It was only when Gregory ordered Phillips and Mathias to stop setting up camp, and to prepare to return to Pietermaritzburg, that she had finally confessed.

'All right, all right, I'm a reporter. For a newspaper, *The New York Times* – at least, they've promised to print my story and my photographs if I can get a picture of the empress to go with the story of her pilgrimage.'

Gregory had shaken his head. 'An American newspaper will *pay* you to print photographs of a grieving mother?'

She had grimaced and put her hands on her hips. 'That's one way of looking at it. The other is that the world was shocked, and moved, by what happened to the Prince Imperial last year. People in America love this stuff – maybe because we don't have royalty of our own. And can't *every* mother in the world identify with Eugénie, feel for her?'

Gregory had bitten his tongue. He was as much impressed by Teresa's grit and determination, albeit grudgingly, as he was disdainful of her profession and employers. But, then, he had suffered the snide undertones of his own local newspaper, the *Natal Witness*, which had been less than glowing in its story of his escape and that of others who had survived the slaughter at Isandlwana. That wasn't Teresa O'Kane's fault, only his.

'Captain . . . Peter,' she had pleaded, 'since we're halfway to hell and gone out here, and it seems like half the British Army and your own Natal Mounted Police are determined to keep me away from the empress, can you at least take me to the Prince Imperial's monument? At least if I get a picture of that I could run it with my article.'

She was right. They had both come some distance, and it was not too much of a detour to visit Nqutu, the location of the memorial. Also, he was waiting on Samuel's return, hopefully with information about the late prince's missing sword. He wanted to question some of the Zulus who had been involved in the engagement in which the prince was killed, if they could be found, to find out what they remembered of the sword and its subsequent handover to the British.

He had agreed to take Teresa to Nqutu. 'And from there I'll have Phillips escort you back to Pietermaritzburg.'

'What were you dreaming about?' she asked now, bringing him back to the moment. Phillips, who was blowing the embers of last night's campfire to life and feeding it with dry grass and sticks, cocked an eye towards him.

'I can't remember,' he lied. Gregory stood, untied the sheet of off-white calico strung between two trees and rolled up the fabric. It was a simple shelter, lightweight, and it kept the dew off him while he slept beside the fire, his Martini–Henry carbine by his side, as it always was when he was out on the veld.

'I should like to see Rorke's Drift and Isandlwana, as well,' Teresa said. 'I understand they're on the way.'

Phillips put the coffee pot on the fire, and Gregory could tell he was listening in to their conversation. 'The Prince Imperial was not at either of those two battles.'

'I know.' Teresa looked at him and caught his eyes. 'But you were.'

He moistened his lips with his tongue, which felt dry. Perhaps it was from the squareface he'd taken last night, after the others had turned in. As usual, he'd told himself the gin would bring him a more peaceful sleep. As usual, he'd been wrong. He broke Teresa's stare and looked across at Phillips, who stood and yawned, raising his hands like a man surrendering. That was a gesture that had not worked in the war that had ranged over these hills. 'We break camp in half an hour, Phillips. Look lively.'

'Sir,' Phillips said. He went to the wagoner. 'Look lively, there's a good fellow. Strike the lady's tent.'

'Help him,' Gregory said.

'Let me fetch some things, first, Mr Phillips,' Teresa said. She moved the fly sheet aside and went into the tent.

Phillips looked back at Gregory and seemed about to object to being ordered to take part in manual labour, but then thought better of it.

Teresa emerged with a small holdall in one hand and a bath towel over her shoulder.

'You didn't answer my question, Captain,' Teresa said.

'It wasn't framed as a question from what I heard.'

'Touché, Sub-Inspector, since we're being literal.'

He shrugged. He'd succeeded in avoiding talking about what had happened last year. 'I can have the wagoner bring you water from the *spruit*, madam. I see you have a hipbath on your wagon, and we can leave the tent up while you wash.'

She waved a hand. 'I'd feel like a baby washing in that little thing. I don't even know what possessed me to buy it, other than the fact that a nice Indian man at the store in Pietermaritzburg positively insisted on it. I'm going for a bracing dip in that creek or *sprite* or whatever you call it. I took a stroll there yesterday afternoon and it looked lovely.'

'It will be cold,' he said.

'I'm tougher than I look, Captain. And I'm not stupid. It was freezing last night.'

'There may be crocodiles.'

'Look on the bright side, Captain. If I get eaten by a crocodile you won't need to worry about me.' She marched past him.

'Shall I strike the tent or not, sir?' Phillips asked.

Gregory harrumphed, and when Mathias passed him a tin mug of coffee he walked off in the opposite direction to Teresa. He gazed out at the Drakensberg Mountains to the west and wished he were up there, alone, exploring some little-known trail or peak. When he had time to himself, when police work or his abysmal attempts at farming were not tying him down, he found the closest thing to solitude in those grassy slopes or in the ice-cold, clear waters of some waterfall's pool.

He thought of Teresa. In the stream. He tried to rid himself of the thought by listening to Phillips babbling on as he heaved on a stuck-fast tent peg.

'I should rather be chasing criminals, or putting down some native rebellion, than striking and erecting tents,' Phillips moaned to Mathias.

Mathias slid a peg from the ground with practised ease. 'The lion is a beautiful animal when seen from afar, Sergeant Phillips.'

Phillips straightened his back and kicked the recalcitrant peg. 'Who said anything about lions? Though I wouldn't mind having a shot at one of them as well. Seems like all the bloody lions have been hunted out in these bloody hills as well as the renegade Zu– I mean, criminals.'

Mathias moved to the next peg. 'It means that battle, killing, looks glamourous when viewed in your illustrated magazines, or heard in the tales of others. It is not the same when you are there.'

'Balderdash,' Phillips said.

'Hush, Mr Phillips.' Mathias looked up, alert, and raised a hand.

Gregory heard the noise as well, a low, rasping sound, like a saw cutting through fresh, soft timber. It came from the direction of the stream, where Teresa had gone to bathe.

'What is it?' Phillips said.

Gregory ignored him. He snatched up his Martini-Henry and broke into a jog. He leapt over a fallen tree, then slowed again as he entered the thick riverine bush – partly because it was too thick to run through, but also because he didn't want to surprise his quarry.

'Lady Beecham,' he called.

He opened the breech of his rifle as he walked, slid a cartridge in with his left hand, then worked the lever to chamber it.

There was no reply from the woman, but he heard the terrible rasping again.

It was close.

He gripped his rifle tightly with his right hand, his index finger resting against the trigger guard. There was no safety catch on the Martini–Henry, just a switch on the right-hand side whose position told him, when he instinctively caressed it, that he was ready to fire.

Gregory had wrapped a sheath of wet cowhide around the barrel more than a year ago and then stitched it so that it was wrapped snuggly. When the skin had dried and shrunk it formed a smooth, tight-fitting cover around the stock that had saved his left hand from blistering and burning at Isandlwana, due to the heat of firing cartridge after cartridge. Now the leather absorbed the sweat from his palm.

'Teresa?' he yelled.

Again, there was the rasping call.

Why? The sound of his voice should have scared the creature off.

They were cunning, dangerous animals at the best of times and had accounted for more than one big game hunter and hapless herdsman that Gregory knew of. They prowled in the darkness, but could, in fact, appear at any time of day. To the best of his knowledge, they only made their calls when searching for a mate.

Gregory took his left hand from the barrel to move a branch out of the way. He had slowed to a pace which made him check every footstep before he placed the sole of his boot on the ground.

He heard the rush and splash of water over smooth river stones and light filtered into the narrow band of forest from his right, where the *spruit* flowed. Gregory cut through the vegetation until he could see the stream.

He stopped and listened. The call was no more, but he heard Teresa singing 'Molly Malone'.

'Teresa!'

The singing stopped.

'Captain Gregory? You're very familiar all of a sudden.' Her voice was faint over the flow of water, but the note was a high one, of surprise. 'I'm not exactly decent.'

'Please just stay where you are. Don't move.'

'Well, I have no intention of coming on back to camp in my birthday suit.'

'No. Don't move. Not even to fetch your clothes.'

He took a few more paces then stopped again. He saw a flash of pale skin beyond grey boulders worn smooth by floodwater. *It must be gone; it must have been scared off by the sound of our voices after all.*

Gregory opened his mouth to speak again, then heard the call, louder than ever.

Uh-uh-uh.

Gregory splashed through mud and shallow water to close the

distance between him and Teresa as fast as possible. He had the Martini–Henry up in his shoulder, ready to fire, and his eyes scanned left and right.

Teresa was knee-deep in the stream. She must have heard his approach, because she looked over her shoulder. Her back was bare, smooth, perfect. She wore white bloomers whose cotton was moulded to the skin of her buttocks, which sat just above the water-line. 'Captain!'

He moved his left hand from the rifle and put his index finger to his lips.

She opened her mouth as if to say, *What?* He shook his head and gripped the rifle again.

A flicker of movement caught his eye from the other side of the stream. He stood stock-still, as did Teresa, moving his head and the tip of the rifle's barrel slowly. Teresa watched him closely, and then followed his gaze.

The leopard emerged from the bush on the far bank.

The cat was not twenty yards from where Teresa stood and Gregory knew the leopardess – it looked like a female, judging by its size and build – could cover that distance in a human's last heartbeat.

He sighted down the barrel.

The leopard locked eyes with him, then lowered itself, compressing its legs like springs, ready to pounce.

Gregory wrapped his finger around the trigger.

Teresa had chosen a pool in which to bathe and ordinarily he would have thought it a beautiful spot. Downstream from her, where the leopard was, the water cascaded between a series of large boulders.

The leopard jumped.

Gregory's heart kicked the inside of his ribcage as he tracked its movement with his rifle. The cat landed deftly on a rock and continued to look at the humans. Gregory registered tiny details – the beautiful contrast of its coat of black rosettes on white and yellow fur; Teresa gripping herself as she shivered in the stream.

He would have only one shot, and he must take it before the

leopard leapt to the next boulder, within even easier striking distance of Teresa. To make it worse, he knew that leopards were adept swimmers, so this feline could choose the means of approaching its helpless prey. There was no other choice.

Gregory's mouth had gone dry. He licked his lips. He peered along the barrel, lining up the sights to a point just above where the leopard's left front leg met its body. He was a good shot and the Martini–Henry's bullet would fly heavy, fast and true at this range. Death would be instantaneous as the lead tore into the animal's heart.

The last time he had pulled a trigger he had been in the thick of the battle. He remembered the men, Zulu warriors, who had fallen in front of him. At first they had been far off, a hundred metres or so, but all too soon they had been almost within stabbing distance. Gregory had seen the horrible power of gunfire and bullets, had been sprayed with blood and gore.

When he and Samuel had been on patrol these last few months, and, more recently, with the fledgling snuff Phillips in tow, it had been the other two men who had shot game for the pot. Eight months earlier, on their first rideout after the battle, Gregory had lined up a shot on a buck, but at the last minute he'd watched the barrel of his rifle shaking, the tremor extending from his hands. He'd felt the sweat dripping from his forehead and down off the tip of his nose. He hadn't been able to do it.

Uh-uh-uh, the leopard called again, but it stayed perched on its rock.

No. With a terrible sense of dread, Gregory realised he'd been a fool. Leopards called to communicate with each other. *There must be another one.*

He re-focused on the aiming point. Teresa was still frozen with fear in the water.

Gregory breathed in and took up the slack on the trigger once more. He hoped he could kill again.

There was another sound. Involuntarily, he and Teresa both turned to their left, to the side of the river where Gregory was standing. These were not the deep, gruff grunts of a big male leopard; indeed, the complete opposite.

Ow-ow, came the high-pitched squeak.

From under a fern grove emerged a tiny cub, its blue eyes glinting in the sunlight. It opened its mouth and gave its call again, showing its small pink tongue at the same time.

The leopardess raised her head, looked to her cub, then sprang from the rock she had been standing on to a second, in the middle of the *spruit*, and then to a third not ten yards from Gregory, and on his side of the stream. He tracked her with the end of the Martini–Henry. When she bounded up to the cub she took the little bundle in her mouth, by the scruff of its neck. The leopard shot Gregory a quick glance, then slunk off into the undergrowth.

Gregory raised the barrel of the rifle into the air and strode along the bank, intending to make sure the cat had gone, and to give Lady Beecham some measure of privacy.

Instead, she hurried from the water, and while she still clutched her arms across her torso, the gesture of modesty did little to hide her bare breasts. She came to him and wrapped herself around him, pressing her naked flesh into the rough wool of his tunic, which was half unbuttoned.

He took his left hand from his rifle to accommodate her, but could not fully hold her as she pressed her face into his chest and wept into his shirt.

After a few moments she raised her tear-streaked face and looked up into his eyes. Teresa sniffed. 'I don't know if that was the most terrifying or the most beautiful thing I've ever seen.'

He cleared his throat. 'Africa, ma'am.'

She put her face back into his chest, perhaps scared, or unwilling to let go. For the sake of modesty he looked over the top of her head, scanning the bush for the leopard, although he knew it would be long gone now.

Gregory was acutely aware of her – the warmth of her body against his, the smell of her hair, which was wet and seemed to have been washed with soap. He felt her hands come between them now, her palms moving up to his chest. He opened his mouth to speak, but she beat him to it.

'Perhaps you might give me a moment, Captain.'

'Of course, Your Ladyship.'

He took a step backwards, averted his eyes and made a smart about-turn. He heard the rustle of clothes being collected from a bush on which she had hung them.

'I'm decent now, Sub-Inspector. You may turn around.'

When he did he saw she was wringing water from her hair, but had dressed again, in her long skirt, blouse and her jacket, although that was still unbuttoned, allowing him another glimpse of the swell of her breasts underneath. He *had* seen them though, and felt them. He coughed again. It did not escape him that she had just used his correct rank, and not the familiar term by which the men addressed him. He, too, had reverted to using her rank, as tenuous as that might be.

She came to him again, but instead of enfolding him in her arms she laid a hand gently on the sleeve of his tunic. It was almost more intimate than pressing her naked body to him. Teresa looked up into his eyes. 'Thank you. When I saw it, the leopard, my first instinct was to run.'

He nodded as she removed her hand. 'That's what the leopard wants. It then sees you as prey, something to be chased and taken down.'

She gave him an enigmatic half-smile and he wondered if she was reading something unintended in his words. Or was it intended? He recalled the way her back had narrowed to her waist above her hips, the way her skin had almost glowed through her bloomers. He swallowed.

'We should get back to camp, assuming you're finished,' he said.

Teresa threw back her head and laughed out loud. 'Oh yes, Captain,' she drawled, back to the familiar, 'I've had enough of this old creek for one lifetime.'

He smiled and it felt as though that simple act put a strain on muscles in his face that had been unused for more than a year. But it was a good feeling. As he set off, she moved to his side, companionably close. He kept his rifle loaded, ready, across his body. A flock of four trumpeter hornbills swooped through the treed canopy above them, wailing like crying babies as they flew. He felt Teresa inch closer, her arm brushing his at the unfamiliar sound.

Gregory saw movement ahead and stopped. Teresa ducked behind him and he felt her hand on his shoulder. He started to raise his rifle.

'It's me, sir.' Mathias emerged from the bush and lowered his own weapon. 'I saw the *ingwe*. The leopard,' he added for Teresa's benefit. 'She is gone.' He grinned and Gregory wondered what else he might have seen while stalking through the undergrowth.

'We need to finish packing and get moving.'

'When I saw the *ingwe* leave, I circled back through the camp, to make sure Sergeant Phillips hadn't been eaten by another one. We have visitors.'

'Visitors?'

Samuel nodded. 'Two, in fact.'

'Who?'

'I don't know, sir. A man and an Indian woman.'

Gregory closed his eyes for a moment. And when he opened them, and emerged from the belt of vegetation back up onto the grassy slope where they had camped, he could see it was her.

'Peter, how *are* you?' Grace said. She was dressed in the brand-new full finery of an English lady. She came to him and kissed him on the cheek.

In her wake was a man decked out in a tweed jacket, shirt and tie, jodhpurs and polished riding boots. He was young, perhaps in his early twenties, with jet-black, pomaded hair and a neatly trimmed goatee beard. He came to Gregory and bowed.

'Allow me to present,' Grace said with a flourish of her hand, 'Count Ferdinand Rosini, from Italy.'

Gregory gave him a nod. 'To what do I owe the pleasure, sir?'

'Ferdi's a historian,' Grace interjected.

'Is that so?' Gregory said.

'Ferdi – Ferdinand – that is, the count, would like to visit Isandl-wana, Rorke's Drift and the place where the Prince Imperial died. He's writing a book. He needs a guide and I told him that you would be perfect.'

'Preeti . . .'

She gave him a fierce grimace.

'Sorry, Grace.' He turned to the man, who hadn't said a word yet. 'Excuse me.'

'*Sì*, of course.'

Gregory took Grace by the elbow and led her aside. He lowered his voice. 'Grace, what the devil is going on?'

She looked over her shoulder. 'He's nice,' she hissed. 'He's a gentleman. *And* he's rich.'

'Grace, I'm very happy for you, but I am not leading a tour group here.'

Grace turned to the others and nodded to Teresa who, Peter saw, was in conversation with the dapper Italian noble. 'What are you doing with her, then?'

'That's different.'

Grace put her hands on her hips. 'How?'

'It's official business. She's . . . American.'

Grace scowled. 'She is officially pretty. And she's your type of woman.'

Gregory ran a hand through his hair. 'What's that supposed to mean? What is a "type" of woman?'

Grace put her hands under her breasts and hiked them up.

'Grace!' He lowered his voice. 'Stop that.'

'Am I too vulgar for you now, Captain Peter? I'm gone five minutes and you've fallen for some rich American floozy.' She gave him a half-smile.

'Don't be ridiculous. And, besides, you made it clear you didn't want the life of a farmer's wife, with me. You told me you'd found an eligible pastor.'

'I found God.' She put her hands together and looked heaven-wards. 'But the pastor wanted me for one thing only, and it wasn't marriage, and it wasn't respectability. I wasn't entirely faithful to him, anyway. I've been trying them all on for size; I started going to the Catholic Church in Pietermaritzburg as well. They don't let their priests marry, but I found Count Ferdinand there. Praying. We got talking, and he told me he needed a guide to take him to Nqutu, where that French prince was killed last year. I told him I knew a man who was going that way.'

Gregory exhaled. Maybe he should invent a business in which he got paid to take people he didn't know on tours around Africa.

Grace looked up at him with her big, dark eyes, and moved closer to him. '*Please.*'

17

KWAZULU-NATAL, THE PRESENT

Adam had left Bhanga Nek ablaze. He'd acted in self-defence, and hadn't killed anyone – that he knew of – but this was only the beginning.

He drove through the night, across KwaZulu-Natal, from the coastal lagoons and forests through dark, silent fields with sugar cane undulating in the moonlight like the surface of a troubled sea. He'd climbed as he'd travelled, avoiding the motorways, passing through towns blacked out by load shedding and townships where paraffin and rechargeable lanterns lit up late-night drinking spots.

The craggy fortress of the Drakensberg Mountains was dark against the blue-black sky, the rock walls turning pink as the sun came up behind him. He wound his way up and across winding passes and through endless grasslands.

There was no time, though, to appreciate the beauty of his home-land. Just as it had been so many times in its history, the land was witness to bloodshed yet again.

Who are they? What do they want? How can they be defeated?

The antique Koran and the sword, which also looked ancient, must be the key. They were both Arabic – there was writing inscribed in the blade of the weapon. The dead men were Middle

Eastern, and the men he had engaged were western military, British.

His phone was connected to the *bakkie* by Bluetooth. He hit a button on the touchscreen.

'Siri, call Schalk Smit,' he said out loud.

The phone rang for so long that Adam thought it would ring out.

'Hello . . .' there was a yawn, 'who . . . Adam? Sheesh, man, do you know the time?'

'Sorry to call so early, Schalk. Howzit, *boet*?'

Schalk coughed. 'Shit. I'd say, *lekker*, man, but what gives, China? Are you in trouble?'

'No . . .' Adam thought again. 'Well, *ja*, a bit. But you're too far away from me to help. Are you in Joburg?'

'Hoedspruit,' Schalk said. 'Let me go to the kitchen. Rozanne's sleeping.'

'Sorry.'

'No, China. I'm awake – now. Rozanne and I moved to Hoedspruit.'

'How are the kids?'

'Kids are fine, but enough of the chitchat, hey. I've got a warm wife to get back to. But I've always got time for you, Adam.'

It was the way of army friendships. Adam hadn't seen Schalk for many years, but their friendship dated back to when Adam had been in 1 Parachute Battalion and Schalk had been his corporal.

'All right,' Adam said into the hands-free microphone as he indicated and overtook a truck. 'You worked as a mercenary in the Middle East, right? Iraq, Afghanistan?'

'Ja, sure, *boet*, but we call ourselves PMCs these days – private military contractors,' Schalk said. It sounded like he was opening a refrigerator and getting something to eat. 'But that Sandland well of money dried up years ago. I was in Mozambique a while back, protecting natural gas plants from the fundamentalists. Adam, this is a hell of a time of night to be asking me for a job, *bru*.'

'No, no, it's nothing like that. It's just that I've got into a bit of trouble with some *okes* who I think are ex–UK military, and there's a connection to some Saudi Arabian nationals. Would they all be mixed up with those ISIS-affiliated guys in Mozambique?'

'Doubtful – the Saudis aren't into that shit,' Schalk said. 'Bin Laden might have been one of them, but he was the black sheep of his family.'

Adam remembered one of the men making a joke about slotting – killing – a policeman somewhere. 'How about Yemen?'

Schalk gulped something. 'Yes, now you're talking – hundred per cent – Yemen's the new hotspot.'

'Really?'

'*Ja.* Horn of Africa. Surely you heard about the Houthis attacking shipping, and the UK and Britain bombing them?'

'Yes, I do remember that. But are the Saudis involved as well?' Adam recalled Andy, sitting by the campfire and taking about the 'Saudi idiots' who had drowned.

'They are, sure as nuts. Like most things in that part of the world it's helluva complex, Adam. There was a civil war, with the Houthi faction overthrowing the government. The Saudis support a guy called Hadi, who used to run the country, and then the United Arab Emirates support the southern province of Yemen, which wants autonomy. Sometimes the Saudi and UAE-backed forces had been in a coalition; other times they've also fought each other. Throw Iran into the mix – they support the Houthis – then you've got yourself a *lekker* shitfight.'

'And foreigners – westerners?' Adam asked.

'*Ja.* The UAE military recruited special forces from outside the Middle East – quite a few Australian ex SAS and commando guys that I know went into UAE uniform, but there's also reports that they've been using PMCs to do some of their proper dirty work, like assassinations and stuff.'

'Like British ex Royal Marines or Special Boat Service maybe?' Adam thought of Andy and his men and their underwater equipment, boat and proficiency as divers.

'Exactly. You'll find the *Engelsman* in any fight.'

Adam thought a moment. 'What do you know about the trade in antiquities – like antique swords or Korans, that sort of stuff?'

'Sure,' Schalk said, 'it's big. Has been since the earliest days of the invasion of Iraq. When Saddam fell there were private operators in Baghdad almost faster than the Americans, looting museums and historical sites and ruins. Same thing happened during all that *kak* in Syria, and I've actually read online that it's going on in Yemen as well, but with a difference.'

'And what's that?'

'In some places it was collectors driving the trade. There were rich *okes* who bankrolled operators to go into Iraq and Syria with a shopping list of, like, Roman and Mesopotamian shit to order, *boet*. They knew exactly what they wanted and where it was. In other places, like Afghanistan, I heard of GIs who were digging up old battlefields – graves even – from the days when the British tried to colonise the country and got their asses kicked. They were selling old rusty rifles and cap badges and kit on eBay. Where there's demand, there's trade, and where there's trade, there's money.'

Adam nodded to himself. 'And Yemen?'

'There it's the Houthi government that's driving the trade. They've got no money as the country's blockaded, so they're selling off their own national treasures and heritage to make some bucks and fund their war. Of course, you know that there'll be *skelms* involved - someone making money on the side.'

'What's all this stuff worth?'

Schalk yawned again. 'You know the drill. It's worth whatever someone will pay for it. Millions of dollars, I'm guessing.'

'Thanks, Schalk, I'll let you get back to bed.'

'Adam?'

'Yes?'

'How much trouble are you in, *boet*?'

Adam debated how much to tell his friend. Schalk lived his life on other people's frontlines, but he had a wife and two young sons. Adam didn't want to put anyone else in harm's way.

'Nothing I can't handle.'

'Bullshit.' Schalk laughed. 'You're a south coast *soutie* surfer, always were. All you *ouens* know is how to catch waves and chicks and smoke DP.'

Adam smiled in return. DP, Durban Poison, was an old South African Army term for a particularly potent strain of marijuana. 'I'll be fine.'

'Listen, Adam, we were tough, back in the day, and we saw some shit in Angola and South-West, no lie. But let me tell you, what goes on in places like Yemen is next-level brutal, my *boet*. Those people are fighting for religion and oil, and it doesn't get any nastier than that. You keep your head down and your ammo dry, and you just call me, any time, day or night, if you need the cavalry. All right?'

Adam licked his lips. 'Will do, thanks, Schalk. Goodnight.'

Adam ended the call and stared out the windscreen. 'Shit.'

Sannie saw a bright light. *Is this what heaven looks like?*

'Sannie?'

Someone was touching her hand. A man was speaking. She began to panic. *Christo?* She forced herself to remember what her first husband looked like. *Tom?* Her second partner in life had died as well.

'Sannie, you're awake!'

She blinked and saw that she was looking into an overhead light, in the ceiling. A machine nearby beeped. She smelled starch and disinfectant. She blinked and looked to her left. It was Adam. Her lower lip started to wobble and a tear escaped her eye.

'Adam . . .'

He leaned over and kissed her on the cheek. She remembered his surfer smell – sunscreen lotion, salt, Sunlight soap. She remembered the beach. He was wearing a Rip Curl T-shirt and jeans.

Sannie felt the fear pierce her chest again. 'Marilyn?'

'She's fine,' Adam said. 'She's out now, talking to some police from your unit.'

'The Hawks,' Sannie said. 'Call Colonel Gita Kapahi. Her cell phone number is zero-eight-two . . .'

Adam placed a comforting hand on her arm. 'It's OK. Marilyn's already called Gita. I know her, remember?'

'Sure,' Sannie said, although she was anything but. Another man, in blue surgical scrubs, came into view. He checked the chart at the foot of her bed. He was older, with grey hair and a moustache. He smiled. 'Susan, I'm Dr Charl Strydom. It's good to see you awake and talking, and your memory seems to be OK, if you can remember the rest of that phone number.'

'I can.' She reeled off the number. 'And call me Sannie.?'

Dr Strydom checked her chart again. "We'll need to run a few tests on you before I can discharge you, Sannie.'

'No tests. We can do those later. What about John Parker?'

Dr Strydom sighed. 'The young safari guide who brought you in?'

Sannie nodded. 'He's fine. But, with respect, Sannie, I can't discharge you yet.'

Sannie reached for the wires connecting her to the monitor, found the sticky pads on her chest and ripped them off. 'Get my clothes for me, please, Adam.'

Adam frowned, but went to the closet.

'Mr Kruger . . .' the doctor began.

Adam took a coathanger with Sannie's shirt and pants on it and passed it to her. 'You try telling her, Doc.'

'Don't talk about me like I'm not in the room,' Sannie said.

The doctor's kindly bedside manner took a turn. 'I'll have a nurse bring you the paperwork you need to discharge yourself.' He wagged a finger at her. 'But I want you to know that it's against my advice.'

'*Ja*, sure, fine,' Sannie said.

OUTSIDE THE HOSPITAL, with an angry doctor standing by the entrance with folded arms, Adam pulled up in his *bakkie* and Sannie got in.

'Where's Marilyn now?' she asked him as she put on her seatbelt.

He drove out of the hospital car park. 'I tried her number while I was waiting for you, but it went through to voicemail.'

'When I called her she said she was going to interview some guy called Deon Meyer. Sure that's the *oke*'s real name?'

She shook her head. 'No, it's a nickname. His name is Matteo Meyer, and he works for a security company. He was one of the first on the scene when David Gregory was killed. *Fok.*'

'Yes, that's right. Marilyn said she was going to the Viking Security office in Dundee. Do you want to go there now?'

Sannie nodded, but said nothing.

'What's wrong?' Adam asked.

Sannie bit her lower lip and stared out the window for a few seconds, remembering, before replying. 'I had a partner, ten or eleven years ago, a Shangaan woman named Mavis. I was with the Hawks at Nelspruit and we were investigating a series of home robberies and insurance fraud – people faking their own deaths. I left Mavis on her own during a stakeout and she was murdered. I've *told* Marilyn we work as a team.'

Sannie took out her Z88 and a magazine of ammunition, and loaded the pistol. She placed it back in her holster. While she was getting dressed, and the doctor was out of the room, Adam had told her about his gun and grenade fight with the veterans at Bhanga Nek.

'And that goes for you, as well, from now on,' she admonished him.

'Yes, Colonel,' he said.

'Stop grinning. This is no joke, Adam.'

He nodded.

She shook her head. 'You look like you almost enjoyed yourself.'

He shrugged. 'I spoke to Schalk Smit, an old friend from the army, on the way up here last night. He had some interesting information about mercenaries in Yemen and the trade in antiquities.'

Adam told her about the sword he had taken from the veterans' camp during his battle with them. He had carefully stowed it, and the antique Koran, in the back of his *bakkie*.

Sannie thought a moment or, rather, tried to mentally reach for a catalogue, something that was hovering on the edge of her mind, just out of reach. She told herself she *was* all right, and fit for duty, but her brain did feel a little fuzzy.

'Around the campfire they were talking about waiting for one more shipment. But I destroyed their inflatable boat. I guess they were waiting for another delivery of something.'

She pinched the bridge of her nose with thumb and forefinger. She loved Adam, and he was normally a man of very few words, but now he seemed to be talking incessantly, making it even harder for her to latch on to whatever it was that was circling her brain, like a moon orbiting a planet.

Was it just a coincidence that David Gregory had been murdered after killing sixteen of his own rhinos? She'd spoken to Richard Tustin and to John Parker about David, and they had both said that David was in favour of the legal trade in rhino horn. What did that mean? She blinked.

'Trade.'

Adam glanced over at her. 'What?'

'Trade,' she repeated. 'It was something I was talking about, when I was interviewing the commander of the veterans. Trade is a two-way thing, Adam.'

He nodded. 'Of course. Yes, I see. You think that maybe Andy and the veterans are waiting to *export* something, rather than staying there preparing to receive another shipment of goods?'

'Yemen.' She closed her eyes. *What about Yemen?* 'Think.'

'What's on your mind?' Adam asked.

She held up a hand for quiet. 'Sorry. Yes. Yemen. Rhino horn.'

'Rhinos?'

She snapped her head around to look at him, pleased to feel that at last her synapses were working. 'Yes. Everyone knows that rhino horn is used in traditional Chinese medicine, and that Vietnam is a big market for horn, but as well as Asia, rhino horn used to be exported up the east coast in dhows in big quantities to the Horn of

Africa, specifically Yemen. John Parker, the guide – lodge manager – reminded me of that, just before we were ambushed.'

'Really?'

Sannie took out her phone and started tapping into its internet search engine as she spoke. 'Yes. It was carved into ceremonial dagger handles.' She found an item on the internet. 'Here it is. The dagger is called a *jambiya* and it's worn on a belt on the front of the wearer's traditional robes.' She scanned the article, and paraphrased it. 'When Yemen had a more secular, left-wing government, traditions like this were being phased out and the importation of rhino horn was made illegal, but with the fundamentalist Houthi militia now in charge there's a return to people having to wear traditional dress, like what's happened in Afghanistan. People can even be jailed for wearing western clothes. *Jambiyas* are back in style, and while many are made with resin or plastic handles, people with money want a proper rhino-horn dagger again. The Houthis have been looting museums and selling off their precious antiquities abroad to finance their war, but you can bet there's a criminal element involved as well.'

'Yes, that's pretty much what Schalk said,' Adam said. 'So, the horns from sixteen dead rhinos would be a good commodity for trade with someone in Yemen right now. And the Arabic sword and Koran I found could have been shipped out of there in exchange.'

'Exactly.' Sannie called Marilyn again, and this time, Marilyn answered.

'Sannie!' Marilyn said. 'Is that really you? Are you awake?'

'*Ja*, and you're in *kak*, Marilyn. You shouldn't be off interviewing people without backup.'

'You were asleep.'

'Yes, well, I'm awake now. What's happening?'

'I spoke to Meyer. I went through all the events around David Gregory's death, and also spoke to him about his time doing security on the farm and game reserve. Nothing new, but he didn't seem particularly surprised about two men trying to kill us. He seemed to think the WildForce guys were all a bunch of crazy Rambos. He also thinks they might have been involved in something criminal, with their coming and going at night.'

'Same thing John Parker told us,' Sannie said.

'*Yebo*,' Marilyn replied, 'affirmative.'

'Does he have any idea what they might have been involved with?'

'He thought maybe drugs, but he did make an interesting observation. Deon – Matteo, I mean – said that he remembered a few occasions when there were incidents with poachers at David's game reserve which happened to be on the same days or nights as stock theft incidents, and at the same times.'

'Serious?' Sannie said. 'Did you check?'

'Of course I checked.' Marilyn could be sassy, but Sannie also knew that she was good at her job. 'I got Meyer to check his company's computer logs. Viking gets calls from landholders who are part of the local Farm Watch scheme, because Viking provides the armed response, and Meyer found four incidents where their on-duty car had been sent to respond to reports of poachers breaching the fence at David's, and then having to divert to cattle-rustling incidents.'

'And the poaching incidents occurred first every time?'

'Every single time,' Marilyn said. 'You're thinking what I'm thinking?'

Sannie wanted to be as sure as she could be. 'Were there any apprehensions of suspects from any of the poaching incidents?'

'*Aikona*, Colonel.'

'None. So, these highly trained foreign military veterans saw poachers, called it in, and on four separate occasions they weren't able to catch a suspect, even though during another incursion they shot a local guy.'

'Yes, and I even checked that one. The man was shot on the fifth reported poaching incident, and there was no stock theft on that night.'

'So, the other poaching reports could have been false, to divert security away from stock theft incidents in-progress. The young guy who was checking his snares for bush meat was maybe the only *real* poacher. Good work, Marilyn,' Sannie said. 'Standby, I'll get back to you soon.'

'All right,' she said, and they ended the call.

They were in the town of Dundee now and Sannie saw the turnoff to The Shed pub and restaurant. She pointed to it. 'Let's go there, please, Adam.'

'Sure. You want food?'

'No.' Her stomach rumbled. It was early afternoon and she'd been unconscious and hadn't eaten since the day before. 'Actually, yes. Maybe order us toasted sarmies for the road. And chips.'

There was a chill in the air when they got out and Adam took his hoodie, also with a surf-brand logo on it, from the back of the driver's seat. Sannie put on her cropped black leather jacket. Both of them were more accustomed to the heat and humidity of the coast.

They walked into the restaurant and Sannie asked if Jan-Maree Ball was working. The waiter on duty said she would fetch Jan-Maree and went to find her. Adam ordered their food from the woman behind the register.

Jan-Maree came in from the outside deck and took off her apron when she got to Sannie.

'Hi again,' Jan-Maree said. 'I'm just finished for the day.'

'Where's Richard Tustin?' Sannie said, without any pleasantries. 'I tried his phone and he's not answering.'

Jan-Maree nodded. 'He's at Isandlwana.' She looked at her watch. 'Or Rorke's Drift. He's got two clients from overseas staying with him and he's taking them on a tour of the battlefields. Phone signal's not so *lekker* out there.'

'What time is he due back? He stays in a house in Dundee, doesn't he?'

'I'm not sure when he's coming back. He can get engrossed in the tours, believe me. Maybe only by six, and yes, he owns a place just outside of town. He alternates between here and the UK. He's also got a place in Cape Town.'

Wealthy, Sannie, thought, but then the price of property in South Africa was very affordable compared to the UK. Sannie thought about where and how to next meet Tustin. She wanted to make sure it was somewhere public, and that she had backup.

Then Jan-Maree said, 'I was going to go meet him, now, after my shift, but my car wouldn't start this morning. I had to walk to work.'

'Why were you going to drive out to meet him?'

Jan-Maree gave a small shrug and glanced away. 'Sometimes he likes me to do the tour of the Prince Imperial's monument. It's something I know a fair bit about. It gives his tourists a bit of variety, and me a bit of cash and a cut of the tips.'

That gave Sannie the course of action she needed. 'You can come with us. I want to see him, and you can navigate us to whichever battlefield he's at when we get there.'

'Sure, thanks,' Jan-Maree said. 'We can start at Rorke's Drift. I'll just change and get my things.'

Sannie went to Adam, who was waiting for the sandwiches.

'I ordered you chicken mayo, your favourite,' he said.

'Thanks. Listen,' Sannie said, 'you know I didn't approve of you taking on those guys at Bhanga Nek and going all Chuck Norris with your guns and hand grenades.'

Adam shrugged. 'Yes.'

'That said, I need to ask you a question.'

'Shoot,' Adam said.

'Let's hope it doesn't come to this, but are you carrying?'

Adam looked around. The woman serving at the register had her back to them, and was berating someone in the kitchen. There were no other waiters or customers at the front counter right now. He gave her a grin and reached into the pocket of his hoodie. He pulled out a grenade.

Sannie exhaled. '*Adam.*'

'Oh.' Adam replaced the grenade, then raised his right index finger to his lower lip, as if just remembering something.

'Oh, what?'

'There may be an AK-47 in the back of the Ranger, in my dive bag.'

Sannie frowned. Adam was a walking, talking arsenal of illegal, unlicensed weapons, but after what had happened to them both, she felt a small measure of comfort. She took out her phone and began tapping on the screen.

'Who are you messaging?' Adam asked.

'Marilyn. I'm telling her to meet us at Rorke's Drift, and to find a gun shop and buy me some more ammo. If we're going to war, we'd better be ready.'

18

ZULULAND, 1880

Gregory rode through the hills, deeper into Zululand, with his odd assortment of travellers.

Ferdinand, the Italian count, spoke some English, and Grace seemed quite taken with him.

The sun was high in the sky and had banished the morning chill. Gregory – and Teresa – had recovered from the scare with the leopard. He had not, however, fully recovered from the feel of her wet skin against him, nor the warmth of her arms around him and the sight of her bare flesh.

'Penny for your thoughts, Captain.'

Surprised, he looked to his right and saw that Teresa had crept up behind him on her horse without him noticing. He tugged at the collar of his uniform tunic and felt his cheeks burn. He looked up to a craggy range towering above their route of march to the left. 'Just watching out, for possible danger.'

'Peeping tom leopards?'

He laughed, something he did not often do. 'Good country for them.'

'To me it seemed like they preferred creeks and thick bush.'

He nodded. 'Anywhere they can hide – vegetation or mountain

rocks. They're ambush hunters; they lie in wait for their prey and then pounce.'

Teresa looked behind her and Gregory followed her gaze, noticing she was watching Grace and the count.

'She's very pretty,' Teresa said. 'How do you know her?'

'Miss Naidoo, ah, used to work as a domestic in my employ.' She *had* cleaned his farmhouse a couple of times. 'You're a journalist . . .' he began.

'You pay attention,' Teresa said.

He cleared his throat, then lowered his voice. 'What are your impressions of our Italian count?'

'He's a handsome rake, I'll give you that. Seems charming enough from what I can gather.'

Gregory raised his eyebrows.

Teresa frowned. 'But, if you're asking what I really make of the count, I'd say it takes a thief to catch a thief. Well, I'm no thief, but I know when to be honest and upfront and say who I am and what I want, and I also know that sometimes there are other ways of getting what you want.'

'Quite,' Gregory said. 'Do go on.'

'There's something shifty about him. He looks slightly familiar to me, like maybe I've seen his picture somewhere. I think he might be another newsman.'

'Really?'

'See that big wooden box he's lugging?'

Gregory turned slowly in his saddle. The count and Grace had arrived not with a cart but with two packhorses in tow. On one was, as Teresa had pointed out, an oversized box.

'Camera,' Teresa said. 'I'll bet my next gin on it.'

'Writing for some Italian publication?'

Teresa shrugged. 'Europe's royalty is a popular source of news and gossip throughout the continent – and in America. I bet he just coincidentally aims to get to the site of Prince Louis's death about the same time as the Empress Eugénie.'

'Well, he won't have much luck there.'

'Of course,' Teresa said.

He tried to read her expression, but her beatific smile was the picture of innocence. Gregory suspected that Teresa would try, at some point, to slip away from his protection and cross paths with the empress, most likely when she arrived at her son's memorial. Short of tying Teresa up, he could not stop her, and he wondered if she was right – would Count Ferdinand try the same shenanigans?

It wasn't his problem. He had a missing sword to locate. Of greater concern to him, though, was a small mount, little more than a rocky outcrop, that lay between him and Nqutu, the place where the prince was killed and his sword taken. His party of misfits would have to cross the Buffalo River and then pass through the old battlefield at Isandlwana, beneath that terrible peak. It was there that he would have to face, again, the terrors that woke him at night. He gripped the pommel of his saddle for a moment to stop his hands from shaking.

At Rorke's Drift they stopped to water the horses in the shallows of the fast-flowing Buffalo River. When they were done, for the drift was several hundred yards from the mission station and out of sight of it, they began heading back to the post to take lunch.

'I'm going to come back and try some fishing after I've eaten.' Grace patted the leather rod holder strapped to her saddle.

'Are you going to beat the fish to death?' Gregory asked.

Grace poked her tongue out at him.

It had been Gregory's idea that she hide the sjambok whip in her prized container when she visited Blundell in jail. She'd told him that the client who had given her the rod holder had refused to pay after she had offered her services. Grace had pulled a knife on him and had also made him give over his saddle.

'Be careful of crocodiles,' he said to her. Gregory lagged behind his charges, glad that none of them sought his company, and walked Bullet through the golden grass, alone at last.

The ordinariness and peacefulness of the place belied the momentous and terrible events that had happened here. Gregory sat down on a low rise overlooking the site of the British holdout against the Zulus. Bullet was content to graze beside him as the others made their way into the camp.

Trader Jim Rorke's house, which had later served as the Reverend Otto Witt's mission station and then as the British Army hospital before the battle at Isandlwana, had been burned during the fighting. It had not been rebuilt, but the commissariat storehouse had been reconstructed, and where the defenders, led by lieutenants Bromhead and Chard, had erected barricades of mealie bags and biscuit tins, there were now stone walls. The newly reinforced complex had been christened Fort Melvill, after one of two other lieutenants who had died on the banks of the Buffalo River trying to save the colours of the 24th Regiment. The embroidered flags, listing the regiment's battle honours, were later recovered downstream.

Gregory had not been at the battle at Rorke's Drift, and nor had Samuel, but its story was well known around the world. Here 139 gallant British soldiers and their allies had fought off four thousand Zulus, who had just missed out on their share of blood and glory on the slopes of Isandlwana.

When Gregory had arrived at Rorke's Drift the last time it had been the morning after the battle. He'd heard gunfire as he rode over the open plains below Helpmekaar, on his new horse, the same one that now snuffled beside him. Bullet, like Gregory, had been a refugee from the battle and they had found each other in the chaos the night after Isandlwana.

The shooting he had heard was not a pitched battle but rather the odd, sporadic shot coming from the red-tinged golden grasslands around the mission station. Mostly the sounds were screams and the sickening squelch of bayonets being rammed into flesh.

'We killed three hundred and fifty of the bastards,' a red-coated corporal with a face blackened by soot and gunpowder told him when Gregory had come to the still-smoking outpost, 'but there's easily that many more wounded to be rid of. Come, help, if you wish.'

Gregory had dismounted and slaked his thirst, as he had done just now in the river more than a year later. He closed his eyes as he heard again the moans of the Zulu wounded, as he watched redcoats roll bodies, some of them still alive, into mass graves and then shovel dirt on them.

There was the story, in the pictorial newspapers in Natal and Britain and throughout the empire, of the bravery of the defence of this outpost – and that could not be questioned – but no word of the butchery that took place the next day. That was not a story, that was just reality.

He came to a low rise from which he could see over the long grass that had covered the mass graves and which obscured the skeletons of those the British had missed. He looked to the old mission.

Teresa was busying herself setting up her camera on its tripod, having untied the apparatus from her wagon. Grace was walking with Count Ferdinand, as though they were out for a stroll in a piazza in Rome. *How can they not be moved by what went on here?*

Phillips was being posed by Teresa. She made him hold his rifle at the ready and stare off into the distance. When Phillips grinned, Gregory heard Teresa rebuking him, even from his perch overlooking the fort.

'Look *fierce*, Sergeant Phillips.'

Gregory snapped off a long stalk of grass and chewed the end. Phillips composed himself and struck a thoughtful pose, pointing at something imaginary. The strip of fast-burning magnesium in the device Teresa was holding up with one hand went off with the flash of a small explosion. Gregory clenched his fists to still the tremors the sight had aroused in him.

Where Phillips was standing, there had been two Zulus hanging by their necks from a wooden frame, which had been pressed into service as a makeshift gallows. While other wounded were being bayoneted to death, another captive was being wrestled into a noose by two redcoats.

'Would have died anyway,' the grubby-faced soldier who had first spoken to him said as he walked by again. The man spat on the ground and Gregory saw the blood on the man's hands and boots.

'Their own lot didn't see fit to take them away and we can't treat them.'

Gregory closed his eyes, then as now, to block out the sight, but he heard the cries of the wounded again, and the butchering of flesh.

'Peter?'

He opened his eyes at the sound of Teresa's voice. She had left her camera, and Phillips, and come walking towards him, one hand up to her brow to shield her eyes from the sun's glare. The ground she walked had once been littered with bodies, the grass red with blood and slippery with brains and innards.

'Tea's made. Would you like some?'

He opened his mouth to speak, but nothing came out. He nodded, stood, and brushed himself down.

She stood there, waiting for him. 'Did you fight here?'

He shook his head. 'No.'

But many times he wished he had, wished he could have told a tale of honour and glory. How could he tell her, as she turned and led him to afternoon tea, that he often wished he had died at Isandlwana?

'Look!' Teresa stood and pointed.

Gregory had been lying, after tea, in the shade of the rock wall, his tunic rolled beneath his head as a pillow. He sat up and saw a party of half-a-dozen Zulus, warriors, walking towards them. One was on horseback and Gregory saw it was Samuel returning. Gregory stood and buckled on his gun belt. Samuel spurred his horse and broke away from the group on foot.

Gregory walked out from the fort to meet and greet Samuel, who swung down from his saddle and gripped Gregory's hand.

'Did you have any luck, my friend?' Gregory asked.

'I did.' Samuel looked past Gregory to where the others had come into the open. 'I see Grace is here?'

Gregory nodded. 'I'll explain later.'

The Zulu party walked up to them.

'*Sanibonani*,' Gregory said, using the polite greeting to more than one person.

'*Sikhona, Siyaphila*,' the tallest, perhaps their leader, replied, telling him they were well.

'They are from far,' Samuel pointed to the east, 'towards Mthonjaneni, from the kraal and family of Mfunzi.'

Gregory nodded.

'I asked them about the Frenchman's sword. They knew of it – many people did.'

This was a breakthrough. 'Good work,' Gregory said.

Gregory's Zulu was good, but he was happy to defer to Samuel in this case. 'Ask them to describe it,' he said to Samuel.

Samuel translated.

The tallest of the Zulus indicated for a younger warrior, his frame still filling out, to step forward from the back of the group. The young man and Samuel spoke.

'This one's father, Mfunzi, actually carried the prince's sword for a while,' Samuel said.

'And what did it look like?'

Samuel and the young man spoke. Gregory followed it and understood most of what was said. The man used his hands to indicate the length of the sword, and mentioned the word '*golide*'.

'He says the grip,' Samuel made a fist and when he looked to the man for confirmation he nodded, 'and the pommel and hilt were made of gold. He said it was a thing of beauty.'

Gregory nodded. Even if it was just gold inlay, this was no cavalry trooper's blade.

'His father let him hold it a few times,' Samuel continued. 'He would sneak a look at it whenever his father was not in the kraal. The young man said he wanted to carry it into battle, but he never had the chance to fight the British. One day, his father left with the sword, and he later told his son that the sword had been returned to the enemy, so that they could send it to the famous man's family, the one who had been killed at the Tshotshosi River.'

Gregory nodded. 'That's the place where the prince fell. Ask him why it was so beautiful.'

The young man pinched the thumb and forefinger of his right hand together and waved it in the air as he spoke. 'It was writing,' Samuel said. 'Words and some pictures, that were on the blade.'

'Engraved?' Gregory asked.

Samuel spoke some more; the young man replied, and Samuel nodded. 'Yes, engraved. He said it was as though a story was carved along the blade. He'd never seen a weapon like it.'

Gregory thought back to what Hellfire Jack had told him. A standard French service sword, like the one Lord Chelmsford had presented the Empress Eugénie, was similar to a British cavalryman's sabre – a plain, steel blade made for killing, not for show, and undecorated. No gold. The weapon the young Zulu had just described did not match that description.

His earlier melancholy forgotten, Gregory felt his senses spark to life. *This* was what sustained him now, the search for the truth in the face of lies and obfuscation. 'He never saw the sword again?'

Samuel translated then shook his head. 'No. His father gave the sword back to the British, as a gift.'

'Yes,' Gregory said. 'The way I heard it, the Zulus brought the sword out on Cetshwayo's orders, as a gesture of goodwill. He was still hoping for a negotiated settlement even as Chelmsford was marching on Ulundi.'

Samuel exhaled. 'That was never going to happen, was it? Not after what happened at –'

'Ask him what else he knows about the sword.'

Samuel nodded. He conversed with the warrior. 'As he said, he never saw the sword again, but he repeated that it was the most wondrous weapon he had ever seen. He says his father was killed at Ulundi.'

Gregory locked eyes with the young man. He saw the hardness there, resentment mixed with an unbreakable pride. The war might be over, and these people were still on this land, but Gregory knew there would never truly be peace in this country.

'*Ngiyabonga*,' Gregory said, and the young man and his leader begrudgingly nodded their thanks. 'Find them some blankets and some food,' he said to Samuel.

'*Yebo, Nkosi.*'

Samuel only ever called him 'Lord' in front of others, when Samuel thought protocol demanded it. Gregory saw how the leader of the Zulu party held Samuel's stare for a second or two longer. Whatever their leader thought of Samuel, who had thrown his lot in with the colonists, Samuel was unrepentant. He held his head high, chin out, then told the men to come with him to the wagon.

'Do you think I might take their picture, Samuel?' Teresa asked.

Samuel translated and the men became wide-eyed and animated, clearly excited by the prospect. Gregory smiled at the way Teresa had instantly lifted the mood and defused any latent conflict. The warriors busied themselves posing.

AFTER LUNCH they crossed the Buffalo River at the drift. The water had been much higher, the river swollen with summer rains, in January of the preceding year, when Chelmsford first invaded Zululand.

The Zulu warriors had departed, heading back to their homes. Samuel led the way, followed by Gregory, Teresa, Grace and the count, and Mathias driving the wagon. Phillips trailed them, making sure no one lagged behind. Once clear of the water, Teresa caught up to Gregory.

'I've read about the Battle of Isandlwana, Peter,' she said to him as her horse trotted alongside his, 'but I'd love to hear a first-hand account from you.'

He could do that. He could talk, dispassionately, about the chain of events that had led to what happened. While he spoke, Teresa said nothing, silently urging him to continue. Gregory gripped Bullet's reins tight as the mount came in sight. The stepped peak of Isandlwana looked like a rough silhouette of the Sphinx, the monument worn as collar badges by the redcoats of the 24th in recognition of their regiment's service in Egypt against Napoleon Bonaparte. It was ironic that the same emperor's great-nephew died while fighting alongside the French's traditional enemy.

Their ride took them up to the mount and Gregory caught his breath as he looked out over the plain. The crackle of gunfire and the clamour of steel spearheads on rifles played at the edges of his sanity as he took in the sights. There was the conical-shaped hill, the higher mountain mesa to his right, and the Ngwebeni Valley to the left. In this vast, almost treeless land it seemed inconceivable that twenty thousand Zulus had escaped detection, like ghosts, only to appear at the time of their choosing, ready to wreak havoc.

Gregory continued his story, and Teresa listened with empathy. Gregory stayed in the saddle as the rest of his small train plodded up the hill behind him. He did not want to linger in this place. Samuel had taken up position some forty yards to their right, perhaps lost in his own memories.

Gregory closed his eyes. The sounds of battle were getting louder in his brain, thrumming against the inside of his skull. It was as if it was happening all over again.

'Peter?' Teresa's voice was soft, her unfamiliar American accent as warm as honey. 'Are you all right?'

It was only then he realised he'd stopped talking. He opened his eyes and blinked at her. 'I . . .' He then pinched the bridge of his nose, trying to squeeze out the shame. He looked at Samuel, sitting astride his horse. *Why has this experience not broken Samuel? How can he be so strong?*

Teresa followed his eyes. 'Samuel was here, then, wasn't he?'
'Yes.'
'Was he with you, in the police, at the time?'

Gregory looked to his friend, who seemed unaware Gregory was watching him. Samuel was looking towards the donga where Durnford had tried to stop the Zulu tidal wave, back straight, head held high, as if he had no regrets.

'He was a member of the Natal Native Horse. I didn't know him, but he saved my life that day.' Gregory nudged Bullet in the ribs with his stirrups and set off down the hill, his back to the outcrop.

SAMUEL WATCHED PETER, on his horse, trot slowly down the slope, away from the rest of them. Sometimes a man needed to be on his own.

The woman was watching him as well, and although the others in their party had caught up, and glanced down at Peter, the red-headed woman's eyes were different. She cared for him.

Teresa steered her horse towards Samuel and greeted him. He nodded.

'Tell me, please, Samuel. What happened here? Not the battle; what happened to Peter?'

Samuel remembered and he told her of that terrible day, when the moon swallowed the sun – a terrible omen if there ever was one – and the myth of the white man's superiority was shattered. Samuel, even as a member of the Zulu nation, could not throw his lot in with his former regimental brothers of the *amabutho*. They clamoured for his blood even more than that of the colonists – there was no question of a last-minute change of side.

'Why *did* you side with the colonists, Samuel?' Teresa asked as their horses moved side by side at an easy pace.

He looked to the sky, then at her. 'A woman.'

'Tell me.'

'I was the son of a chief, and our family were loyal supporters of the king, Cetshwayo. Like all young men I served in an *amabutho*, a regiment, with warriors of my own age. Under the king's system, my brothers and I could not marry, could not settle on our own land with our own cattle, until we had been to battle. It was forbidden, but . . .'

'You met a girl.'

He nodded. 'Like many others throughout the kingdom I grew tired of waiting, and my woman and I – her name was Nandi, she shared the name of the great King Shaka's mother – we crossed the river into Natal. Do you know what "Nandi" means, Teresa?'

She shook her head. 'I'm afraid I don't.'

His smile was a sad one. '"Sweet". We lived as husband and wife, and I sought work. Nandi became infatuated with the white men's God – she had no faith anymore in the king – and I ended up joining a Christian military unit, the Edendale Horse. When not serving I could come closer to where my home had been, on the Natal side of the Mzinyathi, the Buffalo River, where we just crossed. The pull of my heart, to a woman on one side of the river and to my home on the other, was my failing.'

'How so?'

'One day,' Samuel looked to the horizon to avoid Teresa's eyes, 'when I was out tending to my cattle, a raiding party came, on orders of the king. They had come to kill me, but instead they took Nandi. She was carrying my child, but that counted for nothing. They took her across the river . . .'

'Oh, Samuel.' She reached across from her horse and briefly laid a hand on his forearm. He did not need to tell her the horror of what had happened. It had been spoken of throughout his former kingdom, a message sent to those who would side with the enemy.

He drew a breath. 'And so I served the white people. Not really for love of the colony or of a new god, but for my wife, and my unborn child.'

He told her of his part in the battle, and of his first meeting with Peter Gregory. Samuel had been on the verge of leaving the brave, foolish, wide-eyed policeman to his death, but he admired the man's courage in saving the drummer boy.

'"Come with me, *Nkosi*," I said to him again,' Samuel said. 'But he said to me, "No, thank you, I'll –" and then he was shot. The bullet left him unconscious.'

Teresa nodded as she and Samuel set off again 'He wanted to stay there, with Durnford and his friends, even though it meant certain death.'

'Yes,' Samuel said. 'And sometimes I think that in his mind he is there with them still, yet he walks the earth today, like a ghost.'

'Tell me, Samuel, how did the two of you escape?'

Samuel looked away from the lonely, mounted figure of Peter Gregory, back towards that terrible, rugged path on the reverse side of Isandlwana. His thoughts took him back to that hot January day, and he told his story to Teresa.

CATTLE STAMPEDED PAST SAMUEL, Zulus jumping and dodging their way through the herd and the dust, yet rather than turn and gallop away, Samuel dismounted again.

Colonel Durnford and his remaining supporters were encircled, a little way down the hill. Peter Gregory – though at that time Samuel still did not know his future friend's name – had saved the young man, but had then been shot. Samuel dropped to one knee and checked the white man. The bullet had carved a furrow along the skin of his right temple, just above the ear, but it had not penetrated his skull. He was breathing but unconscious.

Samuel slid the ammunition bandolier over Gregory's head and hauled him up and over his shoulders. He was stronger than the Natal policeman had been, and he was able to flip the man up and over onto the back of his own horse. Samuel stooped to pick up Gregory's rifle and bandolier, and chambered a round before remounting.

The right horn of the buffalo formation, the fleet-footed younger men on that flank, had already branched off to begin a mad and murderous pursuit of the black and white fugitives fleeing the doomed battlefield. Down the steep, rock-strewn slope the defenders and their pursuers had run, through the mostly dry watercourse of the Manzinyama stream towards the deep valley of the Buffalo River, the border with Natal.

Any of the redcoats, wagoners and allies of the British who tripped and fell were put to death immediately. Samuel had ridden past Englishmen and Zulus alike as his sure-footed pony dodged or leapt over rocks, sending up a hail of grit, stones and dust in their wake. Around him were bodies, wounded men and Zulus pausing to eviscerate the dead and loot their clothes. A spear flashed across his front and a minute later a stray bullet snatched at the flapping hem of his tunic. For all he knew, the man lying across his horse behind him was dead by now.

At the Buffalo River, chaos was morphing into organised killing. A party of fleet-footed Zulus had outflanked the fleeing forces and crossed at a rocky drift. They were now waiting on the Natal bank – against their king's explicit orders – and taking their time spearing any surviving fugitives who struggled out of the swirling torrents. A warrior stood on every exposed rock in the fast-flowing, pink-tinted rapids, ready to spear the next person who tried to cross.

It was there, on the bank short of the crossing, that Samuel was reunited with the rest of his unit, the Edendale Horse contingent of the Natal Native Horse. Having remained disciplined while other indigenous units had fled after the first shots of the battle, the Edendale troopers had only left Isandlwana at Durnford's explicit command. Now, one of their most steadfast leaders, Sergeant Major Simeon Kambula, had formed up two dozen of them into two ranks.

The sergeant major pointed at Samuel. 'You there, Khumalo, dismount, fall in!'

Samuel slid down from his saddle, unslung Gregory's rifle and joined the right end of the front rank. Although he was not one of those in his troop who had been issued a rifle, he had been trained in its use. The Zulus on the far bank banged their assegais against their shields, taunting the African soldiers. Perhaps they thought they didn't know how to shoot.

'At fifty yards,' Kambula bawled, slow and low. 'Front rank, ready!'

Each of the dismounted horsemen, Samuel included, worked the lever under his Martini–Henry and drew out a cartridge from a pocket or bandolier. Samuel blinked sweat from his eyes and tried to slow his breathing as he slid the fat brass round into the breech and levered it closed.

'Present!'

He had not been with the Edendale troop long, but the words of command had been drilled into him, just as the tactics of the Zulu *amabutho* had been taught to him from childhood. At the second command he raised the butt of the rifle into his shoulder and took aim at the group of warriors on the far bank, fifty yards away.

There was no command given to 'fire' when shooting a volley like this. Instead Samuel, like every man in his rank, said to himself: *One, two, three.* On the third count Samuel squeezed the trigger, and felt the kick in his shoulder. As a communal cloud of burned powder momentarily obscured the enemy from their sight, Samuel and the others in the front rank dropped to one knee, to allow those behind them the opportunity to fire next.

As the smoke dissipated Samuel saw gaps in the Zulu ranks and bodies on the sand. But the warriors were not easily discouraged. A barrage of spears came flying at the troopers as Samuel and the men in his rank reloaded. A spear landed just two or three yards in front of Samuel, but none of the others found its mark.

'Rear rank, ready!' Sergeant Major Kambula barked. Samuel counted to three, waited for the crash of soft, hollow-nosed bullets to leave barrels above his head, then he and his fellow troopers in the front rank stood again.

Samuel breathed in the smoke of the last volley and the vision of fewer warriors on the far bank filled him with nothing but elation. For all he knew, some of them could have been his childhood friends, but right now they stood between him, the man he had rescued, and freedom.

'Front rank, ready!'

A couple of defiant Zulus threw spears. Samuel licked his dry lips and his emotions roiled inside him. Gone was the thrill; now it was just the grim business of killing to survive.

Three. He squeezed the trigger again.

A cheer rose up from the Edendale troopers as the Zulus on the other side of the drift, realising they could not hope to stand against such fire, broke and ran. Those who had been reduced to cowering on their rocks in the river bounded to the Natal side, and also fled. The sergeant major gave the command to mount up.

In the course of their calm, disciplined fire the uniformed

troopers had bought time for more escapees from the battle to group up behind them.

'Take hold of our stirrups,' Kambula called to the refugees as he led the mounted troopers towards the river.

Samuel went to his horse and saw the man he had rescued was now standing beside it, though he looked unsteady. He was holding his left hand to his bloodied head. He reached out his right.

'Sub-Inspector Peter Gregory. My friends call me Captain – it's a nickname, not a rank. *Ngiyabonga.*'

Samuel took his hand and was surprised to see Gregory – Captain – shook it like an African. 'Trooper Khumalo, Samuel,' he said as he let go and climbed up in his saddle.

'How does Constable sound – Natal Mounted Police? The pay will be better.'

Samuel leaned down and helped Gregory back onto his horse, but sitting this time, and holding on to him. 'If we survive.'

Two dishevelled-looking redcoats joined them, grasping on to the stirrup straps on either side as Samuel spurred his horse into the raging river.

TERESA AND SAMUEL rode on in silence for a while after Samuel had finished telling his story.

Teresa stared at Peter Gregory on his horse, now little more than a lonely speck on the horizon, all alone. 'He has nothing to be ashamed of. In fact, the opposite.'

'You are correct,' Samuel said. 'But try telling him that.'

19

KWAZULU-NATAL, THE PRESENT

Adam drove his Ford Ranger, with Sannie next to him and Jan-Maree Ball in the back, giving directions when necessary.

From Dundee they headed back towards Pietermaritzburg, to Helpmekaar, which comprised little more than a police station, a farmhouse and a couple of abandoned old stone buildings.

'This is where Lord Chelmsford launched his invasion of Zululand in January, 1879,' Jan-Maree said.

Adam felt good being close to Sannie again, and wished it were just the two of them. Seeing her again made him realise how much he had missed her. She'd been shot at – as had he – and was deep into an investigation with a number of complex and dangerous threads, but all the same he felt she was being frosty towards him.

He reached over and squeezed her right knee.

Sannie gave him a look that said, *Not now.* He moved his hand. She was probably right, given Jan-Maree was in the back, looking on. His eyes caught Jan-Maree's in the rear-view mirror. She was smiling. Sannie looked out the window to her left.

'We turn off here,' Jan-Maree said.

Adam indicated and left the smooth tar road for a rough gravel surface, which had clearly been churned up during the last rainy season.

'This is Knostrope Pass,' Jan-Maree said. 'It leads down to the Mzinyathi Valley – the Buffalo River Valley.'

Sannie's phone dinged. She took it out and checked the screen. 'Marilyn's at Rorke's Drift already. She drives like a madwoman. She's waiting there for us. She says there's no sign of Tustin.' Sannie whispered to Adam: 'She'd already thought of going to a gun store. She has ammunition.'

'He's probably at Isandlwana by now, then,' Jan-Maree piped up from the back seat.

They started to descend. 'Hell, this is steep.' Adam braked hard as he went into a tight bend. The wide-open valley stretched out below them. 'Must have been tough in ox wagons in the old days.'

'It was,' Jan-Maree said. 'Helpmekaar takes its name from this pass, where locals would have to "help one another" to get up the hill.'

'You're the historian,' Sannie looked over her shoulder at Jan-Maree, 'what are your thoughts on David Gregory's collection of Anglo-Zulu War memorabilia and weapons and so forth? What's it all worth? What will happen to it?'

Adam glanced briefly at Jan-Maree in the mirror – he had to concentrate on the road. She seemed to think a moment.

'The answer to the first question is, I'm not sure. A good deal of money to the right collector or collectors, but it's academic.'

'Why?' Sannie asked.

'David told me not long ago that he had specified in his will that the whole collection would go to the Talana Museum, in Dundee. There'll be a few upset collectors, for sure.'

'Like Richard Tustin?' Sannie asked.

Adam saw Jan-Maree shrug. He gripped the steering wheel tighter at the sound of the man's name. Sannie had warned him that she would ask the questions when they met up with Tustin, and Adam understood that was the best course of action. But he had a score to settle with the man if he was, in fact, the commander of the men who had tried to kill Adam and his student.

It was ironic, Adam thought, that here they were driving the route of an invasion that had taken place nearly one hundred and fifty years earlier, when they might be heading into another battle.

'Tell me about the trade in memorabilia,' Sannie said.

'It's a thing,' Jan-Maree said. 'David was dead against it. Yes, he had a big collection, but much of that was stuff that had been given to him. He'd been working to uplift the communities around the battle-fields for decades and every now and then some old *madala* would give him a shield or a knobkerrie – a club – or an assegai that had belonged to his great-great-grandfather or whatever. He never bought or sold, though, to the best of my knowledge.'

'Even though he was going bankrupt?' Adam chimed in.

'*Ja*, even then,' Jan-Maree confirmed.

'What about others?'

'I was up at Hlobane a while ago, walking the battlefield on my own, or so I thought, when I came across a kid, a local boy of maybe sixteen or so, with a metal detector. I asked him where he got it and he said a white guy had given it to him, and told him to go look for stuff on the battlefield.'

'Where's Hlobane?' Adam asked. It was weird, learning things about his own country's history from a younger person with an Australian accent. However, her pronunciation of Zulu words was very good.

'Up towards Vryheid,' Jan-Maree said. 'It's not as well known as Isandlwana, but it was another disaster for the British and their allies during the war. The Zulus lured them up onto Hlobane Mountain – it's still a hell of a rugged place to get to – and then slaughtered them. There were even accounts of colonial horsemen riding their horses off the top, over sheer precipices, and falling to their deaths while they tried to get away. The battlefield's on private land, owned by a coalmine, and you need permission to visit – or you sneak in, like the kid I came across. Because of its location, and the fact it's not as popular as other sites, you can still find bullets and belt buckles and other remnants of the battle there.'

'Who gave the kid the detector?' Sannie asked.

'He wouldn't tell me, and he became quite aggressive when I pushed him, so I left him to it. I told David, later, and he said he would report it to Amafa, the KwaZulu-Natal heritage body, but I never heard if they followed up. David said he'd heard of a British tourist travelling Zululand, handing out metal detectors and money for finds.'

At the bottom of the winding pass the road flattened out and was in better condition, so Adam picked up speed. They drove across the broad, open, grassy valley towards the Buffalo River. The sun was high, the sky clear, and Adam tried to imagine the landscape at the time of the battles that were fought there when, for a time, this remote corner of Zululand was the centre of the English-speaking world's attention.

Eventually they arrived at Rorke's Drift, the former trading post and mission station that for many years had been a museum to the battle fought there. Marilyn was waiting for them in the car park, leaning against Sannie's Toyota Fortuner.

Adam pulled up next to her and he, Sannie and Jan-Maree got out of the Ranger to stretch their legs.

'Howzit, Marilyn,' Sannie said, 'you been sightseeing?'

'While you were sleeping.' Marilyn grinned. 'This place is boring. I want to see the battlefield where the Zulus won.'

'Next stop,' Adam said. He and Marilyn hugged.

'The missing Mr Kruger.' Marilyn held him at arm's length. 'It's good to see you again. If you have a fine woman like the colonel, you need to stay home more.'

'*Ja.*' Adam looked to Sannie and she just shook her head at Marilyn's bluntness.

'No sign of Tustin?' Sannie said.

'*Aikona*, Colonel. Not here,' Marilyn said. 'I waited for you, as ordered.'

Adam looked at the stone buildings with red tin roofs.

Jan-Maree pointed to one. 'That was the hospital, the other was the storeroom. Both buildings were burned during the battle and have been rebuilt and altered over the years. Do you want to take a quick look inside?'

As a former solider, Adam did – he'd never been to this place, despite growing up less than five hours' drive away.

'We've got a murder investigation on our hands, plus other crimes that need looking into. We agreed to drive you to help us find Richard Tustin, not to be our tour guide,' Sannie said.

Jan-Maree ran her hands down the front of her shirt. 'Point taken.'

The young woman looked nervous, Adam thought, and he wondered if her offering to show them around the museum was a way of stalling their meeting with Tustin. Was she worried about it? Adam thought of the weapons he was carrying. He doubted Tustin would try anything in a public place, with witnesses around, but it seemed the stakes were high and his foot soldiers on the coast had been happy to be dropped into a gunfight in a public camping ground.

They went to their cars. Adam felt Sannie's hand on his elbow. 'Just give us a moment, please, Jan-Maree.' The young woman nodded and got into the Ranger.

Sannie led Adam a few metres away. 'I'm sorry, about before, and just now, if I sounded stand-offish.'

He smiled for her. 'It's OK. You've been under stress; you were wounded. I get it.'

'It's more than that. We'll talk later. It's also that . . . Adam, I missed you, when you were away. I didn't want to come up here and, to tell you the truth, if circumstances had been different, I would have told Gita no, even if it cost me my job.'

Adam tried to process her words. *If circumstances had been different.* Did that mean that if he'd been at home in Pennington, with her, then she would not have left him? Was that what she wanted of him, to be around all the time? He'd wanted to be a marine biologist so much when he was younger, but the army and life had got in the way and he'd spent years in a loveless marriage. He didn't regret his two children, Phillip and Jolene, but it felt like he'd just begun to live the life he wanted, finishing his PhD, being given his own turtle research program to supervise *and* finding Sannie. He tried to think of the right thing to say.

'It's fine, Adam.' She turned and went around to her side of the car.

'Sannie . . .'

She made a show of checking her watch. 'Let's go. I want to catch Tustin at the next stop.'

THEY WERE TOO LATE. Sannie tried to keep her rising anger in check.

'Yes, I know the major, Mr Tustin,' the young Zulu woman in an Amafa shirt at the entry gate to Isandlwana Battlefield said to Adam when he asked if Tustin was onsite. 'He left about twenty minutes ago.'

Sannie put a hand to her forehead. She had a headache. She looked at Jan-Maree in the rear of the double cab. 'Where's he going next?'

'The Prince Imperial's monument, at Nqutu.' Jan-Maree pronounced the name of the place with the correct 'click' at the beginning. 'Maybe half-an-hour's drive.'

'How long will he spend there?'

Jan-Maree shrugged. 'Thirty, forty minutes. Depends how interested his guests are in Louis Napoleon's story.'

Adam turned the Ranger around and pulled over, giving Sannie time to think.

She'd been too abrupt with him in the car park and he hadn't said anything since.

They had both been mostly silent on the drive to Isandlwana, which was not far, but Jan-Maree had prattled on about how the vegetation in the area was different from what it was like in 1879, with far more trees now than in the old days. As a scientist, Adam was interested in her theory about why this was so – Sannie felt like he was taking refuge in talking about stuff he was interested in, rather than their relationship.

She banged the dashboard.

'Are you OK?' Adam asked.

'No, Adam, I'm not OK.' She took a deep breath. She did not want to do this in front of a stranger. What the hell had she been thinking, bringing a civilian along as a tour guide on a police investigation? Sannie felt like control of her life, and this case, was slipping through her fingers.

'Sorry,' Adam said.

She glanced at him. He was so handsome. Could he really be so unfeeling that he couldn't see what his protracted absences were doing to their relationship? Her second husband, Tom Furey, had been similar to Adam in some ways. After Tom had left the Metropolitan Police in London and moved to South Africa to be with her, he'd felt restless, having given up his career. Sannie suspected his ego had suffered and so he'd taken a job as a contract bodyguard, working mostly in Iraq, not just for the money, which had been a fortune by South African standards, but to regain what he saw as his lost self-esteem. She'd also struggled with his absences, but she had said nothing, knowing the work was important to him. And it had cost Tom his life.

Her grief and loneliness had almost killed her. At one point, alone in the Kruger Park one morning, she had been close to taking her own life.

Then she'd found Adam. And he, too, was compensating for what he saw as wasted years in his life, by taking on this new job as a scientist, away from her.

Adam reached out, took her hand from her lap and gave it a squeeze.

She looked at him and fought the urge to snatch her hand away. At that moment she didn't care that Jan-Maree was in the car. She looked into his blue eyes.

Love you, he mouthed.

Sannie gave a small nod. 'All right. Let's get going.' Then she had a thought, and looked again into the rear. 'Give me your phone.'

'What?' Jan-Maree said.

'I said, give me your phone, now.'

Jan-Maree leaned back into the seat, away from her. 'You can't make me give you my phone. I'm not under arrest. Am I?'

'No. But I don't want to risk you sending messages to your *friend*, Tustin, telling him our movements.'

'There's nothing going on between us, if that's what you're inferring,' Jan-Maree said.

'Yet he gave you a Celtic love knot ring?'

Jan-Maree sighed. 'OK. So, he's got a bit of a crush on me. He knew I split up with Deon and then he asked me out, but I said no. He persisted, and, well, he can be charming and he gave me the ring, but I'd also developed feelings for John.'

'How did Tustin feel about that?'

'He wasn't exactly thrilled, but Richard's old enough to be my father. I told him the age gap thing wasn't for me.'

'Give me your phone,' Sannie said again.

'I told you, signal's useless out here.'

Sannie took out her own phone and checked the screen. 'Four bars. Four G.'

Jan-Maree narrowed her eyes. 'Must be the good weather conditions. And no load shedding.'

Sannie held out her hand. 'Give me your phone, or you can get out here and hitchhike back to Dundee. Stop the car, Adam.'

Adam pulled over to the side of the road. A stray cow blinked at them.

'You'll never find your way to the Prince Imperial's monument without me,' Jan-Maree said.

'We'll ask a local,' Sannie said.

Jan-Maree laughed. 'Good luck with that. Tourists travel all the way from France every year on the anniversary of Louis Napoleon's death to visit that place, but for most of the people who live around

Nqutu they couldn't care less who he was, even if they know. They're too busy trying to find work or feed themselves or fetch water from the river.'

'Are you leading us on a wild-goose chase, Jan-Maree?'

Jan-Maree glared at her. 'I'm *not* messaging Richard, and I'm not leading you astray. I told you, he's with two overseas clients – a woman from New York called Goldie someone, and a guy named Piet from somewhere in Europe, I think. The truth is, I want to see Richard again, because if he's up to something illegal, or whatever, I want to know about it. If it was his crazy veterans who shot at you and John and your partner then I want to know why. I'm not going to invest myself in a man who's no good for me. *That's* why I agreed to help you today.'

Sannie was taken aback. '*Invest* in him? So you are interested in him after all?'

Jan-Maree frowned. 'No. Maybe. I don't know. He's offered more than once to pay for my airfare to London next time he goes home. He says he'll take me to the Imperial War Museum and the museum of the Royal Welsh Regiment, which has an amazing Anglo-Zulu War collection.'

Sannie almost scoffed. She didn't know whether Jan-Maree was naïve or a manipulator of the men around her. 'And John?'

Jan-Maree exhaled. 'He's lovely, and handsome, and all he cares about is wildlife, which is cool, but . . .'

Sannie shook her head. 'All right. Let's go, Adam.'

Adam put the car into gear and drove off. Jan-Maree reached through between the front seats, her phone in her outstretched hand.

Sannie checked Jan-Maree's SMS messages and WhatsApp. There was nothing that had been recently sent to or received from Tustin. Sannie handed the phone back to her and Jan-Maree put it in her pocket.

'What's the countryside like, around Nqutu and the monument?' Adam asked as they left Isandlwana, with Marilyn following them.

Sannie wondered if Adam really wanted another lesson on post-colonial botany, or if he was looking for intelligence on the terrain, in case they became involved in a confrontation.

'Sparse. Open. Short dry grass,' Jan-Maree said. 'The landscape's changed since we were up on the high ground, near Helpmekaar and Dundee.'

'Yes.'

Sannie could see it as well. The higher grasslands had been lush and supported fat cattle on farms that had been established by the *Voortrekkers*, her people, and the English had brought sugar cane, along with labourers from their other colony in India, from the coast to the fertile hills around Pietermaritzburg.

'The Zulus would move their cattle to the higher pastures, traditionally, but by the end of the nineteenth century they were hemmed in, restricted to places like this. See how short the grass is, how thin the layer of topsoil here? This is hard country; there are fewer cattle compared to where we were higher up.'

Sannie saw what she meant as they began passing the isolated kraals dotted about the landscape. Each one, a collection of a few modest buildings of brick and tin, was the base for a family, but instead of herds of beasts there was a bony cow here and there, or a few goats. Adam slowed to let a small boy cross the road, pushing a rusty wheelbarrow with an old plastic twenty-litre paint bucket in it – water from a well or a stream, she guessed.

Decades on from the hopes and dreams promised by Nelson Mandela, the people here were still living in poverty without the most basic of necessities.

'What was Napoleon's great-nephew doing out here anyway?' Adam asked.

Jan-Maree lapsed into tour guide mode. 'After the Franco-Prussian war, Emperor Louis Napoleon, the prince's father, was forced into exile, with his wife, Empress Eugénie. Ironically, they found themselves living in England, the home of Bonaparte's fiercest opponents. The emperor had done some good things for France, such as building most of modern Paris as we know it today, but he'd made some foreign policy blunders. He was almost assassinated by a bomb thanks to trying to block another European country's bid for unification, and he bit off more than he could chew by going to war with Otto von Bismarck of Prussia. His son, Prince Napoleon Eugène Louis Jean Joseph Bonaparte – better known as Louis Napoleon, wanted to be a soldier, like his great-uncle, Napoleon Bonaparte, so he actually enrolled in the British Army's officer training school.'

'So, Bonaparte's great-nephew joined the British Army?' Adam sounded incredulous.

'Not exactly,' Jan-Maree said. 'He trained with them, but as a French national he could not join their army. When the Anglo-Zulu War broke out, Louis was desperate to join the fight. His mother, and even the British Prime Minister, were dead against it, but the prince talked his mother around, and thanks to Queen Victoria, who was a friend of Empress Eugénie, the prince was allowed to sail for South Africa, where he was supposed to act as a kind of observer of Chelmsford's second invasion of Zululand – after the first, failed attempt.'

'So this was after Isandlwana and Rorke's Drift?' Adam said.

Jan-Maree nodded. 'The British government had been ambivalent about a war against the Zulus initially – the campaign was really driven by Bartle Frere, the governor of Natal, who had a mandate to bring Zululand more under British control. But after the terrible defeat at Isandlwana the British public was baying for blood. Chelmsford was going to be relieved by another general, Wolseley, so he was in a hurry to go back into Zululand and defeat Cetshwayo before his replacement arrived. More troops were sent from England, and with them came the French prince.'

'How did he get killed if he was supposed to be an observer?' Sannie asked.

'The prince was what we would call today "gung-ho". He was itching for action, even though he wasn't supposed to be a combatant. There are accounts of him riding off solo after Zulu warriors when they were spotted, waving his great-uncle's sword over his head as he did so.'

Adam looked away from the road for a moment. 'He had Napoleon Bonaparte's sword?'

Sannie was leaning around her seat back, listening to Jan-Maree. The historian rocked her head from side to side. 'Maybe, maybe not. There are sources from the time that say he was armed with a sword that Bonaparte had used in his historic victory against the Russians and Austrians at Austerlitz in 1805, but that's confusing.'

'How come?' Adam asked.

'Long story, but I'll try and make it short,' Jan-Maree said. 'The prince was on Lord Chelmsford's staff, where they could supposedly keep an eye on him. He was given a job scouting just ahead of the main British force, and sketching the route that the column would take – remember, there were no detailed maps at the time. He stayed at Helpmekaar and Utrecht, north of here, and was coming into Zulu-land in the direction of Nqutu when he was sent out with a small party of horsemen to look for a site for the army's next encampment. The area was believed to be clear of hostile Zulus, and the prince and the other men stopped at what they thought was an abandoned kraal for coffee. While they were sitting waiting for the water to boil, a group of Zulus emerged from a nearby mealie patch and attacked them. Everyone made a run for it, and the prince's horse bolted. He was holding on to the stirrup leather from his saddle as he ran, trying to mount, but the strap snapped, or became unhooked, and he was left alone. Two of the British escort and a Zulu scout working for the British had already been killed and by this time the others had galloped away. It was just Prince Louis, armed with his pistol in one hand and his sword in the other, facing down all the Zulus. He died, as a book about him puts it, *"with his face to the foe"*. There was a huge fuss afterwards, with the surviving British officer from the patrol charged with cowardice for not going back to try and rescue the prince, and court-martialled. In the end he was acquitted.'

'And the sword?' Adam prompted.

'Right. The prince's body was stripped and his weapons and uniform were taken by the Zulus. Most of his possessions were recov-ered by a later patrol that went looking for them, but his sword was actually handed back to the British by two emissaries from Cetshwayo's court in the run-up to the Battle of Ulundi, in which he was finally defeated. The Zulu king knew the sword had belonged to an important man, and he offered it as a sign of good faith, to try and get the British to negotiate with him. But Chelmsford was hell-bent on a military victory to save his reputation.'

'Ego,' Sannie said.

'Partly,' Jan-Maree replied. 'Chelmsford later took the prince's sword back to the UK and gave it to Empress Eugénie. It ended up in a museum in France. But it turned out not to be Napoleon Bonaparte's sword, but rather a plain French Army general-service cavalry sword. It's such a shame old David Gregory's not with us. He knew more than any of the local guides about the Prince Imperial. I had a theory . . . Well, it doesn't matter now.'

'What was your theory?' Adam asked.

Sannie knew that Adam was interested in swords, having recovered the Arab relic from the men who had tried to kill him at Bhanga Nek. She felt a little tingle in her fingers, which she sometimes experienced when she came across an important or missing piece of evidence or clue in a police investigation.

'I couldn't reconcile the several primary source – contemporary – accounts of the young prince carrying Napoleon Bonaparte's sword into battle, and the fact that it turned out to be an ordinary French cavalry trooper's weapon. I asked David Gregory about it – we had several discussions about the sword. His view was that the prince was a braggart, a bit of a "Walter Mitty", with delusions of grandeur.'

'You didn't buy it?' Adam kept his eyes on the road.

'Yes and no,' Jan-Maree said. 'I mean, we have the hard evidence, that a French sword was presented to the British and Chelmsford later gave it to the empress, and that sword is sitting in a museum in France today. But why would the prince lie about the lineage of his sword? Imagine the scandal and ridicule it would have caused at the time, if someone had proved he was lying. And what reason did he have to lie about the lineage of his weapon when his name and his bloodline spoke for itself? He didn't need to *prove* he was Napoleon Bonaparte's heir – he was.'

'What was your theory?' Sannie asked. 'If the prince really was carrying his great-uncle's sword when he died, then what do you think happened to it?'

Jan-Maree smiled. 'You're the detective, Colonel. You of all people should know what human beings are like, and what they're capable of.'

'You think someone stole it?' Sannie said.

'It's just what you'd probably call a hunch,' Jan-Maree said, 'but I've been spending quite a bit of time scouring old books, letters and archival documents looking for something that might support my theory.'

'The question is,' Sannie said, 'if it was Bonaparte's sword and it was stolen back in 1879 and swapped for a different weapon, where is it now?'

Jan-Maree shrugged. 'It could be anywhere. It might have been smuggled back to the UK and now be in the attic in someone's family home, or sold to a private collector. It might even still be here in South Africa somewhere.'

'How much does Anglo-Zulu War memorabilia sell for?' Adam slowed to allow a cow to cross the gravel road. A little boy in ragged shorts and shirt carried a stick and was trying to tend to the animal. He waved at Adam, who returned the greeting.

'Depends,' Jan-Maree said. 'Individual shields, assegais and rifles from the period can sell for hundreds of pounds, maybe – the UK market is big. The Victoria Cross medals for bravery awarded during the war run into the tens of thousands, or even more. The VC awarded to Lieutenant Bromhead at Rorke's Drift – he was the guy played by Michael Caine in the movie, *Zulu*, is estimated to be worth seven hundred thousand pounds, close to a million US dollars.'

'*Bliksem*,' Sannie said.

'If Napoleon's sword from the battle of Austerlitz was found, what would that be worth?' Adam asked.

Jan-Maree shook her head. 'Who knows for sure, but the last time one of Bonaparte's swords came up for auction, from a private collector, it sold for six-and-a-half million US dollars.'

Sannie thought about that amount. It was more than worth killing for. She glanced at Adam, who nodded that he was thinking the same thing.

Sannie looked back into the rear of the double cab. 'What has your research uncovered so far?'

Jan-Maree exhaled audibly. 'Not a lot. I was hoping that David could help me some more, even though his view was that Louis Napoleon never really carried the Austerlitz sword. David's great-great-uncle, one Sub-Inspector Peter Gregory, was a member of the NMP – the Natal Mounted Police – and I found a few references to him in the police archives. I was looking through old investigation reports and came across an entry dated May, 1880. Peter was tasked by the commander of the NMP, Major Dartnell, to escort an alleged noblewoman who was travelling in Zululand at the same time as the Empress Eugénie was visiting the area, on the first anniversary of the death of her son, the prince.'

'What's an "alleged noblewoman"?' Adam asked.

'It was a woman named Teresa O'Kane. She was an American who claimed to be an English aristocrat, Lady Beecham, even though her titled husband had left her. She was actually a journalist for a New York newspaper and she was in South Africa trying to get a scoop – a picture and an interview with Empress Eugénie, like an olden-days member of the paparazzi. Royal Watching's nothing new. The empress found out Teresa was in the country and gave orders that she be kept away from her. I think Peter Gregory had been sent to keep an eye on Teresa and to keep her away from the empress, but there was a second entry in the archives which said something like: "*. . . also investigate report of alleged valuable missing property*". I wondered if it was more than a coincidence that Gregory was looking for something important at the same time, and in the same general area, as the empress was travelling.'

Sannie thought it was an optimistic stretch. She asked the next obvious question. 'What do the police logs say about the outcome of Gregory's mission?'

'There's nothing more,' Jan-Maree said. 'The next entry in the record noted that on the first of June, 1880 – incidentally, a year to the day after Prince Louis was killed – Sub-Inspector Peter Gregory was killed while trying to apprehend a suspect. He was stabbed to death, run through by an unnamed man armed with a sword.'

20

ZULULAND, 1880

Samuel, who knew this part of Zululand better than Peter, led them to the monument that had been constructed at the place where the Prince Imperial had been killed.

It was the day after they had passed through Isandlwana. Gregory had been quiet throughout that afternoon, preferring to ride ahead of the rest of the party but behind Samuel, who had scouted ahead. They had spent a cold night on a windswept hill and not even his customary morning coffee could lift Gregory's spirits.

There was nothing special about the place where the French royal bloodline had come to an end.

Nqutu, a cluster of huts and a largish kraal, was the bastion of the Hlubi people, Zulus who had sided with the whites and whose chief had then been installed to rule over this part of Zululand. Samuel and Gregory had paid their respects to the chief, whose protruding belly was the only sign that he enjoyed a marginally more privileged life than the other people of his district.

The young man whose father had, for a time, held custody of the prince's sword had been adamant that the sword was returned to the British, and that he had never seen it again. That meant that if the sword had been switched – a standard French cavalry sabre substituted for the real sword carried by Napoleon Bonaparte – then the deed had been done by someone in Chelmsford's army.

A river – little more than a narrow stream a yard or two wide in places at this time of year – ran through a donga.

'This is the Tshotshosi,' Samuel said. Further downstream a boy of nine or ten was collecting water in a clay gourd.

Gregory dismounted, and while he waited for Phillips, the wagon, the women and the Italian count to catch up, he and Samuel watered their horses. A short distance away some trees had been planted to provide shade, one day, for the marble cross that marked the place where the prince had been killed. He would take the others there when they arrived.

Gregory looked around. Apart from the man-made monument, there was nothing to distinguish this forlorn place from any other in this blood-soaked kingdom where thousands on both sides had died.

He kicked the dirt and golden grass at his feet. *Was it really worth dying for?*

In contrast to the steadily increasing noise of creaking axles and the squeaks of the loaded wagon, he heard the drumbeat of hooves and looked up out of the donga towards a hill. A horseman was approaching, at speed.

Gregory raised his hand to his eyes, to shield them from the glare. The man on horseback was British. Cavalry. Gregory spat in the dust.

'You there,' the man called as he came within earshot and reined in his horse. 'Sub-Inspector Gregory. You're to move along, away from this place, at once.'

Gregory moved his hands to his hips and glared up at Second Lieutenant Llewelyn Walters, who stopped his horse a few yards from him.

'Under whose orders?' Gregory asked.

'General Wood. Damn it, man, I told you before, we have orders to keep that meddlesome person,' he nodded in the direction of Teresa's approaching wagon, 'away from the Empress Eugénie. Her Majesty and General Wood and their attendants will be here tomorrow.'

'Calm yourself, Lieutenant,' Gregory said. 'I know the empress's wishes and I don't need you to parrot them at me.'

Walters looked at the additional riders and packhorses, trundling towards them in the distance. 'And who might they be?'

'An acquaintance of mine, and a gentleman friend from Italy, who is touring the colony.'

Walters narrowed his eyes and kept staring. 'Wait. I know her. She's that Indian whore, from –'

Gregory closed the distance between them in a couple of bounds, reached up and grabbed Walters by his pistol belt. Before the officer could react, Gregory hauled him out of the saddle and he fell to the ground.

The silent rage and shame and terrors that had been bottled inside Gregory for more than a year burst from him as he stood over the fallen Walters, his fists bunched tight by his side.

'Peter!' Samuel ran to him, but Gregory ignored his friend's call.

'Apologise, damn you,' Gregory said.

Walters said nothing but started to get up, and as Gregory took a step closer to him, Walters kicked out and swooped his leg crossways, catching Peter below one knee and knocking him over.

Walters scrambled and leapt on Gregory, then slammed his right fist into Gregory's jaw. Peter was older, but he'd been in his share of brawls. He brought his knee up into Walters' crotch and the lieutenant rolled over, sucking in air through his mouth. Gregory was on him and landed blows to the other man's stomach and chin before he felt Samuel's big hands on his shoulders, dragging him away from the fight.

'Enough,' Samuel said.

Samuel held him back, but Gregory fought against his friend to free an arm and deliver a killing blow. In that moment he knew he could pound the other man until he died. His anger needed an outlet, a target, and it was in front of him.

Walters stood and wiped a cut lip.

Gregory tried to reach for the pistol in the holster on his belt.

'No,' Samuel said in a steady, even voice into his ear, his lips as close as a lover's. 'He's not worth it.'

Walters had seen Gregory's move and now he, too, drew his service revolver and aimed it at the two men still locked in an embrace.

Gregory heard the metallic *click* of a rifle lever being worked and flicked his head around.

'I wouldn't if I were you, Lieutenant,' Teresa O'Kane drawled as she sighted down the barrel of a Martini–Henry rifle aimed at Walters' head.

Teresa's wagon had pulled up and Grace and the count stopped next to her. Grace jumped down from her horse.

'What are you stupid men up to?' Grace demanded as she strode to them and placed herself between Gregory and Walters.

'Go back,' Walters paused to spit blood, 'to the den of sin you came from, miss.'

'Sin?' Grace pointed a finger at Walters. 'You hypocrite. I *know* you. You're the one who Marigold said likes to wear her bloomers while she spanks you, when you're not hurting her.'

'What . . . How *dare* you, you slattern.' Walters' face went red. He raised his gun hand and shifted his aim to Grace.

A shot rang out, echoing across the barren plains, and Gregory saw the puff of dirt erupt in front of Walters' boots. He looked around and saw Teresa eject the spent cartridge then chamber a second round.

'You can get on your horse and mosey along right about now, Lieutenant,' Teresa said.

Gregory shook himself free of Samuel's grip and stepped around Grace. 'And apologise to the lady.'

Walters half rose, then lowered his pistol and shoved the weapon back into its holster. His face remained vermillion. 'I will do no such thing.' He paused for a second then turned and remounted his horse. As he wheeled it around he pointed at Gregory. '*You* take charge of these insolent women and make sure you're gone by nightfall. The empress and her party are due here tomorrow. If any of you are here, and that includes you as well, Sub-Inspector, I'll have you arrested under General Wood's orders.'

Walters kicked his horse and galloped away.

Gregory turned back to Grace and raised an eyebrow. 'Marigold's bloomers?'

Grace rocked her head a little and smiled. 'Well, it was a rumour I heard.'

Gregory strode to Teresa. 'That rifle's got a kick like three mules. You're lucky you didn't kill him.'

The rifle was across her lap. 'I'd say he's the lucky one, Captain. And I know guns, so don't lecture me.'

'Well,' he raised his voice so that they could all hear him, 'as much as we may have cause to dislike young Lieutenant Walters, his orders do come from a general and an empress. We will camp here the night, so that those who wish can take pictures and so forth, and we *will* be away from here by first light.' Gregory looked around. 'Where's the count?'

Ferdinand appeared, somewhat sheepishly, from behind Teresa's wagon. He straightened his tie and smoothed his oiled hair.

'I am sorry, *Capitano*, I am not, how you say, a man of action.'

Grace went to him and picked imaginary dust particles from the lapels of his expensive tweed jacket. 'It's all right, Ferdi. Not all men need to behave like Neanderthals.'

Gregory shook his head. Samuel came to him and lowered his voice so only the two of them could hear. 'I thought you were going to kill him, Peter.'

'I might have, if you hadn't taken hold of me. Thank you. You may have spared me a court martial, and the gallows.'

They still hadn't had time to inspect the monument. Gregory and Samuel walked to it. In the small yard fenced in by a dry-stone wall was a marble cross with the details of Prince Louis's life and death engraved upon it. Weaver birds chirped in the saplings planted nearby in the prince's honour. Gregory walked past the impressive crucifix to the far end of the tiny cemetery where two simple crosses marked the actual resting places of the troopers who had been killed in action on that fateful day and buried here. The prince's body had been taken back to Pietermaritzburg and from there on to Durban and London, where he was finally buried. Gregory remembered the funeral procession – as a member of the Natal Mounted Police, he had been a member of the honour guard.

He stopped by the graves of the troopers.

Gregory took off his helmet and looked down at the smaller, simpler crosses. The prince, by all accounts, and like many a young officer fresh out of training, had wanted to make his mark on the world and prove himself on the field of battle. But what of these two men, and the Zulu scout who was with them that day? The scout's body was never found or, if it was, not given a decent burial. These men had been in this forgotten corner of Zululand because it was their job, and it paid and fed them. Gregory had learned, in the shadow of Isandlwana, that no death was noble or heroic. Durnford, along with men who Gregory knew personally, had made a last stand, but for what? Empire? Their queen? The desires of men such as Shepstone and Bartle Frere to colour a map red had left a land drenched in blood.

It could have – should have – been him lying under one of the rock cairns at Isandlwana. To die because of a general's inability to follow his own orders about creating defences around encampments, or because of a young royal's impetuous need for fame, was bad enough. But to live knowing other men – good men – had died in one's place was an endless torture.

Gregory started at the touch of a hand on his shoulder. He spun around.

Teresa looked up into his face, trying to read it. 'Did you know these men?'

He shook his head. 'No. Many like them, but not these two.'

'War is senseless.'

Was it? Cetshwayo had been a tyrant of sorts, but he had not crossed the Buffalo River into Natal, as many had feared. One reckless commander, Dabulamanzi, had done so and attacked Rorke's Drift against his king's orders. By handing Chelmsford a victory, he had bought the British commander a reprieve and perhaps negated any negotiating advantage that Isandlwana might have given Cetshwayo.

Also, Prince Louis's great-uncle had been an infamous tyrant who sought to conquer much of Europe. Had it not been *sensible* to stop a man like Napoleon Bonaparte?

'I suppose,' he said. 'Sometimes.'

'You've been quiet, since we crossed into Zululand.'

He looked into her eyes and saw the kindness there. He noted how she was searching for answers to what tormented him. It was not quiet in his dreams, nor in his mind.

Teresa glanced around her then took a step closer to him and wrapped her arms around him. 'Come here.'

Gregory stiffened. He was not inexperienced in the ways of women, but public displays of affection were no more the norm in the colony than they were back in England. Perhaps things were different in America.

He felt the heat of her body, smelled the soap in her hair and a hint of perfume. His resistance, his gruffness, his fears and his torment dissolved in the power of her embrace.

'Oh, Peter. Let me help you.'

He closed his eyes. If only it were that simple. The others would surely come to the monument now, to inspect it and pay their respects. Even now they might be watching this . . . show. He wanted to push her away. He was a broken man, a husk emptied of whatever value he'd once had. Gregory had been kidding himself that police work would fulfil him, or that it might help him find redemption for his crime of having survived when so many better men had been killed that day.

He had to tell this woman, as beautiful and unorthodox – and kind – as she was, that she was wasting her time with him.

But, as he felt her cheek against his, the press of her breasts through her riding clothes, he didn't care. He clung to her as if she were the last thing to stop him sliding into the dry African dirt, and descending into the hell that awaited him.

'I...'

She put a finger to his lips. 'Hush, now. You saved me, back at the river. I would have run if I'd seen that leopard first, and I know, now, that if I had I would have died. I was terrified, but you stilled me. Let me do the same for you.'

He drew his head back, to better take in her face, her eyes, and her full lips. He wanted to kiss her now, but to do so would have pushed the bounds of decency, and signalled to her that he thought himself worthy of her attention.

Teresa drew herself up onto her toes and kissed him on the mouth.

They had to stop, however, for in that instant they heard the crunch of a footfall on dry twigs and leaves. Gregory and Teresa hurriedly parted and looked around in unison.

Grace stepped from behind the young tree that would one day overshadow the prince's memorial. She put a hand to her mouth for an instant, then gathered her skirts with the other, turned and ran.

Gregory stood there, confused. He looked at Teresa.

She gave him a small, sad smile. 'She's sweet on you.'

'She's . . .' He didn't want to insult Grace, nor to give any credence to the vile things Walters had said about her. In truth, he had no idea what feelings, if any, Grace had for him. He'd been more than happy to give her refuge in his home when she needed it, and he had taken solace in her arms, and her body. He'd still felt, however, that while no money had changed hands between them, she saw him as providing her a service, and that she was repaying him in kind. Certainly, she'd been shockingly honest in telling him of her conversion to Christianity in order to find herself a 'decent' husband and respectability in the colony.

Does she actually care for me? He stared after her.

'She's a woman, Peter. If I'd known you two had some . . . history, I wouldn't have been so rash. Please forgive me.'

He looked at Teresa now. 'No. Yes. I mean . . . well, I don't know what I mean.' He ran a hand through his hair.

She smiled. 'You're a man. It's all right. You should maybe go and see Grace.'

'I . . . I suppose you're right.'

He left Teresa in the memorial grounds and walked to the wagon. Samuel and Phillips were supervising the unloading and preparation of their campsite.

'Don't unpack everything,' Gregory said to Phillips. 'We'll be leaving at dawn.'

'Yes, sir,' Phillips said. 'Oh, sir?'

'Yes?' Gregory said.

'Miss Grace just walked past in quite a state. She was crying, sir.'

'Yes, very good, Phillips. I'll see to her. Get on with it.'

Phillips touched the brim of his helmet.

Gregory spotted Grace off in the distance. She had gone into the veld, in the direction of the kraal that stood on the top of the small rise, above the river's high-water mark. The Italian count watched Gregory walk by. He had a puzzled look on his face and Gregory thought that he must be wondering what was wrong with Grace as well.

'Grace?' he called. 'Don't go far.'

The Zulu nation was nominally at peace now, at least with Britain, but there were old rivalries resurfacing, and some fighting had been reported between clans. Gregory didn't want any of his charges wandering off by themselves too far from camp.

'Grace?'

She strode on, arms swinging, although he saw her raise a hand to her face; it looked like she was wiping her eyes.

Grace came to within twenty yards of the small settlement. A young boy came out of a hut to look at her. She stopped, hands on hips.

Gregory stepped out and caught up to her. She wheeled on him.

'Grace, I . . . I don't know what to say. I didn't think you cared for me or saw a future between us.'

She wiped her eyes, then glared at him. 'There was *never* going to be a future for us, and that's what makes me angry, Peter.'

'You made it quite clear you didn't want to stay on the farm or be a policeman's wife.' He said it not as an accusation, but rather as a statement of fact.

She waved his words away like smoke. 'I know what I said. But it was more than that.' She jutted her chin at him. 'You're too wrapped up in your own melancholy, feeling sorry for yourself because you didn't die like the rest of those red-coated fools, marching around someone else's country and subjugating the damn natives.'

Gregory tried to form a reply, but couldn't.

'What's *wrong* with you, Peter? Would you rather have died? Is *that* why you won't let anyone love you? Do you think you're on borrowed time, that you can only find peace, or happiness eternal, if you die?'

He looked away, not wanting to confront the truth of her accusations. He knew Grace saw things differently; she came from another world, a harder world, where the weak or the pitiable or the infirm were cast aside.

'Look at me, Peter Gregory.'

Something she'd said came to him. *Love*? Had she used that word?

'Grace, I never knew you . . .'

'Yes, indubitably. Exactly. You never knew me, Mr British Army officer turned accomplished policeman and inept farmer. How could you *know* a lowly coolie like me? How could you ever think that I might need something more than money, or shelter, or a warm bed? Do you think that other people have no feelings, no emotions?'

'No, not at all, but –'

'Pah!' She waved him down again, then made a shooing gesture with both her hands. 'I left your home because I needed more, Peter. I needed more money, yes, and I need the things that even a white man down on his luck and plagued with misery has as his birthright – status, respectability, class, privilege. Those of us not born British need to work for those things, or sell our bodies for them, or steal them. Do I shock you?'

He looked down. 'No.' It was a moment before he could meet her eyes again. 'What do you want, Grace?'

She folded her arms, hugging herself tight, and then turned her gaze on Teresa, who was helping Samuel, Mathias and Phillips put up her tent in the distance.

'I want to be *her*. To have the money and means to travel the world if I want to. To help put up a tent because it seems like a nice gesture to share the work of the servants for five minutes, instead of having to sweat in the choking, sickly sweet smoke of a sugar cane mill, or suffer being fondled by the master of a house where I scrub the floors by day and fend him off by night.'

'I'm sorry.'

'What for, Peter? For being a man and not thinking?'

He shrugged. 'I suppose.'

Again, she fixed him with her penetrating eyes. 'I'll tell you what I don't want, Peter Gregory.'

'Yes?'

'You.'

DARK CLOUDS BROUGHT an early sunset and the temperature plummeted.

Grace and the count dined together, and it seemed to Gregory that Grace laughed out loud at every quip the handsome nobleman made. Teresa sat with Phillips, and Samuel went off to the kraal where he shared *putu* and gravy with the herdsmen and Mathias.

Gregory was unsettled, by what Grace had said to him, and by letting his guard down with Teresa. While she flashed him a discrete smile from where she sat with Phillips, she seemed to know, intuitively, that he might need to be by himself at this moment and did not beckon him to join them. He shrugged on his heavy greatcoat, pressed some cold beef into a hunk of crusty bread baked by the wagoner in the coals of the campfire and walked away from their encampment. He sat on the same rise where he and Grace had argued – or, rather, where he had been lectured.

He was adrift, not welcome with the Zulus like Samuel was and disconnected from the whites he was escorting. Grace was right; he'd had no true concept of the life she had led. Gregory chewed his food and listened to the forced gaiety.

Too much of his previous life in the military had been spent on the march, in the absence of female company. He had never been one for prostitutes, but Grace had fallen into his bed and his arms by accident. If he hadn't been scarred and racked with guilt over his survival at the Battle of Isandlwana he might have been more attuned to her needs and more likely to better himself and find a future for the two of them.

Despite what she had alluded to, he cared nothing for the conventions of colonial society. The whole thing was a hypocritical sham, in any case. While Boer burghers and English gentlemen sat through sermons on Sunday about the sins of the flesh and the need to preserve white culture and supremacy, many of those same men had Indian or African mistresses or simply had their way with the servant girls.

Other men he knew, soldiers, police officers and farmers, lived with their dark-skinned partners. Their unions might not have been sanctioned by the church or law, but they were open secrets in the colony. Grace was wrong to paint him as a racist or hypocrite.

But she was right about one thing: she did not need him. And what could he offer her? Neither the status nor the comfort she desired and deserved. Grace had *told* him before that she wanted respectability, which was why she had converted and set her sights on a husband – the pastor, at first. Had Grace secretly been in love with Gregory and been waiting, hoping, for him to propose to her?

A week ago, he might have entertained the idea. But then he had met Teresa. The truth, however, was that both women would be better off without him.

A cold wind rolled over the veld, rippling the grass. Gregory tilted his face to the starless sky and smelled the sweet tang of far-off rain spattering on dry, dusty Africa. A storm was coming; it was unseasonal, unusual.

As he got to his feet his forehead was stung by the slap of fat drops. Thunder boomed like kettle drums and a lightning bolt hit somewhere nearby with a crash. The clouds opened, sending people to their tents and smoke hissing up from the near-drowned campfire.

Gregory's wet coat hung heavy on his shoulders as he walked through the mud towards the tent he shared with Samuel, although he knew Samuel would have stayed in the kraal. Rather than enter the tent, Gregory turned right, where a lamp glowed warmly through sodden calico beyond the wagon. He took three steps then hesitated. The rain cascaded off his face and down his collar. It chilled but also invigorated him, like a bucket of ice-cold water tossed on an unconscious drunkard.

He walked on, his determination renewed. Grace had slipped through his fingers; she was a good woman and she had made a choice that was best for her. He couldn't blame her for not wanting the hollow, washed-out version of himself that he had become.

He paused at the entryway to the tent.

'Miss O'Kane?'

'Captain? Peter?'

'Yes, it's me.' The rain pattering on the tent meant he had to raise his voice a little, but he doubted anyone else in the encampment heard.

The calico parted. She held an oil-filled lamp in her hand and her eyes glittered with the flame's reflection.

'Come in out of the rain, Peter. You'll catch your death out there.'

He nodded and she held the tent flap for him as he ducked his head and went in.

Teresa set the lantern down on the camp table beside her cot. She straightened and stood there, facing him. Then she reached out, took hold of the lapels of his heavy woollen coat and shrugged it from his shoulders.

She wore a nightdress, plain white, starched. It was tied at her neck with a drawstring. Rainwater dripped from his fingers as he undid the bow. The droplets landed on her breast and plastered the cotton to her skin. When he was done, he brushed the backs of his fingertips against one of the two mounds that strained against the fabric. Teresa shuddered.

Gregory looked into her eyes and she gave the slightest of nods.

He hooked an arm around her lower back and pulled her to him. He kissed her, and where before he had clung to her like a ship-wrecked fool, now he took her like an explorer claiming a new-found land.

Teresa opened her mouth to him, seeking him out, moulding her body to his, on her toes again, reaching for him. He paused, taking half a step back to unbutton his tunic and to watch her as she bent, grabbed the hem of her long nightgown, then slowly lifted it up and over her head.

He savoured the sight of her unveiling, then unbuckled his pistol belt and let it clatter to the canvas sheet on the ground. He pulled off his boots, took off his jacket and unbuttoned his shirt.

Teresa lay on the bed, proudly, shamelessly showing herself to him. The lamplight painted her gold, a treasure to be wondered at.

Gregory kissed her mouth and her body and she wound her fingers in his dark hair, drawing him down to her, into her, as Gregory reached for the blankets and cocooned both of them against the wind and rain that pushed the snapping tent walls towards them.

He reached over and turned down the lamp, lest their silhouettes give them away. The darkness intensified the taste of her, the sweet scents, the heat of her, the deliciously teasing trail of her fingernails as she found him under the covers, encircled him and guided him into her fiery core.

Gregory paused above her, now a part of her body, and looked down at her. She reached up, brushed a lock of his hair out his eyes, and smiled. She gave her little nod again and he began to move.

No drink, no drug could banish his demons but here, now, he was lost in a different world, where nothing existed except her, and the sense that the two of them were locked in an embrace that could, should, last forever. Teresa's nails dug into his flesh now and she met his every thrust, clinging to him, her heels against the backs of his legs, spurring him on. He revelled in the sheer, unbridled lust of being with her, and when he glimpsed her eyes, he saw his desires reflected.

She gripped him tighter and pushed her mouth into his chest to stifle her cry as her body shook beneath him.

Gregory felt like he was tumbling over the edge of a waterfall, savouring the feel of falling, weightless, but knowing there was someone to catch him. He lay beside Teresa on the narrow camp bed.

She rolled over and kissed him, then pulled back and grinned. 'Better?'

21

KWAZULU-NATAL, THE PRESENT

Jan-Maree had been right, Sannie thought. They would never have found the Prince Imperial's monument without her.

The town of Nqutu was a cluster of shops and market stalls and a school, and the gravel-road turnoff she had told them to take had not been signposted. Even if they'd made it that far, it was then several kilometres through an almost featureless landscape of open, dry grassy plains and low rolling hills.

Family kraals were dotted over the area, each consisting of a few simple roundhouses or brick and tin buildings and enclosures for livestock. The layout would have been similar to what was encountered by the invading army in 1879, Jan-Maree had said, although there were many more people living in the area today.

The memorial itself was only distinctive at a distance when Jan-Maree pointed out a mature tree that rose incongruously from an otherwise open vlei in the banks of a narrow stream.

'This is the Jojozi River,' Jan-Maree said as they crossed a low-water concrete bridge. 'Though they called it the Tshotshosi back in the 1800s.' Half-a-dozen women stood on the edge of the stream, washing clothes. A couple gave them bored stares as they crossed the river.

The other thing that stood in stark contrast to the surrounds was a late-model white Range Rover parked by a dry-stone-walled enclosure where the tree was.

'That's the memorial,' Jan-Maree said, 'and Richard's car.'

They were still half a kilometre away, approaching a kraal. 'Stop here,' Sannie said to Adam.

'But we can park –' Jan-Maree began.

'We stop here,' Sannie repeated. 'Jan-Maree, please wait in the car.'

Adam pulled over and Marilyn, who had been hanging back to avoid driving in their dust wake, caught up with them a minute later. She stopped behind Adam's Ranger. Sannie and Adam were already out of the car.

Marilyn got out. 'What's happening, boss?'

Sannie looked to the mostly dry donga which the river trickled through, and over the open plain on either side of it. 'A prince got ambushed here nearly one hundred and fifty years ago. We're not going to let the same thing happen to us. Marilyn, please go check out the kraal. Talk to the locals, find out if there are any other *umulungu* hanging around here. Adam, go with her for backup, please, but let Marilyn do the talking.'

'What about you?' Marilyn smiled at Sannie's use of the Zulu word for white people.

'I'll carry on with Jan-Maree.'

'Is that safe?' Marilyn asked.

'It's higher ground here. We'll be in overwatch,' Adam said, reading Sannie's mind. 'Up here out of the way, but close enough in case Sannie needs a ready reaction force.'

Marilyn waved a fly away from her face. 'Sounds like a military operation.'

Sannie nodded. 'We've all been in gunfights with some bad *okes*. They don't mess around.'

'I'll take my dive bag with me,' Adam said.

Sannie bit her lower lip. She knew what he meant. In his bag was the AK-47 he'd taken from the military men he had come up against at Bhanga Nek. As a police officer she should tell him that no, she did not want a civilian backing her up with an assault rifle. It was fine to have him as a lookout, she should tell him, but not as a would-be sniper keeping an eye out for bad guys to shoot.

However, she knew Adam was cool under fire. He'd foiled an armed robbery once, by shooting one of the thieves and saving the life of a wounded security guard. He was a former paratrooper, and she loved him. That sudden thought, clear and free of doubt, comforted her.

'All right,' Sannie said at last.

Adam went to the back of his vehicle and fetched his bag.

Marilyn went with him and looked over his shoulder as he unzipped it. She gave a low whistle as he took a grenade from his pocket and put it in the bag with the assault rifle. 'I see what you mean, now.'

ADAM WATCHED as Sannie got into his Ranger and drove down the low hill towards the memorial. He and Marilyn waited until they could identify who Sannie was going to meet there.

Three people emerged from the walled enclosure and the shade of the tree.

'The one on the right is Richard Tustin. He's the retired British Army major who was running the WildForce operation around here, using military veterans in an anti-poaching role. *Haibo*, I don't trust him,' said Marilyn.

Sannie parked near the memorial and Adam watched the trio greet her and Jan-Maree. One of the group, Adam could now see, was a woman, shorter than Tustin, and the other was another white man. Nobody pulled a weapon of any sort.

'Jan-Maree said Tustin had two foreigners with him, a man and a woman. That checks out,' Adam said.

'OK. Let's do as the boss lady instructed,' Marilyn said.

Adam and Marilyn covered the short distance to the kraal, the rifle hanging heavy in the bag by Adam's side.

Marilyn greeted a woman who emerged from a building, carrying a baby on her hip. Adam had grown up in KwaZulu-Natal and been cared for by a Zulu nanny when he was younger. He had a good grasp of the language and was able to follow the conversation Marilyn had with the woman.

'Hello, sister, how are you?' Marilyn held up her police ID. 'I'm Warrant Officer Marilyn Msani. I need to ask you some questions.'

'Hello, I am fine,' the woman said. She had thin arms and legs and although she was younger than Marilyn she looked very tired. 'We have done nothing wrong here.'

'No, no, I'm sure you haven't.'

Marilyn asked if the woman had seen any strange people in the area lately, other than the three who were at the memorial now.

'*Aikona.*' The woman shook her head.

Adam had an idea, and said in Zulu: 'We need to find a gun.'

Both of the women looked at Adam. The baby grizzled and the woman bounced it a little.

The look Marilyn gave him was meant to scare him, and it worked, but Adam continued, in halting Zulu.

'A *skebanga*, a thief, he robbed and killed a man. We think he dropped the gun in the river.'

The woman shook her head. 'I know nothing about that.'

'What we need,' Adam said, 'is one of those machines that finds metal. A metal detector.'

Marilyn's lips were pursed, but she picked up where he was heading and stepped in. 'Yes, *sisi*,' Marilyn said. 'One of those detectors would help us, but, of course, as you know, the police service has no money and we wouldn't know where to find one.'

The woman looked around, glancing at her house.

'We know some people who live around here, near the old battlefields, have such things,' Adam said. 'Of course it is not illegal to own a detector, and we would only want to borrow it for a short time. I could even afford to pay five hundred rand to hire one.'

The young mother's eyes widened. She looked again to the small house behind her. A goat bleated nearby, and a chicken clucked and pecked at the ground at Adam's feet.

'I could maybe find one for you. My husband is not home, though. He is away working, on a farm. Let me look.'

The woman took her baby inside. Marilyn cast her eyes up at Adam. '*What* are you playing at?'

A dog trotted towards them across the trampled dust and sniffed at Adam's boots. Adam reached down and held his hand out to it. It cowered at first, then let Adam pat it. 'Jan-Maree told us that someone, an Englishman, she thought, had been handing out metal detectors to people who lived around the battlefields.'

'Ah, I see,' Marilyn said. 'Good thinking.'

The woman came back. She had set her child down inside, but now cradled a metal detector, as if it were as precious as her baby.

Marilyn took off the fleece jacket she was wearing and used it to cover her hands as she accepted it from the woman. 'I will take good care of it, and we will return it to you soon.'

Adam knew that Marilyn was trying to keep her fingerprints off the device, and that she would have it dusted for others. 'Who gave this to you?' Marilyn asked.

The woman shrugged and looked away.

Marilyn changed her tone, from good cop to bad cop. 'Your husband stole this.'

The woman glared at Marilyn. 'No! He did not. A guide gave it to him, and asked him to search for things of metal, on the battlefields.'

Marilyn shook her head. '*Ai*, I don't believe you. I am going to have to question your husband. When will he be home?'

'No. I don't know. Please, he will be angry with me.'

Marilyn tutted. 'You will have to tell me who gave you this thing, if you do not want me to take your husband to Dundee and question him at the police station. Do you know it is a crime to take anything of heritage value from a historical site, like a battlefield?'

The woman looked shocked and Adam couldn't tell if she was faking it or not. 'No. The guide, the one who gave it to us, said that this was our land, our history, and that we had a right to share in the profits from it.'

All of a sudden, Adam thought, there was a lot more information coming out about the mystery man who handed out metal detectors.

'Do you know the name of this guide, who gave you the detector?' Adam said.

Marilyn's frown told him to shut up and let her ask the questions. He nodded.

'No,' the woman said.

Marilyn softened her tone again. 'Would you recognise the guide?'

The woman couldn't help herself. She looked down into the shallow valley, to where the Prince Imperial's monument lay shaded under the tree. And where Richard Tustin and his two guests were talking to Sannie and Jan-Maree.

'Does the guide who gave your husband the metal detector visit the battlefields often?' Marilyn asked the woman.

She bit her lip, but nodded. '*Yebo.*'

'Yes,' Marilyn echoed. She pointed to the memorial. 'Is the guide down there now?'

The woman looked to heaven. 'I don't want to get my husband in trouble – from anyone.'

'Has your husband ever found anything with this thing?' Marilyn held up the detector, still cradled in her fleece jacket. 'Has he sold any relics from the battlefields to that man down there?'

The woman shook her head. 'No. Not at all. My husband said that thing is useless. All he finds is old screws and nails and rubbish.'

'Then he has not committed a crime yet,' Marilyn said. 'If you tell me who gave your husband the detector, and if I then find out your husband has never sold that guide anything, then I can promise you there will be no charges against your husband.'

The woman drew a deep breath then looked again towards where Sannie was standing with the others. They were all in clear sight now. The woman pointed. 'The one on the end.' Tustin stood on the far left of the small group.

'My husband was told that anything he found would be taken to a museum in England, and that he would be paid. He was told that it was all official, and legal.'

'Thank you,' Marilyn said. She paused a moment then handed the detector back to the woman. 'Maybe we don't need this after all.'

The woman nodded, took the device back, then walked into her home.

Adam watched as Marilyn took out her phone and sent a message to Sannie. Down below, he saw Sannie take out her phone and check the screen.

Tustin is the one who has been distributing metal detectors. Claims he is working for a British museum gathering artefacts and paying for them.

SANNIE PUT HER PHONE AWAY.

Richard Tustin had just introduced her to Piet Van der Ploeg, whom he described as a businessman from Holland, and an American woman, Goldie Faul, from New York. Jan-Maree had described them as such, more or less, on the drive here.

'Are you two here on holiday? Travelling together?' Sannie asked the people she had just met.

'We're not travelling together, but we do share some common interests,' Faul said.

She was attractive, aged in her mid-thirties with black hair cut in a bob under a wide-brim green felt hat and wearing expensive designer safari clothes. Not the usual zip-on, zip-off trousers but well-cut khaki pants, green blouse and a tailored bush jacket. Her gold necklace and bracelets were understated, yet probably worth more than a South African police officer earned in a year.

'What interests would those be?' Sannie asked.

Faul gave her a tight smile. 'History, for one. I have a PhD in history from Cornell University in the States, and a double major in art and archaeology.'

'First time in South Africa?' Sannie asked.

'No, Colonel. By the way, should I call my lawyer and have him join us via Zoom?' Faul took a phone from her jacket pocket and wiggled it in her hand.

Faul was smiling, but Sannie thought she was only half joking. 'No need,' Sannie said.

Van der Ploeg, older, distinguished-looking, was dressed in chinos and a blue Ralph Lauren polo shirt. He wore a South African–made Rogue bush hat of nylon mesh and canvas, and his *veldskoen* shoes indicated he might have a local connection.

'Are you originally from South Africa, Mr Van der Ploeg?'

'Call me Piet,' he said to Sannie. 'Yes, I'm from Johannesburg originally, left here in 1994 when things changed.'

She nodded, and wondered why he'd felt a sudden need to leave the country when the African National Congress took over. He was in his mid-fifties and had the upright bearing and sharp haircut of a military man. That in itself wasn't unusual, as nearly all white men up until then had been subject to conscription. Her first husband had served in the army, as had Adam. Van der Ploeg's blue eyes met hers without wavering, as if daring her to ask another question.

'Colonel,' Tustin interrupted. 'I *am* in the middle of a tour.'

'I know. And now it's time for the lecture to stop and for you to come answer some more questions that I have.'

Tustin looked at his Rolex. 'I'll be back at my house in Dundee in about an hour and a half. I'd be happy to meet you there, if that's convenient.'

Do retired British officers earn such a pension that they can afford a Range Rover and a Rolex? Sannie shook her head. 'It isn't. I'm sure Jan-Maree here can tell your guests all about Prince Louis Napoleon while you and I go over to my vehicle and talk.'

Tustin held up a hand. 'Colonel, no. Sorry, I really must insist –'

Sannie reached behind her back and took out a pair of handcuffs from a pouch. She took a breath and paused to remember the online research she'd been doing in the Ranger while Adam drove. 'Richard Tustin, I am arresting you for contravention of sections 20 and 33 of the South African National Heritage Resources Act in that you exported or caused to be exported certain heritage objects from

South Africa, not by a recognised customs port, and without the necessary permits, and that you imported or caused to be imported foreign cultural items, not via a recognised –'

'All right, all right.' Tustin held up his hands. 'Enough, please. Let's talk.' He turned to his guests. 'Piet, Goldie, please excuse me, this is all a terrible mistake, as I will soon explain to the colonel here. I'm sure Jan-Maree can answer any questions you have. I'll be with you in a few minutes.'

'It will take longer than that,' Sannie said.

Faul, clearly more used to giving orders than taking them, turned to Jan-Maree. 'Take us back to Dundee, *now*.'

'I don't have my car here,' Jan-Maree said. 'It's why I came with the colonel.'

'I don't give a damn,' Faul said. 'You can drive Richard's Range Rover, or I will.'

'Goldie, wait –' Tustin began.

'Ms Faul, I need you to stay here, for now, as well,' Sannie said. 'I may have some questions for you, and pending my discussions with Mr Tustin here, I may need to search you and any luggage you have.'

'The hell you will. I'm an American citizen and you're doing no such thing without a warrant. In fact, I'm going to call my lawyer in the States right now.'

Van der Ploeg spoke up as Faul took out her phone once more. 'Colonel, you won't find anything on Goldie or me, even if you did get a warrant out here in the middle of nowhere before we flew back to Johannesburg. I doubt you have enough evidence – if any at all – to arrest two foreign nationals.' He smiled and spread his hands wide. 'But we can wait for Richard to clear up this unfortunate misunderstanding.'

Van der Ploeg walked off to talk to Faul, who was striding away from the memorial, holding her phone high as if searching for a signal. Jan-Maree trailed after them.

'We know you've been handing out metal detectors to locals, to scour the battlefields for artefacts,' Sannie said to Tustin, now that they were alone.

He glared at her. 'I have done *no* such thing. I'm fully aware of the provisions of the heritage act and, like all reputable guides, I do not encourage the looting of historical sites.'

He was putting on a good impression of the outraged innocent. 'So, at your other house in England you have no assegais, no knobkerries, no bullets dating from the Anglo-Zulu War?'

'I . . .'

She said nothing. His face was turning red.

'I have received gifts, here in South Africa, from a couple of Zulu chiefs. When I've brought veterans out here from the UK, as part of their ongoing rehabilitation for mental health issues and physical wounds, we visit some of the local communities and help out where we can. I've been given an assegai and a knobkerrie, and two cowhide shields, yes.'

'Antiques?'

'Yes. So the chiefs claimed.' He wiped sweat from his brow. 'One never knows. But, OK, I didn't have permits for them.'

'I'm not talking about gifts, and you know it.'

He took a deep breath. 'I can assure you, Colonel, that I do not deal in stolen artefacts and I most certainly have never given anyone a metal detector. I hate the damn things – they remind me of IEDs in Afghanistan.'

He was a good liar. She nodded towards the man and woman she had just met. 'What are they here for?'

Tustin glanced at Van der Ploeg and Faul, then back at Sannie. 'They're tourists.'

'A hard-nosed American academic and a South African expat businessman happen to end up on the same tour of an obscure corner of the Anglo-Zulu War battlefields?'

'They . . .'

'We can continue this at Dundee Police Station,' Sannie said.

Tustin held up a hand. 'Wait.' He seemed to be mulling over his words. When he spoke he lowered his voice. 'Let me start by saying that I have no indication that either Piet or Goldie are involved with anything illegal at all, whatsoever.'

'Go on.'

'Piet Van der Ploeg runs a boutique auction house, based in the Netherlands. I've had contact with him on and off over the years as he deals quite a bit in militaria. From time to time, collections of Zulu and British Army memorabilia come on the market. It's usually private collections, artefacts gathered from the time of the wars or the early twentieth century when there were no, or fewer, restrictions on exporting heritage items.'

'And what's your role in these auctions?' Sannie asked.

'Piet emails me pictures when lots come up for auction. I do my best to advise him on the age and authenticity of the items and their likely value, even though I'm not a collector myself.'

'I see.' Sannie studied the man and woman for a moment. They were talking to Jan-Maree, who had led them into the low-walled enclosure surrounding the prince's memorial and the graves of the troopers who had been killed on the same day as Louis Napoleon.

'And Goldie Faul?' Sannie asked.

'She is who she says, an expert in African history, but she works for a dot-com billionaire in the States who's a keen collector of art and historic artefacts – military-related stuff.'

Sannie had her notebook out. 'Name?'

Tustin shrugged his shoulders. 'I tried to engage her in a bit of small talk in the car on our way here, but I couldn't get much out of her. Piet was here in South Africa visiting his mother – she's ninety-five – and he'd had dealings with Goldie over the years and offered to show her around, with my help.'

'What's she doing here?'

'Business and pleasure, she said,' Tustin said. 'Piet told me that Goldie is the curator of her rich boss's private museum and gallery. She said that while she was here, she was going to do some "shopping",' he made air quotes as he said the last word, 'for her boss, but when I asked her who that was she told me that he likes to protect his privacy.'

Sannie frowned. She thought about what had happened to Adam on the coast, and the Koran and sword he had found.

Sannie gestured to the tree-shaded memorial. 'Why did you bring them here? I'd never heard about the French prince until just now. Surely this isn't part of the regular Zulu War tourist trail?'

Tustin shook his head. 'No, not really. The French embassy holds a memorial service here every year, in June, on the anniversary of the prince's death, and I get the occasional French client who knows the story and wants to visit the place, but you're right – most tourists just go to Rorke's Drift and Isandlwana. Goldie wanted to see the memorial and learn more about the prince.'

'Anything in particular she wanted to know?' Sannie asked.

Tustin put his hands on his hips and looked around. 'I told her and Piet the story, about how the prince and his escorts unsaddled here and were making coffee when a party of Zulus emerged from a maize field. It would have been over there.' He pointed over his shoulder towards an area closer to the river. 'She was quite interested in his last stand – what weapons he was using.'

'And what *was* he armed with?' Sannie asked. She felt her curiosity growing, and again felt the tingling in her fingertips she got when she felt like she was close to breaking a case.

'A pistol and a sword, although accounts from the time suggest that he had dropped his sword and did not get the chance to use it in his defence. Goldie quizzed me at length about what happened to the sword.'

'And?' Sannie prompted.

'He was killed; the Zulus took his sword, and it was later returned to the British by an envoy from King Cetshwayo, who was hoping that by giving it back, as a gesture of goodwill, he might prompt the British to negotiate peace with him. He failed. Lord Chelmsford eventually took the sword to the UK and gave it back to the Empress Eugénie, the prince's mother.'

Sannie glanced at the memorial again. Jan-Maree looked like she was giving her own version of events to Piet and Goldie. She was talking animatedly, using her hands. 'Jan-Maree has a theory –'

Tustin cut her off. 'Yes, yes, I know, that the Prince Imperial was carrying his great-uncle's sword with him when he was killed. It's a nice theory, like something out of a novel, but I'm afraid it's not true. The prince's bog-standard French cavalry sword is in a museum dedicated to Napoleon Bonaparte, along with all of Boney's other swords.'

'Yet your American guest and her friend the auctioneer are here, in this remote place, asking about Napoleon's sword?'

Tustin gave a small laugh. 'And yes, Jan-Maree's probably filling their heads with her bizarre theory right now, and getting their hopes up. Jan-Maree is a lovely girl, and she can be very persuasive, but I'm afraid there is no Napoleon's sword lying about in South Africa somewhere.'

Jan-Maree was a woman, not a girl, and one who had set more than one heart aflutter in Dundee. Sannie had seen the connection between her and Tustin, yet now he was being dismissive of her. She wondered what games they played together.

'How can you be so certain that the prince never carried Bonaparte's sword?'

'Louis Napoleon was a boaster, full enough of himself and close to delusional. He might have told people back in 1879 that he was carrying his great-uncle's Austerlitz sword, but the facts suggest otherwise. In fact, it was poor old David Gregory who knew most about Louis Napoleon and his sword, and he was trying to set Jan-Maree straight.'

'Why was he such an expert?'

Tustin scoffed. 'Oh, yes, David thought himself an expert on everything to do with the Zulu War, but in this case he really did know more than all of us. You see, his great-great-uncle was a copper, like you, a Sub-Inspector Peter Gregory of the Natal Mounted Police. David was the great-great-grandchild of Peter Gregory's younger brother, who came out to live in South Africa after Peter's death.'

'Yes, I had heard about this Peter Gregory. But Jan-Maree believes he was on a mission to find Napoleon's sword when he was killed in the line of duty.'

Tustin nodded. 'Yes, yes, yes. I know all about that as well. Gregory was killed by a suspect with a sword. But Jan-Maree's wrong if she still thinks that it was some criminal armed with Louis Napoleon's sword.'

'Who said anything about the sword belonging to Napoleon?' Sannie asked.

'I spoke to David a couple of weeks ago, before we had our argument in The Shed, which you know about. Jan-Maree had come to me with a theory about Louis Napoleon's allegedly lost sword and I wanted to hear firsthand what David had to say about it. I went to his home and he told me that Jan-Maree had asked if he had any more letters or diaries relating to Peter Gregory – she had already used one of Peter's diaries to write her thesis on the Natal Mounted Police. David told me that he hadn't, and had already told Jan-Maree that. However, he had let slip to Jan-Maree that he had the sword that was used to kill his great-great-uncle Peter.'

Sannie tried to get her head around the lineage and ages of the people involved. 'What was the story behind the sword?'

'According to David's family history, which had been handed down verbally from generation to generation, Peter was killed by someone armed with a British cavalry sword. All David knew was that Peter was supposedly trying to apprehend a man and was killed in the tussle. Somehow – the collective memory was a bit hazy – a Zulu constable, known only as Samuel, who was apparently a good friend of Peter, eventually brought the offender to justice and presented the sword to the family.'

'Did Jan-Maree know that?'

'Yes. David had told her about the sword and Jan-Maree had asked him if she could see it. She told me that each time she went to see David he had a different excuse about why he couldn't show it to her – it was locked in an old steamer trunk and he couldn't find the key; or the trunk was in the attic and he was too old to get up there and get it out or break the lock,' Tustin said.

'Did you think he was hiding something?' Sannie asked.

'I wasn't sure, but Jan-Maree was certain he was, so she asked me to go see David – he'd been becoming less and less patient with her and didn't want to talk to her anymore. Jan-Maree is young, impetuous, and she has a view of history influenced by movies such as *Tomb Raider* and *Raiders of the Lost Ark*. She was looking for intrigue and mystery and she was certain that David had Napoleon's sword hidden in his home somewhere – perhaps in this trunk he'd mentioned – and that he'd regretted letting slip that he had a sword at all.'

'So you went to see David,' Sannie said.

'Yes, I did, and when I told him why I was there he became angry. He said something to the effect that Jan-Maree and I should stop pestering him with nonsensical theories. He went to his bedroom and came back with a British cavalry sword. 'There,' he said to me, 'once and for bloody all, here's the sword that killed Peter Gregory.' He told me that he'd asked John Parker to get up into the attic, break into the trunk and get the sword out. David and I had always argued, as I told you, but I think this really was the beginning of the end of any vestiges of friendship we may have had. Our next meeting at The Shed was, well . . . you know how that ended.'

Sannie nodded. 'How did Jan-Maree react to the news?'

He shrugged. 'She didn't want to believe it at first, and still thought that she'd caught David out in a lie. However, she later quizzed John, who confirmed David's story. Jan-Maree still thinks Napoleon's sword is somewhere in South Africa.'

'Why is Faul so interested in the sword?'

Tustin rubbed his chin. 'I don't know. To the best of my knowledge, Jan-Maree has never met or spoken to her or Van der Ploeg before – though no doubt she's filling their heads with all kinds of nonsense right now.'

Sannie parked the discussion of a missing sword that may or may not still exist. 'What are your military veterans up to on the KZN coast, down at Bhanga Nek?'

'How should I know?' Tustin said. 'Swimming and fishing, probably. And by the way, they're not "my" veterans.'

Sannie had to tread carefully. She had no evidence, other than one woman's claim that Tustin had been doling out metal detectors, that Tustin was involved in the international illegal trade in antiquities and what had happened to Adam.

She decided to ask her next question obliquely. 'Have you ever used a metal detector to search a battlefield?'

'Never. And I don't condone amateurs who do. They're just glorified treasure hunters. Anyone who does so on a protected site here in South Africa can be, and should be, arrested.'

So that was a no. 'Tell me about a man named Andy, a member of the veterans' group that was formerly working on behalf of your organisation at David Gregory's game reserve.'

Tustin exhaled audibly. 'He's a psychopath. He was drummed out of the British Special Boat Service after getting into a bar-room brawl and putting a civilian in hospital. There were also allegations of war crimes from his time in Afghanistan. The rest of his crew seemed just as rough. They had an American Special Forces veteran with them, but he was the one that fled the country after shooting the local man on the game reserve.'

'You don't check the veterans who take part in your program?'

'It's open to all UK military veterans, and a few from the US. Some – many – are troubled. This just seemed to be a particularly, bad crop.'

'Tell me –' Sannie's phone dinged. She took it out and looked at the screen. It was a message from Marilyn.

We're being watched.

22

ZULULAND, 1880

Teresa lay in the crook of Gregory's arm, and it felt like her warmth had stilled the tremors in his mind and his heart. Yet he had questions for her.

'Your husband?' he whispered in the pre-dawn dark. 'You are still married, in the eyes of the law.'

'Soon to be ex. He finally agreed to admit to infidelity, even though he would be publicly shamed for a time, because he wants to marry again. This time it's a proper English rose he wants to deflower, fifteen years his junior.'

'I see.'

'His mother never approved of me,' Teresa said. 'The gossipmongers on both sides claimed I was after his money, or a social climber putting on airs and graces, but that wasn't true. It was worse.'

'How so?' He stroked her hair and ran the backs of his fingers over the smooth skin of her cheek.

He sensed her smile in the dark. 'I plain fell in love with him. We met when he visited the university where I was studying.'

'What were you studying?' he asked.

'English literature. I wanted to write. Freddy – Lord Beecham – wooed me, and I fell for him, but I think he was after me as a conquest, rather than a wife. I let him – conquer me, that is – and I would have been happy to have his baby.'

Gregory held her tight and kissed her. In his arms, he felt her draw a big breath.

'He was unfaithful to me right from the time we got married, maybe even before.'

He kissed the tears from her cheeks and she clung to him.

GREGORY LEFT Teresa's bed before the dawn. He coaxed the fire to life and was standing by it, warming himself in the dark, when the wagoner rose and began to strike camp.

Samuel came to him. 'Good morning. Are you well?'

Gregory smiled, for what felt like the first time in a very long time. 'I am, Samuel. I am.'

Gregory poured Samuel a cup of coffee and the two of them stood in companionable silence.

'What the devil?' Phillips called in the dark.

Samuel and Gregory turned as one and Peter tossed his coffee cup to the ground and instinctively reached for his revolver in its holster.

In the half-light of the dawn Gregory saw a figure dart between two tents and watched as Phillips also came into view and rugby-tackled a man to the ground. The man was quick to get back on his feet. As Phillips went to stand up the man racked a foot back and delivered a savage kick to Phillips' chin.

'Stop!' Gregory called.

But the man was running fast out of camp and across the veld in the direction that the Prince Imperial's escort would have taken when they left the young royal to his fate.

'Stop or I'll shoot!' Gregory yelled.

Gregory was aware of the others coming out of their tents and Mathias the wagoner ceasing his work to watch. The man kept running towards the crest of the low hill above the Tshotshosi River.

Gregory sighted down the short barrel of the pistol and fired. The gun bucked in his hand.

At this range it was an almost impossible shot, and he missed. He took aim again and pulled the trigger. Gregory fancied he saw the man's right arm jerk outwards, but he kept running.

Phillips, rubbing his jaw with one hand, made for the horses, but they had been knee-haltered for the night. Phillips swore as he fumbled with cold hands to untie his horse.

Samuel had left the camp and was running after the man. He carried his rifle by his side. Phillips at last had his horse free and he jumped up onto it, bareback. Gregory fetched his Martini–Henry from where he'd left it, lying on his bedroll, but it was too late to get another shot off.

'Off you go,' Gregory said to Phillips, 'but don't pursue him to the ends of the earth. If he's got a horse over the hill he'll be long gone.'

'Yes, sir.' Phillips kicked his horse in the ribs and the animal shot away.

'What was all that about?' Teresa was standing by her tent, clutching an unbuttoned overcoat closed. Her hair was tousled. She'd never looked lovelier.

'I'm not sure.' Gregory felt his cheeks flush. They'd just had an intruder in camp, but his thoughts were elsewhere. She gave him a private smile.

'What is all the commotion?' Grace emerged from her tent. There was no sign of the Italian count and Gregory wondered if Ferdinand was in Grace's bed, still.

'We seem to have had a visitor in the camp,' Gregory said.

Grace shielded her eyes and turned to see Samuel standing at the crest of the hill, and Phillips galloping up to him, then reining in his horse. Phillips leaned down, offering Samuel a hand, and hoisted the other man up onto his horse's rump. The two trotted back towards camp.

Like Teresa, Grace had pulled a coat over her nightgown. She looked at the other woman, then raised her nose in the air. 'I'm going to pack.'

'Tell the count to be ready to leave in an hour,' Gregory said.

Grace spun around. 'He is not in my bed, Peter.'

Gregory felt himself blush deeper. 'My apologies, I meant . . .'

Grace wagged a finger at him. 'I *know* what you meant.' She turned on her heel and stormed back to her tent.

'*Signor . . .*'

Gregory looked around and saw Count Ferdinand coming up out of the donga, from the river.

'I was, just a, making my toilet, yes?'

'Fine,' Gregory said. 'We had an intruder in the camp.'

The count's eyes widened. '*Un ladro*? A . . . how you say, thief?'

'Perhaps. You saw nothing from the river?'

'No.' He shook his head. 'I must go . . . look my tent.'

Ferdinand went to check on his belongings while Gregory went to Mathias and questioned him in the pre-dawn darkness. It seemed no one had noticed the man sneak into their laager.

Phillips and Samuel returned to the campfire and dismounted.

'He was gone, sir,' Phillips said. 'He had a horse ready, on the other side of the hill. He was too far away for me to even take a shot at him.'

Gregory nodded. 'Did you get a look at his face?'

'Not really, sir,' Phillips said. 'He had a balaclava on, but he was white. Dark clothes, riding boots – polished.'

Gregory rubbed his chin. 'Hmm. His build looked familiar to me.'

'One of those cavalry chaps, sir?'

Gregory nodded slowly. Was it Walters, the arrogant young officer who had come to warn them off? Was he spying on them, or was he looking for something in particular? Walters was an associate of the murdered Major Morrison, who had been one of the officers who had been presented with Prince Louis Napoleon's sword.

But why was he sniffing around Gregory's laager? Had he heard that Samuel had been out and about in Zululand enquiring about the sword? Did Walters think that he, Gregory, had somehow got hold of the missing blade, and so he'd come to steal it?

Gregory gathered his charges together once the tents had been packed and they had all breakfasted.

'I'm leaving you for a while,' he told them. He saw how Teresa tilted her face up to him at the news, but did not acknowledge the questioning look she gave him. 'I have business to attend to with the Empress Eugénie's entourage and General Wood. Phillips, I want you to take command of our party and see them safely back to Dundee the same way we came, via Isandlwana and Rorke's Drift.'

Phillips puffed out his chest a little at the news of his first command. 'Thank you, sir. I won't let you down.'

Gregory looked to Samuel. 'Make sure it happens, Samuel.'

His Zulu friend smiled a moment, then looked serious. 'After what happened this morning, in the dark, I should come with you.'

Gregory shook his head. The sun was rising fast and soon it would be warm. They needed to start on their respective journeys. 'No, I'll be fine alone. I want you,' Gregory looked to Phillips, to rebuild his bruised ego, 'Sergeant, to make sure the empress's orders are respected and no one slips away from the convoy to try and rendezvous with the royal party. Understood?'

Phillips nodded. '*I* will make sure your orders are followed, sir.'

Teresa scowled at Gregory. He had feelings for her, without a doubt, and she now perhaps felt that he was casting her adrift. 'I'll be back with you all soon. Hopefully by nightfall,' he said.

'I'll come looking for you if you are not,' Samuel said.

'That won't be necessary,' Gregory said, though he wasn't sure what awaited him when he met up with General Wood's column and a French empress.

Teresa was angry as she rode.

She hadn't slept with Peter Gregory in order to convince him to let her get a photo of the empress and hopefully a worldwide scoop on an interview. But now he was actually riding out to meet the royal party and she was being banished.

Poor Sergeant Phillips was watching them all like a sheepdog worried he was going to get a beating for losing one of his lambs. He kept moving from the head of their small party to the rear to make sure no one hung back.

Grace and the count were riding side by side, as usual, and every reporter's instinct that Teresa had honed over her last few years as a newspaperwoman told her they were plotting something. Grace kept looking around to check where Phillips and Samuel were positioned. Teresa was sure they were planning on slipping away.

Teresa had some pictures from her trip, of the battlefields and of the new memorial that had been erected at the site of the Prince Imperial's death, but she dreaded sailing back to New York without the story she had promised her editor that she would bring home – an exclusive interview with the Empress Eugénie.

Heck, she wasn't happy about the prospect of returning to city life in the United States at all. In a very short time there was something about this wild continent of Africa that had grabbed her. She didn't know whether she'd been bitten by something or had drunk something or breathed something in, but the place had taken hold of her. Rather than heading home she wanted to explore more of Africa, to learn more about her people and the wildlife.

She hadn't been lying to Lieutenant Walters – she *was* an amateur ornithologist – and every African bird she had seen so far had only fuelled her passion to see more of what the colony and continent had to offer. As terrifying as her encounter with the leopard had been, she now found herself wanting to see another one, though perhaps from the safety of a carriage or some distance away. She'd seen an elephant once in a circus, in Syracuse, but she wanted to see one – or a herd – living free and wild. She scanned the wide-open plains around her and the distant hills, hoping to spot a buck or maybe even a zebra.

And then there was Peter.

Looking back, it seemed that Freddy had been all about the chase and *that* conquest, and less about love. She'd known there would be trouble when she'd told him that she was pregnant. He'd married her, but she knew it was under sufferance, and his mother had made no secret of the fact that she did not approve of her titled son marrying a commoner from America – let alone one who'd had the temerity to study at university, something she considered most unladylike.

But what of Peter Gregory? It was as plain as day that he'd been involved with Grace, and that she was now madder than a cut rattlesnake. Teresa was no keener to be perceived as someone who would steal another woman's man, any more than she wished to be seen as a greedy schemer, but it had seemed to her that Grace had something going on with Count Ferdinand.

She eyed those two again. They were riding close enough together for their boots to be touching, and Grace was whispering something.

Teresa spurred her horse forward, past the wagon, and drew alongside the conspirators.

'Well, hello, y'all. Is this a private conversation or can anyone join in?'

'Ferdi's been teaching me Italian, and I've been trying to improve his English. *Y'all* could do with some lessons as well,' Grace said.

Teresa laughed off the barb. 'What are your plans when you get to Dundee?'

'Well, unlike you, I live in the colony,' Grace said. 'Some of us have to work.'

'And what is your occupation, Grace?'

Grace cleared her throat. 'I am a lady. I volunteer at the local church and have been assisting the parish priest with his household matters.'

A maid? Teresa didn't think less of Grace because of that, but Grace was the one putting on airs – and Graces. 'And you, Count Ferdinand?'

'Me? *Sì*. I go back to Italy very soon.'

'You don't want to stay and see more of Africa? I do,' Teresa said.

Grace raised her nose. 'I'm sure you do.'

'Have you seen enough of the countryside and the battlefields, Count?' Teresa pressed. 'Maybe I could write an article about you. I think it's very brave and intrepid, and very worldly of a nobleman, to be spending his time and money exploring the world in the name of researching a book.'

'Ah, *no, grazie*, I do not like the newspapers, as you call them. I wish to travel in private, like a peasant.'

Teresa couldn't stifle her laugh completely.

'Peasants don't take boat trips around the world, Ferdi, trust me,' Grace added.

'*Scusa...* my English ...'

'It's fine, Count,' Teresa said. 'We're only joshing you. I bet you've got a hell of a story to tell, somewhere in there, though.'

Phillips galloped back to them, doing his sheepdog impression again. 'We'll stop soon, for morning tea. There's a stream up ahead that we passed through on the way here. We'll water the horses there.'

'Good,' Grace said. 'I am cooking in the saddle today. I need to freshen up.'

It was warm, with the sun high overhead. Teresa had found she'd had to use every item of clothing she had brought to keep pace with the hot sunny days and the bitterly cold evenings. Africa was not exactly how she'd imagined it would be.

A flicker of movement caught her eye, and she followed it. 'Oh my! Zebras!'

Grace gave a disinterested look, but Ferdinand was more animated, pointing wildly at the fleeing creatures and saying something in Italian to Grace, who didn't seem to comprehend. The drumbeat of the zebras' hooves echoed across the plain. Teresa, who prided herself on her excellent eyesight, caught a quick glimpse of something else as the zebras disappeared over the crest of a low hill. Silhouetted, just for a second, was a dark-coloured horse and rider. They were too far away to make out any details of the person. She wondered if it was a lone Zulu. Was he going about his business, or were they being shadowed? Perhaps it had been the man on horseback who had spooked the wild animals. Was it the intruder who had fled earlier that morning?

Teresa looked to Phillips and saw that he, too, had been watching the mystery man. He nodded to her and frowned, signalling that he perhaps shared her concerns.

Soon they came to a line of trees beside the narrow river they had splashed through the day before. They all dismounted, and Samuel and Mathias set up chairs and two tables before Mathias began preparing a lunch of cold meats, bread and pickled vegetables.

Grace wiped her brow. 'I'm going to the river. It was too cold for me to wash properly yesterday.'

'Want some company?' Teresa asked.

'No, thank you. But I heard what happened to you at the stream with the leopard.' Grace looked pointedly at Ferdinand.

'Oh, *si*. Yes, I will accompany the *signorina*. With a gun.'

He slid a short-barrelled Snider carbine from the bucket strapped to his saddle, and stood ready to accompany Grace.

Phillips had dismounted and tied his horse to the wagon. He strode towards them. 'What's going on here?'

'I'm going to bathe and Ferdi is going to be my lookout, in case of wild animals or marauding Zulus,' Grace said. 'I may also do some fishing.'

Phillips' pink cheeks coloured. 'I say, Preeti,' she gave him a look, 'sorry, Grace, that is not acceptable. You know I'm not supposed to let any of you out of my sight. I think I should be your chaperone.'

'No.' Grace pointed a finger at him. '*You* need to keep an eye on her,' she nodded at Teresa, 'to make sure she doesn't go rushing back to her new lover.'

Phillips' jaw dropped and Teresa, who considered herself open-minded and not easily shocked, was stunned. Samuel shook his head and laughed quietly to himself.

Grace spun around. 'Come, Ferdinand.'

The count, who had been looking from person to person, seemingly having trouble keeping up with what was being said, responded to a direct order. '*Si, grazie.*' He shouldered his rifle and marched after Grace as she strode to her packhorse, removed her fishing rod holder, then carried on towards the river.

The count followed her.

Phillips came to Teresa and Samuel, who had also dismounted.

'I apologise,' Phillips said to Teresa, 'for any offence that woman's ill-judged remarks may have caused.'

Teresa smiled. 'You don't have to apologise on her behalf, Sergeant. She's angry, but I can't help but think the count's up to something.'

'The count?' Phillips said.

She nodded. 'I've known a few newspapermen who would masquerade as someone else to get a good story.' The irony of the fact that she had been guilty of the same offence was not lost on her. 'The European pictorials and newspapers will pay as much, if not more, than an American editor for an exclusive photograph of the empress at her son's grave.'

'They won't get far on foot,' Samuel said, 'if their plan is to escape us. They'll most likely try at night.'

'I'll make sure the horses are secure and you and I will provide a security picquet from dusk to dawn,' Phillips said to Samuel.

Teresa had a thought. 'If he's who and what I think he is, then he'll need his camera if he's going to try and get a picture of the empress.'

Teresa went to Ferdi's packhorse and checked his belongings. 'There's a case missing. I recalled seeing it, because I thought it looked about the same size as my camera box.'

Phillips came to her side. 'I deduce the same.'

Samuel had been watching them. 'The count's big box is missing. He told me to be very careful with it when I was helping him with his belongings after striking camp. He came with it tied to his packhorse.'

'Exactly,' Teresa said. As miffed as she was at Peter's dismissive tone that morning, she was now downright mad at the 'count', or whoever he was. He was going to try and beat her at her own game, and she would not let any man get away with that.

'Has he lost his camera?' Phillips asked. 'And if so, he would have been sure to notice and raise a stink.'

Phillips was back to being his dimmest. 'No, he hasn't lost it.'

Teresa shook her head. 'I think he left it behind at the Prince Imperial's memorial.'

'Why would he do a silly thing like that?'

Samuel turned to Phillips. 'Because it's heavy. You can't just slip a camera in your pocket. He can ride – or walk – better without it. He's hidden it somewhere by the memorial.'

'I'm sure of that,' Teresa said. 'Maybe he's going to try a photographic ambush there somewhere – set up at night-time and snap a picture of the empress when she appears in the morning.'

'The cad,' Phillips said. 'How could someone invade another's privacy in such a way? It's just … it's just not done.'

'Oh, it's done all right,' Teresa said. 'People are fascinated by royalty. Some newspapers will go to any lengths to get a story.'

Even as she said the words she felt her own guilt and complicity in such endeavours, and for the first time ever she questioned her desire to be a newspaperwoman. Maybe she was not cut out for this life after all. She had lied about being a friend of the empress to get Peter to escort her here into Zululand. The fact that he and his superiors had seen through her ruse did not absolve her in any way.

'A mother should be left to grieve in private,' Samuel said.

'You got that right, Samuel.' Teresa looked to the watercourse where Grace and Ferdinand had now disappeared.

'I should go down there and see what they're up to,' Phillips said.

Another thought crossed Teresa's mind. Grace and Ferdinand had become close – for whatever reason – and there was always the possibility that Grace was not bathing alone. 'I think I'd better go,' Teresa said. 'If Grace is bathing it won't be as shameful if I see her in the altogether.'

Phillips cleared his throat again. 'Of course. But, um, Miss O'Kane, may I have your word that you won't try to abscond as well?'

She crossed her heart with a finger. 'Yes, Sergeant, I promise.'

Teresa set off through the dry golden grass down a gentle slope to where a donga had formed last time the river had been in full flood. She heard voices. If Grace was naked and bathing, then Ferdinand was close enough for them to be having a conversation. She felt her cheeks colour at the thought of what she might see.

When she got to the edge of the small gully she drew a breath, preparing herself for what she was increasingly thinking would be a romantic tryst. She remembered the feel of Peter, and it annoyed her anew that he had left her.

Teresa peered into the donga but saw nothing, just a narrow stream winding its way through the cutting and around a bend about thirty yards to her left. She carried on along the edge of the high bank, watching her footing in case of collapse. The voices became louder, though were still not distinct. It was like they were trying to keep the noise down. She felt her own heart quicken.

A movement in the grass startled her and she stopped just as a monitor lizard, a yard long with green and brown stripes, ran in front of her and slid over the lip of the bank and down into the water below.

She caught her breath and carried on until she was close to the bend in the river.

'I want it, now,' a man's voice said. It was familiar, British. Upper class.

'You can't order me about. You're not paying for a woman here,' Grace said. 'And you can't go back on our deal.'

'I could just take what I want,' the man said again.

Teresa dropped to her knees and crawled slowly forward through the grass until she was nearly at the edge of the precipice. She inched her way forward.

'That's why I've got the count here, with a gun on you.'

'*Sì.* Don't try anything or I'll cut you down.'

Ferdinand's English had improved suddenly and dramatically.

'You need me. General Wood won't let you anywhere near the column without me and even then I'll have some explaining to do to get you close enough to the empress to photograph her,' said the man Teresa was sure was Llewellyn Walters.

'Trust me,' Grace said. 'When the empress hears what we have to say to her she'll do whatever we ask her to. I've heard she's a generous person.'

'That she is,' Walters said. 'She had her own maids care for one of my men who became ill. And on the way to Hlobane, when one of the wagons broke a wheel and a local farmer came to our assistance, the empress gave the farmer's wife a new sewing machine.'

Grace shook her head. 'I don't know what is more absurd – travelling with a sewing machine, or giving one away to someone who helps change a cartwheel.'

Teresa dropped to her stomach and crawled forward using her toes and elbows. She wanted to get close enough to the donga that she could peer in. Her face was obscured from the people below by a tuft of grass. She saw Walters, Grace and Ferdinand – all fully clothed – and that Walters held the reins of two horses.

Teresa knew that she needed to get back to Phillips and Samuel as quickly as possible. It seemed she was right about Ferdinand being a journalist who was trying to beat her to the story she had been chasing, and it looked like he and Grace were about to leave with Walters on the two spare horses the officer had brought with him. If she couldn't be there to interview and photograph the empress, then no one else was going to beat her to it.

She had started to ease herself back, away from the riverbank, when she heard a rustle in the grass behind her. For a second she thought it was another lizard, or a snake, but when she rolled over to check, she saw a man in a British Army uniform with a tea-stained off-white helmet on his head.

Before Teresa had time to cry out, the man was on her, clamping his hand over her mouth.

She screamed into his palm and tried to lash out, but he pinned her right arm to the ground with a knee on her wrist. The pain was so bad she thought the bones in her arm would snap. She flailed with her left hand, but to no avail, and in an instant he was kneeling astride her chest.

'Quiet now, miss. You don't want me to hurt you more than I have to. You shouldn't have been spying on the good lieutenant, so you're going to have to take your punishment now. You know we shoot spies in the British Army?'

She widened her eyes. What the hell was happening here?

Teresa wiggled under him and tried to fight, but when he put his hand under her skirts she froze in terror.

'That's better. Quiet now, missy.'

There was no way Teresa O'Kane was going to quietly acquiesce to anything. She raised her knee up hard into the man's crotch. He bellowed like a dying buffalo and she thought she would be able to roll out from under him.

But the trooper lashed out in wounded rage and Teresa's world went black.

23

KWAZULU-NATAL, THE PRESENT

Adam heard the high-pitched buzz and held a hand to shield his eyes as he scanned the sky.

'There,' he said.

Marilyn looked up, following where he was pointing. Again, she caught sight of the drone she had just messaged Sannie about.

Adam looked to the young mother from the kraal, who had re-emerged from her house, having returned the metal detector. She was carrying her young son again.

'*Ngubani umnikazi wale* drone?' Adam asked her.

She shrugged, indicating she didn't know who owned it. Adam didn't imagine it was the sort of thing one found flying in this remote corner of Zululand every day. The drone did a lower circuit, this time over them, and the mother pointed it out to her child, who gurgled with joy and tried to reach his little arm up to catch it.

'*Ngena ngaphakathi*,' Adam said to her, and the woman clearly understood this was an order. She went back inside her house.

Adam unzipped his dive bag and took out the AK-47 he'd souvenired from the veterans at Bhanga Nek. He fitted a thirty-round banana-shaped magazine to the weapon and yanked back on the cocking handle, chambering a round.

'Adam . . .' Marilyn began.

He brought the rifle up into his shoulder and pointed skywards. Adam stopped tracking the drone and looked to Marilyn. She was a police officer, and he was just the extra muscle here. If she ordered him not to fire, he would have to comply.

'Don't miss. And watch your fall of shot.' Marilyn smiled at him.

He liked her, and he had already scanned the horizon to make sure that any falling bullets weren't going to rain down on a house or kraal. The landscape beyond the Prince Imperial's monument was empty.

Marilyn was messaging Sannie, and Adam glanced away from the drone to the people down the hill near the monument. Sannie was ushering them all to their vehicles.

The drone did a lazy arc around the monument then started coming back towards him.

It was coming in faster now, and lower, as if the operator had zoomed his camera in on Adam.

Good. It would be the last thing the bastard saw.

Adam took aim.

'Adam, what is that thing underneath it?' Marilyn said.

Adam had thought it was some kind of camera pod slung under the drone. He aimed down the open sights of the old Russian-made rifle and used his right index finger to push the selector switch all the way down to semi-automatic. This would allow him to fire one round at a time. The drone was no gadget-shop hobby model; it was big, maybe a metre across, with four rotors, like the ones he'd seen in the cache at Bhanga Nek. As he moved his finger to the trigger and took up the slack, the thing came closer and better into view. It wasn't carrying a camera.

'Marilyn, take cover!'

Adam had read online about these machines and what they could do, via news reports from the war in Ukraine. He never dreamed he would come up against one in person.

He squeezed the trigger and the rifle kicked back into his shoulder. The drone kept coming.

Adam registered Marilyn running towards the hut where the young woman lived.

He fired and missed again. It was nearly on him.

He took a breath and flicked the selector switch up a notch to full auto. He aimed low and to the left, compensating for the expected pull, and squeezed the trigger. A stream of rounds burst from the rifle's barrel and Adam saw at least one of them slam into the drone.

As rotors and bits of plastic and metal separated from the body and rained to the ground, Adam registered the sight of the green orb being released from under it.

'Grenade!' He lowered the rifle and ran for the scant cover of the low mudbrick and rock wall of the kraal. If Marilyn hadn't already guessed what the drone was carrying – there hadn't been time for him to explain – she knew now.

Adam heard a thud as he vaulted over the wall and threw himself down on the ground, the rifle still in his hand. For a couple of seconds he thought the grenade might not have been armed, but then he heard, and felt, a sickening *whump*.

The ground shook as the hand grenade exploded and Adam was buried in a shower of debris.

'STAY HERE,' Sannie ordered Tustin.

'With someone dropping hand grenades? I don't think so.'

'Is that what that was?' Goldie Faul said. 'Get me the hell out of here, Richard.'

They had all been surprised when Adam started firing, with Van der Ploeg, the South African Border War veteran, correctly identifying the popping noise of an AK-47.

Short of pulling a gun on them, Sannie didn't have the time or means, or probably the legal right, to force any of the group to do what she wanted. Right now, all she cared about was Adam. Neither Marilyn nor Adam was answering her calls. She got into Adam's Ranger, started the engine and accelerated up the hill towards the kraal.

The dust cloud and chemical smoke from the explosion had nearly cleared by the time she pulled up and opened the *bakkie*'s door.

Sannie saw Marilyn on her knees, scrabbling in a pile of rubble. A woman with a baby stood behind her, looking on.

'Adam!' Sannie ran from the car, nauseous with dread. She'd lost two husbands to violent deaths and now the man she loved had just been blown up. 'No!'

Marilyn looked up, her face streaked with sweat and dust. 'Sannie, help me. He's alive.'

Sannie glanced heavenwards and mouthed a quick, silent prayer. She dropped into a slide on her knees in the grass. Adam was moving, his body still partly covered in rubble from the wall, which had been built to keep livestock in, not to survive a grenade blast. Marilyn shifted a rock from Adam's chest which allowed him to sit up. He shook his head.

'Adam? Adam? Can you hear me.'

He coughed and spat dirt and dust. When he answered he was almost shouting. 'I'm OK.'

'Your hearing?'

'What?' he asked.

She asked again, louder.

He nodded. 'I can hear.' He shook his head then smiled. 'Though you sound like you're under water.'

As the two women shifted old bricks, rocks and clumps of hard-dried mud mortar, Adam was able to dust himself off and, eventually, roll over and get to his knees. He stood, patting himself down. His exposed arms and face were covered in scratches, raw abrasions and small cuts where blood was starting to appear. He shook his arms and legs out.

'Nothing major.' He ran a hand through his fair hair, now dust-choked brown. His voice was returning to a more normal level. 'We've got to move. They know who we are and that I'm armed.'

'They?' Marilyn asked.

'The people who were flying that drone. I'm sure it's the same ones I took on at Bhanga Nek. They're Tustin's military veterans. They had a couple of drones with them in their camp.'

The white Range Rover raced past them, leaving a cloud of dust in its wake. It was Tustin, with his two clients and Jan-Maree Ball. Tustin glared at Sannie as he floored the accelerator.

Adam spat again. 'Where are they going?'

'Your guess is as good as mine,' Sannie said. 'Tustin says he's not involved in any of this and has no time for metal detectors or treasure hutners. He says that Andy, the veterans' leader, is, quote: a "psychopath" who was dishonourably discharged from the military.'

Adam watched the car leave. It was headed in the direction they had come from, back towards Nqutu. 'Do you trust Tustin?'

'Not particularly,' Sannie said.

Marilyn gestured to the hut where she had taken cover. The young woman stood in the doorway, trying to soothe her baby, who had been crying since the explosion.

Sannie took out her phone and dialled a number.

'Who are you calling?' Adam asked.

'I'm reporting what just happened to Gita. We need backup.'

'YOU'RE THE FORMER SOLDIER, ADAM,' Marilyn said. 'What do we do next?'

Adam had been scanning the low hills around them, pondering that same question. Andy had eyes on them, thanks to the drone, but there was no sign of him or any of his men. That was the beauty of drones.

'He's got at least one more of those drones.' Adam pondered Marilyn's question. 'Are you ready for a fight, Marilyn?'

She gave him a grin. '*Yebo*.'

He nodded and climbed up into the rear of his truck. He had the AK-47 in his hands again.

Sannie had finished one call and then made another in quick succession. She ended it and came to them. 'What are you doing?' she asked Adam. 'Riding shotgun?'

'Yes.'

Sannie looked at him as if she were about to tell him that would not be legal, but instead, she just nodded.

'We lead,' Adam said, 'back the way we came, and if we reach a choke point – like a cutting through a hill, or a bridge, somewhere they could ambush us, I'll get out and scout ahead.'

Sannie opened her mouth to say something, but he looked her in the eyes and she thought better of any objection she wanted to voice. 'Just be careful.'

He nodded. 'I've got too much to live for.'

Sannie nodded. 'I called the Dundee Farm Watch, and Deon Meyer from Viking. I'm hoping that if a police tactical unit can't get to us, they might be available. He's getting some people together.'

Adam smiled. 'Those Farm Watch *okes* don't need an excuse to get out their AR-15s and head to a gunfight.'

'That's what worries me – that we might be provoking a response. I don't know . . .' Sannie sniffed.

He loved her, right then. Not only was she beautiful and smart and principled, but she could admit her vulnerability, that she didn't have all the answers all of the time. He could see, now, for the first time, why his going away had been difficult for her. He'd found a renewed purpose in his own life and it had been good for him, but he needed to remember that there was someone else in his world now and it was she who had helped him recover from the depths of despair.

Adam went to her. Sannie wiped her eyes and he took her in his arms.

'You two,' Marilyn said, 'I'd say "get a room", but we've got bad guys to catch.'

SANNIE DROVE the Ranger while Adam stood in the rear load area, AK-47 at the ready as she scanned the ground ahead and on either side of them. He watched the sky for drones.

In her rear-view mirror, Sannie saw that Marilyn, in Sannie's

Fortuner, was hanging back, as they'd discussed. If the lead vehicle was ambushed, Marilyn would call for backup and, hopefully, be ready to provide assistance.

Adam banged on the roof of the *bakkie*. Sannie craned her head out of the driver's side window, which she had left open.

'Vehicle ahead,' Adam shouted.

Standing higher than her, he'd seen the Range Rover four-wheel-drive first. It was parked on the side of the road just on the other side of a small rise. It came into Sannie's view. One person was standing outside, and as Sannie drove a little closer she could see it was the American woman, Goldie Faul.

Sannie slowed to a stop, a hundred metres short.

'Stopping for a *veltie*?' Adam asked, perhaps half in jest.

'I don't think they've pulled over so that she can have a wee,' Sannie said. 'She strikes me as the type who needs porcelain.'

Faul was walking towards them, alone.

Sannie opened her door.

'Careful.' Adam was leaning on the roof of the cab now, scanning the terrain around them.

Sannie got out, adjusted the Z88 pistol on her belt so that it was in easy reach, and started walking down the road. She heard the crunch of tyres on dirt as Marilyn slowed to a halt behind them. The air was warm and dry, a soft breeze rippling the golden grass at the road's edge.

Faul halted around the halfway mark, hands on her hips, and waited for Sannie to get closer before speaking.

'Like the gunfight at the O.K. Corral,' Faul said, 'except the new sheriff in town's a woman.'

Sannie stopped a few metres short. 'What does that make you, Miss Faul? The bad girl?'

She laughed. 'Not me. I'm a white hat in this little drama, and I didn't come to Africa for a shootout.'

'Tell me,' Sannie said, 'what *did* you really come here for?'

'A few things, and I think that good-looking specimen in the back of the pickup truck might be able to assist me with a couple of them.'

Sannie raised an eyebrow. 'Tell me.'

'I'd rather talk to him in person.'

Sannie shook her head. 'We travel as a team. Anything you say to him, he'll tell me in any case.'

'Oh.' A look of understanding passed over her face. 'Lucky you.'

Sannie said nothing. Her right hand rested on her pistol. It was not a showdown – not yet, at least – but someone had just tried to kill her boyfriend and partner.

'Your Mr Adam Kruger souvenired something, maybe two things, that were meant for me.'

'An antique Koran and an Arabic sword.'

Faul gave a tight smile. 'You two do share, don't you.'

'Get to the point, Miss Faul. I don't like standing in the open when there are people somewhere around here who like to drop hand grenades from drones.'

'You're safe here with me.'

Sannie narrowed her eyes. She tried to control her anger. Her country had enough crime problems of its own without meddling foreigners coming along with military hardware and explosives.

'I could arrest you now and charge you with conspiracy to commit murder.'

Faul shrugged. 'It's your country, and you're the police. You can do whatever you want, but I think we both know that if you did, I'd lawyer up, call the US embassy and be on a plane back to New York by this time tomorrow.'

'That might be a good idea, Miss Faul. And you can take your band of mercenaries with you.'

She pouted. 'Oh, I'm sure I have no idea what you're talking about. In any case, I'm a businesswoman. I don't deal with the help.'

'Oh. I thought you were a historian?'

'I am. So I can tell you that a certain sword that your Adam may or may not have in his possession right now – unless he's stashed it somewhere – is not just any old antique. It is, almost certainly, the *Zulfiqar*, the missing double-tipped sword of the Prophet Muhammad, and the Koran is purported to be one of the earliest editions left in the world.'

Faul had all but admitted to being involved, in some way, with the man who had tried to kill Adam twice and who had shot Adam's student with a spear gun. 'You're dealing with criminals on behalf of your rich boss.'

Faul shrugged again. 'People sell, I buy. Go on back to your boyfriend, Colonel and tell him I'll give him a million dollars for the blade and the book.'

Sannie tried to keep a straight face, but the number unnerved her. If that was Faul's opening offer then the items must be worth much more.

'Priceless antiquities are being destroyed every day in places such as Yemen and Ukraine,' Faul added, 'where fighting rages. It's better for the world's history to be safe in the hands of people who care about it, rather than barbarians who are killing for money or their God.'

Sannie shook her head. 'Don't try to justify your boss's greed as anything more than what it is.'

Faul said nothing.

'What about Napoleon Bonaparte's sword, the one he carried at Austerlitz?' Sannie asked.

A shadow passed over them and Sannie shot a glance upwards, fearing it was another drone, either spying on her or about to attack them. But it was an eagle, riding a thermal.

'Just watch that trigger finger of yours, Colonle,' Faul said. 'But in answer to your question, what about it? Bonaparte had several swords and they're all in a museum in France. Jan-Maree Ball's talked us through her theory that Prince Louis was carrying his great-uncle's sword when he was killed and that someone did a switcheroo back in 1879, and that the real sword is still somewhere here in South Africa. I don't buy it – literally. Also, I don't want to be accused of exporting an Anglo-Zulu War artefact out of South Africa without a permit. That would be very bad.' She turned down the corners of her mouth in an exaggerated frown.

Faul was taunting her, willing her to pass on her offer to Adam. The Arabic sword and Koran had not originated from South Africa, but, rather, had probably been in transit. Maybe Faul and her mercenary 'help' had thought the law wouldn't catch up with them if she did business in a third-party country, outside of Yemen and the United States.

'You're wondering why I'm here, of all places, aren't you?' Faul prompted.

'The thought had crossed my mind.'

'Piet Van der Ploeg and Richard Tustin talk often. Tustin had mentioned his young female friend's theory and that got Piet – and me – interested. I won't lie to you. My employer is not in the business of breaking laws; even if Napoleon's sword was here, we would have to find a way around those export laws.'

'Around?' Sannie asked.

'What do they say: "TIA", right? "This is Africa"? I'm sure there would be a way if someone senior willed it.'

'You think that everyone in South Africa is corrupt?'

Faul shook her head. 'No, far from it. Not you, I'm sure. But do you want to see your boyfriend killed because he stole some things that didn't belong to him? You don't need to answer that. One million dollars. In the bank account of your choice or his by this time tomorrow.'

Sannie needed to buy time. 'And Tustin?'

Faul looked her in the eye. 'What about him?'

'Is he in league with you and your mercenaries?'

'Mercenaries?' She gave another laugh. 'I told you I don't deal with the help.'

'Does Van der Ploeg?' Sannie asked.

'Piet's a middleman. He knows plenty of people. But as to Tustin, to answer your question, no, I'm not in business with him and neither are the help.'

'He doesn't trade in artefacts?' Sannie asked, for confirmation.

'No. He's too high-minded. I've had to watch what I say around him.'

Sannie noted the way Faul held her eye, but she was clearly a shrewd businesswoman who sailed closed to the edges of the law. Perhaps she was just a very good liar. 'So why are you here now?'

'I told you. I heard about Jan-Maree's theory about Napoleon's sword and I wanted to hear it for myself. I'm grateful to you for bringing her along, since her car broke down. She was supposed to meet us at the battlefields earlier.'

Giving Jan-Maree a ride had almost cost Adam his life.

'Look, I get it,' Faul continued. 'You're a South African cop and you want a South African scalp for what's gone on. Your boyfriend got roughed up, but the way I hear it he gave as good as he got. They're all big boys and they play by their own big-dick, pissing-competition rules. Adam took something that wasn't his and instead of calling the antiquity police I'm talking to you. I want what he's got, and my boss and I don't want to make more trouble in your country.'

'Your "help", as you call them, just tried to kill a man, and shot a young South African woman with a spear gun.'

Faul shook her head. 'No, they were trying to *scare* the man you clearly care about and keep an eye on him from the sky at the same time. Your guy shot the drone out of the sky and it went boom. No one was going to drop anything on anyone anytime soon. As for the woman on the boat, I'm told that was something called an accidental discharge.' She pointed to Adam. 'And word is that your friend had the air hose to his diving cylinder cut. *He* did a better job of trying to kill my help than they did on him. Of course, I'll deny everything if you try to charge me.'

Sannie scoffed. 'I can charge you now for conspiracy to commit murder.'

Faul reached into her pockets and turned them out to show they were empty. 'No grenades in here. Take the money, Colonel. It's best for everyone.'

On the one hand, Faul's offer made sense, especially when it came to saving lives – especially Adam's. But Sannie doubted she could trust Faul or her small army of henchman to honour any deal.

'You tried to kill me once already,' Sannie said.

Faul rocked back on her heels a little. 'Say what?'

'You know what I'm talking about. Two of your thugs ambushed my partner and me and the head guide from David Gregory's game reserve.'

'I have no idea what you are talking about.' Faul stared into Sannie's eyes.

'You expect me to believe that?'

Faul put her hands on her hips and jutted out her chin. 'I've told you more than I should have, in order to get you to negotiate with me, Colonel, but trust me, I did not tell anyone to ambush you. When your boyfriend went all Chuck Norris on my guys they responded in kind, but that's it.'

Sannie narrowed her eyes. 'Tell me about the rhino horns.'

'Now you're just talking in riddles, Colonel. I'm not in the business of trading in wildlife products and neither is the man I work for. In fact, he has donated a significant amount of money to anti-poaching ranger projects in Africa.'

'If you're looking for a medal you won't get it from me,' Sannie said. 'I suggest you radio or call your men and tell them to pack up their kit and head to the nearest airport and get out of my country, Miss Faul.'

The other woman glared at Sannie. 'Not without what I came for.'

Sannie heard the creak of a vehicle's suspension and glanced around. Adam had just climbed down from the back of his *bakkie*. Marilyn had left Sannie's Fortuner and was standing beside the Ranger. Adam said something to Marilyn, then started walking towards Sannie and Faul, his rifle half raised, at the ready.

Adam came to Sannie and stood by her side. 'Need any help?'

Sannie nodded to the woman in front of them. 'Adam, this is Goldie Faul, from New York. She's come to South Africa looking for the items you found at Bhanga Nek. She doesn't need me to introduce you to her – she already seems to know about you. She's the person paying that man, Andy, and his group of veterans. She's offering you a million US dollars for the sword and the Koran.'

Adam gave a low whistle and looked sideways at Sannie. 'We could buy half of Pennington with that much money.'

Sannie smiled. 'I like the piece we've got. Besides, they seem to be priceless antiquities looted from a country at war. I think it would be better if they were in a public museum somewhere.'

Adam looked from Sannie to Faul. 'I think you have your answer.'

Faul shook her head slowly. 'You've just made a bad decision, both of you, and I hope you understand the consequences. Too bad you play by the rules, Colonel.'

Sannie drew her Z88 pistol from its holster. 'Not always.'

24

ZULULAND, 1880

Gregory located the column on the open veld between Koppie Alleen and the Prince Imperial's memorial.

He crested a rise and saw the lonely peak – the direct English translation of the landmark was 'Hill Alone' – first, and then the long train of a dozen wagons and numerous people on horseback who made up part of the caravan escorting the Empress Eugénie. He had heard that in all, there were no fewer than fifty wagons, but all those carrying the tentage, stores, and food needed for the royal's camp would be ahead of this component, setting up for the night. Gregory spurred Bullet in the ribs.

As he drew closer, two men in dark tunics identical to his broke away from the procession and galloped out to intercept him.

They were two snuffs, part of the escort detail, and as they neared he recognised them. Taft was a drunkard ex-soldier and Dunphy a farrier, an idiot who had managed to fail in his almost foolproof in-demand trade and so had joined the police.

Constable Taft pulled up in front of him first. 'Sub-Inspector Gregory.' There was no hint of respect in the way Taft greeted him.

'Taft, I've come to see General Wood.'

Taft spat on the ground. 'No one's to approach the empress's column, except by invitation. They're our orders.'

Dunphy rode up and reined in his horse. 'What are you doing here?'

'You'll do me the courtesy of respecting my rank,' Gregory said to Dunphy, a younger constable.

Dunphy picked at a tooth. 'The regulations say I *have* to respect the rank, Sub-Inspector.'

Gregory knew the unsaid remainder of the sentence: *but not the man*. He had little time for these two morons. 'Where's Walters, the cavalry escort officer? He'll know what I'm here for and he will want to see me.'

The constables looked at each other, then Taft spoke. 'Lieutenant Walters is out scouting the path ahead.'

'Very well, I'll join the column, pay my respects to General Wood and then wait for Walters to return.'

'Orders say –'

Gregory unbuckled the flap on his holster and drew his revolver. He levelled it at Dunphy, whose protest died on his lips. 'Shut up, Dunphy.'

Taft gave a small chuckle. 'Don't worry about him. He won't shoot. He's got no nerve. That's how he survived Isandlwana – he ran away.'

Gregory nudged Bullet in the ribs and used his knee to steer him until his horse stood side by side with Taft's. 'Kill many Zulus in the war, did you, Taft? Way I hear it, you were on garrison duty, suffering from a dose of something nasty you picked up at the Red Lantern.'

Taft sneered. He deserved the 'snuff' nickname. Gregory could smell his body odour and the stale booze on his breath.

'If I did, I picked it up from your Indian lady friend.'

Gregory twisted his right hand as he brought it up and smashed the butt of his pistol into Taft's nose. Blood sprayed as the constable screamed and raised his hands to the shattered cartilage. Taft's horse was spooked by the noise and bucked. Taft toppled backwards, crying out in further alarm as he fell heavily to the ground.

'You can't do that,' said Dunphy.

Gregory turned towards the other man and spurred Bullet into a charge towards him. Dunphy wheeled around and urged his horse to put distance between himself and Gregory.

'Coward,' Gregory said to Dunphy's back.

Before Taft could catch his breath, or Dunphy decided to return, Gregory kicked Bullet and galloped across the plain to the wagon train.

As he drew closer another member of the Natal Mounted Police, Brian Grace, a fellow sub-inspector, rode up to him.

'Peter? What the devil are you doing here?'

Ruddy-faced and greying, Brian's tone was friendly. He was a good man, older than Gregory, but also a former army officer and, having seen a fair amount of war in the Crimea and India, he had not been judgemental of Gregory's escape from Isandlwana. The two of them had discussed the events after the battle and Brian had also spoken with Samuel about Peter, when Brian processed Samuel's recruitment to the NMP.

'I need to pay my respects to General Wood and inform him about a matter involving a member of your cavalry escort, Lieutenant Walters.'

Brian shook his head. 'How someone can become such an insufferable little prig at that stage of life is almost beyond my comprehension. He's off on some self-appointed scouting mission at the moment.'

'So I heard.' Gregory looked back out over the plain. Taft had remounted and was riding slowly back to the column, with Dunphy by his side. 'I'm sorry, Brian, but I just had to discipline Taft and Dunphy. They didn't want to let me approach the column.'

Brian sighed. 'Not an ounce of common sense between them. You're one of us, for goodness' sake. That Walters you speak of has continually been trying to undermine my command and tell my men what they can and can't do. What did Taft say to you, Peter?'

'Taft impugned my honour and that of a lady with whom I'm acquainted. I resorted to fisticuffs.' Gregory left out the part about the pistol butt for now.

Brian nodded. 'I know what some of the men say about you, Peter, and I often find myself explaining the reality of your situation at Isandlwana. If Taft insulted a superior officer, then he got what was coming to him.'

'Thank you.'

'I'll introduce you to General Wood. He's a good fellow,' Brian lowered his voice to a conspiratorial level, 'and between you and me, I think he's quite besotted with the empress. She, by the way, is a marvellous person, Peter, just marvellous. Generous to a fault, but the poor woman grows more melancholic by the day as we get nearer to the anniversary of her son's death.'

Gregory nodded. He knew how she felt. 'Tomorrow?'

'Yes. We'll make camp at the memorial later today.'

Brian led Gregory along the length of the column. Here and there he saw an NMP member he knew and returned the salutes of those who did him the courtesy. One of a pair of ladies' maids riding on a carriage gave him a smile and he greeted Zulu servants and wagoners in their own language as he passed them.

Brian swung wide of the procession as he neared its head. 'We're all under orders to give the empress her privacy, particularly as the big day looms,' Brian said from the saddle as he steered Gregory out to the flank.

From a distance, Gregory glimpsed the empress's profile. Everyone in the colony had seen pictures of her in the newspapers and even this far away he could see that she sat with the erect bearing of a royal beauty.

'The general drives her carriage himself some days,' Brian said as they made a line back towards the column. 'But he's riding ahead today, so that should make it easier for you to speak to him.'

Brian spurred his horse on, and Gregory matched him, but then reined Bullet in as Brian rode up alongside General Wood, who was a short distance behind his forward scouting element, a pair of cavalry troopers and two NMP constables. They exchanged words and Brian then turned in the saddle and waved Gregory forward.

'Sub-Inspector Peter Gregory, sir,' Brian said by way of introduction. Brian looked around him and saw that Taft and Dunphy were almost back in the column. 'I'll just see to my men.' He rode away.

'Good morning, sir,' Gregory said as Bullet fell into step beside the general's horse.

Wood was in his early forties, his receding hairline balanced by a luxuriant, drooping moustache. 'Gregory. You're aware I gave orders that the column was not to be approached by outsiders, including that bothersome American writer. I've been told you were given the job of escorting her.'

'I was, sir, but this is of the utmost importance.' Gregory was impressed that Wood knew who he was, and that he'd been tasked with chaperoning Teresa.

The general gave the smallest of nods. 'Go on, then.' Wood kept his eyes on the horizon. An old soldier who had been awarded the Victoria Cross for his service in India, and had seen both victory and near defeat in the war with the Zulus, he would be alert to any sign of unforeseen danger.

'I'm conducting an investigation for Major Dartnell into the possible theft of the late Prince Imperial's sword, sir.'

Wood flicked his head around. 'What? Why wasn't I informed of this? It was my understanding that Lord Chelmsford returned Prince Louis's sword to his mother last year. The empress has mentioned nothing of this to me.'

Gregory didn't know how much detail he should go into. 'I don't want to betray confidences, sir, but it seems the prince's sword may have been switched with a substitute at some point before it left Africa with Lord Chelmsford.'

'By whom?'

'That is what I'm investigating, sir. One of the officers who originally received the sword, when it was returned by the Zulus during Lord Chelmsford's march on Ulundi, was a major named Morrison, 17th Lancers. He left the army and was recently found dead at his farm outside of Pietermaritzburg. He was murdered, with some hallmarks of a Zulu attack. His body was eviscerated.'

'You think he may have been involved in this . . . deception?'

'I was the investigating officer, sir. Major Morrison was a man of extremely undesirable character. He'd been disciplined for sexual transgressions in the field and was reputed to be a pederast.'

Wood grimaced. 'Disgusting.'

'Sir, I've come to you because I need to question one of the officers currently under your command, a Lieutenant Walters.'

'Young Llewellyn?'

Gregory nodded. 'Yes, sir.'

'Hmm. It was Walters who told me that you were escorting the American woman. He's a self-starter – he volunteered to ride out to intercept your party and keep tabs on your movements. What does he have to do with any of this business?'

Gregory noted that Walters had 'volunteered' to come to him, but held his thoughts on that fact for now. 'My investigation revealed that Walters was an associate of Morrison. They both frequented a house of ill repute in Pietermaritzburg and were known to each other.'

The general looked surprised. 'Walters wasn't . . .'

'For a man of his age, sir, Walters reputedly has quite some experience in pursuits of the flesh, but, no, sir, there is nothing I have learned that indicates his desires run to the criminal, such as corrupting minors.'

'Something, at least,' Wood said. 'Go on, man. Why do you need to question Walters – simply because he and this disgraced major frequented the same bawdy house?'

Gregory shook his head. 'In addition to his many transgressions, Morrison was a drunkard and a bankrupt. His farm was failing.' Even as he said the words, Gregory could not help but feel a hypocrite. He, too, drank too much and was no good as a farmer, but at least he had not resorted to crime. 'He needed money, and my investigations uncovered another witness who, while also of dubious character, spun a believable story that Morrison was in the midst of a business deal of some sort. He had something purportedly of great value that he was about to sell, and Lieutenant Walters, who comes from a moneyed family, was intending to buy said item from Morrison.'

'The missing sword?' General Wood had come to the same conclusion.

'I can't be sure, sir, but this is why I need to question the officer.'

Wood rode on in silence and Gregory wondered if he was running through the same hypotheses. Had someone murdered Morrison in order to steal the sword? Had Walters killed Morrison, and if so, why? Had Morrison reneged on the deal, or had he sold to another bidder? Had Walters killed him in a fit of rage, or had he tortured him first, in search of information? There were many possibilities and Gregory was wary of the temptation to try to make a theory fit what little evidence he had, rather than the other way around.

Wood cleared his throat. 'Walters is under my command, so when he returns from his patrol, I'll see to it that you have access to him. If Walters is involved in any sort of business that might possibly affect the empress – even if he was, say, trying to do the right thing by retrieving her son's sword – then I want to know about it.'

Wood seemed to be protective of an officer under his command, which was understandable, so Gregory did his best to sound conciliatory. 'Yes, it is possible the lieutenant wanted to find the sword to present it to the empress.'

'My thoughts as well.' Wood stroked his moustache. 'Walters is a driven young fellow, I can imagine that he would think that such a gesture might advance his career, but I enforce a strict chain of command, here, Gregory.'

'Of course, sir.'

Wood shot him another look. 'Which means that once your business with Walters is finished, you'll be departing from my location. My orders about no one approaching our column without official business remain extant.'

Gregory nodded. 'I had hoped that I might be able to question the empress in order to get a better description of the prince's sword, sir.'

Wood narrowed his eyes. 'Out of the question. If, and I stress *if*, there is a need to involve the empress in any of this, then it will be through me. As I am sure you will appreciate, Her Majesty has been in a very . . . delicate state these last few days, and tomorrow is the anniversary of her son's death. She is to be afforded privacy and other considerations in this moment of reflection.'

Gregory had known his chances of speaking to the royal would be slim. 'Of course, sir.'

Gregory had little to link Walters to the scene of Morrison's murder – only the word of a prostitute and another degenerate that Walters and Morrison were cooking up some deal or other, and the fact that he had seen cavalry bootprints in the mud outside the dead man's house. He'd noted the size of the prints and that was one thing he could check. There was also the bullet he had found in Morrison's house, which he was sure came from a British service revolver.

Gregory saluted and let his horse fall back down the line, sensing that his time with the general had run its course. He gave the empress's buggy a wide berth, spurring Bullet out to the flank, though he glimpsed her upright silhouette again.

He returned to the procession in time to come alongside another carriage with two ladies' maids on board. He tipped his helmet to them and one smiled and then covered her mouth coquettishly. He thought of Teresa, and let himself fall further behind.

Why? Why had he allowed himself to feel again? His army life had kept him celibate, or as near as damn it, and the only other time he had felt an inkling of a true romantic connection to a woman was with Grace.

But now there was Teresa. Beautiful, forthright, intelligent – and passionate. It somehow felt wrong, disrespectful to those of his comrades cut down in their prime, that he might even consider anything resembling a future with her, or be allowed to experience a measure of happiness. But he could not keep her off his mind for long.

Gregory raised his hand to the brim of his pith helmet and looked around him. General Wood, near the head of the column, was pointing off to the left, and Sub-Inspector Brian Grace was riding beside him. Gregory knew this area well now, and while they were approaching the site of the Prince Imperial's memorial, it seemed that General Wood had given an order for the empress's entourage to head off on a tangent.

Thinking a mistake may have been made, Gregory spurred his horse forward. At the same time, however, Brian wheeled his mount around and met him before Gregory could reach the general.

'If you're riding up to tell the general he's going the wrong way, then save your breath and his wrath, Peter.'

Gregory nodded. 'So why the change in the direction?'

Brian turned again until he was riding alongside Gregory. 'As you probably know, that white marble cross and plinth they've erected stand out like a redcoat in a snow field. The general gave orders to alter our course, so we are to ride along that wide donga over there.'

Gregory looked where Brian was pointing. It was a circuitous path, but there was method in Wood's madness. The new route would take them below a low rise in the deceptively featureless short-grass plain. 'If we took the direct route, she'd be able to see the cross from miles away.'

Brian nodded. 'Precisely. Spending the better part of a day fixating on the cross commemorating her son's death will be too much for the empress – or so the general fears.'

Another thought occurred to Gregory. 'That also means that if anyone wanted to surprise the empress they could be waiting at or near the memorial and not be seen until the last moment, when the general cuts across this rise and arrives at the cross.'

Brian smiled. 'He's not a general for nothing. He's thought of that already. He ordered Walters to ride out yesterday and bring the local Zulu chiefs to him for an *indaba*. They met and General Wood convinced them, with the promise of some blankets and other trinkets, to set up a cordon in the vleis and hills around the memorial. If they see anyone approaching the monument, the Zulus will intercept them and ward them off.'

Gregory had underestimated General Wood. He might have lost the battle at Hlobane Mountain – and been spared the humiliation of being relieved of his command because the debacle at Isandlwana had overshadowed his loss – but he had scored a sound victory at

Kambula. Probably more than many other commanders, he had relearned the importance of choosing one's terrain.

'Walters was supposed to ride out ahead of our column to secure the memorial after his current reconnaissance mission, but he's now overdue,' Brian said.

Gregory checked his watch. 'He'd be hard-pressed getting to the Tshotshosi River and the cross even if he reported back now and left again.'

'Likely as not he's cut straight to the memorial from whatever has held him up today.'

Gregory made a quick decision. 'I think you're right, Brian. Thank you for your help. I think I'll take my leave now and ride to the memorial. Maybe I'll find Walters there. Please pass on my respects to General Wood.'

Brian raised a finger to his helmet in a parody of a salute. '*Hamba kahle*, Peter.'

'I'll go well, and you stay well, too, Brian.' Gregory tugged Bullet's reins to the right, administered the spurs again, and galloped away, directly towards the memorial.

As he took a final look at the empress and her entourage over his shoulder, the sight reminded him of a funeral procession. Gregory looked forward again, which was all one could do at times like these.

The wide open plain stretched away from him and he gave Bullet his head.

GRACE RODE behind Lieutenant Walters and his sergeant, and watched the officer's back and hands for any sign of unexpected movement. She was pleased that she had insisted that Walters bring the two spare horses.

Before leaving Pietermaritzburg Grace had sent word to Walters, via another member of the 17th Lancers who had been a client, that she was riding out to join Peter Gregory's party, and wished to meet, discretely, with the lieutenant. Walters' brother officer had smirked, thinking that Grace was talking about a different kind of liaison.

When Walters had snuck into the encampment in the early hours of the morning, Grace had finalised her demands. The plan had nearly unravelled when Walters had been discovered.

Ferdi was at her side.

The Italian count was rich and handsome, and, unlike many white men she had bedded, he knew what to do under the covers. He had 'confessed' to her the night before that he was, as Teresa O'Kane suspected, a newspaper reporter, from the *Gazzetta di Mantova*.

'It is a very historic publication,' he had whispered in her ear. 'It has been in print for more than one hundred years. It will be a grand honour for me and my editor if I can get a photograph of the empress and an interview with her. You are sure she will see you?'

'Yes. I am sure,' Grace had replied in the dark.

Walters had met them in the donga where she had supposedly gone to bathe, chaperoned by Ferdi. In truth, she would have felt more comfortable dealing with the British officer if Samuel had been with her, but he was probably too honhourable to get involved with her scheme. She liked Samuel a good deal and she knew, from snippets she had gleaned from Gregory – who never wanted to talk about the war – that Samuel was a fierce warrior.

Ferdi, though, had surprised her.

When Walters and his sergeant had splashed their way on horseback up the narrow donga, riding through the water, Walters had been rude to her, despite the fact that they had arranged to meet and she had been waiting for him.

'You'll come with me, alone,' he had ordered her, even though he had brought the second horse, as planned. Already he had been trying to double cross her.

Ferdi had stepped out from behind a boulder at that point, bringing his Snider carbine up into his shoulder and aiming it at Walters.

'*Signor*, that is no way to talk to a lady.'

Walters had grimaced, but Ferdi had held his eye with a hard stare. 'Miss Naidoo,' he cleared his throat. 'If you will accompany me, alone, I would be obliged.'

'Ferdi's coming with me,' Grace had replied. 'He's going to record my meeting with the empress for posterity, in the written word and by photograph.'

'That is not going to happen, Miss Naidoo,' Walters had protested. 'We had a deal.'

'Yes, that you would bring two horses and take me to the empress, and that you would bask in her favour for having delivered me to Her Majesty. And, as we agreed, you and I will share in whatever reward the empress decides to present either one of us,' Grace had said. 'And the reason I asked for two horses was because I always intended on bringing a companion, to make sure that I arrive safely.'

'You should be thankful I even agreed to meet with you last night,' he had said.

Grace had pointed to the tear on the right sleeve of his tunic. 'You should thank the Good Lord that Peter Gregory's bullet didn't take you in the back, instead of making a hole in your overcoat.'

Walters had opened his mouth to speak again, but at that moment a shower of stones had cascaded down from the high bank of the donga to Grace's left and Walters' right. They had all looked up.

'Sergeant, get up there, now. Find out who's spying on us.'

Walters had given her a hard stare, but Grace had jutted out her chin and said nothing. She, too, wondered if someone was above them, watching what was going on. If it was Samuel, then her deal with Walters would end here and now and she and Ferdi would be frogmarched back to camp and Sergeant Phillips. Perhaps it was an animal, a small buck come to drink at the river. For the moment, she had been content to let Walters think that she might have had another pair of eyes watching him, in case he tried something tricky. She had known Walters from the house of ill repute and though she had never bedded him, she knew the young man was one of those who needed to hurt a girl to experience fulfilment – even if sometimes he also needed to be spanked. He made her skin crawl, the same way that the cobras in the cane fields had terrified her as a young girl.

As she rode now, still keeping an eye on Walters, she remembered his brutish sergeant returning to the donga a few minutes later.

'It was the other woman, sir,' the sergeant had said. 'The American.'

'And?' Walters had asked him.

'She won't be bothering us, sir, and she won't be following us.'

What had the uniformed thug meant? Had he killed Teresa? Grace had not liked the nosey American when she first met her. The woman put on airs and graces but, in the end, was just another muck-raking journalist, like Ferdi. Grace had let Peter think that Teresa's plainly obvious – well, obvious to everyone but Peter – attraction to Peter had got under Grace's skin. The truth was that she did not want Peter mooning after her, in case he got too close and tumbled to what she was planning with Lieutenant Walters. There was a time when she could have seen herself staying in Peter's farm cottage, poor but happy, but now a bigger world awaited her. Who knew, perhaps she might board the ship with Ferdi and sail to Italy?

Walters led them away from where poor young Phillips was standing watch over no one except Samuel.

Whatever the sergeant had done to Teresa unsettled Grace. She spurred her horse and it broke into a canter. When she drew up alongside Walters she reined in her mount.

'Yes?' he said, turning towards her.

'I want money. Now.'

Walters shook his head. 'No. I told you we'll conduct whatever transactions we have to at a place of my choosing, after we have met with Her Majesty.'

She spat on the ground. Walters grimaced. 'Yes, and at this place of your *choosing*, you'll have half-a-dozen of your soldiers waiting to ambush me and take whatever I have, and give me nothing.'

Walters lowered his voice. 'I assure you, miss, that I am a gentle-man. I would never go back on my word, and I did not bring any money with me in case *you* and your cohort decided to ambush me.'

No honour among thieves. Grace still felt like she could not trust Walters, but she had backed herself into a corner. He was her only chance of meeting the empress before she left the colony. It was frustrating, but there was no one else with whom she could deal.

She sighed. 'And you stand by your promise to share whatever gratuity the empress gives you when you hand over what she wants?'

'You have my word, as an officer and a gentleman,' Walters said.

She felt the bile rise in her throat. It was a mix of nerves and disgust. She had heard the words of so-called gentlemen too many times in her life. 'I will make sure I stay around long enough to find out how generous she is going to be.'

Walters shrugged. 'If General Wood and Her Majesty allow you to linger, then that is up to you.'

Grace exhaled. *What else can I do?* She looked around to check on Ferdi, and saw that while she had been talking to Walters, the cavalry sergeant had moved his horse next to the count's and they, too, were conversing.

'Break,' Walters called.

The other two horsemen stopped, and the cavalry sergeant reached into his uniform tunic. For a moment Grace panicked and thought he might produce a hidden knife or gun. She felt relief when he withdrew a white tobacco pipe and handed it to Ferdi. The count smiled, slid his rifle back into the bucket strapped to his horse's side and took the pipe.

As Ferdi held the pipe closer to his face, to inspect a carving or something on its bowl, Grace realised she was thirsty and needed a drink. She looked down to retrieve the water canteen hanging from her saddle.

A flash of movement made her look up. The sergeant's free hand had balled into a fist, and he smashed it square into Ferdi's face, sending him flying from his saddle.

Wide-mouthed, Grace looked back around. She heard a *click* just as she found herself looking down the barrel of Llewellyn Walters' pistol.

25

KWAZULU-NATAL, THE PRESENT

Andy had deployed his troops into a classic L-shaped ambush – not because he expected a gunfight, but because he didn't want to be surprised again, as he had been at the beach. They were on the Isandlwana side of the Buffalo River, in the bush on either side of the approach to the bridge.

He'd smiled when Adam Kruger had shot the drone out of the sky, and for a moment he thought that the ex–South African Parabat might have actually blown himself up with the grenade attached to it.

Andy had been told to scare Kruger and the female police detectives, not kill them, but his gut instinct told him the order should have been for the latter option. Whatever happened, he needed to get himself and his crew out of South Africa as soon as possible.

He looked at his phone and read the WhatsApp message from Goldie Faul.

Stand down. We're coming to you. Cops have called for backup – need to investigate the drone crash. We're falling back to Dundee.

It was classic Faul. No-nonsense, and she'd talked about 'cops' in previous messages – telling him to keep their backup vehicle under surveillance, like he needed to be told how to do his job.

Tustin's Range Rover was coming down the gravel road towards them now.

The significance of their location was not lost on Andy. He'd read about the battles that had been fought in this area, and he'd learned the lessons of Chelmsford splitting his forces and underestimating his enemy. Both Adam Kruger and Sannie van Rensburg were worthy adversaries.

'Get eyes on that fucking car,' Andy said to Willis.

'On it, boss.'

Willis was watching the oncoming four-by-four through a pair of high-magnification, toughened binoculars.

'Tustin's driving. The Dutchman's next to him. I can see Faul in her safari hat in the back seat. Another female next to Faul.'

Andy tapped Willis on the shoulder and the former sergeant handed him the binoculars. He refocused and peered through them.

'That's Jan-Maree Ball,' Andy said.

Andy swung the binoculars up and along the road. There were no other vehicles visible and no dust clouds over the hill that might indicate a tail hanging back.

'Stay in position until they've reached us.' He handed the binoculars back to Willis.

SANNIE LIFTED the brim of Goldie Faul's hat slightly, so she could get a look at the man standing by the roadside, holding an AK-47 at the ready.

'Not too tall – maybe one-comma-seven metres; black hair and beard, big biceps, lots of tattoos,' Sannie said.

'That's Andy – their boss,' Adam said from the rear luggage compartment of the Range Rover, where he sat cradling his own Russian assault rifle.

'You sure you want to mess with these *okes*?' Van der Ploeg said with a smile from the front passenger seat.

'You just let me do the talking,' Sannie said.

Van der Ploeg held up his hands. 'I'm not arguing with you, Colonel. I just don't want to get caught in the crossfire.'

Tustin's knuckles showed white on the steering wheel. 'That man is dangerous and unpredictable.'

Sannie nodded. She did not underestimate the former Special Forces soldier. 'I'm counting on him not wanting to kill either of you.'

'Don't be so sure,' Tustin said.

Sannie filed that remark away for future reference.

'All of you, stay in the car,' Sannie said.

'Sannie . . .' Adam began.

'You as well. Stop here, Mr Tustin.'

Tustin pulled up twenty metres short of Andy and kept the engine running. Sannie half wondered if Tustin was going to make a run for it. Sannie got out of the vehicle and revealed herself.

'Colonel van Rensburg, I presume,' Andy said, in an appalling approximation of an Afrikaans accent. 'You fooled me.'

'How do I address you?' Sannie asked.

He smirked. 'Whatever turns you on.'

She straightened her shoulders and put her hand on her Z88 on her hip. 'Tell your men to stand down. Surrender your weapons, which I am sure you do not have the required permits for. Oh, and get out of South Africa on the next flight.'

He widened his eyes in mock surprise. 'What? You're not even going to read me my rights and try to arrest me?'

'I'm making you a good offer, Andy. You'd be unwise not to take it.'

He shook his head slowly. 'Not without my property, which your boyfriend stole. He's got a sword and a Koran that I paid for, and now I need to sell them to someone else.'

'I doubt very much that you had the required permits to export them from Yemen, or wherever they came from.'

He grinned. 'Somebody has been doing her detective work. You're only trying to deal with me because Adam Kruger's now in possession of the sword and the book. That makes him a criminal in your eyes as well, right?'

'Those things will be repatriated in due course. Now's the time for you to do the smart thing, Andy.'

'Where's Goldie?' Andy said.

Sannie kept her eyes on his. 'She is assisting the South African Police Service with our enquiries as we speak.'

He laughed. 'You're going to be drowning in lawyers before you know it, Colonel.'

She shrugged. 'I don't care. I want answers to some questions.'

Andy rocked his head from side to side. 'Maybe we can parlay. Ask away. Maybe if I tell you what you want to know then you'll give me back my treasures.'

Sannie thought a moment. She gave nothing away. 'Who killed the sixteen rhino in the boma on David Gregory's farm?'

He held her gaze. 'Not me. Nor any of my men. Promise you.'

'Why should I believe you?'

He kept his right hand on the pistol grip of his rifle, but ran the left through his thick mane of hair. For a moment he broke eye contact, then stared at her anew. 'I don't know if you can understand this, right, but I'll try and explain. My lads and I have killed – for our country, and for money, as operators and military contractors. From Afghanistan and Iraq to, yes, Yemen, and a few other places. But not one of my lads, or me, would harm the hairs on the back of a defence-less animal. Believe it or not, the boys really enjoyed the time out on old David's game reserve.'

'What about the rhino horns?'

He shrugged, the corners of his mouth turning up a little at the same time. 'What about them?'

'They're a valuable commodity, once more, in Yemen, from what I understand.'

'That may be, Colonel, but I don't understand the point you're trying to make.'

She narrowed her eyes. If he was a liar, then, like Goldie, he was a good one. Special Forces soldiers, she knew, were trained to resist interrogation. 'The rhinos were killed, from what I know, just after you and your men were told to leave David Gregory's reserve, where you had supposedly been doing anti-poaching work.'

'There was nothing "supposed" about it. We trained David's existing rangers and a few other locals, and when he had to let them go, and he couldn't afford to pay Viking Security, we hung on until the cranky old bastard kicked us out. We did a good job. I can tell you here and now that those rhinos would not have been killed if we'd still been there on patrol.'

'You didn't answer my question about the horns.'

Andy sneered. 'You didn't ask one.'

'All right,' Sannie said. 'If you didn't kill those rhinos, were you aware of someone wanting to sell the horns, perhaps to you? Do you have a plan to ship those horns out of South Africa?'

Andy looked around him, and Sannie thought he might be checking on the position of his troops, and maybe wondering how many of them were in earshot. When he spoke, his voice was quieter.

'Where I grew up, in Liverpool, we don't grass on people, but I'm also what you might call an entrepreneur, like. And, as I said, my boys and I don't go in for killing animals. Of course, if someone offered me a cargo weighing maybe thirty or forty kilograms and I figured that I could make fifty to sixty grand per kilo at the other end, I might be tempted to act as the middleman.'

The money he was talking about showed he knew something about the trade in rhino horn, even if he was not a poacher. And the fact that he had indicated he knew something about the rhino horns told her he was keen to do a deal, and that the sword and Koran Adam had taken were of more importance – and probably of greater value. Was the rhino horn deal an afterthought? She deliberately said nothing, waiting for him to fill the void.

'You work in Stock Theft and Endangered Species, if I'm not mistaken,' Andy continued.

'You're well informed.'

He smiled. 'As Sun Tzu said in *The Art of War*, time spent in reconnaissance is seldom wasted. Anyway, I know that your unit is responsible for counter-poaching. I think it might be a feather in your cap if you could seize, say, sixteen rhino horns.'

Sannie saw the way that Andy's eyes shifted to the Range Rover, his own assault rifle at the ready.

'Let me guess,' she said, 'you'll tell me who has the rhino horns, and who killed the animals, if I get you your sword and Koran.'

'And I'll be out of South Africa on the BA flight to London tomorrow night.'

Sannie bit her lower lip. Dealing with a criminal like this went against everything she stood for, but Adam, impetuous as he was handsome, had stumbled into an international smuggling ring and found himself in possession of property that was, if not stolen, then illegally trafficked.

'Goldie Faul will make life hell for you,' Andy goaded.

That made her angry. 'I'm an officer of the South African Police Service. No one intimidates me, least of all some New York lawyer or a tourist.'

'I'll give you and your boyfriend a cut of what I get from Faul. Ten per cent.'

It was Sannie's turn to smile. 'Your boss, Faul, who, incidentally, refers to you and your men as "the help", has already offered Adam and me a million dollars to give her the sword and the book.'

Andy did not have a strong enough poker face to hide his disgust.

Sannie raised her eyebrows. 'No honour among thieves?'

'*I* had to pay for those relics, and I bought them from a representative of the government of the country they came from,' Andy said. 'I'm out of pocket a significant amount of money, Colonel.'

Sannie wanted to spit on the ground in front of him. 'And I'm sure you're charging Ms Faul double or more for your troubles. I don't care what you're owed, and if I deal with her direct, you get nothing.'

Andy lifted the AK slightly and his right hand tightened around the pistol grip.

Sannie saw the implied threat. 'Careful, there's a police tactical unit, plus the Dundee Farm Watch and Viking Security, on their way here, right now.'

Andy relaxed a little and grinned. 'Now *that* is funny. What next – "Behind you?". I'm not going to start a shootout, Colonel, but I'm also not leaving here without my property.'

Sannie looked over her shoulder to the Range Rover, then back to Andy. 'Tell me about Napoleon Bonaparte's sword.'

'He was the short French geezer, right?'

Sannie adjusted her hand on her pistol. 'Don't play games with me.'

Andy gave the slightest of nods. 'I'm a trader, Colonel. I don't give anything away for free. I want something in return.'

Sannie ignored this. 'Do you think it really exists?'

'In the spirit of good faith, I'll level with you, Colonel. I don't know. Jan-Maree Ball thinks the real Bonaparte sword was switched with a fake back in 1879 by some crooked British Army officer. I was paid by certain individuals to do a recce, to have a good look around this part of South Africa to see if someone might have some concrete proof to back up the girl's theory.'

'And you had to be in South Africa at the same time to take delivery of the Prophet Mohammed's sword and an ancient Koran, which were being landed, illegally, on the South African coast at Bhanga Nek from – let me guess – Yemen?'

He smiled again. 'No comment.'

'And these "certain individuals" would be Piet Van der Ploeg and Goldie Faul.'

He gave a little shrug. 'Still no comment.'

'What did your "good look around" uncover about the sword?'

'Not much. Like I said, Jan-Maree is desperate to prove her theory and old David Gregory would have been the best person for her to get information from. I overheard Jan-Maree, Tustin and David talking about it one day – David was adamant the prince never carried his great-uncle's sword while he was in Africa and that the historical accounts from the time that said that was the case were just conjecture. David thought the prince was probably a bit of a poser as well, who might have encouraged people to think he was grander than he really was.'

'I see,' Sannie said. 'Jan-Maree said she found archival documents that indicated that David's ancestor, a policeman, was investigating a missing property case – she thought it was the sword.'

'Yeah.' Andy nodded. 'The three of them discussed that as well.'

'I won't ask how you happened to overhear all this.'

Andy smiled. 'Technology is a wonderful thing. But no, David said that whatever his great-great-whatever-uncle was up to around the time of the French empress's visit, it got him killed. No sword hiding in David's attic, or anywhere else. They were David's words, about the "attic", by the way.'

Sannie glanced back at the Range Rover again, and then to Andy. 'So why was Jan-Maree coming out here today?'

'Beats me. I'm just an old operator, following orders. Maybe Jan-Maree thought Goldie and Piet would help her with her quest. There's the smell of money in the air whenever those two are around. Now, enough chitchat, Colonel. If I give you the name of the person who approached me, wanting to sell me sixteen rhino horns, will your boyfriend give me –'

There was a sound like a tree branch cracking and Andy pitched backwards.

Sannie ducked instinctively, and when she looked over at Andy his AK-47 was lying in the grass and he was clutching his chest. Blood welled through his fingers.

He stared at her, his eyes wide open, his face already turning pale. 'What the fuck?'

Sannie crawled to the fallen man and placed her left hand over his, helping him staunch the blood flow. She drew her Z88 pistol at the same time.

Gunfire erupted from the bush a few metres away from her and there was the sound of metal on metal as bullets stitched a line of bright holes in the side of the Range Rover.

Sannie looked around and saw that Adam had thrown open the vehicle's rear hatch. 'Adam, no!'

As Richard Tustin gunned the Range Rover's engine and drove off at speed in a cloud of dust, Adam leapt out and hit the ground in a parachutist's roll. He kept his own rifle tucked in by his side.

Sannie watched in horror as someone else – one of Andy's men, she presumed – fired from the trees on the side of the road and kicked up a line of bullet strikes in the dust next to Adam.

'Cease fire!' Sannie yelled. 'It wasn't him.'

Adam shifted himself so that he was lying on his belly in the middle of the gravel road, but facing where the gunfire had come from.

A man emerged from cover. 'You heard her, Jones, you pillock. Cease fire!' the man called as he ran to Andy and Sannie and dropped down to one knee.

The gunfire stopped. Adam raised his head, and when Sannie nodded to him he got up and came to her. 'Sannie, get behind a tree. We need to find cover.'

The other man grabbed hold of Andy's collar and dragged him, on his back, deeper into the bush, away from the road. Adam and Sannie followed. The man, dressed in khaki bush shirt and cargo pants, shrugged off a desert tan hiking pack and unzipped it. He pulled out a wound dressing. 'I'll take over here. I'm a combat medic.'

Sannie saw that he knew what he was doing. The man took a haemostatic dressing from a pouch, removed if from its wrapper and pressed it to Andy's chest wound. Chemicals impregnated in the dressing would help slow the bleeding. Andy moaned. The man then jabbed a small syrette of something into Andy's arm; Sannie guessed it might be morphine.

'Where did that shot come from?' Adam said.

Sannie searched the rocky high ground across the road from where she and Andy had been having their discussion. She pointed to a ridgeline. 'Up there, somewhere.'

Adam raised the barrel of his rifle as he scanned the rocks.

'Careful,' Sannie said. 'We don't want whoever it was taking a shot at you.'

The man treating Andy looked at Sannie after he'd tied off the bandage around Andy's chest then run an IV line into his arm and connected a saline drip. 'Andy needs a hospital, now, medical evacuation chopper.'

'Out here?' Adam said.

'We're military contractors. We've got fookin' travel insurance like you wouldn't believe, pal.' The man opened another compartment in his pack and took out a bulky handheld satellite phone. He selected a number from the phone's memory and waited for his call to connect.

'What's your name?' Sannie asked him.

'I'm Willis. Ex-sergeant, Royal Marines.'

Adam narrowed his eyes as he looked at him, then recognition dawned on Adam's face. 'You nearly killed me.'

Willis snorted. 'Aye, and you me, chum. I think that makes us even.' His call went through and he started giving details of Andy's condition and their location. He was put on hold.

'Who shot at us – my partner, plus a game ranger – when we were on David Gregory's game reserve?' Sannie asked Willis while he waited. It was the question she'd been about to ask Andy.

'Not us, ma'am, and that's the truth,' Willis said. 'Our whole detachment was down the seaside.'

'It was men in camouflage fatigues. One of them was African, or of African descent.'

Willis shook his head. 'All our lads were born in England or Wales, ma'am. And not much diversity in our crew. All white.'

Sannie closed her eyes for a second. Just when she thought she was getting to the bottom of this case there was another twist.

'Hang about,' Willis said. 'You say an African man in camo?'

'Yes,' Sannie said.

'Old David's rangers, the ones he employed before he went bankrupt, all wore plain green uniforms, but like I said we also trained some local lads. It was kind of a job creation program, taking unemployed youngsters from Sibongile township, near Dundee, and giving them basic ranger skills. It was promoted by a local businessman, who was also a politician, and WildForce. Tustin organised uniforms for them from the UK – former soldiers sent out their old kit for them and it was all camouflage pattern.'

'What was the name of the businessman?' Sannie asked. She felt her pulse quicken.

'George someone. Spivvy-looking bloke, all designer labels and bling. Shaba-shaba or something like that.'

'George Tshabalala,' Sannie said. 'An ANC councillor and businessman.'

'Yeah, that's the geezer,' Willis said. 'Tustin said he was all about taking land from rich people and giving it to the poor.'

Sannie nodded. If Tshabalala had a pool of young men, trained and armed and dressed in camouflage, then maybe they were up to no good on David's game reserve, and his farm. 'Could Tshabalala have killed David's rhinos? Did Andy ever say anything to you about that?'

Willis shook his head and looked down at his commander, who was breathing but barely conscious. 'Not that he told me, but the skipper keeps things on a need-to-know basis.'

It wasn't much to go on, but if they could get out of their current predicament then Sannie had more questions to ask. She knew Marilyn already had her suspicions about Tshabalala and once they had a positive ID on the men who had been shooting at them, they might be able to tie him to the politician-cum-entrepreneur.

Adam had a question for Willis. 'The two *okes* who were killed when the boat sank off Bhanga Nek. Who were they?'

'Omani Arabs. Smugglers. Not very nice people. They run all kinds of shit up and down the coast from the Horn of Africa down to Mozambique. It's the old slave route, but today they use it to ship heroin from Afghanistan. They move gold stolen from the mines in South Africa out to the Middle East and India – even women and kids. Bastards.'

'Yet still you and your boss used them.'

Willis checked Andy's pulse. 'Only this once. The shipment we were waiting for down on the coast was coming out of Yemen so we couldn't get the gear ourselves. The Arabs were a day late, so we figured they'd been wrecked in that big storm.'

This business stank and Sannie wanted nothing to do with these people or the artefacts they were trading in. This was treasure soaked in the blood of civil war. But she also wanted to make sure Adam was safe.

Another gunshot rang out.

Adam raised his head to look up at the rocky cliffs. 'He's definitely up there somewhere.'

Two shots cracked out from their side of the road.

'Bastard just took a shot at me,' a third man called out in a Welsh accent, and Sannie assumed this was the man named Jones who Willis had spoken to before.

'Then keep your head down or fookin' take him out,' Willis said back. He looked to Adam. 'We need a safe LZ for when the evacuation chopper comes.'

'You want me to help save the man who tried to have me killed?' Adam said.

Sannie tried calling Marilyn, who had been hanging back, deliberately, in Sannie's Fortuner, but the signal was too weak – the phone beeped in her ear. There was just one bar, so she typed a WhatsApp message. *We are under fire. Lone gunman. Tell tactical unit to hurry up. Stay put for now.*

'Who the hell is shooting at us?' Sannie asked Willis. 'Who wanted your boss and your men dead?'

Willis snorted. 'The list is long in some parts of the world. But here in South Africa, I don't know. To tell you the truth, Colonel, I like your plan that I overheard, that we get the next plane out of this country. But, if Andy survives, he'll kill me if I leave without our gear.'

Sannie looked at Adam, and she was sure he could read the question in her expression. *Should we just give these men the sword and Koran and get out of here?*

'What were the terms of the deal for the sword and the book?' Adam asked Willis.

'Andy paid his contact in Yemen half the asking price and he was going to transfer the other half once the geezers on the boat had delivered the goods. And the Arab crew was going to be paid a shipment fee, in cash.'

Sannie pictured the deal, and the situation. 'Yet according to Adam you and your boss were waiting with a rigid-hulled inflatable boat, diving gear, assault rifles and hand grenades.'

Willis turned his gaze back to Andy, and made a show of checking his pulse and breathing again. He didn't meet her eyes. 'We don't travel light.' Willis looked up at the slope opposite them again. 'I'm not sitting here waiting for some sniper to pick us off one at a time whenever we show our heads.'

Adam stood up and started to run.

'Adam!' Sannie couldn't believe what she was seeing. Adam sprinted from where they had been taking shelter, in the tree line, across the road. A puff of dirt erupted at his feet, and he dived and slid into a drainage ditch on the other side.

'It's not just Andy's guys they're aiming at,' Adam called. He grinned at her from his new place of cover.

Sannie thought her heart was about to explode. 'Don't do that again!'

'Your boyfriend's right,' Willis said to her. He leaned over Andy, closer to his commander's face. 'Hang in there, skip. We'll sort this muppet out and then it'll be clear for the chopper to come in and CASEVAC you.'

Sannie thought the men's heroics – Adam's included – were foolhardy, but it was true that it would be incredibly risky for a helicopter to land in the middle of a gunfight.

'Kruger, did you see where that shot came from?' Willis said to Adam.

'Affirmative.'

'Give me some covering fire in fifteen seconds.'

'Will do,' Adam called back.

'Jones, prepare to move,' Willis barked, 'and push out to the left flank when you do.'

Sannie, like Adam, was mentally counting down the seconds, and when she reached fifteen Adam popped his head up over the rest of the ditch and opened fire with his AK-47. He fired in bursts of three rounds as Willis and Jones, who emerged from the tree line further along, leapt to their feet and charged.

Sannie watched the men surging forward, up the hill. Adam continued to pour fire from the right flank, while Jones, as ordered, swung wide to the left.

A gunshot rang out from the cliff. Willis paused to fire back, while Jones ran forward now, scaling the hill in front of them. When Jones was a good way up, he dropped to his belly and fired, and Willis used the covering fire from Jones and Adam to move forward.

Sannie's phone rang. 'Van Rensburg.'

'Colonel, it's Richard Tustin.' He sounded agitated and she heard an engine revving hard. 'Sorry to leave you in the lurch back there. It's Jan-Maree . . .' He seemed to be having trouble speaking.

'What is it?'

'She's . . . she was shot. It's a head wound. Piet Van der Ploeg's tending to her, but it doesn't look good. I'm taking her to Dundee. I just thought you should know.'

26

ZULULAND, 1880

Teresa, Samuel and Sergeant Phillips rode hard.

Their horses' hooves kicked up divots of soil and yellow grass as they thundered across the veld. The sun was falling – Teresa still wasn't used to how quickly day turned to night this far south of the equator – and the air was turning chilly.

The back of Teresa's head and her hair were crusted with blood from the blow the sergeant had inflicted on her, and she felt a dull ache. She still wasn't sure exactly how long she'd been unconscious before Samuel found her. The cavalryman had not raped her, but she still wanted to kill him.

And Walters.

And Grace. She was doing some deal with Walters – that much Teresa had overheard – and the Italian count was in on it as well. As angry as she was, Teresa's heart was pounding, no longer with fear but with excitement. Something was afoot and every journalistic instinct she had told her it was a big story, perhaps the most important of her life.

Samuel was riding ahead, and Teresa could see that every now and then he leaned forward and to one side, to look for the tracks of the people they were pursuing. A thought struck her and she spurred her horse to catch up with him.

'Samuel,' she called as she drew alongside him, 'slow down.'

He reined in his horse. 'What is it?'

'I've been thinking.' Teresa slowed her mount to a canter. 'Grace has something that Walters wants – that the empress wants, right?'

Samuel frowned, but gave a small nod a few seconds later.

'Walters seems to be a blusterer,' she continued, 'a braggart. It doesn't make sense to me that he'd share the limelight with Grace if there was a grand gesture to be made.'

'Perhaps,' Samuel said.

'*Perhaps*? Come on, Samuel, what's all this about?'

Samuel looked behind him. Phillips was still some distance away, and Teresa guessed that whatever Samuel knew, Phillips didn't.

'Peter – Sub-Inspector Gregory – is looking for a valuable sword that belonged to the empress's son. It was carried by his great-uncle, Napoleon Bonaparte, in a battle. I think Grace might have it, and is planning on returning it to the empress, in the hope that she will be rewarded.'

'What makes you think that?' Teresa asked.

'Grace . . .' Samuel looked up for a moment, then back at her, 'knew many men – not all of them good. She told Peter certain things, about a man Walters knew, a Major Morrison. That man was killed. He – Major Morrison – supposedly took possession of Napoleon's sword, but it was never returned to France. Someone, perhaps the person who killed Morrison, has the sword.'

'Grace?' Teresa had thought Grace a manipulator, but not a murderess.

Samuel shrugged.

Teresa looked to the setting sun, which was big and orange and right in front of her, in the direction in which they were travelling. She looked at the ground, at the hoofmarks in the grass that Samuel had been following. 'Something's wrong, Samuel.'

Samuel slowed his horse to a walk. He looked across to Teresa.

Realisation dawned on his face. 'Walters . . . Grace. These tracks are heading west. Nqutu, where the empress will camp, is to the north.'

'DISMOUNT,' Lieutenant Walters said to Grace.

She pouted, but when Walters thumbed back the hammer on his pistol, she slid down from the saddle. 'I can't believe you are double-crossing me.'

He gave a laugh. 'You think I'd let a whore hand over a priceless family heirloom to an empress?'

Grace glared at him, then glanced over at Ferdi. He was lying facedown on the ground, not moving. She was unarmed and alone. Walters took aim at her. She stared into the barrel of his revolver. After all she had been through, all that she had survived, was this how her life was to end?

'Unbuckle that fishing rod case of yours and take out Napoleon Bonaparte's sword. Slowly. No tricks.'

Grace gritted her teeth. She stood her ground.

'Very well,' Walters said. 'I'll just shoot you now and have my sergeant get it.'

'And if I give it to you now, what will you do to me? Kill me?' Grace said.

'Whatever you think of me, *madam*, I am not a cold-blooded murderer. Now unbuckle that fishing rod holder of yours, slowly, and extract the sword from it.'

Liar. 'You killed Morrison,' Grace said, and had the satisfaction of seeing the sergeant, still on his horse, turn to stare at his officer. 'Not that I blame you, mind. He was indubitably an odious specimen of a human being.'

'I –' Walters' words were cut short by the crack of a gunshot. The lieutenant pitched over and fell from his saddle with a thud.

Grace spun around and saw that Ferdi had rolled over onto his back and was brandishing a pistol of his own. She hadn't even known that he had such a weapon. Walters' sergeant was sliding a Martini–

Henry from the bucket next to his saddle, but he was too slow. Ferdi fired again.

Grace put a hand to her mouth as she saw the red dot appear in the sergeant's forehead. His horse reared up and then bolted. Its rider fell from his saddle and was dragged, hanging upside down, bouncing on the ground for several strides until his boot came free of the stirrup.

Ferdi stood and ran his free hand through his black hair, smoothing it.

Grace turned on him. 'Ferdi, you killed them!'

He brushed grass and dirt from his tweed jacket. 'They were about to do the same to us.'

Grace looked at the two British cavalrymen, lying motionless in the grass. She couldn't quite believe she had just seen two men killed. 'How . . . Ferdi, I thought you were a journalist.'

He stuck the pistol into the waistband of his trousers. 'The newspaper world in Italy is, how you say, quite competitive. We must leave, quickly.'

Ferdi, however, did not get straight back onto his horse. Instead, he went to the cavalry sergeant he had just shot in the head, knelt down, and began removing the man's bandolier, belt and sword, and unbuttoning his tunic.

'What . . . what are you doing, Ferdi?' Grace felt light-headed. Walters was a bastard and his sergeant had been a common thug, but Ferdi had just shot both of them and seemed not to be bothered at all.

'This one, he is a, more the same size as me.'

'Yes, but what are you proposing?'

Ferdi tugged the dead sergeant's uniform from his body and then took off his own jacket. He stood, dressed in the sergeant's tunic and buckled on his sword belt. 'I am proposing that when we approach the empress's camp, the sentries will be less likely to stop us if they see you riding in with a uniformed guard.'

'You're crazy, Ferdi. We have to think of another plan now. Walters was known to the British, to the general escorting the empress, and probably the royal herself. As soon as we get within a stone's throw of them they'll know you're not Walters or the sergeant.'

Ferdi looped the bandolier of ammunition around his neck and arm, and slid the sergeant's carbine from the bucket on his saddle. He opened the breech, took a round from a cartridge pouch on the bandolier and chambered it. 'All we need to do is get close enough for me to get my picture, then I will leave. You can stay and talk your way into the camp. I know the empress won't see me in person, but that is not a problem. She will see you once you explain that you have her dead son's sword in that fishing rod container of yours.'

Grace wasn't sure, but she was still in shock and could not think of a better plan. Following Ferdi's lead, she got back up on her horse, took a last look at the two dead men, then spurred her mount onwards, into the gathering gloom.

WHEN GREGORY ARRIVED at the Tshotshosi River and the newly erected memorial to the Prince Imperial he found that the empress's encampment had been set up. A welcoming fire burned in the centre of the laager of wagons and and there was the smell and sound of meat sizzling on a spit.

A couple of snuffs he knew saluted as he rode into camp. He reined in Bullet when he came to a cavalry trooper carrying a bundle of firewood.

'Where can I find Lieutenant Walters?' he asked without preamble.

The cavalryman looked him up and down, trying to ascertain his rank. 'He's still out on patrol . . . sir. Went out with the sarge earlier, and not been back since.'

'Thank you,' Gregory said. He thought a moment. 'Where is Lieutenant Walters' accommodation? I need to leave a personal message for him.'

The trooper pointed to an encampment on a low rise overlooking the river. 'The lieutenant's tent is third from the left, sir.'

'Thank you.'

He rode to the line of tents and dismounted outside the one the man had indicated. A couple of troopers were sitting on boxes outside another tent. One cleaned his rifle while the other looked up at Gregory from the cup of tea he was drinking. 'Evening, sir.'

'Evening,' Gregory made a show of opening his saddle bag, taking out his notebook and a pencil, scribbling some gibberish on a page and tearing it out. He folded the sheet of paper and held it up for the men to see. 'Personal message for Lieutenant Walters.' He moved the calico flap of Walters' tent aside and went in.

There was a camp bed, haversack, and a spare uniform left out, draped over a crate. Gregory looked under the stretcher upon which Walters slept. He found a pair of leather sandals, locally made, perhaps a practical souvenir of the officer's campaigning in Africa. He took one out.

For a man of average height, Walters had very big feet. Gregory nodded to himself, replaced the sandal, and let himself out.

Gregory wondered where Walters was now. He doubted that Walters had circled around him and linked up with General Wood and the empress – who were probably an hour behind him; the countryside was too open, and Gregory would have seen Walters and his man from a good distance. He wondered what the cunning young officer was up to.

'I need to check on your sentry posts,' Gregory said to the soldier drinking his tea, sounding as convincing as he could.

The man nodded towards a higher hill. 'One picquet's up there, sir.' The soldier then looked in the other direction, to his left. 'And there's a screen of friendly Zulus out there somewhere, with orders to stop anyone who approaches. That's if you can call any of them friendly.'

'Thank you,' Gregory mounted his horse,

'Who shall I say the bearer of the message was, sir?'

Gregory kicked Bullet in the ribs and rode off. On the hill the trooper had indicated he came to two more snuffs, Dolahenty and Davidson, who had made a small fire to brew tea. Dolahenty put down his pipe and stood as Gregory rode up. Davidson squatted and blew on the hot coals.

'Mr Gregory, sir. Fancy seeing you here,' Dolahenty said in his Irish brogue.

'Evening, Dola,' Peter said to the short, stocky trooper. 'All quiet?'

'Aye, sir, as the grave.'

'Lieutenant Walters?'

Dolahenty sneered. 'No sign of him since yesterday.'

'Yesterday?' That was news to Gregory.

'Aye, him and that . . . well, that sergeant, left the column late yesterday, in the evening. The Good Lord alone knows what they were looking for out in the dark last night. Not been seen by me since.'

Gregory's suspicion that it had been Walters he had seen fleeing from his camp in the pre-dawn suddenly seemed more likely. He was involved in all of this, in some way.

The other constable stood, holding two steaming mugs. 'Coffee, sir?' Davidson spoke with an American twang, having come to South Africa a few years earlier from California, to try his luck finding gold at Barberton. He'd failed and ended up in Natal, in the police.

'Thank you, but no, Davidson. What are your orders, men?'

'Not to let anyone approach the camp, especially a certain lady from America,' Davidson said. 'But, hell, sir, if I came across a filly from my old home country, she wouldn't be gettin' past me.'

Gregory frowned. 'New orders. I've been assigned to take over camp security. If you see anyone approaching – and I mean anyone – you're to notify me immediately.'

'Anyone, sir?' Dolahenty said. 'Even if Lieutenant Walters and the sergeant show up?'

'*Anyone.*'

'Yes, sir,' the two constables said in unison.

SAMUEL SPOTTED a riderless horse in the near darkness and, when they rode to it, Phillips pointed out that from its saddle and accoutrements it was a British cavalry mount.

Teresa felt her senses sharpen as Samuel followed the horse's tracks, which were invisible to Teresa's eyes in the poor light. They came upon two bodies lying in the grass and all three of them dismounted.

'This one, it's the cavalry sergeant who visited us; you took a picture of him and his chaps, and their obnoxious lieutenant,' Phillips called. 'He's dead.'

Teresa knelt by the other man. It was the odious Lieutenant Walters, but all she could feel for him now was pity. He had been shot through the shoulder and was unconscious, but he was breathing. At first, she thought he'd taken a bullet to the head – his forehead and temple were crusted with dried blood. On checking, she saw it was a gash and wondered if the fall from his horse had knocked him out. He did, however, seem to have lost a lot of blood from the gunshot wound; the grass beneath him was soaked. 'Help me.'

Samuel came to Teresa and knelt beside her. He unwound the red scarf from around his neck, rolled it into a ball and pressed it against Walters' wound.

Walters opened his eyes, and parted his lips as if trying to speak.

'What were you up to?' Teresa demanded.

'The . . .' he began, 'the Italian . . .'

'The Italian be damned,' Teresa said. 'Your sergeant assaulted me. What were you and Grace doing, Walters?'

He blinked at her, as if trying to understand. 'The Italian,' he said again, 'is dangerous.'

Ferdi? The seemingly innocuous Italian aristocrat? Dangerous? Teresa remembered how Ferdi had drawn the rifle and stared down Walters. There was an edge to him. She'd thought he was a newsman, and that was partly because she thought she'd seen him somewhere before.

'Murderer . . .' Walters mumbled.

Teresa froze. She looked at Samuel, who had begun binding Walters' wound with a linen bandage. 'What is it, Teresa?' Samuel asked.

'I just remembered where I've seen Ferdi before,' Teresa said. 'We have to hurry. We have to get to the empress.'

'You're forbidden from approaching the empress,' Phillips reminded her.

'I don't care. Her life's at stake.'

'What?' Phillips looked shocked.

'Come with me, both of you,' she said. 'We have to go.'

'What about the casualty?' Phillips looked down at Walters, who reached out and plucked at Phillips' sleeve. 'He might not be a very nice chap, but he is a British officer.'

Teresa had to make the call and there wasn't time to sit and explain everything, including her reporter's hunch. 'He's survived this long; he'll live a little longer. They say only the good die young. We can come back for him. Come on, we're leaving.'

'But . . .' Phillips protested.

Samuel silenced him with a look, then added: 'We will need all of us.'

Phillips nodded. 'Righto.'

GRACE WAS ALMOST RELIEVED when two Zulu warriors stood up from their hiding place in the grass, under the rising moon, and spooked their horses. Hers rose up and Ferdi had to hang on tight to keep from falling off when his mount did the same.

The elder of the pair told them to stop, in Zulu, which Grace understood, then ordered the younger man to take a message to the police. The young warrior set off at a run. The senior man confronted Ferdi, who had no idea what he was saying.

Grace interpreted: 'He says we're to stay here and wait for the mounted police to come. No one is allowed to move closer to the monument.'

'Out of the way, man,' Ferdi barked in his best English accent.

Grace would have laughed if she wasn't so worried about how the Italian count had begun acting.

'Ferdi, please,' she said. 'I don't think we can go on. I'll try and get a message to Peter. He might be able to escort us close enough to the camp for you to get a picture. In any case, it's dark now. Doesn't your camera contraption need daylight to work?'

He turned on her. 'Have you never seen magnesium being burned to produce artificial light for a photograph?'

'Don't talk to me like I'm an idiot. I've still never seen a camera operated after dark.'

'You there,' Ferdi addressed the Zulu man, 'take care of this woman. I must report to the general. Understand? Gen-er-al?'

The Zulu smiled. 'I understand per-fect-ly,' he said in English. 'And I have my orders. You will wait here, for the police.'

'I –' Ferdi began reaching for the cavalry sergeant's pistol in the holster on his belt, but the Zulu stepped forward and thrust a long spear up until the tip rested in Ferdi's stomach. Ferdi slowly moved his hand away from the gun. 'Damn you, man.'

The Zulu said nothing more and simply stood there, like a statue, for several minutes until they heard the drum of hooves.

A Natal Mounted Police constable galloped up to them and reined in his horse.

'Who are you two, now?' the constable said in an Irish accent.

'Sergeant Cortez, 17th Lancers,' Ferdi said, carrying on with his Music Hall upper-class accent.

The constable screwed his mouth up. 'Foreigner?'

'I'm from Gibraltar. I'm as British as you are,' Ferdi said.

'Fact of the matter is, I'm Irish. To the bone. Dolahenty, from County Cork. And what would you be wanting here, Sergeant?'

'I've orders to report to General Wood. Lieutenant Walters has been severely injured in a riding fall. I need to mount a mission of salvation . . . er, a mission of rescue.'

'Rescue mission? Do they not speak the queen's English on Gibraltar, then? I think you'd better stay put, chum, while I go fetch my sub-inspector.'

The senior Zulu warrior had stepped back with Dolahenty's arrival. Grace wanted to speak up, but didn't know what to say without compromising her own reason for being there. 'Please,

Constable,' she chimed in, 'the sergeant is correct. Lieutenant Walters is really rather poorly.'

'What about the sergeant who rode out with him?' Dolahenty asked.

'He's tending to the lieutenant,' Grace improvised. 'Time is of the essence. Lieutenant Walters has a fractured skull. We need a surgeon.'

Dolahenty rubbed his jaw. 'Well, Her Majesty is travelling with everything from a chef to ladies' maids, so I've no doubt there's a doctor hiding somewhere in the baggage train. Just let me fetch the sub-inspector. Now, dismount, please, the pair of you.'

Grace looked to Ferdi who gave a little nod, and they both swung down from their saddles.

Constable Dolahenty looked down at the Zulu. 'Good work, man. Keep an eye on this pair and I'll be back, directly, with Sub-Inspector Gregory. No need to tie them up or anything like that, especially as the sergeant says he's with the Lancers. It won't take a moment for me to check on that.'

'Hurry, please,' Ferdi said, as Dolahenty wheeled his mount around and then set off.

'Very well,' the Zulu man said. 'It appears we are to wait together.'

Ferdi nodded. 'Will you join me in a cigarette?'

The man smiled. 'Of course.'

Ferdi reached into the dead sergeant's tunic, but instead of withdrawing a pipe or tobacco tin he produced a long, narrow-bladed stiletto. He drew the knife back over his right shoulder then threw it. The Zulu man clutched at his heart, which had just been pierced, then fell backwards.

'Ferdi, no!' Grace took two steps towards him, but a savage backhanded blow from him across her cheek sent her to the ground as well.

27

KWAZULU-NATAL, THE PRESENT

Adam and the two British soldiers of fortune, Willis and Jones, pulled back to where Sannie was waiting with their wounded commander, Andy.

'The shooter got away,' Adam said. 'We heard a trailbike up in the hills somewhere. Just as well, as I'm out of ammunition.'

Marilyn pulled up next to them in Sannie's Fortuner and got out, with her pistol drawn.

'It's OK, Marilyn, the threat's passed – for now. Can you maybe take Adam back to pick up his Ranger?'

Marilyn holstered her firearm. 'Sure.'

Adam looked to Sannie as if making sure she was alright. She nodded, and Adam got into the car with Marilyn, who then did a U-turn and sped away.

Willis knelt and checked on Andy, then looked at his phone screen. 'Damn, I missed a message while we were chasing that sniper. Our medical evacuation company has a fixed-wing aircraft coming to Dundee – no helicopters available. They suggested we call an ambulance, but I think it would be better if we drive Andy to Dundee.'

Sannie nodded. 'I agree. Jan-Maree Ball was hit in the exchange as well. Tustin and the others are taking her to hospital at Dundee now. Marilyn had driven off like a maniac and they soon saw a dust cloud coming their way.

The two vehicles arrived and between them they all lifted Andy into the rear seat of Adam's Ranger.

Marilyn held up her phone. 'I've got news.'

'In a minute,' Sannie replied. 'Adam, you drive the Ranger, with Willis and Jones. I'll follow in the Fortuner with Marilyn. We have to hope that you guys scared the sniper off.'

Adam nodded and fetched his dive bag out of the rear of his Ranger and transferred it to the back of Sannie's Fortuner. She knew he had a grenade, and imagined he thought it would be safer in her vehicle, now that the immediate danger seemed to have passed. 'I love you,' Adam said to her when he was done.

Sannie nodded. 'Let's go.'

Adam gave her a small smile, then got in his vehicle. Sannie climbed in next to Marilyn, who was happy to drive. Sannie needed to make some calls of her own. Her phone had being dinging with messages throughout the gunfight.

'Tell me what you've got, Marilyn,' Sannie said as Marilyn floored the accelerator to keep pace with Adam on the gravel road that led back the way they had come, through Rorke's Drift, up to Help-mekaar, then on to Dundee.

'I got a call back from the Hawks. They've traced all the registra-tion plates on the list that George Tshabalala's personal assistant gave me, for vehicles he owns. I went through the pictures of the trucks in his compound in Dundee. Of course, some of the trucks were out on jobs, but there was one that was in the yard, but not on the list.'

'They left it off deliberately?'

'I don't know,' Marilyn said, 'but here it is.' She passed Sannie her phone. 'Open the first picture – it happens to be the last one I took.'

Sannie looked at an image of an Iveco prime mover with a large trailer. 'Yes?'

'Check the registration plate, and the dent on the front right-hand fender.'

'OK,' Sannie said, studying the picture.

'Now scroll back about ten pictures. I took some shots of the info and pictures on Derick le Roux's pinboard in the briefing room.'

'I remember you doing that.' Sannie swiped through the pictures until she found the one Marilyn wanted her to see. 'It's the photo of the truck the military guys took – the cattle transport vehicle that Derick thought was used by the rustlers – the Cheetahs. The plate's obscured, but –'

'But the make and model and the dent are identical,' Marilyn said.

'They are. Good work Marilyn,' Sannie said. 'I'll call Tshabalala.'

'Use my phone,' Marilyn said. 'You'll find his number in my recents.'

Sannie found the number and dialled. She put the call on speaker so Marilyn could hear.

'Warrant Officer Msani. What a pleasure,' Tshabalala answered. 'Can we meet for a coffee, something stronger or –'

'It's Lieutenant Colonel Susan van Rensburg, Mr Tshabalala.'

'Oh. Well, I heard there was a new sheriff in town.' He laughed. 'How can I help you? Your colleague has already been in touch with my office, and me.'

'I know. I'm calling because there's a vehicle in your yard which is not on the list of trucks that your office supplied to Warrant Officer Msani.' She gave the registration number from the picture.

'The Iveco? With the livestock carrying trailer?'

'Yes, that's the one,' Sannie said.

'It's not mine,' Tshabalala replied.

'Then what is it doing on your premises?' Sannie asked.

'I'm sorry if you were hoping this was your big break in some case you two are investigating, Colonel, but that vehicle does not belong to me. It's just in my yard because my mechanics have been working on it. My business also services heavy goods vehicles.'

Sannie looked to Marilyn, who shrugged.

'Who is the owner?' Sannie asked.

'I'd have to check, or you could call my secretary again and ask her.'

'Thank you, I will.'

Sannie was about to end the call when she had a thought. 'Mr Tshabalala, why have you been driving your cattle onto David Gregory's game reserve?'

Tshabalala laughed. 'I haven't. uBhejane belongs to the people, but we will continue to operate it as a safari destination once we take rightful possession. The difference will be that the money will go to previously disadvantaged people from the local community. I would never send any of my cattle onto that land – there are too many lions and other predators there.'

Though she doubted the man's intentions were as altruistic as he claimed, his answer was exactly what Sannie had been thinking. She thanked him, ended the call, checked the recent numbers again and showed the screen to Marilyn, who pointed out Tshabalala's personal assistant's number. When Sannie called it went through to voicemail, so she left a message, asking for the details of the owner of the truck and telling the assistant that her boss had authorised her to release the information.

Sannie settled into the passenger seat and checked her emails. There was one from Hudson Brand, which she read.

'You know,' Sannie said to Marilyn, 'I have a feeling we might already know the owner of that truck.'

'Who's that?'

Before Sannie could answer, her phone rang. It was Adam, and as she accepted the call she could see, up ahead, that Adam had switched on the hazard lights on his Ranger and was slowing.

'You won't believe this,' Adam said, 'but there's a helicopter coming in to land up ahead. Farmer's field, on the right.'

Marilyn slowed down and closed up to Adam, who was making a right-hand turn through a farm gate. Richard Tustin's Range Rover was parked in the grass and a white air ambulance helicopter was descending slowly as the pilot and crew checked for hazards.

As soon as it touched down, two paramedics in orange jumpsuits hauled a collapsible wheeled stretcher out of the helicopter and went to the Range Rover. As Sannie and Marilyn pulled up behind Adam's

Ranger and got out, Sannie saw Piet Van der Ploeg and Goldie Faul walking alongside the stretcher.

'Get Andy into the chopper as well,' Tustin called to Willis and Jones. 'As much as I dislike you lot, he's an ex–serving member of the military and I don't want to see him bleed out.'

Adam lent a hand and the three of them carried Andy to the helicopter. Just before the aircraft's rear door closed, Goldie Faul climbed in.

'I thought there were no choppers available,' Marilyn said as the noise of the chopper's engine receded into the distance.

Tustin looked back to them now that the helicopter was out of sight. 'Money talks. Goldie got onto the phone to the insurers and said she'd pay for Jan-Maree to be transported, as well as Andy. She said it was a matter of life and death.'

'Was it?' Sannie asked.

'I'm not sure,' Tustin said. 'Jan-Maree's wound wasn't as bad as I thought it was when I first called you. The round creased the side of her skull. She was lapsing in and out of consciousness. Of course, she was in shock and needed to get to expert care as quickly as possible – but, well, there was also a renewed sense of urgency.'

'How so?'

Tustin took a deep breath.

'Tell me,' Sannie pushed.

'Jan-Maree told Goldie Faul that she has Napoleon Bonaparte's sword.'

'What?' Sannie said. 'She wanted to sell it to Goldie?'

Tustin nodded. 'Jan-Maree said she would get it for her, but she would have to agree to meet her somewhere in Dundee, in a public place, on neutral ground of Jan-Maree's choosing.'

'She's scared someone else wants it, and might kill to get hold of it.' Marilyn looked to Jones and Willis, who were standing by Adam's Ford Ranger. 'Like them.'

'Or someone else,' Tustin said. 'It was just after Jan-Maree confirmed she had the sword that she was shot.'

'So where did Jan-Maree find the sword?' Marilyn asked.

Tustin shrugged. 'David Gregory was adamant that the sword didn't exist. I knew his house very well and stayed there a few times overnight. I never found any sign of a sword or special hiding place.'

'You snooped around while you were there?' Sannie said.

Tustin grimaced. 'I'm not a thief. But, from my, er, cursory looking, I couldn't see anywhere where he could have kept it.'

Sannie had done enough house searches in her early days in the police to know that people could hide anything – drugs, guns, money – in the most imaginative places. 'In a wall cavity?'

Tustin shook his head. 'That house is over a hundred years old. A few of the walls are from the original dwelling built by David's ancestor, the one who was in the Natal Mounted Police. The walls are solid.'

Sannie closed her eyes for a moment. She forced herself to remember what she'd seen on her brief visit to David's home and blood-spattered lounge room.

Sannie opened her eyes again and snapped her fingers. 'The TV.'

Tustin raised his eyebrows. 'I beg your pardon?'

Adam came to them; the military contractors stood off to one side by themselves, perhaps unsure what to do now their leader was gone.

Sannie nodded to herself, then addressed Tustin. 'Did David Gregory watch much television, when you stayed with him?'

Tustin shook his head. 'Not at all. He said he detested television. He only had it to watch the rugby, and as times got tougher he eventually cancelled his DStv. He said he couldn't justify the satellite subscription.'

'David's lounge room was like a museum, from what I remember of it, full of antiques that could have been worth a small fortune,' Sannie said.

'Yes,' Tustin agreed.

'And above his fireplace and hearth, flanked by flags and spears, in a place of prominence in any home, was, what? A flatscreen TV, not even connected to a satellite, set in a wooden cabinet with a padlock.'

'Of course.' Tustin looked up, like he was mentally slapping his forehead. 'He must have kept the sword in there, safe under lock and key.'

Sannie nodded. 'And in that empty TV cabinet, I remember now, were two sets of racks. I knew there was something not right about that installation; it didn't seem right just to hang the television. One of the mountings must have been for the sword.'

'The old bugger,' Tustin said. 'He probably opened the cupboard and took down the TV when there was no one around so he could gaze at his sword, all the while telling anyone who asked that it never existed. You're right, it really would have been the centrepiece of his collection. But why wouldn't he have sold it, especially when it was worth a fortune and he was probably about to lose his farm and his game reserve?'

'That's a good question,' Sannie said. 'And I need to talk to the person who now has the sword.'

'Jan-Maree,' Adam weighed in.

Sannie nodded. 'The other question is, how and when did Jan-Maree get hold of the sword?'

'Maybe David gave it to her because he wanted her to act as a broker for him,' Tustin said.

Sannie looked at him. He clearly still carried something of a torch for Jan-Maree. Also, all she had was Tustin's word about Jan-Maree supposedly having the sword. Nothing was certain, though things were starting to fall into place in her mind.

'Or Jan-Maree stole it,' Marilyn said.

Sannie and Adam looked at Marilyn.

'Jan-Maree's not a thief,' Tustin said.

Marilyn put a hand to her mouth.

'What is it?' Sannie asked.

Marilyn glanced at Adam. 'You remember when we were talking to that young mother, at the kraal overlooking the Prince Imperial's monument?'

Adam nodded. 'Yes, what about it?'

'We asked her who the guide was, the one who gave her husband the metal detector, and we were looking down at the people by the memorial.'

Tustin interrupted: 'I told Colonel van Rensburg, I have *never* had anything to do with metal detectors.'

Marilyn held up a hand. 'Adam, that woman said to us that the guide *on the end* of the group was the one who handed out the detector ...'

Adam pointed to Tustin. 'He was on the end of the group.'

'And Jan-Maree was on the other end,' Marilyn said to Sannie. 'We got the wrong guide. Jan-Maree was the one who was doling out metal detectors to local people, to look for archaeological finds that she could sell illegally to collectors.'

Tustin was shaking his head, but had nothing more to say. He and Piet Van der Ploeg had moved off to one side and were talking to each other.

'Where to now?' Adam asked.

Sannie was about to answer when Adam's phone rang. He took it out of his pocket and looked at the screen, then at Sannie. 'It's Jenny. I should take this.'

Sannie felt guilty that she'd all but forgotten that Jenny had been injured. 'Of course – send her my best.'

Adam walked a few paces away to answer the call and Sannie looked to the mercenary, Willis. 'Adam says you have a drone.'

Willis nodded. 'Yeah, luckily we have a spare, since your friend destroyed our other one.'

'I'll try and ignore the fact you were carrying illegal explosives under your drone,' Sannie said. 'I need it. Now.'

Willis jutted out his jaw. 'Will it help you find out who shot our skipper?'

'I think so.'

'All right, ma'am. Just tell me where and when.' Willis gave a grin. 'Will you be wanting a grenade with that?'

Sannie knew he was joking, but she thought about the carnage that had ensued so far on this investigation. 'Maybe.'

Adam ended his call and came back to her. 'Jenny's fine.'

'I'm glad.'

'Sannie, she knows Jan-Maree Ball. Apparently they're best friends.'

Sannie was taken aback. 'What?'

Adam shrugged. 'Not so much of a coincidence, I suppose. They're about the same age, and both did undergrad degrees at the University of KwaZulu-Natal. They're also both doing PhDs at the moment. Jan-Maree's mother just got a message from her, and she SMSed Jenny. Jan-Maree's mom is in Australia and she knew Jenny was working in KZN – even though we were hundreds of kilometres from here. She's asked Jenny if she can go to the hospital where Jan-Maree's being flown to.'

'That will take her a day's drive,' Sannie said.

'Um,' Adam looked up, then back at Sannie, 'Jenny checked herself out of hospital and she's already on her way here. She wants to visit Jan-Maree and come see me while she's in the area. She's only about an hour away.'

Sannie put her hands on her hips and glared at Adam. 'I don't want any more civilians involved. She's already been injured once! She could've died on your watch, Adam. You're being reckless.'

Adam held up his hands to her. 'Sannie, wait. Maybe we can use this connection between Jenny and Jan-Maree. If we're lucky, Jan-Maree hasn't made a connection between me and Jenny.'

Sannie reluctantly agreed, but didn't want to admit it. 'Well, you'll be held responsible if anything goes wrong.' She turned back to Willis. 'Let's go. David Gregory's farm. Now. You two travel with Adam.'

'I'll get our back-up to bring the drone and our gear,' Willis said.

Sannie nooded then looked around. Seeing Tustin she called: 'Follow us to the Gregory farm. I'm not finished with you, Major.'

Tustin exhaled. 'Very well.'

'Sannie . . .' Adam began in a conciliatory tone.

'You as well. We'll talk at the farm. Message your protégé and tell her to meet us there.'

. . .

THIS TIME SANNIE drove and Marilyn sat beside her, arms folded, saying nothing.

Sannie glanced away from the road. 'What?'

Marilyn frowned. 'It's not my place to give you relationship advice.'

'But you're going to.' Sannie slowed for a goat.

'I told you before, the goat will move.'

'Marilyn knows all.'

'*Haibo*, no, but in some things, Marilyn is wise, especially in the ways of men.'

'But you're not married, and you don't have a boyfriend.'

Marilyn leaned around so Sannie could see her raised eyebrows. 'You see how clever I am? My mother is a single mom and she has worked as a domestic all her life. It was tough for her and she was determined that I not get pregnant at a young age, like she did. She used to supervise me getting contraceptive shots, but she didn't need to worry – I've always been careful, and not just about the sex. I am going to marry a man who truly loves me for who I am, and not just my fabulous body.'

Sannie gave a small laugh.

'I am serious,' Marilyn said. 'But you have a problem.'

Sannie glanced over again. '*I* am the problem?'

Marilyn shook her head. 'You're mishearing me, or projecting. No, you are not the problem, you *have* one. You have found a genuinely good man and you're too scared to commit to him.'

'What?' That was outrageous. 'I moved in with him and he packed his Billabong beach bag and went up to Bhanga Nek to hang out with his teenage acolytes on the beach, Marilyn!'

'No, sister,' Marilyn wagged a finger, 'the way I heard the story, Adam is following his dream and finally getting to do the job he always wanted. When I met you six months ago you were bursting with pride about your boyfriend who had turned his life around, got help with his PTSD and became a university professor. Now he goes away for a month, and you think you've been abandoned. And let's not forget, your job takes you away sometimes, like now, and has crazy messed-up hours, *is dit nie so nie?*'

Sannie pursed her lips. Marilyn was almost young enough to be her daughter and she was giving Sannie relationship advice. What annoyed Sannie most of all was that there might be something in what Marilyn was saying. 'Yes. I suppose that is so, Marilyn.'

Marilyn gave a satisfied nod.

They came to the farm gate. It was easier for Sannie to focus on a murder scene than her own love life. 'We'll talk more later.'

'Exactly why are we here again?' Marilyn asked.

'I'll let you know when I know. In the meantime, call John Parker, please, and ask him to come here. We might need an expert tracker.'

Marilyn took out her phone as Sannie drove along the dirt driveway to David Gregory's house. Rather than stopping, she carried on around the house to where the business side of the farm began. She passed cattle pens enclosed with tubular steel fencing, and pulled up outside a stouter boma made of thick treated-pine logs. She stopped the car and got out.

Adam and Willis had followed her in and Adam stopped his Ranger behind Sannie's Fortuner. A WildForce four-by-four came up the driveway behind them.

'What's on your mind?' Adam asked as he closed the door of his Ranger.

She ignored the question as she lifted the latch on a gate and walked into the boma. The large rectangular enclosure was the size of a soccer pitch and, inside, was divided into sixteen individual pens.

'This is where the rhinos were kept,' said Willis, who was lifting a large Pelican case out of the back of the vehicle that had just pulled up.

'You never saw the carcasses,' Sannie said to Willis. It wasn't a question.

'No. We were gone by then. The old bastard – if we'd been here –'

'Save the rage,' Sannie said. She sniffed the air; there was the scent of dung, still. From her time in Kruger, she recognised the desiccated, dried piles of old white rhino dung, deposited in middens. She scanned the ground, then walked out of the boma.

About a hundred metres to the south the farming operation ended, and a three-metre-high electrified fence marked the border with the adjoining uBhejane Game Reserve. A big double gate was set into the fence, but like the main entrance to the reserve, the fence and gate here looked to be in poor condition. The gate itself was bent, and even when it was closed and padlocked, as it was now, it looked like a decent-sized animal could still squeeze through the gap where it was warped. Sannie walked towards it along a dirt road, studying the ground as she went.

'You wanted the drone, ma'am?' Willis called to her.

She stopped, turned around and nodded. 'Yes. Get it ready, send it up.'

Willis opened the case and carefully lifted out the large unmanned aerival vehicle. Jones had taken a folding chair and table from the back of the WildForce vehicle and was setting them up.

'Sannie . . .' Adam began.

She held up her hand to Adam. 'I want to say something.'

'Sure.'

'I love you, Adam. I know that maybe I don't say it enough, and with our work schedules and your time away supervising your students, maybe we still haven't had enough time together, just the two of us, to make this work.'

A look of fear crossed his face. 'You're not ending it, not like this?'

She shook her head. 'No, no. It's just . . . something needs to change, Adam, and I –'

They both turned at the sound of a car honking. A white Ford EcoSport came bouncing down the access road, too fast for the corrugations and erosion. The car stopped and a young woman, red-haired and pretty, got out. Her left arm was in a sling.

Adam and Sannie went to her.

'Sannie, this is Jenny Ellis, my student,' Adam said. 'Jenny, this is my partner, Lieutenant Colonel Sannie van Rensburg.'

Sannie smiled and shook hands with the young woman. She

thought 'partner' was an odd – but also nice – way to describe what they meant to each other. More fitting than 'boyfriend' and 'girlfriend'.

Adam gave Jenny a quick hug, then stepped back from her.

'I just wanted to say, Sannie, that it's nice to meet you in person,' Jenny said. 'Adam – the prof – talked about you a lot when we were in Bhanga Nek.'

'He did?' Sannie looked at Adam, who gave a sheepish smile and shrugged.

The noise of the four-bladed drone screaming up into the air interrupted their meeting.

Willis's offsider, Jones, was sitting on a fold-out camp chair, looking at a laptop on the portable table. He had the drone's controls in a chest rig.

'Shift your arse,' Willis said to Jones, who looked to Sannie. 'Colonel, over here, if you please?'

'Excuse me, Jenny.' Sannie went to the men, sat on the chair Jones had just vacated, and peered at the screen. Willis, behind her, pointed out the drone's elevation and tracking.

'Jones has a screen on his chest unit. He can watch that and fly wherever you want him to. You've got the feed there on the screen.'

'Over the game reserve. Can you take it higher?'

Jones responded and Sannie watched the view of the reserve zoom out. There was a mix of open grassland and lines of thick vegetation that clung to the rivers and streams running through uBhejane. The drone flew over a high granite peak that Sannie could see from the farm, and a broad valley came into view.

'We're fairly familiar with the layout of the reserve, having been on ops here,' Willis said.

'This road that leads from here on the farm into the reserve, is it well used?'

Willis shook his head. 'Not at all, ma'am. As it leads here to old David's home it wasn't ever used, so we were told, by game-viewing vehicles. More like a private access road and short cut for David and

John Parker and the other staff if they had to get from the lodge to the farm or vice versa for any reason.'

'What's along the road? Any dwellings, satellite camps, anything like that?'

'No,' Willis said. 'We drove it a few times – like I said, to get from the farm to the lodge if needed.'

'Follow the road; drop down a little lower,' Sannie ordered the operator.

'Yes, ma'am,' Jones said.

Sannie had a sensation of ground rush as the drone dove, then raced over the landscape. Sannie touched the screen, with Willis looking over her shoulder. 'What's that road, leading off to the left, deeper into the reserve?'

Willis scratched his chin. 'Oh, yes. I remember. Dead end. David said there were the remains of another old farmhouse down there. His family bought up land over the last hundred years or so and incorporated a couple of other old cattle farms into the reserve. I remember him saying the road was washed away and not traversable, so we never went down there.'

'Follow it,' Sannie told the operator.

The drone swung left, the side road now in the centre of the screen as the operator navigated along it. Sannie tapped the screen again. 'There's a bridge. Looks in good order.'

Willis leaned in closer. 'Yes, it does.'

'Take it right down,' Sannie called to the operator.

The drone dropped to maybe five or ten metres off the ground. 'That road looks clean – used,' Sannie said. 'There are no trees overgrowing it, no branches or dung on the ground. Bring the drone up again.'

'What's that?' Willis asked.

Sannie could see it as well. In the distance ahead of the camera was a large circular cleared area, surrounded by a fence. There was movement.

'Animals,' Sannie said. 'It's like another big boma. And look, there's a couple of tents and a vehicle.' There was a *bakkie* in the upper right quadrant of the screen. Sannie saw a human, running. The boma was still a long way off, but there was definitely a few hundred head of game or livestock of some sort milling about within the enclosure. Sannie looked over her shoulder at Willis. 'Did David have any other stock or game out there?'

He shook his head. 'Not that I knew of.'

'Shit,' Jones yelled. 'There's a geezer with a gun.'

The camera's screen was obscured for a second by the sight of something falling off the drone; the image rocked from side to side, and then it went black.

'Shot down, again,' Jones said in disgust.

Sannie's phone rang. She looked at the screen. It was her boss from the Hawks, Colonel Gita Kapahi.

'Colonel?' Sannie said.

'Sannie, howzit? I managed to pull off a minor miracle for you. There was a police tactical unit from Durban doing helicopter training with 15 Squadron. I've got a team in an Oryx chopper heading your way. Are you still in trouble?'

Sannie thought a moment. 'The situation's changed. The contact I was in is over, with two gunshot wound casualties on their way to hospital by air ambulance. But we've got a new threat, Gita; armed poachers or maybe cattle thieves holed up in the middle of David Gregory's game reserve east of Dundee. I've just had a visual on at least one man armed with a rifle.'

'All right, Sannie. It's your call,' Gita said. 'The chopper's in the air. I'll WhatsApp you the tactical unit commander's number. You can brief him on the change of mission. I trust you to run with this.'

'Thanks,' Sannie said. 'I think it's all linked – the rhinos, the cattle, the sword. I'm just putting it together now.'

'Sword?' Gita sounded surprised. 'What sword?'

'I'll explain later.'

They said their goodbyes and Sannie's phone dinged with the incoming number. The tactical unit's commander was Captain Brian Shozi. Sannie had worked with him before; he was young, smart and tough. Sannie sent him a pin with the location of the farm. His six-person team would touch down here, where she was now, and mount any assault from this location.

Adam came over to Sannie. As Sannie looked around she saw Jenny Ellis, Adam's student, get back into her EcoSport, start the engine and drive back up the farm access road.

'Jenny's going to the hospital, to visit Jan-Maree and talk to her,' Adam said.

Sannie nodded. She filled Adam in on the drone being shot down, and the inbound South African National Defence Force Oryx helicopter and its cargo of elite police personnel.

'I asked Jenny to see what she can get out of Jan-Maree. If Jan-Maree's hiding something, like the sword, she might let Jenny know where it is. She'll know other people are trying to get their hands on it, like maybe the person that shot Jan-Maree and Andy.'

Sannie wondered about the shooter and their motive. As she'd just said to Gita, it *was* all linked. There were just a couple of pieces of the puzzle floating about the edges. She tried to concentrate.

'Sannie?' Marilyn sidestepped awkwardly to avoid some dung and walked to Sannie.

Sannie needed some time to think, but everyone was looking to her, asking her questions. She closed her eyes for a second and composed herself. 'Yes, Marilyn?'

'I can't get hold of John Parker – he's not answering his phone – but I just took a call from Sergeant Nyathi, from the stock theft unit.'

'All right. What did she want?'

'They've picked up on the radio chatter from Farm Watch and Viking Security. It seems everyone's now on their way here. She says she's sending a *bakkie* with two extra officers as backup.'

Sannie waved a hand in the air. 'Fine. Sure. If everyone wants to get involved, then the more the merrier.'

'Sergeant Nyathi asks if I can meet the *bakkie* on the main road to guide them in.'

Sannie really needed to think. This was detail she did not need to know. 'Fine, Marilyn, go, and when the Farm Watch guys show up bristling with guns, take control of them too, bring them here along with the reinforcements, and keep an eye on them. I don't want people going off doing their own things. We'll hold a joint briefing here. There's a tactical team on its way by helicopter as well.' Sannie reached into her pocket and gave Marilyn her car keys. 'Take my Fortuner.'

'*Eish*, this thing is getting bigger than the Rugby World Cup,' Marilyn said. She turned to leave.

'Keep in contact with me, Marilyn,' Sannie said.

'I will, and . . . *haibo*!' Marilyn winced and lifted her shoe. 'And now I have stepped in the shit.'

Sannie smiled, but she had other things to think about. Marilyn walked off, dragging her dirtied boot in the grass to wipe off the mess.

'Where do you want us, Colonel?' Willis asked.

Tustin and Van der Ploeg had done as Sannie ordered and had also arrived at the farm, and reported to her.

'And what about us?' Tustin interrupted.

Sannie was about to tell them to make themselves scarce, but then she looked at the ground where Marilyn had just trodden.

Adam was watching her. 'What is it, Sannie?'

'Shit!'

28

ZULULAND, 1880

Gregory galloped on Bullet, sticking so close to Constable Dolahenty that stones and dirt dislodged by the other man's horse flicked up into his face.

He'd been circling the camp in the twilight, far enough out not to bump into General Wood; Gregory didn't want to have to explain that he was staying around the empress's encampment on a hunch. Walters had come to Gregory's small band of travellers in the night to try to fetch something – Gregory suspected it was the sword that Napoleon Bonaparte had carried at the Battle of Austerlitz, and which his great-nephew had lost in Zululand a year earlier.

Exactly who had that sword came down to two people in Gregory's mind. By the end of the night he would, he was sure, know who had stolen the sword from Morrison and who had killed the despicable major in the course of that theft. Gregory was a policeman and an officer, and as much as he might dislike the victim, he could not let a murderer – or a thief – go untried by the courts.

And there was other danger about. He could sense it.

Dolahenty had said that man and woman he had encountered had told him that Walters was injured. That may very well be the case, but Gregory did not trust Walters, nor his brutish sergeant.

Dolahenty reined in his horse. 'I could swear, sir, that they were around here.'

Gregory slowed Bullet to a walk and pulled in beside the trooper. They scanned the plain around them. It was dark, the moon not yet up, and a chill had descended on Zululand.

'Sir!' Dolahenty swung down from his saddle and ran a short distance. He dropped to kneel next to a form that Gregory could now see was a man. 'It's the Zulu I left in charge of the prisoners. He's . . . he's dead, sir. Been stabbed, by the look of it. When I left it was just this woman, a pretty one with brown skin, and a rum sort of a fellow who claimed to be a cavalry trooper from Gibraltar.'

'Slicked-back hair, olive skin, handsome, about five foot ten?'

'That'd be the fellow, sir.'

Ferdinand. There had been something odd about him all along and Teresa had first identified that he might not be what he claimed to be. But if he was a journalist, was he prepared to kill for a story, or a photograph? That seemed unlikely.

The drum of hooves reached their ears and both Dolahenty and Gregory turned. Gregory reached for the revolver at his belt, and the trooper for his rifle.

'Peter!' Teresa spurred ahead of the other two horsemen, Samuel and Phillips.

'It's dangerous here, Teresa.' Gregory was annoyed, while also pleased to see her face again. He looked past her to Phillips. 'I told you –'

'There's been quite a turn of events, sir,' Phillips said. 'We – that is, Miss O'Kane and Samuel and I – thought it best to come to you. Also, Grace and the Italian chap absconded.'

Samuel pointed to the body on the ground. 'Did the count do that?'

Gregory nodded. 'Seems like it.'

'Peter.' Teresa drew a breath. 'Ferdi's come here to kill the empress.'

. . .

GRACE RAN THROUGH THE NIGHT, stumbling a couple of times and picking herself up as she tried to catch up with Ferdi, who had taken their horses and abandoned her after killing the Zulu. Her fishing rod container with the sword in it bounced on her back.

Every now and then she caught a glimpse of Ferdi on his horse, her mount behind him. She thought she would never catch him, but then he slowed and dismounted next to one of the few trees that irregularly punctuated the open veld.

Grace, too, slowed, then dropped to a crouch and watched. Ferdi looked around, but seemed satisfied that no one was following him. Beyond Ferdi, Grace could see the glow of lanterns and the flicker of a fire that indicated the presence of the empress's encampment.

When he had started killing people, Grace had thought Ferdi was after her sword – for that was how she now thought of the blade – and that he would turn on her at any moment and demand it from her. But he had not even mentioned it. She had known a couple of journalists in her time and while they could be pushy and arrogant she had never met one who would literally kill for a story or a photograph. If not the sword, then what was driving him?

As to her sword, that pig Morrison had stolen it, but Grace had 'liberated' it from him, and was now intent on returning it to the mother of its former owner. Grace had become an expert at wafting through the Red Lantern, enthralling men with a wink and a smile, or a glimpse of skin, and fools such as Morrison and the others hardly bothered to lower their voices even when they were talking about the trade in stolen goods – or human beings.

She had gone to Morrison's filthy farmhouse and pretended to offer him a child if he gave her enough money, and while the degenerate had made her tea they had civilly negotiated a price for a young life.

'What a wonderful collection of swords you have,' Grace had said to him, and when Morrison had gone to the racks on the wall, caressing one of the blades like it was his puny member, Grace had produced a small bottle of laudanum and tipped some drops into his tea. When Morrison was in the grip of the poppy's spell, she had searched his home until she found the ornately engraved emperor's sword under his bed, then she had taken it and fled.

Morrison had been found dead, later, and as far as Grace was concerned, he had deserved his violent end.

From what Grace had heard of the empress, she was sure that the noblewoman would reward her handsomely for the return of her son's sword, which had also belonged to the great Napoleon Bonaparte. But what on earth was this madman Ferdi up to?

Ferdi had the sergeant's gun, and he had pulled that wicked-looking knife from the Zulu man after he had killed him. Grace had only one thing to protect herself with – a priceless antique.

Ahead of her she could now see two horses, alone and tied to the tree. As she crouched lower, she unbuckled her leather case, reached in, and drew out the sword. It was long and heavy, and while she was no expert in its use – she'd never wielded a blade like this in her life – she was sure she could cause some damage with it.

Looking past the horses she saw Ferdi, who was now moving forward on foot. He walked bent at the waist, now with the sergeant's revolver drawn. Grace followed him.

'WHAT DO YOU MEAN?' Gregory asked Teresa. 'Why does Ferdinand want to kill the empress? And how?'

Teresa reached into her jacket and took out some pieces of paper. She held them up, and although they looked like pages that had been torn from a book, the light was too poor for him to read them.

'As part of my research into the empress I read everything I could about her,' Teresa said. 'I found this book back in the States. These pages are an account of an assassination attempt on the life of the Emperor Louis Napoleon III and his wife, the Empress Eugénie, in Paris back in 1858.'

It was twenty-two years earlier, but Gregory vaguely remembered it. 'A bomb?'

Teresa nodded and held her horse steady with her knees while she riffled through the pages and found the one she was looking for.

She handed it to Gregory. 'The emperor was against Italian unification at the time and this man, Felice Orsini, and some British radicals came up with a plan to kill him by throwing a bomb at him. Orsini failed to injure the royal couple, but ten people were killed.'

Gregory held the picture close. When he looked at the engraving of Orsini's face he saw a definite resemblance to Ferdinand 'Rosini'. 'A relative?'

Teresa nodded. 'That's what I'm thinking. I'm worried Ferdi's here looking for revenge. Orsini was put to death by guillotine.'

'Ferdinand had a rifle. Do you think he means to shoot the empress?'

'I'm worried it's something more ... dramatic.' Teresa held up another page and paraphrased it. 'Orsini's bomb a metal sphere studded with spikes, which were fuses containing a substance called mercury fulminate. When one of those little spikes hit something – like a carriage or a person or whatever, it was compressed and then detonated the explosives inside the ball. After you left us, and Grace and Ferdi did a bunk, Phillips and I did an inventory of his baggage. There was a box missing, and I thought it was his camera, and that he had hidden it near the Prince Imperial's monument. I thought he was sneaking back to take a picture of the empress.'

'But you now think it contained a bomb, Come on,' Gregory said. 'Let's spread out, line abreast, and ride to the encampment.'

Gregory wheeled Bullet around and spurred him in the ribs. Phillips pushed out to the far right; Samuel was on Gregory's left, and Teresa and Dolahenty off to his right as they rode down the hill towards the lights of the camp above the Tshotshosi River.

The memorial cross came into view, stark and white in the rising moonlight. Gregory scanned the low wall around it, looking for hiding places.

'Over there,' Teresa called. 'Someone's running.'

Gregory looked to where she was pointing. A lone figure was running towards the first line of white canvas tents. It was a woman, holding up her skirts with one hand. In her other she carried a sword. It was Grace.

'Hah!' Gregory spurred Bullet on.

GRACE'S CHEST was heaving and she wished, for a moment, that she'd worn riding breeches. The sword was heavy in her right hand and its tip clanged on rocks and dirt as she felt her arm muscles tiring.

Ahead of her, to her left, she could see a tent set apart from the others and a figure emerging from it. It was a woman, her silhouette against the lighted canvas tall and slender, her bearing erect.

To her right, also still a long way off, Grace saw movement. It was Ferdi. He'd been crouching, as if retrieving something, and now he was standing. In his right hand he seemed to have a ball of some kind. He lowered himself again to a crouch and started creeping towards the empress and her tent, which were still maybe a hundred yards from where he was.

Grace calculated the distances. She would never make it. Just then she heard a whinny and looked to her left. There was a two-person carriage and two horses, both tethered to a metal spike driven into the ground.

Grace went to the buggy, untied the horses and climbed up into the driver's seat. The horses were spooked by her urgency, and one reared up a little.

'Calm down!' She was no expert horsewoman, but Grace grasped the reins and flicked them as hard as she could on the horses' rumps. The horses took off and Grace held on tight as the carriage wheels bucked and slid over the uneven ground. 'Faster now!' She found a whip and used it to encourage her steeds on. The sword rested against her right leg and threatened to fall out of the buggy as she careened on. She still did not know exactly what Ferdi was planning, but every instinct told her that she needed to prevent him from getting close to the empress.

'Your Majesty!' Grace yelled.

She was still a way off, and while the royal woman heard something, she was looking around her as if not sure where the noise was coming from. All the while, Ferdi was moving closer.

. . .

BULLET WAS galloping and Gregory knew he had far outstripped the others. He'd watched Grace climb into the buggy and saw how she was charging to intercept Ferdi and the empress, who had emerged from her tent.

In his peripheral vision Gregory sensed more movement within the camp, bodies rushing past campfires, voices shouting, but it was clear that if anyone was going to reach the empress and the would-be assassin first, it would be Grace.

He gripped Bullet's reins tight in his left hand and drew his pistol with his right. As he rode, he tried to take aim at Ferdi. Gregory fired, but at more than two hundred yards he knew he had little to no chance of hitting the Italian. It appeared Ferdi might not even have been aware of the shot, for he continued moving with his stalking, half-crouching gait, the studded orb held up high in his right hand. *Teresa was right. It's a bomb.*

Gregory and the others thundered down the hill and a moment later Bullet was splashing through the shallow waters of the stream and onto the bank where the Prince Imperial had met his fate a year earlier. Gregory fired again, and while he thought he saw a puff of dirt near Ferdi's feet, the Italian did not slow down.

Grace raced across Gregory's front and he had to raise his gun hand to avoid shooting her.

'Run, Your Majesty, he means to kill you!' Grace yelled.

The empress looked from Grace, whom she had now identified as the source of the warnings, to Ferdi, and put a hand to her mouth.

Ferdi, now no more than thirty paces and an easy throw from the empress, stopped, drew back his arm and threw the object.

Gregory carried on unchecked, and so, too, did Grace. She was utterly fearless.

Gregory watched as Grace's buggy cut between Ferdi and the empress. As if time had slowed, he watched the wicked, spiked ball spin in the air as it carved an arc across the night sky. It must have been made of brass or some similar alloy as, for a moment, it glittered in the reflected light of a campfire.

The spinning orb connected with the tail end of the carriage. It was just a glancing blow, but enough to divert the bomb from its intended path.

A noise like a cannon firing split the night and Gregory's vision was seared with a flash bright enough to light up the camp beyond the veld for a hundred yards or more. Even Bullet, battle-tested and used to gunfire, whinnied in fear and checked his pace, nearly sending Gregory flying over his head. As Gregory fought to stay in the saddle, he saw the wagon roll onto its side and the left-hand wheel dig into the ground as the terrified horses pulling the carriage charged on. He spurred Bullet on and saw Grace, at first obscured by the light and flame of the explosion, sail through the air like a child's doll tossed aside. She landed heavily on the ground.

Gregory looked back to his front to see he was almost on top of Ferdi who, having seen his bomb detonate prematurely, had now drawn a pistol. He swung at the waist, aimed and fired at Gregory.

There was the sickening thud of a bullet hitting somewhere below him and Gregory knew that his horse, his friend, had been hit. Bullet carried on, but his momentum was slowing. Gregory saw the ground rush up towards him and slid out of his saddle as his horse went down.

Gregory hit the ground hard and rolled. He came to rest not far from Grace. She lay in the grass, motionless and bloody. He needed to see to her, but when he looked up, his neck aching from the fall, he saw that Ferdi was running, gun in hand, towards the empress's tent. Gregory patted himself down, feeling his empty holster, and looked around. He couldn't see his pistol. He hauled himself to his feet and stumbled towards Bullet. The horse was down, neighing and writhing on the ground, but lying on the side where Gregory stored his rifle. There was no time for him to try to retrieve it.

Lying beside Grace was a sword – he imagined it was Napoleon Bonaparte's. He went to her and scooped up the weapon. 'I'll be back, Grace.'

He ran, his right ankle protesting in pain, the sword gripped tight in his right hand.

Gregory looked around. Teresa, Samuel and Dolahenty were on the scene. Phillips was nowhere to be seen. Gregory raised his sword arm and pointed towards the empress's tent. 'That way!'

The wagon was on fire and the horses that had been dragging it had come to a halt. They were rearing, panicking, and possibly injured. There was the smell of burned cordite and blood in the air. Bullet was up on his feet again, but had wandered off, out of Gregory's immediate reach – at least it appeared he was not seriously injured.

Gregory struggled up the slope away from the river towards the noblewoman's tent. He could not let Grace's sacrifice, nor her bravery, be in vain. He charged onwards, yelling a garbled war cry at the top of his voice.

Ferdi stood outside the entrance to the white canvas tent, his pistol up and ready. He turned and aimed at Gregory, who ran headlong at him. The pistol bucked in Ferdi's hand and Gregory felt the blow of a round punch into his torso somewhere. But when Ferdi aimed and pulled the trigger again, the hammer clicked on an empty chamber.

Gregory raised his arm and slashed down with the sword as he careened into Ferdi, but the younger, lither man was quick on his feet. He pivoted, avoiding the downward slash, then drew Gregory to him in a lover's embrace. Gregory brought his right hand up, thinking to smash down on his opponent's head with the sword's pommel. However, at the last minute he remembered the hole in the dead Zulu guard's heart. Gregory forced a hand between them, onto Ferdi's chest, and pushed himself away.

He was just in time to avoid the flash of the pointed stiletto as Ferdi swung his right hand in an arc. Gregory slashed again, but now Ferdi stepped back out of range.

'Give up, Ferdi. The others will be here, soon, with guns,' Gregory said.

Ferdi smiled at him. He struck a street fighter's pose, legs apart, balanced on the balls of his feet with the knife in his outstretched right hand. 'That may be the case, but you will not take me alive. Why do you protect a foreign aristocrat, and a failed one at that?'

Gregory raised his eyebrows. 'Why travel halfway around the world to kill a woman who, as you say, has no real power?'

He spat. 'Do you know the Italian word, *vendetta*?'

Gregory nodded. 'A blood feud. Give up, man. It's over.'

From the corner of his eye Gregory saw a woman run from the tent. It was the empress. Ferdi moved with a ballet dancer's grace, spinning on one foot. He tossed the stiletto in his hand and caught it, by the blade. Ferdi drew back his arm.

'No, Ferdi! Just drop it.'

Ferdi had turned away from Gregory and posed no more immediate threat to him, but if he threw that knife . . . Gregory lunged and ran the tip of the sword through the back of Ferdi's rib cage, into his heart.

The stiletto fell from Ferdi's hands.

Gregory heaved the sword from Ferdi's body; the weapon now felt so heavy he could barely hold it. His vision was becoming dim.

'Peter, no!' Teresa ran to him and took him in her arms as his knees buckled.

He looked into her eyes, then saw the alarm, and the fresh blood on the smooth white skin of her hand. She was crying.

He focused on her green eyes, glittering with tears, but beautiful all the same. Others were arriving. He felt Samuel's big hand clasp him on the shoulder.

'Stay with us, my brother,' Samuel said.

It was getting hard to hear – his ears felt like they were stuffed with cotton wool, but he was vaguely aware of other people crowding around him as he sank to the ground, Teresa still holding him. There was General Wood, with a face like thunder, and a dark-haired woman, older, still beautiful, clutching the cotton of a fine nightdress to her bosom.

'Your Majesty,' Gregory croaked. He reached out, fingers clawing the grass beside him. 'The sword. Your . . . your son's . . .'

Samuel retrieved the sword from the ground, dropped to one knee and, head bowed, held it out to the empress.

Gregory looked at her. She took the sword, looked at it, but shook her head and passed it back to Samuel. She gave Gregory a small, sad smile. 'Regrettably, this is not the Emperor Napoleon Bonaparte's sword, but thank you, sir, for saving me.'

'Grace,' he said, wanting them all to know that Grace had saved the empress's life, putting herself between Ferdi and the tent when he threw the bomb.

Gregory looked up, beyond all the faces, to the stars. He smiled. Others would have seen what Grace had done. He hoped she was alive. She was a survivor; tougher than him. The empress was alive; he had done his duty. He would miss Teresa, but it was time.

His time to die.

29

KWAZULU-NATAL, THE PRESENT

Sannie's phone was going crazy as Adam drove into the uBhejane Game Reserve in his Ford Ranger. She had enlisted Richard Tustin and Piet Van der Ploeg to come with them – the more eyes the better.

There were messages from Hudson Brand and Marilyn which were helping her slot the final pieces into the puzzle.

You'll never believe who owns the truck used to move the stolen cattle, Marilyn typed. Sannie thought she could guess. She waited for the rest of the message to appear, but before it did, Adam touched her on the arm.

'There!'

Sannie looked up from her phone. Fifty metres to her right, in a sunny clearing, was the great, grey, placid bulk of a white rhinoceros, minus its horn, grazing on grass.

'Bloody hell,' Tustin said. 'It's a rhino!' The creature raised its enormous head and twirled its ears like antennae, trying to zoom in on the unfamiliar sound of people talking.

Piet Van der Ploeg was sitting in the rear cargo compartment of the *bakkie*. He leaned around to get their attention through the windows of the double cab. 'There's two more,' he whispered.

Adam reversed a little, and they could all see the trio of giant creatures.

'Look for ear tags,' Sannie said.

'I can see one has a tag,' Adam said, 'but not the others.'

'They don't all have tags,' Sannie said to herself.

'No,' Tustin interrupted. 'Eight of David's sixteen rhinos were tagged with GPS trackers a couple of years ago. He never received the rest of the funding to tag all of them.'

Sannie looked to Tustin. 'And David only ever had sixteen rhino – there weren't any wild ones roaming around that he might not have known about?'

Tustin shook his head. 'No, he was certain of that. But what are they doing here? They were all supposedly shot, burned, and the bones buried.'

Sannie had seen the fresh rhino dung by the boma and she had *known* the rhinos, or at least some of them, were still alive. The gate to the reserve was askew, and she was sure that it would have been just like a rhino who was used to being fed to wander back looking for a source of food. She'd had a hunch she would find them on the reserve, close to the farm, and she was right.

'WHAT NOW?' Adam asked.

'Drive back into the farm, please, Adam.' Her mind was racing with tasks. She could not complete them all. She checked her phone again, hoping to read the rest of Marilyn's message about the truck. There was nothing.

Sannie dialled Marilyn.

'You've called Warrant Officer Marilyn Msani. I can't answer the phone right now, but –'

Sannie hung up. 'Drive to the main road, Adam.' She tapped out a quick message to Marilyn. *Call me asap.*

Adam nodded, and he must have been able to read the look on her face because he floored the accelerator, causing the others in the vehicle to hang on as he bounced along the access road leading from the farm to the main gate. When they arrived, there was no one at the gate.

'Marilyn's gone,' Sannie said. 'She was supposed to be meeting some officers from Dundee here and bringing them to the farmhouse.'

Sannie phoned Dundee police station, and when a constable answered the phone Sannie asked to speak to Sergeant Nyathi from the Glencoe Stock Theft unit.

'Sergeant Nyathi is not at work today, Colonel. It is her day off,' the constable said.

'*Kak*,' Sannie said, then: 'Thank you.' The fear rose up inside her, almost paralysing her. With dread she realised she'd been too busy to spot the trap Marilyn had been lured into. Marilyn had been asked to drive to the main road to guide the local police into a farm that was well signposted, and that they had most likely visited before, given its history. She needed help. Sannie checked her phone and dialled another number.

'Meyer,' the man's voice answered. Sannie heard the drone of a car engine.

'Deon . . . Matteo . . . whatever,' Sannie said, 'it's Colonel Sannie van Rensburg.'

'Yes, Colonel, can I help?'

'*Ja*. I need to find John Parker, now. He's not answering my calls.'

'I saw his old Land Rover game viewer in town, just now, in fact. Do you want me to, like, make a citizen's arrest or something?'

It was no time for a complex debate, but Deon was a big *oke* and there was no love lost between him and Parker, since the lodge manager was now with Deon's former girlfriend. 'Find him for me, Deon, and sit on him if you have to. Call me when you're with him. He's avoiding me, but I suspect him of being involved in a crime.'

'*Jislaaik*. Affirmative, Colonel, you can count on me. I'll go look for him now.'

'Deon, wait . . .'

'Colonel?'

'Deon, Jan-Maree Ball's been taken to hospital,' Sannie said. 'She's been shot.'

'*Bliksem*, I'll kill whoever did that.'

'Calm down, Deon. But maybe check the hospital. Parker might try to go to her there.'

'Yes, Colonel.'

'And while you're there, check on that British veteran, Andy, the commander of the WildForce guys. He was also shot.'

'Affirmative.'

Sannie ended the call.

'Parker?' Adam asked.

Sannie nodded. 'He's in on it. The rhinos, the cattle rustling, all of it. Those animals we could see in the boma, in the game reserve, on the drone's camera. I'm sure they're cattle stolen from local properties. I think that John wanted Marilyn and me to find those cows when we met him on uBhejane Game Reserve. He was going on and on about how the reserve had no money, and he couldn't even patrol most of it because he had no fuel for his vehicle, but he was taking us on a *moer* of a long game drive deep into the reserve, and I'm sure, now, knowing the layout, that he was leading us to those old bomas where the cattle are now stored.'

'And then someone started shooting at you,' Adam said.

Sannie nodded. 'Precisely. I think Parker wanted to get out of whatever he was into, and maybe wanted us to just stumble onto where the stolen cattle were being held, but his business partner, or partners, had other ideas and they ambushed us. I'm sure they were trying to kill Parker, and Marilyn and me, to keep their secret.'

'You don't think Parker was maybe leading you into the ambush?'

Sannie shook her head. 'No, the gunmen were trying too hard to kill him as well. Right now, I'm more worried about Marilyn.' Her phone dinged and Sannie stared at the screen.

'What is it, Sannie?' Adam moved closer to her and looked over her shoulder.

The message had come from Marilyn's phone and it was a video, of Marilyn, but she had not filmed it. Marilyn was lying on her side, with her hands cuffed behind her back, in the rear of Sannie's Fortuner. Adam's green dive bag was crunched up under her. Marilyn was wide-eyed with fear and the person shooting the video was holding a pistol pressed to her head in a gloved hand.

The short video clip ended, and the phone dinged again, this time with a typed message. *You have found the cattle.*

Sannie typed a reply. *Yes. And the rhinos. Let Warrant Officer Msani go.*

Call off the tactical unit. Your investigation is over. Go back to Port Shepstone, where you came from. I will release her.

Sannie thought a moment. *Who killed David Gregory?*

The reply came a minute later. *Tsotsis working for that criminal politician Tshabalala. It was his truck that was used to steal the cattle. He is the head of the Cheetahs.*

Let's talk. Who are you? Sannie thought she knew the answer to the question. The person sending the messages, the one who had kidnapped Marilyn, was the real head of the stock theft gang.

A farmer, sick of the killings. David only wanted to make some money from his rhinos, like any other farmer. The government was coming to investigate him, to take DNA samples from his herd to match with some horns seized in Vietnam. He did not harm those animals, but he had to make it look like they had been killed by poachers, to save himself from prison. He was selling rhino horn on the black market – a market which this government should LEGALISE! The same criminals who prey on us farmers killed him in his home.

Sannie composed her next message carefully. *With a good lawyer you can avoid prison time for stock theft, but not for kidnapping a police officer. Let's meet.*

Leave and call off your officers. Last chance.

Sannie drew a breath. *We can talk.*

She watched the screen, seeing the other person was typing. She hoped they would see sense. *I gave you a chance. Sorry, I'm going to kill her now.*

.   .   .

ANDY CAME to in the hospital. He blinked at the bright overhead light that was hurting his eyes. His throat was sore – he was on a ventilator.

He heard a soft beeping noise, a monitor, and tried to look around his room, but his neck was in a brace. The light above him was eclipsed.

It took Andy a moment to focus and then he saw that the cause of the darkness was a man standing over him. He wore scrubs and a surgical cap and mask. Andy looked into the man's eyes. Although he couldn't see the man's mouth, he could tell the man was smiling. It was the same man who had offered Andy sixteen rhino horns, to smuggle out of South Africa to Yemen. Andy had been about to tell Sannie van Rensburg this man's name when he had been shot. This, then, was the shooter.

The man lifted his hands from beside him and then the light went out completely as the man placed a pillow over Andy's face.

DEON MEYER'S rubber-soled combat boots squeaked on the linoleum floor of the hospital corridor.

Luckily, he'd gone to school with Colleen, the nursing sister on duty, and she had given him the information he'd asked for – Jan-Maree's room number, and the name of another nurse he could talk to in the ICU, who would update him on Andy's condition. John Parker's Land Rover game viewer was in the hospital car park, so when he saw that little English-speaking prick he'd take him into custody. Exactly how, Deon still wasn't sure.

ICU was closest, so Deon pushed through a set of swinging doors and followed the sign on the wall. Ahead of him, further down the corridor, he heard an alarm begin to sound. A nurse burst from a room off to his right and pushed past him, running towards the noise.

She went through the next set of doors and half collided with a doctor coming towards Deon. The man was tall, dressed in green surgical scrubs with a mask and cap.

'Doctor, come, please, patient crashing in ICU,' the nurse said to the doctor in Afrikaans.

'I've got another emergency,' the doctor said to her, then carried on towards Deon. Elsewhere, people were shouting and the nurse, clearly annoyed, shook her head, swore in Afrikaans and ran on.

The doctor noticed Deon for the first time and raised his eyebrows.

Deon stopped. He looked into the other man's eyes.

'Hey...'

The doctor put a hand under his shirt and reached into the waistband of his pants. Deon could see now that he wore jeans under the scrubs and on his feet were not those surgical over-slippers, or whatever they were called, but hiking boots.

Deon reached for the nine-millimetre pistol in the holster on his chest, but the man in the doctor's outfit was quicker. He pulled a small-calibre pistol, maybe a .38, with a long suppressor screwed to the end of the barrel.

Deon had practised drawing his piece so many times in front of the mirror that he was sure he could out-draw anyone. He was wrong.

The doctor fired once, twice, three times, and with the alarm bells ringing and medical staff converging on the ICU ward, no one heard or saw Deon fall back and slide down the corridor wall. Blood ran from his neck, down over his arm and dripped from his fingertips onto the gun in his hand, then to the floor.

JOHN PARKER and Jenny Ellis steadied Jan-Maree between them as they worked their way through a labyrinth of hallways to the hospital kitchen.

A cook yelled at them in Zulu, telling them they shouldn't be there, but John waved an apology to the woman and they ushered Jan-Maree out into the sun. Behind them, somewhere deeper in the hospital, they could hear alarms going off.

'Are you sure we should be doing this?' Jenny asked. 'Jan-Maree doesn't look well.'

'Get me to my flat, please, Jenny,' Jan-Maree said. 'If I stay here, I'm worried I'll be killed.'

Jenny knew she should tell someone. When they got to the Land Rover, she said to John: 'Where are we going, anyway?'

He glared at her. 'You'll find out when we get there. Look, you might be one of Jan-Maree's varsity friends, but I can't trust anyone right now. Help me get her in.'

'I'll follow you in my car,' Jenny said.

Parker pursed his lips. 'No. Come with us. I need you to hold on to her, to watch her while I drive.'

Jenny hesitated. Parker looked desperate and she didn't like the way he seemed to casually rest his right hand on the gun in a holster on his right hip as he spoke to her. But Adam had told her to stay with Jan-Maree and to find out what she could about what she'd been up to. It was something about a sword. 'OK,' Jenny said.

They lifted Jan-Maree into the tiered seat behind the driver's position. Jenny winced – she was still in pain from the wound from the spear gun, and the bandage on her shoulder was spotted with fresh blood. Jan-Maree's eyeballs rolled backwards, and she slumped against Jenny.

Parker started the truck and looked back. 'Oh, no! How is she?'

Jenny felt for a pulse. 'Still conscious, but she's, like, half passed-out again, I think. She did get shot in the head, you know?'

'I know, I know.' He banged the steering wheel then started the engine. It coughed smoke and then he lurched out of the car park. Keeping her hand low, Jenny pulled out her phone and selected WhatsApp. She found Adam's number and started a video call. She kept the phone out of sight, but angled it so that the camera would track their path.

THREE *BAKKIES* full of heavily armed farmers pulled up at David Gregory's home at the same time as a camouflage South African National Defence Force Oryx helicopter came in to land in a field next to the farmhouse.

'You Farm Watch *outjies*, over here,' Sannie began, addressing them as a group as they got out of their vehicles. They wore an assortment of camouflage and khaki, and bristled with assault rifles and pistols. 'Five kilometres up the road through that gate are a few hundred head of stolen cattle in old pens, and a couple of guys with AK-47s. I want you to move in and set up a cordon in the bush around the bomas. I need you to contain the offenders until we can return with more police personnel. Does anyone want to leave now?'

She surveyed them. They were smiling and nodding to each other, and a few were fist-bumping. 'Not on your life, Colonel,' a burly man with a beard said to her.

'Good. These ex-military men,' she nodded to Willis and Jones, 'have a recording of drone footage of the target. They can brief you on the terrain and best avenues of approach. Remember, I said *contain*, not eliminate.'

The men laughed. Sannie hoped they would stick to the mission at hand, but if the cattle thieves tried anything, she knew these farmers would give as good as they got. She half hoped the stock theft foot soldiers had seen the drone as a harbinger of doom and left the reserve already.

She turned to Captain Brian Shozi and his four men and two women from the police tactical unit, all heavily armed and wearing body armour and helmets. 'We're going to a farm not far from here where I believe a SAPS member, Warrant Officer Msani, is being held captive.'

Brian looked taken aback. 'Marilyn?'

'You know her?' Sannie asked.

'Yes, she's . . .' he smiled, 'well, she's Marilyn.' His face turned grim. 'If anything's happened to her . . .'

'Let's hope not. Let's go. I'll brief you in the air.'

Sannie turned to Adam; as much as he would want to go with her and Brian, she could not take a civilian on such a raid, even if he had been a Parabat. Adam was staring at his phone. 'What is it?' Sannie asked.

'It's Jenny.' He looked up from the screen. 'She's driving in an open vehicle, a game viewer, and she's got Jan-Maree Ball with her.'

Sannie looked at the live video feed. 'And that's John Parker driving. I need to get to them next, as soon as we find Marilyn. She has to be my number one priority.'

Adam checked the screen again. 'Let me try and pick up their trail from this video. I'll stay in touch via WhatsApp.'

Sannie took a deep breath. There were far too many moving parts to this operation, and people she cared about were in danger. She drew Adam to her in a hug and kissed him. 'Be careful and don't do anything stupid. Like with these other guys, contain and call for backup.'

'I understand,' Adam said.

She nodded. 'I have to tell you who's behind all this, so you know how much danger you're in – we're all in.'

Sannie told him and they kissed again.

A couple of the tactical unit officers were hooting and whistling. Brian Shozi stilled them and brought them back into mission focus with a stern: 'Mount up!'

Sannie went with the officers and boarded the Oryx. The 15 Squadron pilot, a handsome South Asian–looking man with gelled hair, put on his flight helmet, grinned back at her, then flicked the switches to start the helicopter's engines. As they lifted off, Sannie saw Adam's Ranger racing away and a convoy of farmers' HiLuxes and Cruisers invading uBhejane Game Reserve.

She felt like she was going to war.

Jenny had to stop videoing and hide her phone as John Parker pulled up at a house on a small holding outside of Dundee. She had managed to video a street sign and the entry gate to the property. There appeared to be no one home.

'Jan-Maree stays in a flatlet out the back,' Parker explained as he got out and reached up for Jan-Maree.

Jenny helped Jan-Maree down then climbed out of the Land Rover after her. Jan-Maree seemed lucid again and could walk with just a little support from the other two. They made their way along a pathway to the small building at the rear of the larger house. John lifted a pot plant by the door and retrieved a key.

As soon as they were inside, John rounded on his girlfriend. 'Where is it, Jan-Maree?' he said. Jan-Maree just stared at him. 'The sword – tell me where you've hidden it. We've got to get it and then we have to leave. That's why we're here, right? Why you wanted us to get you out of the hospital? We can arrange a time to sell it to the American woman later, once things die down.'

Jan-Maree shook her head. 'No, John. That's not why we're here. Yes, we'll get it. It's in the ceiling, but there's something more important I need to show you.'

'More important than six and a half million US dollars?' he said. 'You told me we'll share the money and we can save uBhejane. I know David's left the reserve to me. We can make it work.'

She didn't seem to hear him. Instead, she went to her small kitchenette and unscrewed the lid of a cylindrical tin that said *Rusks* on the outside. She fished out a USB stick. 'You need to see this; it's the only thing that will save us, John.' Jan-Maree turned to Jenny. 'Sorry, Jen, I need you to see this as a witness. I have to warn you, though, it's not nice.'

Jan-Maree hobbled to a TV sitting on a cabinet and dropped slowly to her knees. She reached around the back and plugged the USB stick into a port, then eased herself back onto a tattered sofa. She motioned for John and Jenny to sit, then picked up a remote and turned the television on.

'I'm not proud of myself, but this is how I found out where David hid Napoleon's sword.'

On the screen, a video began. It was taken from a camera with a wide-angle lens, clearly set up high in a lounge room. There was antique furniture and an assortment of Zulu shields, spears, old military uniforms and rifles lining the walls of the room. In the centre of the frame was a fireplace with a TV cabinet above it.

'David Gregory's home,' John Parker said for Jenny's benefit. 'He was killed. I was there the day it happened.'

Jan-Maree fast-forwarded the video then let it play until an elderly man, who John identified as David, came into view. Jenny watched as David went to the fireplace then bent down and retrieved a key hidden under a brass coal scuttle. He used the key to unlock the cabinet above the fireplace and then proceeded to lift down a television that did not seem to be connected to any cables. Behind the TV was the metal rack it had been hanging from and, below that, another rack that cradled a sword.

'Napoleon Bonaparte's?' Jenny said.

Jan-Maree nodded.

David took down the weapon, wiped it with a polishing cloth and seemed to stare at it lovingly for a few moments before replacing it. Jan-Maree advanced the video to show him then replacing the TV and closing the cabinet, before returning the padlock key to its hiding place.

A short while later Jan-Maree herself came into the lounge room, wearing activewear. David returned to the screen carrying two cups of tea or coffee.

'There's more.'

When Jan-Maree cued up the video, it showed her entering the lounge room and recovering the key to the TV cabinet. Jenny and John watched as Jan-Maree, glancing over her shoulder often, opened the doors, took down the TV and then removed the sword. She replaced the TV and locked the cabinet and then went to a nearby window and slid the sword outside.

'I retrieved the sword after I had tea with David, then brought it to your place that morning,' Jan-Maree said to John. 'I told you I'd been out for a run.'

He nodded. 'You planted a hidden camera – that's how you finally proved he had the sword and where he was keeping it. Almost in plain sight, all this time.'

'Yes,' Jan-Maree said. 'I'm not proud of myself.' She looked down at her hands and the remote in her lap. 'I'm a thief. But someone was worse.'

They all watched as Jan-Maree played the rest of the events of that morning. A man that Jenny did not recognise entered the house, and in the lounge room, although the camera did not record sound, it was clear the man and David Gregory were arguing. Taller, younger than David, but still a mature-aged man, the new visitor took David by the shoulders and shook him. David stepped to one side and picked up a poker from beside the fireplace, but the man was bigger and stronger. He warded off the blow from David, then lashed out with a fist, punching the older man in the face.

The man picked up the steel poker and used it to rip the lock from the TV cabinet. He wrenched it open and lifted down the television, but then pointed to the space where the sword had been. David put his hands to his head, in disbelief, or anger. The man stood there a moment, as if willing the sword to reappear. John, Jan-Maree and Jenny watched in silence as David moved to a side wall of the lounge room and reached up for a military bayonet hanging on a hook. David unsheathed the knife and moved on the bigger man, lunging for him.

Perhaps David made a noise, or a sixth sense alerted the man, because he spun at the last moment and dodged to one side, avoiding the tip of the bayonet. The newcomer reached for his belt, drew a pistol and brought it up. Although there was no sound, the effect of the single shot was plain.

Jan-Maree stopped the video. 'I'll spare you the horror, Jenny. David dies and the murderer ties him to a chair. He then uses the bayonet to . . .' for a moment Jan-Maree looked like she was going to be sick, 'to open David up and to fish out the bullet from inside him, so it couldn't be found and used as evidence. Cutting him open like that was also an amateurish effort to make it look like David had been ritually disembowelled by a Zulu warrior. He then makes a call, probably to a couple of his hired thugs, to tell them that David's house is unlocked and they can come and rob the place and take what they want.'

John's face turned pale. 'I . . . I killed them.'

Jan-Maree nodded. 'I didn't want you to leave that morning, to respond to David's alarm call, John. You helped David's killer, inadvertently, to cover up his crime. I snuck back, after all the crime scene people had left. They never found my camera – I hid it too well.'

'Who . . .' Jenny began. She was in shock, having just witnessed a man's murder. 'Who was that man?'

The door to Jan-Maree's bedroom creaked and they all looked around.

A man dressed in doctor's scrubs entered the small lounge room and pointed a gun at them. In his left hand he held a sword, which he pointed at Jenny. 'I'm Captain Derick le Roux, and I really wish you hadn't asked that question, young lady.'

ADAM STOPPED his Ford Ranger down the road from the house with the Land Rover game viewer parked out the front. He had driven past once already and confirmed it was the entry to the property that he had seen on Jenny's video, just beyond the street sign that she had also managed to capture.

He went to the back of his vehicle and looked for a weapon. All he had was the antique-edged weapon, the sword he had purloined from Andy and the other mercenaries at the coast.

Adam cursed the fact that he had put his dive bag with the hand grenade in it in Sannie's Fortuner and that he had not asked one of the veterans for more ammunition for his empty AK-47.

He unwrapped the antique sword and hefted it in his right hand. It was long and heavy and had a wicked-looking double point at the end of the blade. It wouldn't be much use in a gunfight, but it was deadly.

He advanced onto the smallholding, moving tactically from cover to cover, darting between trees and finally to the Land Rover. He saw a motorcycle, a trail bike, on its stand, but pushed between some bushes as if the rider wanted to conceal it. He pressed himself against the side of the Land Rover, then dropped to a crouch. The main house looked closed and locked, but the front door of the flat at the rear was half open. He moved to the smaller building, making his way down one side.

When he reached a window, he slowly raised himself up so that he could peek into the lounge room, his eyes just above the level of the windowsill. He could see, immediately, that Sannie had been right.

'It's Derick le Roux,' she had said to him just before he left the farm. 'He and his sergeant, Eva Nyathi, are listed as the investigating officers on a string of questionable stock theft insurance claims. Also, I saw his investigation photos of the alleged killing of David Gregory's rhinos. All of the rhinos in the pictures had ear tags, but Tustin told me David only had money to tag a few rhinos, remember? Le Roux's briefing room was full of images, posters, of rhinos crossed with humans and a cheetah with a gun – he told me his wife was a whiz with Photoshop. I think he helped David fake the death of his rhinos, for whatever reason, by getting his wife to fake crime scene pictures of dead rhinos. There are so many of these pics online that it would have been easy for the wife to cut and paste one or more into the background of David's farm.'

'Another insurance scam?' Adam had asked.

'More likely just smoke and mirrors. We've long suspected that some of the private rhino owners in South Africa are illegally selling horns into the black market – they think they're right and the law is wrong, and they're harming no one. The authorities were homing in on David and he needed his herd of rhinos to disappear for a while, just as Derick and his sergeant were making stolen cattle disappear into uBhejane when it suited them. I think the way they worked it was that cattle were allegedly stolen from local farms, but hidden in pens on the reserve, and once the insurance money was paid and more stock were bought, the cattle were returned to the farmers. Le Roux probably thinks he was being some kind of Robin Hood figure to the farmers. But everyone pays in the long run. Also, the actions of John Parker, trying to show Marilyn and me what was happening, made me think that there's more to this, and that David wasn't killed by common criminals robbing a farm. I think maybe Le Roux and David and John had a falling out and somehow that got David killed.'

Now, Adam took in the scene in the flat. Jan-Maree Ball, Jenny

Ellis and John Parker were all on the floor, handcuffed, and Derick le Roux was splashing liquid from a red jerrycan around the flat. Red always meant petrol.

There was clear and present danger. Adam cursed. If he'd had the loaded AK-47, he would have shot Derick right now and worn the consequences later. Within reach of Derick, on a coffee table, were two pistols and a sword.

Adam dropped down and circled around to the front door. It was ajar and he could still see and hear what was going on inside, as he waited for the right moment to strike. Adam sent Sannie a quick WhatsApp message to say where he was and what he was about to do.

'The police know what's happening. They're at the farm where the killing happened, right now,' Jenny said.

'I don't care,' Le Roux replied.

'Derick,' Jan-Maree said, 'that's not the only copy of the video that I have, of you killing David.'

Le Roux laughed. 'And what, your other copy is hidden in another rusk tin? I'm prepared to take a chance. Shame, you shouldn't have been spying on poor old David, and you shouldn't have stolen his sword. We had a good thing going, him, me, and even you, hey, young John? And then you and David had to go and get cold feet, just because some armchair warriors on Facebook started criticising David and claiming he'd killed his rhinos.'

'Captain, please,' John said. 'Can't we talk some more, make a plan?'

Le Roux laughed again. 'I've made my plan. I'm leaving for New Zealand. I've delayed my flight once already, thanks to my over-zealous replacement, but now it's time go. I just wish those local clowns I used to guard the cattle had killed you and Sannie and her partner when you tried to tip them off about where we were hiding the cows, John. You were stupid; you should have just sent Sannie an anonymous message about the livestock. Van Rensburg might have got the jump on me sooner. Your little bit of theatre cost you, but no doubt you wanted to make it look like it was a big surprise to you when you *discovered* the missing stock.'

Le Roux tossed the empty fuel can aside and wiped his hands on his scrubs, then slipped off the stolen pants and shirt. 'Right. It's time for me to leave.'

Adam ran in through the front door. He leapt over Jenny, lying on the lounge room floor, and barrelled into Le Roux. The police captain fell backwards, and Adam raised the fist not holding the sword and brought it down into the other man's face. Le Roux had been taken by surprise, but, like Adam, had probably been in his share of fights. He brought his knee up into Adam's crotch, and Adam felt the breath forced from his lungs.

Le Roux rolled underneath Adam and reached around him. He grabbed the leg of a coffee side table and swung it up and across Adam's back, shattering the flimsy little piece of furniture. Adam slid away, rocked back on his haunches and popped back up on his feet. He still surfed and his legs were one of his strongest assets.

Le Roux, however, had also recovered and scooped up what Adam assumed was Napoleon Bonaparte's sword, just in time to block an arcing slash from Adam's Muslim weapon. Steel rang on steel.

Adam watched where he stepped, not wanting to stand on one of the captives, who were trying to wriggle away. He saw the two guns on the side table, and Le Roux caught his eye. Adam lunged with his sword and Le Roux parried the blow.

Adam's move had been enough to distract Le Roux from the pistols. Jenny, who had been watching what was going on, kicked out at the side table, and the two firearms fell to the ground. None of the three handcuffed captives could get to the guns, and Le Roux couldn't dare risk reaching to the floor for a pistol with Adam closing in on him.

Le Roux went on the attack, thrusting back at Adam and taking a step closer to him. Their blows rang off their respective weapons as each of them stepped over and around the three prone young people. Adam met blow with blow, and also pushed closer until the two of them were face to face, blades pushing against each other.

Adam shot his left hand out to try to punch Le Roux in the face, but the policeman ducked and kicked out at Adam's shin. Adam took the blow and the pain, then drew back his head and snapped it forward again, head-butting Le Roux on the nose. Adam felt cartilage shatter and the vicious strike was enough to break the impasse. Le Roux, momentarily dazed, staggered, and Adam drew back his sword arm and swung it back again in a savage blow. The blade connected with Le Roux's left bicep and opened the skin.

Adam tried to press home the advantage. Le Roux, wounded, took a step back and half tripped over John Parker. However, the stumble put him out of reach of Adam's next swing and saved him from another injury. Adam had to sidestep to stop from falling and Le Roux recovered his balance and composure. He came back fighting, arm swinging hard and fast and forcing Adam to take a step backwards.

The smell of petrol was strong in Adam's nostrils and he worried a spark from their swords ringing off each other might set the flat ablaze. Jan-Maree was writhing on the floor and Adam thought it looked like she might be trying to get to her feet – a difficult prospect with her hands cuffed behind her back.

'Stay down,' Adam ordered her.

'Yes, stay out of the way,' John said.

Le Roux came at Adam, ignoring his obvious pain and the blood streaming from his nose. His arm swung like a machine, and each parry by Adam seemed harder and harder to sustain. Le Roux reached down with a free hand, grabbed one of Jan-Maree's potted plants by its stem and hurled it at Adam's face. Adam took another step backwards and lost his footing. Le Roux's next swing came in under Adam's defensive move and the tip of Bonaparte's sword carved a deep furrow across Adam's stomach. Blood flowed.

Adam felt his skin opening and the shock of it weakened him. He tried to recover, but as he took a step backwards his foot rolled on the discarded clay flowerpot, and he started to fall.

Le Roux raised his sword hand high over his head and grinned as he began to bring down his killing blow. Adam had his free hand out to break his fall and his sword was hooked on the arm of a chair. He thought of Sannie and his children, far away in Australia.

Jan-Maree appeared between them.

'No!' Adam yelled. He didn't want his mistake to cost someone their life.

Le Roux, however, was committed to his sweeping cut, the weight of Bonaparte's sword creating a momentum of its own.

The blade came down and hacked into Jan-Maree's left shoulder, in the crook of her neck.

She stared wide-eyed up at Le Roux as her chest cavity was opened, from her clavicle down across her heart.

Adam rolled out of the way as Jan-Maree began to fall backwards. He swung his sword around in a wide arc and it, too, travelled with its own impetus as it cleaved into Le Roux's midriff.

Jan-Maree reached out in vain as she fell, and her hand knocked a lamp from a table. The lampshade fell off and the bulb shattered, causing a spark. The lounge room erupted in flame.

MARILYN, handcuffed and lying in the boot of Sannie's Fortuner, with the rear hatch open, watched as Lettie Pienaar laid out an arsenal of weapons on a workbench in her barn. There was an AR-15 semi-automatic rifle, two pistols, a heavy-calibre hunting rifle, a crossbow, and a pair of shotguns.

'Lettie, I think we should just leave,' Sergeant Eva Nyathi said.

Marilyn could have laughed. Nyathi was finally seeing the light.

'Eva's right,' Marilyn said, 'you can probably avoid jail time for cattle rustling, but not for killing a police officer.'

Lettie scoffed. 'Your Colonel van Rensburg said the same thing to me in a message. But you police, you do nothing. Only the captain cared for us farmers. He protected us, and showed us how to make a living in this terrible time when all the . . . all the local people want to take our land and kill us for our guns.'

'Well, technically, we were here first,' Marilyn said.

Lettie picked up a pistol and pointed it at Marilyn. 'You be quiet.

Everything was fine until you came . . . until the captain decided he must go to live in New Zealand, like everyone else.'

Marilyn had been gradually shifting her position in the Fortuner for some time. Eva had parked it inside the barn, under Lettie's orders, to make sure it was not visible from the road or the air. Slowly Marilyn had moved until she could get her cuffed hands into the folds of Adam's dive bag, which her captors had ignored. At last, she had what she wanted.

'Lettie?' Marilyn said in a beseeching voice.

'What?'

'I need to pee.'

Lettie screwed her face up. 'So what?'

'So, I do not want to do it lying down in the back of a car. Not my boss's car.'

Lettie frowned. She looked to Eva, who had, Marilyn thought, a very uneasy expression on her face, as though she was regretting several decisions she had made recently.

'*Sisi*,' Marilyn said to Eva in isiZulu, 'help me down and then make yourself scarce, OK?'

Eva stared at her.

'Talk English or Afrikaans,' Lettie barked. 'Eva, help her go to the toilet.'

Eva went to the rear of the Fortuner, reached in and grabbed Marilyn by the arm. Then she half swung, half dragged her to the open door.

'Thank you,' Marilyn said to Eva. 'And now, ladies . . .'

They all paused, because the air was suddenly full of the growing crescendo of helicopter rotors and a screaming engine overhead.

'Now,' Marilyn raised her voice, 'it's time for me to leave the building.'

Marilyn did a smart about-turn parade-ground movement so that Lettie and Eva could see that in her hands was a grenade, from which she had just pulled the pin. Marilyn dropped the grenade and ran for the barn door.

Lettie seemed to half think about bringing the pistol around to shoot Marilyn, but the sight of the hand grenade on the floor made her and Eva also break into a run.

As the three women emerged into the sunlight the Oryx helicopter touched down, and armed police and Colonel Sannie van Rensburg spilled from the door.

'Down!' Marilyn yelled. 'Down!'

The barn exploded.

EPILOGUE

Natal, 1880

'To track a man, one needs to do more than follow his footsteps in the mud.' Samuel pushed the broad-brimmed straw hat back on his head, exposing his smiling face to Teresa and Grace.

A steamboat's whistle blew and gulls wheeled and cried overhead. The smell of the sea was strong in Teresa's nostrils.

'I understand,' Teresa said. 'We know his habits and his weaknesses, thanks to Grace.'

Grace smiled. 'Like the others – all of them except Peter, of course – he used to visit the Red Lantern. He pretended he was an innocent; he thought the girls would find that charming. But always, he was asking, listening, seeking information. He was too late for the war, too young for glory, so he sought his fortune by any means he could find. His greed is his weakness.'

Teresa nodded. 'We know he will be here. He needs to get out of the colony and today is the next sailing.'

'It is ironic,' Grace said, 'that he would be on the same ship as you, and the empress.'

'Yes,' Teresa agreed. 'Perhaps there's some kind of thrill in that for him.'

Samuel had swapped his snuff's uniform for the stained off-white shirt and ragged trousers of a dockside porter. Grace wore an intricately patterned green sari and Teresa a tight-nipped frock with a plunging neckline that diverted men's attention from her face to her bosom. Her hat, also broad-brimmed, hid her features. She felt daring, dressed as she was, hoping to blend in among the women who plied their trade on the waterfront.

'Maybe he won't come,' Teresa said.

Samuel nodded slowly. 'He will come. He needs to leave Africa's shores. He is bold, because of the news of Peter's death. He thinks he will get away with his crime, and that no one has noticed his absence.'

They retreated to their places – Samuel into the throng of porters and stevedores, Grace into the portico of an Indian trader's store, and Teresa to the shadows of the warehouses that lined the dock. Other women affected the same casual air as her, while keeping watch for their prey with the sharp eyes of raptors.

It was less than half an hour to departure before he finally showed himself.

He strode along the dock in a new suit and top hat. Like a dandy, he carried a cane, which he tapped on the stone beneath him in time with the heels of his new boots, and in his left hand was a carpet bag, unusually long.

'Boss, boss, can I help you with your bag?' Samuel said.

The young man barely turned his head. 'No, thank you.'

Samuel carried on behind him, keeping pace with him. 'Please, boss.'

'No, thank you.' Still he did not look back, chin up, eyes forward.

Samuel closed the gap and reached into the pocket of his trousers. He withdrew the revolver and pushed it into the young man's back. 'This way, if you please, Mr Phillips.'

'What?' Phillips spun around and, for the first time, laid eyes on the man who had been calling him. 'Samuel?'

Teresa strode out of the dank shadow of a warehouse, and marched over to the pair. She hooked an arm in Phillips'. 'This way, darlin',' she said in a cockney accent, 'we've got some business to attend to.'

Phillips began to struggle, but Samuel pressed the pistol barrel harder and Phillips complied. The three of them were joined in a narrow dockside alleyway by Grace. Her right arm was still bandaged from the injury she had suffered when the bomb exploded and the carriage rolled.

'You've got my sword, Gavin, you damned miscreant,' Grace said.

'It's not your . . .' He looked to all of them. 'Damnit.'

Samuel raised the revolver to Phillips' chest and poked him with it. 'Best you hand over what does not belong to you, *Gavin*.'

Phillips scowled. 'How dare you?'

Grace rounded on him. 'No, how dare *you*! You stole that sword from me and left us to die, what with that crazy Ferdi trying to kill the empress.'

Phillips' Adam's apple bobbed and he spread his hands wide. 'I . . . well, it's different for all of you.'

Samuel raised his eyebrows. 'Care to explain?'

Phillips frowned. 'Samuel, you're brave as a lion.' He looked next to Grace: 'And you're smart as a whip and beautiful and resourceful.' Next, he turned to Teresa. 'And Miss O'Kane, well, you're . . . American.'

'Gee, thanks.' Teresa was unable to hide her sarcasm.

'The point of it is, you're all doing just splendidly, and I'm just, well, me. This sword was my chance to make my fortune.'

'Mine, as well,' Grace chimed in.

'Yes, but look at you, Grace, in your fine dress. I *know* the empress has given you enough money to start up your own business, selling clothes for well-to-do Indian ladies. I've been in hiding, but I've been watching. And Samuel, I hear you're up for a commission.'

Samuel gave a small nod. 'You killed a man, Mr Phillips. A British officer.'

Grace spat in the ground. 'And he was a pig.'

Phillips looked at Samuel and nodded. 'I was working at head-quarters and had to open Hellfire Jack's correspondence. I saw the letter from Lord Chelmsford about Napoleon's missing sword and the reference to Morrison being the one who took possession of it. I knew him from the Red Lantern.' Phillips looked at Grace. 'I knew what sort of person he was.'

Grace shivered.

'When I went to him, to offer to buy the sword from him, he was up in arms. He said you'd visited him, Grace, to offer him – well, to offer him what he wanted, and he told me you had drugged and robbed him. He wanted me to help him find you, Grace, and kill you. I couldn't do that. We argued, Morrison and I and, well . . . a struggle ensued, during which my firearm discharged, and Morrison was killed. That is all I will say on the matter, in court or otherwise.'

Samuel nodded. 'In other words, you shot the pig in cold blood.'

Phillips said nothing.

'The captain suspected it was you,' Samuel said.

Phillips raised his eyebrows. 'He did?'

'He told me that you were too clever, spotting the cavalryman's bootprint outside of Morrison's farmhouse. You were trying to misdirect our attention, making us think that maybe Lieutenant Walters was the one who killed Morrison. We knew that Walters and Morrison knew each other from the Red Lantern, and that Walters wanted to ingratiate himself with the empress.'

'How . . .?'

Samuel smiled. 'Captain Gregory looked at Lieutenant Walters' footwear. His feet are very big. Yours are very small.'

Phillips frowned. He turned to Teresa, then Samuel. 'The captain . . . I'm so sorry that he was . . .'

'You heard that he died,' Teresa said.

Phillips nodded. 'It was in the *Natal Witness*. Sub-Inspector Gregory was killed apprehending a murderer. Nothing about an assassination attempt on the empress at all. You all kept that jolly quiet.'

'Yes,' Samuel said. 'But the captain is alive. Peter was wounded, quite badly, by Ferdi, but it was his idea, in the aftermath, to put out a story that he had died simply doing his job, trying to apprehend a common criminal. As I said, Peter thought you were involved in the killing of Morrison and stealing the real sword, and your disappearance on the night of the attack confirmed it. He wanted you to think that you had slipped away without anyone knowing the truth about you, and said that if you thought he was dead, then you would drop your guard and be easier to catch.'

Phillips frowned. 'And here you all are. He was right. Although I'm very pleased he didn't die.'

'We also kept news of the assassination attempt quiet out of respect for the empress,' Teresa said. 'And for that same reason, we will now take the sword from you.'

Phillips opened his mouth as if to protest, but thought better of it. Samuel took the carpet bag from his hand, set it down, opened it, and nodded.

'I should arrest you, Gavin,' Samuel said.

Phillips jutted his chin out. 'But?'

'But Her Majesty is adamant that there be no publicity about what happened,' Samuel said.

'And what am I to do?' Phillips asked.

Samuel looked him up and down. 'You arrived too late for the war, yes, but there will be more trouble in this colony. You can follow the path of crime you have embarked upon, Mr Phillips, or you can start again. You wouldn't be the first reformed or out-of-work rogue to join the snuffs. You can return to the Natal Mounted Police as a constable. If you are willing to serve under me, we can start again.'

Phillips started to speak, and for a moment Teresa thought he would say no, that he could not work with Samuel. Instead, he smiled and put out his hand.

Teresa hugged Samuel and Grace and shook hands with Phillips. She boarded the lighter and took the short but nonetheless nerve-racking and rough voyage across the sandbar out to sea and the steamship that would take her to the Cape of Good Hope, where she would board another vessel to New York.

Once on board, she made her way to the first-class deck and knocked on the door.

'Come,' the Empress Eugénie said.

In a very short time, the two women had struck up something of a rapport, if not a friendship. The empress, naturally, could perhaps still not completely trust a journalist to abide by her promise to publicise nothing of perhaps the most sensational news story of the decade, if not the century.

Teresa walked into the cabin with the carpet bag, curtsied, then set the bag down and undid it. She reached in and lifted out the sword, which she presented to the empress with two hands.

Eugénie put a hand to her mouth. 'Oh, *Mon Dieu . . . I . . .*'

Teresa saw the tears well in the other woman's eyes. Here, in Teresa's hands, was the last link between a grieving mother and her cherished son. There was no doubt in Teresa's mind that this was the sword that the Prince Imperial had carried with him, nor that it had once belonged to their famous ancestor, the greatest ruler France had ever known.

The empress reached out a hand, but seemed almost afraid to touch the weapon. She eventually laid a fingertip on the ornately inscribed blade. She looked up from the polished steel into Teresa's eyes.

'This is it. *Oui.*' She blinked, several times, and a tear rolled down her cheek. 'But not even holding this thing, that was perhaps the last *objet* that he held before he died, can give my son back to me.' She sniffed.

'It belongs to you, Your Majesty,' Teresa said.

Eugénie reached out and put her hand around Teresa's left wrist, gently encircling it as she held the sword.

'You will swear to respect my privacy, so that I might grieve in private, without the world knowing what happened here?'

Teresa nodded. 'I will.' She had come to Africa looking for a story, and even though she had been privy to a scandal so momentous it would have set tongues wagging around the world, at the same time she had met a woman who had lost a son at war and wanted nothing more than to honour him in her own way, by herself. Eugénie had also spoken sympathetically of Ferdi, whose soul had been tortured for most of his life by his own demons and the terrible memory of a beloved uncle who had been executed by guillotine.

'Perhaps, Teresa,' Eugénie had hinted during their last meeting, 'instead of reporting on the sadness and tragedy in other people's lives, you can write something of your own, something that will bring joy or wonder, instead of sadness or scandal.'

'I always wanted to write a novel, Your Majesty,' Teresa had admitted.

'Then perhaps you now have some ideas.'

They had both laughed.

'Teresa,' Eugénie said now, bringing her back to the present. 'Take this sword to *Monsieur* Gregory. Tell him he may keep it, in thanks for saving my life. I have rewarded Miss Naidoo, so it is only fitting that he has some recompense as well. But I will make this gesture on one condition.'

Teresa nodded. 'What is that, Your Majesty?'

'My son's sword must stay in his family in perpetuity, and he must never sell it for profit. If I hear of it, then I will break my silence and reclaim it.'

'I understand, Your Majesty.'

The empress smiled. 'You are close to him. I see it in the way you look at him.'

She nodded. 'I am.'

'Then I hope it stays in *your* family.'

Teresa let herself out of the empress's cabin and carried the bag two decks down to where Peter rested. She let herself in.

He opened his eyes. The sun streamed in through a porthole and lit his face. He was still pale, but there was a hint of colour in his cheeks. He smiled at her. She was taking him away from Africa, for now, to America, to recover, although they had agreed they would return to Natal one day.

'The empress has given you a gift.' She set the bag on his bed and opened it. He raised his head, with some effort, and looked at the sword.

'I thought I was going to die. I was ready for it,' he said.

Teresa nodded. 'Yes, but you didn't – die, that is.'

'No.' He smiled and held out his arms. She came to him. 'Perhaps I'm not quite ready yet.'

KwaZulu-Natal, **the present**

Once Sannie and the tactical unit had arrested Lettie Pienaar and Sergeant Eva Nyathi, they flew straight to the smallholding where Jan-Maree Ball lived.

Adam had managed to drag Jenny and John Parker from the burning building, but Jan-Maree and Captain Derick le Roux died in the fire.

Three days later, Sannie and Adam, his stomach stitched and bandaged, stood by a bed in the hospital with the name *Meyer, Matteo* written on a card above it. Sannie reached up and slid the card from its holder. Then she took a pen out of her handbag, crossed out *Matteo* and wrote *Deon* instead.

At that moment, the patient opened his eyes; he'd been resting.

'Howzit, Colonel?'

Sannie replaced the card. 'Now I can tell all my friends I know Deon Meyer.'

He smiled up at her. 'I'm sorry I got shot.'

'The medical examiner says Andy was killed by suffocation. Derick le Roux killed him. He might have had time to go on to kill John Parker and an innocent woman, Jenny Ellis, who were also here in the hospital, if you hadn't interrupted him, Deon. As it was, he had to follow them to Jan-Maree's house, which gave us time to stop him. You did good.'

He gave a small smile. '*Baie dankie*, Colonel. But I'm still sad about what happened to Jan-Maree.'

Sannie nodded.

'Oh, hi.'

They all looked over as Jenny Ellis, wearing a hospital gown, appeared in the doorway.

'The sister said I'd find you here, Prof, Colonel,' Jenny said to Adam and Sannie.

'Howzit, Jenny,' Sannie said. 'Can we have a quick word in private?'

'Sure.'

Sannie and Adam led Jenny into the hospital corridor. There was a loose end that Sannie needed to tie up.

'I arrested John Parker and charged him with conspiracy to commit a crime – stock theft. I doubt he'll do any jail time,' Sannie said. 'He asked me about the Bonaparte sword and I thought he was going to demand that we give it to him, since he'd inherited David Gregory's farm and the game reserve and all his possessions.'

'But he didn't?' Jenny asked.

'No,' Sannie said, 'he thinks the sword is cursed and despite its value he said he wanted nothing more to do with it. I told him that like other unclaimed police evidence it would eventually be disposed of.'

Jenny nodded. 'That sounds like a good idea. After I saw what that thing did to Jan-Maree I never want to see another sword again. She did wrong, but she was my friend.'

'It'd be good if the story of the sword stayed where it was up until now,' Adam said to Jenny, 'consigned to history.'

Jenny gave him a smile. 'You can count on me, Prof. All I want to do is get back to the sea turtles.'

Sannie reached out and gave Jenny a hug.

'Thank you, Jenny,' Adam said, 'for all that you've done.'

'I'm just pleased I could help, Prof.' Jenny looked back to Sannie. 'Colonel?'

'Yes?'

'Seeing what sort of person you are, how brave you are, and smart, I can see why the prof is so in love with you.'

'Oh.' Sannie didn't know what to say.

'I hope I can find a love like that some time.'

'I hope you do.' Sannie led them back into Deon's room to say their goodbyes.

Jenny looked down at Deon in his bed. 'Hi, I'm Jenny.'

Deon smiled. 'They call me Deon Meyer.'

'No way,' she said.

'Way.' He laughed.

'So,' Deon said to Jenny, 'do you like crime fiction?'

Jenny smiled. 'I do.'

'We need to go, Jenny, but we'll be back to visit again tomorrow,' Adam said.

Jenny sat down on Deon's bed. 'No problem, Prof. You two enjoy yourselves.'

Sannie and Adam left Deon and Jenny and walked out of the hospital into the open air. Adam breathed deeply. 'Are you ready to do this?'

Sannie looked to him. 'I am.'

They got into Adam's Ranger – Sannie's Fortuner had been wrecked by the grenade explosion – and drove out of town. Brian Shozi had offered to fly Marilyn home to Durban in the helicopter, and Marilyn had accepted the offer. Sannie directed Adam to David Gregory's farm.

'You said there was something you wanted to show me?' Adam said.

She nodded. 'Up behind the boma. When I went back to the farm yesterday I had a good walk around. I found a small cemetery. There are just two graves there; the original occupants of the farm.'

Sannie pointed the way and Adam drove around the farmhouse and past the enclosures where David's rhinos had been kept for a time.

'The crime scene techs have been going over David's house. They found a secret compartment in the TV cabinet, behind where the sword was hanging, which was behind the TV,' Sannie said.

'Secrets within secrets.' Adam smiled. 'When were you going to tell me this?'

'Today,' Sannie said, 'for dramatic effect.'

Adam pulled up within sight of a wrought-iron fence overgrown with long grass. They got out of the *bakkie*.

'You have a spade, right?' Sannie asked.

Adam went to the rear of the Ranger, where he kept his four-by-four recovery gear, and took out a small fold-out spade. He assembled it. 'Where must I dig?'

'Come with me,' Sannie said.

She walked through the waist-high grass and heaved open a rusting gate in the iron fence. Inside the small enclosure were two graves.

'*Here lie Peter Gregory and Teresa Gregory,*' Sannie read. '*Dearly beloved in life and eternity.*'

'Nice,' Adam said. 'Here?'

Sannie nodded. 'Give me the spade, please.'

'But I ... '

'You need to take care of yourself. I don't want that wound in your stomach opening up.'

'OK, Colonel.' He handed her the tool.

Sannie smiled and started to dig. 'The investigators found an old envelope with a letter on parchment in the hidden compartment. It was written and signed by Peter Gregory.' Sannie paused to catch her breath and pointed to the grave. 'It said that Napoleon's sword must never be sold or given away outside of members of the Gregory family – those were the wishes of Empress Eugénie when she presented the sword to him as a "reward for services rendered", whatever that meant. It seems the family line died out with David. And

David was determined to keep to his forebear's wishes. When Jan-Maree Ball uncovered some old police reports that seemed to link Peter Gregory to an investigation into the loss of Napoleon Bonaparte's sword, David tried to throw her off the trail by directing her to an item in the *Natal Witness* reporting that Peter was killed in the line of duty. Clearly, from the dates on this headstone, Peter didn't die then; indeed, he lived for another forty-five years – it must have been some kind of ruse at the time.'

'I see, and also looking at those dates it seems his wife, Teresa, died just a few weeks after him. You don't want to bury the Arab sword and the antique Koran as well?'

Sannie had resumed her digging, but took another break to stretch her back. She shook her head. 'No, I think that now we've had your history professor friend confirm the provenance of both that your plan is better. Get Goldie Faul to pay you for them and put the money into a charitable trust to benefit wildlife research and anti-poaching projects, starting with training some proper, honest rangers to protect the rhinos on uBhejane.'

Adam nodded. 'Good. I like it when you agree with me.'

Sannie laughed. 'So do I.' Sannie had spoken to Faul again and learned from her that Andy was an orphan and had never married. The military, and, subsequently, his band of mercenaries, had been his only family. He had paid his contact in Yemen for the treasures, but there was no one who would be the poorer for his death. Faul had told Sannie she would cover the wages Andy had promised his men – Sannie wondered if the American had future plans for them.

Sannie continued digging and Adam went to the Ranger and opened the rear door of the double cab. He took out Napoleon Bonaparte's sword and held it out in both hands, to Sannie.

She set down her spade and took it, then lowered it into the long, deep trench she had dug next to the combined graves of Peter and Teresa Gregory.

Adam stood watching her as she began shovelling earth back into the hole to cover the weapon. 'You know that thing is worth a fortune, right?'

She looked up at him. 'Yes, but this is the right thing to do, Adam.'

He smiled, glanced down at the headstone, and read out loud the same words Sannie had said. '*Dearly beloved in life and eternity.*' Adam looked into Sannie's eyes. 'There's something else that's the right thing to do.'

'What's that?' Sannie asked.

Adam got down on one knee, reached up, and took Sannie's hand in his.

ACKNOWLEDGEMENTS AND HISTORICAL NOTE

So, how much of this story is fiction, and how much is historical fact?

The answer to the first question is, most of it; the answer to the second is, a surprising amount.

As incredible as it sounds, Prince Louis Napoleon, son of Emperor Napoleon III, and great nephew of Napoleon Bonaparte found himself living in exile in the United Kingdom, studied at a British military academy, and wangled himself an attachment to Lord Chelmsford's army in South Africa during the Anglo-Zulu War.

Thirsting for action, perhaps to prove himself a worthy successor to his great uncle, Louis Napoleon met his fate as outlined in this story in a lonely corner of Zululand in 1879. The chance encounter during a coffee stop that saw the exiled heir, two British soldiers and a Zulu scout killed caused a stir that echoed around the world.

Much has been written about this incident, but as I noted in this novel, probably the definitive book about the death of Louis Napoleon and its aftermath is *With His Face to the Foe, The Life and Death of Louis Napoleon, The Prince Imperial Zululand 1879* by the highly respected Anglo-Zulu War historian Ian Knight. I drew heavily on this book for my research.

In the aftermath of the attack and during subsequent investigations Louis Napoleon's uniform and pistol were recovered, but not his sword. As mentioned in this work of fiction, his sword was, indeed, presented to British forces in the run-up to the battle of Ulundi, in a failed gesture of goodwill by the Zulu king, Cetshwayo who wanted to bring Lord Chelmsford to the negotiating table.

But was it *his* sword?

I had read about Louis Napoleon many years ago and had long wanted to write a book at least partly set during or around the time of the momentous battles of Rorke's Drift and Isandlwana. While I was researching *Die By The Sword* I noticed something peculiar. Several accounts from the time of the prince's death, and repeated many times since, referred to him carrying Napoleon Bonaparte's 'Austerlitz' sword.

Later, I stumbled upon an interesting website and blog online called www.ageofrevolution.org which had a thread about the sword. An article posed the question: where was the sword now, and was it the same weapon Bonaparte had carried at the Battle of Austerlitz? The conclusion, backed up with evidence from the Napoleon museum at the Château de Fontainebleau in France, was that young Louis Napoleon's sword was in the museum's collection and that rather than being the ornate blade carried by his Great Uncle it was a standard French service sword.

Why, I asked myself, were there so many reports from the prince's time in Zululand that specifically mentioned not only that he was carrying Bonaparte's sword, but a particular weapon from a particular battle? That seemed pretty precise and, as one of the characters in *Die By The Sword* notes, why would a prince lie about something like that?

That question was enough to get me started on this novel.

Knight's excellent book, *With His Face to the Foe* deals not only with the prince's death, but the controversy following it, and the visit by his mother, the Empress Eugénie, to South Africa a year later to honour her fallen son.

A good deal of what I've written is based on the real events surrounding Eugénie's pilgrimage. General Evelyn Wood, and Major 'Hellfire Jack' Darnell, are real people and based on Knight's work, and other contemporary sources, including *Natal Past and Present*, by Major Arthur A. Wood (a history of the Natal Mounted Police), I have tried to portray them as realistically as possible. My apologies to their descendants if I've missed the mark, but I think they both come out of this story as fairly decent chaps.

And what of the feisty female American journalist, a prototype paparazzi putting on airs and graces, using a dubious title and claiming to be a friend of the Empress Eugénie, in order to get the scoop of the decade and interview a grieving royal? Surely, dear reader, you might suppose that is pure fiction.

No.

Stalking Eugénie's caravan was one Theresa (with an 'h') Longworth, an undercover correspondent for an American newspaper who had convinced the Natal Mounted Police to assign two troopers to her, in order for her to intercept her 'friend' the Empress. Theresa was using a title, Lady Avonmore, which, like Teresa O'Kane in *Die by the Sword*, she claimed she was entitled to use, having been seduced and married by a rotter of a Lord who later dumped her.

As I like to say, in Africa – even in 1880 – truth is stranger than fiction.

The Empress Eugénie and Louis's father, Napoleon III, were the subject of a near-miss assassination attempt in Paris in 1858 when the Italian revolutionary Felice Orsini did indeed try to do away with them using an early-model hand grenade. The 'Orsini Bomb', as described in my book and carried by the fictitious Ferdi, went on to become the preferred weapon of anarchists for some time.

However, there was no attempt on the Empress's life in Zululand in 1880 – at least as far as I'm aware!

The Battles of Isandlwana and Rorke's Drift have been the subject of many books and movies over the decades and I found the most useful source of research for these was another volume by Ian Knight: *Zulu Rising, The Epic story of Isandlwana and Rorke's Drift.*

Certain events in *Die by the Sword* are based on actual incidents, including Colonel Durnford's last stand, his ordering of the Edendale Horse to retreat, and the heroic decision by Sergeant Simeon Kambula to halt his men at the Buffalo River and have them lay down orderly, disciplined fire to cover what was otherwise a disorganised exodus.

My thanks go to Anglo-Zulu War battlefield guide Tony Coleman, from Dundee, South Africa, who took my wife and me on a tour of the key sites, including the Prince Imperial's memorial (don't try and find it without a guide – you'll get lost!).

Thanks, also, to Vincent Nixon from the Dundee Diehards re-enactment group, for permission to use the picture on the cover of the US/UK version of *Die by the Sword* showing a redcoat and Zulu in hand-to-hand combat.

In the 'modern' era my thanks go to Andy Coetzee for sharing his wealth of knowledge on endangered sea turtles and pointing me towards Bhanga Nek beach, where my wife and I were able to see hundreds of tiny hatchlings heading for the sea.

Stock theft is a real issue in South Africa, but I wish to point out that I had no specific evidence of insurance fraud in relation to farm animals being stolen – that's something I made up. Thank you, to Farmer Hendy Davis, from Swartberg, for putting the idea of stock theft in my head as a theme for a novel (though I'm sure she didn't expect the farmer to be doing anything crooked – apologies for that).

General Johan Jooste (Retd), with whom I co-authored the memoir, *Rhino War*, gave me some valuable insights into the challenges facing private rhino owners in South Africa today and read and checked the manuscript for me. *Baie dankie,* General.

It was not my intention to discredit private owners of rhinos in South Africa in this book. In fact, I have met a few over the years and they are good people whose hearts are in the right places. Private owners of rhinos are crucially important for the survival of the species and they deserve the thanks of all South Africans and anyone with an interest in conserving these magnificent animals. Keeping rhinos is an expensive, largely unprofitable business. The debate over whether the sale of rhino horn should be legalised is a complex and emotional one. I've tried to briefly cover both sides in this work of pure fiction.

As with many of my past books I was pleased to 'outsource' the naming of characters to several charities and good people who paid money to good causes for the right to have their name, or that of a loved one, assigned to a character. They couldn't all be 'good guys', but they are all heroes and heroines.

If you think it's weird that I named a character after South Africa's number-one-best-selling crime author, Deon Meyer, it isn't. Deon (a thoroughly nice guy as well as a brilliant writer) contacted me and said that he would make a donation to the Cape Leopard Trust in order to have his name used. Thank you, Deon.

Thanks, also, to the following people and the charities they supported: Peter Gregory, on behalf of himself and David Gregory; Teresa O'Kane; Audrey Uren, on behalf of John Parker; Jenny Ellis and Richard Tustin (who all donated to Painted Dog Conservation Inc). Thanks to: Jan-Maree Ball (Aussie hero quilts); Derick le Roux (SANParks Honorary Rangers Project K9); Heike and Andrew Millar on behalf of Schalk Smit (SANParks Honorary Rangers); Deon Van der Ploeg on behalf of Piet Van der Ploeg (Nourish NPO); Gavin Phillips (PROVET Pangolin conservation, Hoedspruit); and Danni Faul, on behalf of Goldie Faul (the Koala Hospital, Port Macquarie).

If the name of that thoroughgoing rotter Llewellyn Walters sounds familiar, that's because Llew paid money to charity to have his name in an earlier book, *Ghosts of Past*. He appears in *Die By The Sword*, as his younger self thanks to his donation to the Umoya Khulula pangolin rescue centre.

Thank you, again, to my dedicated and unpaid first readers and editors: wife, Nicola; mother, Kathy; mother-in-law, Sheila; Afrikaans expert Annelien Oberholzer; firearms expert Fritz Rabe; and newcomer proof-reader Melissa Macgill.

Thank you, as always, to my publishing 'family' at Pan Macmillan Australia and South Africa – in particular, Alex Lloyd, Danielle Walker, Terry Morris, Andrea Nattrass, Gill Spain, and Nkanyezi Tshabalala – for getting this book print-ready.

Last, but by no means least, whether you read in print or e-book, or listen to audiobooks, thank you. In the world of publishing, you are the most important person of all.

If you've enjoyed this book, you can find more of my African adventures at www.tonypark.net